THE BLIND SPOT

Special Agent Ricki James Thriller Book 9

C.R. CHANDLER

Editing by: https://www.behestins.com/about.htm

Cover Art by: https://cheekycovers.com/

Also By C.R. Chandler

SPECIAL AGENT RICKI JAMES

(Mystery/Thriller)

One Final Breath October 2020

One Last Scream January 2021

One Life Gone May 2021

Waiting In The Dark October 2021

Running In The Night February 2022

Hiding In The Shadows July 2022

Colder Than Ice October 2022

Dead Of Winter February 2023

The Blind Spot June 2023

No Place To Hide November 2023

FOOD AND WINE CLUB MYSTERIES

(Cozy Mysteries)

A Special Blend of Murder 2017

Dinner, Drinks, and Murder 2017

A Burger, Fries, and Murder 2017

Champagne, Cupcakes, and Murder 2018

Tea, Dessert, and Murder 2018

Prologue

A HARD JOLT struck the nerves in his arms, raced up his spine and along the back of his neck, causing him to bolt upright. His sleeping bag slid off his shoulders as he let out a loud groan of protest as the sudden, jarring movement magnified the jackhammer pounding in his head. The pain forced him to gingerly lie down again, carefully lowering one vertebra at a time until he was lying flat and motionless on the ground once more.

Sonofabitch. He gritted his teeth against the pain relentlessly spreading across the top of his skull like an oil slick on water. His eyes stayed glued shut while he took long, deliberate breaths, patiently keeping to a slow rhythm of a deep inhale followed by an extended exhale until the pain eased off. Not that it left entirely, but enough for him to risk opening his eyelids to a small slit. Still, even that tiny bit of light almost blinded him. It also revved up the jackhammer once more. But he didn't shut his eyes, instead visibly bracing against the pain seeping in.

Sheer force of will had him drawing on the discipline instilled over twenty years in the military to keep his eyes open. That, and a hardheaded determination not to let anything, even the mother of all headaches, get the best of him. He absolutely refused to give in to the black curtain creeping around the edges of his vision, and went back to his controlled breathing.

When the pounding in his skull receded again, he risked opening his eyes a little more, stopping and gritting his teeth against the renewed pain, repeating the steps of slow inhales and exhales. He went through several cycles of pain followed by breathing and then grinding his teeth together until his jaw hurt more than his head. He finally managed to open his eyes enough to make out something besides the dark insides of his own eyelids.

At first, all he could say for sure was that now everything looked like a solid sheet of white. It took him a full two minutes to recognize the bright light as sunshine. Frowning, he concentrated on the blurry shapes that began to emerge, focusing on the fuzzy objects until they settled into something he could recognize. A tree branch, holding up a cover that stretched out over his head. The ends of the olive-green tarp swayed in the same gentle breeze that also swept over his face. He carefully took in another breath, letting his chest fill with the crisp air, grateful when it finally pushed back the edges of the fog clouding his mind.

He stared at the crooked branch, vaguely recalling coming across the makeshift pole lying on the ground a few feet from the stream. He blinked, frowning at a constant noise in the background. Water. It was the splash of water tumbling over and around rocks. Camping. They had set up camp on a site surrounded by streams. Kelly had groaned about having to hike the extra mile and a half, but he hadn't meant it. His brother Marine hadn't blinked an eye at walking a couple of extra klicks, despite his dramatic show of complaining about it.

He turned his head to look beyond his tarp shelter and frowned. Judging by the amount of light, it was well past his usual rising time of daybreak. When he looked over at the second tarp shelter on the other side of the campsite, he didn't see any movement. Whatever brand of bourbon Kelly had brought along for them to share had really packed a punch. Apparently they were both still feeling the effects, and that was saying something. Kelly could drink any man alive right under the table, then walk away whistling, with a spring in his step.

Reaching over, he unzipped his sleeping bag and flipped the top back, not overly surprised he was still fully dressed in his clothes from the day before, including his heavy coat. But it startled him that he also had his boots on. The last time he'd slept with his boots on, he'd been in a combat zone, not camping in a national park.

Still puzzled, he slowly got to his feet, closing his eyes again as a sudden wave of dizziness washed right over the worst hangover he'd ever had in his life. He planted his feet a hip distance apart, hunched his shoulders, and dug his heels into the ground until the world righted itself again and he was confident he'd stay upright. He straightened his back until he was standing his full six feet three inches and ran a big hand lightly over the top of his short buzz cut. Thinking he was about halfway back to feeling normal again, he took another look over at Kelly's shelter.

It was a replica of his own, right down to a tree branch anchoring the center. He couldn't see Kelly's bright orange sleeping bag, but that wasn't any big deal. The man had probably been up for hours with no aftereffects from their encounter with a potent bottle of bourbon.

It will be two lifetimes before I hear the end of this. Broad shoulders lifted in a small, resigned shrug at the thought as he automatically looked over to the right of his sleeping bag. When he saw nothing but empty space, his frown returned. He quickly scanned the surface of the packed pine needles and dirt that made up the floor of his shelter until he spotted his rifle near one edge. If it had been years since he'd slept with his boots on, it had been twice that long since he hadn't set his rifle next to him, on his right side, whenever he slept in the field. And while this wasn't a combat zone, it was still not as safe as the bed back in his apartment. Keeping his frown, he walked over, picked up his rifle, and stepped out into the sunshine.

The fire they'd cooked over the night before was nothing but cold ashes in the cool morning light. At least they hadn't burned down the campsite, not to mention the entire forest around them. He slowly walked over to Kelly's shelter and squatted to look around. His friend's sleeping bag was missing, for some odd reason that his still-clouded brain wasn't processing, but Kelly's backpack was lying on its side, right where it should be. He smiled when he realized the brand-new rifle Kelly was so proud of was nowhere to be seen. It was no surprise that his longtime friend had decided to do some exploring while his much bigger camping buddy, who was clearly more lightweight when it came to liquor, slept it off this morning. If there was one thing he'd learned about Kelly over the years, it was that the man liked to keep moving.

Wondering where his friend had wandered off to, he strolled over to the edge of the campsite, intending to look down the path that led to the nearest stream. Kelly had a Tennessee fishing license and had brought along lines and hooks that they'd used successfully the previous afternoon to catch their dinner. So it could be he was down by the water, trying his luck again.

He took his time walking to the head of the path. The long hike the day before, and now the soothing sounds of the forest, were just what he needed. After spending the better part of the winter chasing killers and cooking up a storm at the diner he was a partner in, it was good to be greeting spring in the middle of these old mountains. Especially with the light breeze dancing through the trees overhead, perfectly in harmony with the noise of the constantly rolling water.

"Norman Beal?"

A deep voice that he didn't recognize stopped him in his tracks.

"Stay where you are and toss that rifle a few feet to your side."

When he didn't move, the voice took on a hard edge.

"I know who you are, Mr. Beal. Toss that rifle to the side, and do it now."

"I'm setting it down." Norman slowly bent his knees, keeping both hands out to his sides and in plain sight as he gently laid his loaded rifle on the ground, then, just as slowly, stood up again.

"Mr. Beal, I'm Ranger Jerome Johnson, with the law enforcement unit assigned to this park. Now I'd appreciate it if you'd put your hands behind your head and turn around. Very carefully. I don't like the thought of shooting someone in the back, but I will."

Shoot him in the back? What the hell was going on here? Norman took a slow breath as he lifted his hands and laced his fingers behind his neck. Doing exactly as he was told, he inched his way around until he was facing not one but three men with high-powered rifles pointed right at him.

Both sides silently stared at each other for a long moment.

"Care to tell me what this is all about?"

The ranger closest to him watched from deep brown eyes, half hidden underneath the broad brim of his hat. The badge of the National Park Service was pinned to his thick jacket, and from the way he stood and held his weapon, it was clear he knew exactly how to use his rifle.

The ranger didn't smile as he dipped his head in a quick nod. "Now, you just keep still. Like I said, I know who you are, Mr. Beal. And how you earned that nickname of yours. I don't want any trouble here, but we're taking you in on suspicion of murder."

The trapped man's chin hit his chest as his mouth dropped open. "Murder? Who the hell do you think I murdered?"

"His dog tags have identified the victim as Sergeant Kelly Dorman. And you, Norman Beal, are under arrest. Or would you rather I address you as Anchorman?"

Chapter 1

SOME THINGS just couldn't be rushed. Which was why she paused and took a moment to admire the rectangle of fried perfection, just waiting for her to take that first bite of absolute heaven. Sam had outdone himself this time. The bread had been toasted in melted butter to a rich, golden brown, and then topped-off with a heavy dusting of powdered sugar. The peanut butter and jelly in the center had been stirred into each other before being slathered on in a thick layer that had melted together under the heat of the grill.

It really was perfect. Using only the thumb and forefinger of each hand, Ricki lifted her favorite sandwich, smiling in anticipation. Planting her elbows firmly on the table, she held it in front of her mouth for another long moment before her teeth sank in. Her eyes closed in bliss at the satisfying crunch of toasted bread, followed by the mouth-watering blend of salty and sweet chunky peanut butter mixed with strawberry jam.

She chewed slowly, savoring every second as she opened her eyes and glanced around the large kitchen. It didn't get much better than eating a fried PB&J while sitting at a table in a warm kitchen. Especially one that still had the shine of being brand new since the entire space had recently been rebuilt. A necessary remodel following the fire that had been started by a killer trying to distract her from a murder case. Of course it hadn't worked. Now he was behind bars, and the diner had a new kitchen. Definitely no fun at the time, but now was a win-win as far as she was concerned.

"This could be the first incident of a man being jealous of a sandwich."

Sam's mild voice rose over the sizzle of burgers on the grill and had Ricki turning her head to look at him. "What are you talking about?"

The wiry cook with thinning hair pointed his spatula at her. "I'm talking about Clay seeing you make moony eyes over a sandwich."

"I am not," Ricki instantly denied, before her midnight-blue eyes narrowed. "And what are moony eyes, anyway?"

The cook grinned before glancing back at his loaded-up grill. "It's a term you younger people don't use anymore."

Ricki laughed. "You sound like you're eighty years old, Sam, instead of that fifty-something on your driver's license. And I doubt anyone, no matter how old they are, says 'moony eyes' either." She took another bite of her sandwich, keeping her gaze on him as she chewed and swallowed. "I think you made that up."

"Nope." Sam shook his head, then winked at her. "Heard it on TV. And I still say the chief would rather you saved all those gooey-eyed looks for him and not waste them on two pieces of bread plastered together with some peanut butter and jelly."

The comical picture of the tall, imposing chief of police getting annoyed over her attention to a sandwich had Ricki grinning back at the diner's fill-in cook. Sam usually manned the greeting desk up front and made sure everyone got a seat to their liking when they stopped by for a bite at the Sunny Side Up. But their usual cook, who was also one of Ricki's two partners in the diner, was on a much-deserved vacation. Which left her and their other partner, Marcie, running the place. Which was why Sam was behind the grill, keeping an eye on the various pots bubbling away on the stove while she and Marcie looked after the customers.

Luckily, Ricki's regular job as a special agent for the Investigative Services Branch of the National Park Service had been relatively quiet while Anchorman had been off on his camping trip back east. Which had left her with more time to help at the diner, although Marcie had definitely been picking up the lion's share of the load. Just like the top-notch waitress was doing right that minute. Feeling a twinge of guilt, Ricki popped the last bit of her sandwich into her mouth and stepped down from the tall stool she was sitting on.

"Heard from him?"

She blinked before refocusing her attention on Sam. "What?"

His eyes crinkled in amusement as he flipped two burgers before glancing her way again. "Anchorman. You said his name out loud, so I was wondering if you'd heard from him?"

Resigned to her habit of thinking out loud, Ricki suppressed a sigh and shook her head, sending the long fall of thick, dark hair pulled back into its usual ponytail at the nape of her neck gliding across her back. "No. But I don't expect to. I've spent a couple of weeks in the park where he and Kelly were headed, and it has its fair share of dead zones when it comes to cell service. And by fair share I mean that most of the park is in a dead zone."

The double doors separating the dining room from the kitchen flew open, followed by a short, comfortably built woman carrying a large gray plastic tub filled with dirty dishes, backing her way into the room. She stopped halfway to the big sink at the far end of the kitchen and turned to frown at Ricki.

"Dead? Did you say the word 'dead'? Please don't tell me

you'll be taking off to track down another killer who left a body behind, rest his or her soul." Marcie set the tub down on the nearest counter and slapped her hands onto her hips. "After barely getting back from catching that maniac near Crater Lake, your boss can't possibly expect you to go chasing after another one already? You need some time off."

Ricki smiled at the woman who was her partner and a full-time waitress at the Sunny Side Up. Over the years Marcie had been her babysitter, and now stood in as part mother, part friend, depending on what the older woman thought was needed at the time. And from the sound of it, Marcie was in full "mom" mode.

"I was talking about cell service. There's a lot of dead zones in the park Anchorman was headed to." Using her lean, athletic build and long legs to her advantage, Ricki's deep midnight-blue eyes crinkled in amusement before she deliberately stood up to her full height of five feet eight inches so she could tower over the much shorter Marcie. "I've been back for over a month, and not doing a lot for most of that, so I've managed to get plenty of rest."

Not the least bit intimidated at having to tilt her head back in order to look up at Ricki, the seasoned waitress snorted as she rolled her eyes. "Rest? You spent one week chasing after Eddie and those friends of his when he came home from that fancy school for spring break. And wasn't it you who was tramping around the mountains the last two days, looking for that lost hiker?"

Ricki's son was in his second year at a high school for advanced students located on the other side of Seattle. He also came home most weekends since it was only an hour away, and his long string of friends liked to visit the Bay.

The three small towns of Brewer, Edington, and Quinlan were nestled along the 101 Highway on the eastern border of Olympic National Park. Each of them was too small to afford much on their own, so they had banded together to share most of the public services, including the police department with its two deputies and part-time chief.

Eddie's friends enjoyed the rustic conditions around the Bay's towns, as well as the chance to go camping in a park that was the only genuine rainforest on the continent. Since Eddie's father also lived in town and ran an adventure tours company, he was more than happy to spend the extra time with their son and his pack of friends.

It took some work, and a lot of compromise, but Ricki was still on good terms with her ex, making it easy for her to tag along on the camping excursions whenever her job allowed. So all in all, things were going pretty well at the moment.

She gave a mental "knock on wood" as she picked up her empty plate and stepped around the counter. Setting the dish in the tub Marcie had abandoned, she scooped the whole thing up and carried it the rest of the way to the large sink. She carefully set it down before turning back toward Marcie. "I had a lot of company, so I didn't have to do much tramping around. And we did find the guy still breathing and in one piece, which made any tramping that had to be done well worth it."

Marcie shook her head, sending her short curls streaked with gray bobbing around her face. "It isn't even your job anymore to go searching for stray hikers."

"I was available, and I know the backcountry," Ricki stated simply. She loved the forests, especially those in the enormous park that cast its shadow over her hometown. She'd spent many happy hours exploring the trails and little-visited areas with all their incredible beauty. But she also knew how dangerous the backcountry could be. The tales of both beginner and experienced hikers getting lost in Olympic Park didn't always end with only a few cuts and bruises, and a thrilling story to tell your friends.

"Of course you know that park as well as anyone. But right now it's the customers who need our attention, not lost hikers, or all those criminals you chase around." Marcie's tone still held a note of admonishment as she gestured toward the dish-filled tub next to the sink behind Ricki. "There are more of those tubs under the counter out front, and plenty of tables with dirty dishes that need to go into them." She lifted both hands and made a shooing motion. "And be sure to do some mingling while you clean off the tables. I've heard grumbles that no one sees you much anymore."

Ricki made a scrunched-up face as she passed Marcie, dissolving into laughter when the older woman simply pointed at the swinging door. Despite what Marcie had claimed, she'd spent more time at the diner in the last few weeks than she had the entire two months prior to that, so she doubted if the grumbling from the locals was too loud. Pushing through the doors, she sent a smile to the three men sitting at the counter, who all grinned back in unison.

Walking over to the counter, she leaned down and grabbed one of the empty tubs, straightening up again with her smile still firmly in place. "Hey, guys. How's the fishing going?"

The man sitting closest to her, who wore his plaid shirt buttoned all the way up to his neck, gave her a morose look from beneath sagging eyelids. "Not so good, Ricki. Not so good. Was going to get an early start, but this rain isn't letting up any."

That made her laugh as she balanced the gray tub on one hip. "That's not surprising. It's April in the Northwest, so it's always raining."

He nodded back at her, his fingers wrapped around a steaming mug of coffee. "Yep. But since it's wet out there and dry in here, I think I'll just let the fish get lucky today and stay where I am."

"Sounds like a good plan to me." She looked at his half-empty mug. "Can I top that off for you?" When she got a headshake, Ricki lifted a questioning eyebrow at his two companions.

"None for me," they both chimed in, earning another grin from Ricki.

"Well, just shout out when you're ready for a warm-up." She gave the trio a wink before moving off to clear tables. Since she was a disaster of a cook herself, and Marcie had the waitressing duties all under control, busing tables had become her usual job by everyone else's unspoken but firm agreement.

She didn't mind. It gave her a chance to talk to her customers, most of whom were also her neighbors. Especially today since it was midweek, and the tourist season wouldn't get into full swing for another month.

Pete, the undisputed king of the town gossips, was planted at his usual table at the center of the room. He was surrounded by his regular entourage—all older men happy to pass the afternoon eating lunch and drinking coffee at the Sunny Side Up, while exchanging the latest scraps of news floating about.

Ricki approached the table with a small feeling of dread and a huge smile. On more than one occasion, Pete and his posse had inexplicably known all about her latest case almost as soon as she had. Which had caused her no small headache in the past. And since she currently didn't have any gruesome cases, she sincerely hoped old Pete wasn't about to let her in on something she hadn't yet heard about through the official channels.

She balanced the plastic tub on one hip and nodded her thanks as several congratulations rang out over her finding the missing hiker. "I appreciate that, but it's really the rangers' search and rescue team that deserves all the credit. They stayed with it no matter how much rain got dumped on them." As the murmurs of agreement came from all around the table at the unusual intensity of the recent weather, Ricki smiled.

Once the noise had died down to normal levels again, Pete took the opportunity to loudly clear his throat. "Even though you were busy with misguided hikers, I guess you heard Chief Thomas had to break up a bar fight over at Tom Madison's place the other night."

Since she hadn't heard that, Ricki's eyebrows lifted in surprise. "Really? At the Mountaintop Bar? Who got into a fight?" She smiled at the bald-headed man with the long beard who was sitting in a place of honor right next to Pete. Bill Langly was the bartender and commander of the local Veterans of Foreign Wars post located just a few blocks from the Sunny Side Up. He'd spent twenty-five years in the service and, despite his tours in various war zones, was as easygoing as the relaxed grin he sent back to her.

"Some truckers passing through, I guess," Bill volunteered. "It wasn't any of our guys since I didn't recognize the names, or get a call to bail someone out."

Pete tapped a long, gnarled finger on the tabletop, deliberately drawing her attention back to himself. "I'm surprised the chief didn't mention it to you." His gaze shifted to the bare third finger of her left hand. "And I would have thought there would be more news coming from the two of you by now."

Ricki stared back at him without batting an eye. "It's tough to hear any news when you're camped out on a mountain, but I appreciate you filling me in." She shifted her gaze to take in the rest of the group. "Can I clear some of those lunch dishes away so you have more room?"

Not put off in the least by her cool response, Pete immediately organized a makeshift assembly line, happily in his element as he cheerfully barked out directions while a mountain of empty plates and silverware was passed down to Ricki. Her tub was completely full by the time she carefully placed the last saucer to precariously perch on top. She thanked them for the help before making her way back to the kitchen, sidling past Marcie on the way.

The waitress was taking an order for a group Ricki hadn't seen before, who had settled into a booth tucked along one wall. Mentally placing them into the category of early tourists passing through the area, she sent over a friendly nod and continued to the kitchen. It took her less than a minute to set the tub near the sink and return to grab the last empty one from under the front counter.

For the next thirty minutes she cleared tables, wiping down the tops and then doing the same to the seats of the chairs before laying fresh silverware on a large squares of paper towels that served as place mats. Keeping Marcie's comment in mind, she took the time to stop and talk with what seemed like an unending parade of customers.

She returned from her fourth trip back to the kitchen just as the bell over the front door tinkled, announcing another arrival. When she looked over that way, her automatic smile grew even wider, and this time it was accompanied by a sparkle in her eyes.

That same sparkle gleamed back at her from a pair of gray eyes as Clay caught her gaze. A huge grin lit up his Hollywood-handsome face, making Ricki's heart rate jump a notch. Since she hadn't seen him in several days, the warmth of her smile didn't even dim when his runway-model-ready partner, Tipper, came in right behind him.

The two made a striking pair and would have turned Ricki several shades of green with envy if Clay hadn't already made it crystal clear that Tipper wasn't his style at all. She was his partner whenever he was involved in a case as an investigator in the Seattle District Attorney's office—something he did when he wasn't busy with his part-time job as chief of police in the Bay. Which was most of the time. While his flat reassurance about his stunning partner had made Ricki feel better, it didn't negate the fact that Penelope Tipper was a very beautiful woman.

Tipper added a nod of greeting to Clay's before gliding her way across the diner, heading for the empty seats at the far end of the back counter.

As every male eye in the place was glued on his partner, Clay walked up to Ricki and leaned over to give her a lingering kiss on the lips. "I heard you found that hiker last night, so I was hoping you'd be here today."

Ricki briefly leaned against him, breathing in the fresh scent of rain that still clung to his parka. When she reluctantly stepped back, she smiled. "We were too far out to get back last night, so we decided to set up camp and hike out first thing this morning. I meant to call you." She looked around at the packed tables. "But it's been crazy here all day."

Clay frowned. "Customers are important, but so are you. Why aren't you home resting? It was a miserable two days to be out in this."

She shrugged that off. She'd grown up in the Northwest, which meant rain had been a regular part of her childhood experience. "It wasn't a bad hike out." She tilted her head toward the nearest occupied tables. "And we're short on bodies to help here." She lifted one hand and gave him a light poke in the chest. "I've heard you've been busy breaking up bar fights."

"I think a punch or two has to be thrown for it to be considered a bar fight." His lips curled into a wry grin. "This was more a case where everyone stood around hoping someone would show up so they wouldn't actually have to do any fighting." He lifted the still-empty tub from her hands and gestured toward the counter where Tipper was sipping a cup of coffee. "Have you got a few moments?"

"Sure." Ricki sighed when a customer stopped Clay to ask him about a parking ticket. Taking the tub back, she left him to listen to the man's earnest explanation of why the ticket had been issued by mistake and made her way to the back counter. Returning the tub to its shelf, she walked over to where Tipper was sitting half sideways on a tall stool, her legs crossed and her full body profile visible to the entire room.

When Clay had gone part-time as police chief for the Bay

and then filled his newly freed-up hours with becoming a special investigator with the DA's office, it had allowed him to get back to his roots as a homicide cop. Which was good. But his new partner? In Ricki's opinion, not so great. The woman might be drop-dead gorgeous, but as far as Ricki was concerned, Tipper had a weak skill set as an investigator. Clay didn't think much of her job performance either, but he was willing to give her time to learn. Not feeling as generous, Ricki silently conceded that was probably because she and Tipper had gotten off on the wrong foot.

But lately the woman had become more friendly toward her, and less of a hindrance to Clay, so Ricki had been withholding judgment on Tipper having any role in law enforcement in general, and specifically as Clay's partner. And while there was zero chance she and Tipper would ever be the best of buddies, at least they'd been maintaining a civil relationship. More or less.

It's a work in progress, Ricki admitted silently to herself, remembering to stretch her lips into a smile as she approached the section of the back counter where Tipper was sitting.

"Hey, Ricki." Tipper nodded, her short blond hair remaining perfectly in place as she frowned into her coffee cup. "Did you get a different brand of coffee?"

"No. Just a different coffee maker." At Tipper's puzzled look, Ricki smiled. "Anchorman usually makes the coffee, but he isn't here this week. He's on vacation."

Tipper's light blue eyes widened slightly. "Oh yeah? I'm about to do the same. Where did he go?"

"Camping in the Great Smoky Mountains."

That caused an immediate wrinkling of Tipper's nose in obvious distaste. "Definitely not for me. I'm looking for a nice warm beach. No rain, no snow, and especially no pine trees."

Trying to keep it light, Ricki smiled. "You picked an odd place to live if you don't like pine trees."

"That is definitely the truth," Tipper muttered before

turning at the sudden noise coming from the front door. "Isn't that Cheron? I guess she didn't want to go camping with Anchorman."

"He went with a Marine buddy," Ricki said absently as her smile faded away. The bookish-looking Cheron Garrison was Jefferson County's part-time medical examiner. The rest of her workday was spent at her own forensics lab that she had built right on the outskirts of Brewer. With the help of Anchorman. Which had surprised no one. The big, former Marine sniper was crazy about the mousy-looking doctor, who had a painfully thin build and large, oversized glasses with thick black frames to go along with all the impressive degrees to her name.

Right now she looked more frantic than a calm, controlled scientist, as she waved her arms wildly back and forth over her head. Concerned that something had happened at the lab, Ricki lifted her hand and waved back. Once Cheron spotted her, she broke into a sprint, dodging around the tables as she ran straight for Ricki. She skidded to a stop in front of the counter, almost dislodging Tipper from her stool as she leaned over the willowy blond, her chin trembling and her voice a good octave higher than her usual quiet tone.

"I just spoke to Norman. They've arrested him. You have to do something." The doctor reached a long, thin arm across the counter, and her fingers latched on to Ricki's shirt with a death grip. Giving the cloth a hard yank, she forced Ricki to lean in closer or have her shirt ripped down the front. "They're claiming he murdered someone. We have to go. We have to go right now!"

"Who's Norman?" Tipper asked.

Ricki ignored the question as she caught and held Cheron's gaze with her own, silently willing her to calm down as she reached up and pried the frightened woman's hand from her shirt. She didn't let go even as Cheron tried to jerk away, but kept the doctor's hand imprisoned in her own as

Clay came up silently behind her. Cheron visibly cringed when Clay laid a gentle hand on her shoulder.

Once she was sure Cheron couldn't wiggle away, Ricki dropped her hand and inclined her head toward the kitchen's double doors. "We'll go right now," she promised, giving an affirmative nod just to settle the doctor down. Cheron immediately stopped struggling and blinked her eyes several times as she stared back at Ricki from behind the thick lenses of her glasses.

"Let's find a more private place to talk, and then you can tell me exactly what's going on."

Cheron blinked again before nodding as Clay smoothly turned her toward the kitchen. The two of them walked the length of the counter with Ricki on the other side, matching them step for step. She held the doors open to allow Clay to usher Cheron through, then swiveled around so her gaze swept the dining room.

Every head was turned toward the kitchen. Not sure what to say, and futilely hoping no one else would say anything, Ricki slowly narrowed her eyes, deliberately sending a warning look across the width of the entire space before turning on her heels and marching through the doors.

Chapter 2

WHILE CLAY COAXED the visibly shaking Cheron to sit on a tall stool that was tucked underneath the edge of the long food-prep table, Sam stood in front of the stove, still holding a spatula. His forehead creased with deep worry lines as his gaze stayed fixed on the upset woman. He crossed his arms over his chest and shifted his stare to Ricki as she came through the double doors.

Catching his accusatory look, she frowned and gestured toward a small kettle on the stove's back burner. "Can you make Cheron a cup of tea?" As her fill-in cook stepped toward an open shelf displaying large mugs and cups all neatly lined up in two rows, Ricki walked over to Cheron and pulled out the stool next to hers. Slowly sitting down, she waited patiently until the doctor lifted her watery eyes. "It's going to be okay. Now tell me exactly what Anchorman said."

"I don't remember every word." Cheron pressed her hands against the sides of her cheeks. "I was so shocked." Her eyes pleaded with Ricki for help. "It was as if he was speaking another language, and then he was just cut off." She sucked in a quick breath, then let it out on a sob. "He sounded sick, or maybe hurt. What if they were beating him? They do that sometimes, don't they?"

Ricki leaned forward and wrapped her fingers around Cheron's wrists, forcing the woman's hands back down onto the table. "No one on this earth can beat up Anchorman. You know that." She waited until she could pin Cheron's gaze with her own. "You do know that, don't you?" She kept her expression calm and her eyes steady while she mentally crossed her fingers. Anyone could be beaten within an inch of his life. Even Anchorman. At least if there were enough very big guys delivering the beating. But she needed information, and the only way she was going to get it was to calm Cheron down.

The doctor took in a longer, deeper breath as her teeth gnawed on her bottom lip. "Of course not. He would never allow that." The words were soft at first, coming out stronger as she straightened her back, sitting up taller. "Norman would never allow that."

Feeling an inner wave of relief as Cheron's trembling subsided, Ricki nodded in satisfaction. "Of course he wouldn't. You're a scientist, Cheron, and a damn good one. You know how to take in and remember details. It's what you do. Small things, like how a blood spatter sprayed out, or hearing the alarms and beeps from all that equipment in your lab."

"Yes, yes. Of course I can do that."

With another satisfied nod, Ricki softened her voice. "Okay then. You heard Anchorman. You know what he said. All you have to do is close your eyes and listen to his voice. Just listen. You can hear him. You know you can. Tell me what he's saying."

The doctor pressed her lips together and lowered her eyelids. The rise and fall of her chest settled into an easier rhythm as her breathing gradually slowed and her face relaxed. "He said he didn't want to upset me, but I needed to listen because he didn't have much time. He wasn't calling from his own number, either. He was using someone else's cell phone." She paused. When she frowned, lines appeared around the corners of her mouth and over her eyebrows, which were barely visible above the rim of her glasses. "I could hear a loud motor in the background. I think he was in a car, or maybe a truck, and he said he was on his way to the county jail. That they were taking him there directly from the park. They arrested him for murder." Her eyes flew open and some of the panic leapt back into them. "He said they have witnesses, and they took his rifle to test."

Ricki's mouth dropped open until it hit her chest. Witnesses? To Anchorman murdering someone? She shook her head. That couldn't be true. No way in hell was that true. Her gaze flew over Cheron's head, seeing the same stunned look of disbelief on Clay's face that she could feel on her own.

Biting her lip to keep from blurting out a vehement protest, Ricki took a long moment to regain her balance. "Did Anchorman give you the names of these witnesses?"

"No, no. He was cut off right after that." Cheron blinked once, then stared blankly past Ricki's shoulder. "But there was something else. I remember he said something else. I'm supposed to tell you something else, but I didn't understand him."

Sam quietly placed a cup of tea in front of her and then retreated to his position in front of the stove. Cheron automatically lifted the cup to her lips, taking a small sip before immediately setting it down again. "Thirty."

"Thirty?" Ricki repeated. "That's what he wanted you to tell me? Thirty?"

Cheron nodded, sending the straight-cut edge of her brown hair brushing across her shoulders. "That's what he said."

Ricki's eyes slowly narrowed as she kept a careful watch on Cheron's face. "Thirty. You're sure?"

The doctor's emphatic nod had her glasses sliding down

her nose. She lifted her forefinger and absently shoved them back into place. "I'm sure. It sounded like he was yelling it, as if the phone had been taken away and he wanted to get that last thing out." She shifted her gaze to look Ricki directly in the eye. "Thirty. Does that mean something to you?"

"Maybe." Ricki slid off the stool and slowly stood up. "You sit here and drink your tea while I check a couple of things." She held out a hand, palm up. "Can I borrow your cell phone?" At Cheron's confused look, Ricki managed a tight smile. "Just for a little while."

The doctor squeezed her eyes shut as she dug into the oversized pocket of her jacket. "Of course." She opened her eyes and gave Ricki an anxious look. "You know all the parks, and all the rangers, don't you? So you'll know how we can find him and bring him home."

There were over four hundred parks spread across the country, and thousands of rangers worked in them. What Cheron believed was damn near impossible, but Ricki curved her mouth upward into a smile. "We'll find him," she assured Cheron. Finding him wouldn't be the problem. She knew where he was. Or at least where he was supposed to be, she amended silently. But making sure he got home again was an entirely different can of worms.

She gave Cheron's forearm a gentle pat before lifting the cell phone from her hand. "Give me a minute to make some calls and then we'll figure out what to do from there." Gesturing to Sam to take her place on the stool next to Cheron, Ricki moved off to the far corner of the kitchen, with Clay following close behind.

"This is bullshit," Clay hissed under his breath so Cheron wouldn't hear. His voice vibrated with fury.

Ricki only nodded her agreement as she traversed the entire length of the kitchen, coming to a halt when she reached the door leading into the back alley.

Clay stopped next to her and jammed his fists into his coat

pockets. "The only reason Anchorman would ever have pointed his rifle at another human being would be to protect his own life or someone else's. Maybe his Marine buddy was in trouble. What was his name?"

"Kelly." It was weird that Cheron hadn't mentioned the man Anchorman considered his closest friend and brother, which meant her cook had said nothing about Kelly. Who was supposed to be on the camping trip with him. So where was the man he considered a brother while he was being arrested for murder?

An uneasy feeling settled into the pit of her stomach. Doing her best to ignore it, she turned to squarely face Clay. Slipping Cheron's phone into the front pocket of her plain wool shirt, she reached for her own, which was tucked into the back pocket of her jeans. Pulling it out, she tapped the screen several times as she started an Internet search. "I'm getting a trail map of the park."

"Did he tell you where they'd be camping?" Clay moved so he stood next to her, with a good view of the cell phone's screen.

"Not directly." Ricki continued to scroll through Internet images until she came to the one she wanted. Opening it up, she enlarged it using two fingers, leaving them on the screen as she slowly moved the image to the right. "I'm not sure he knew when he left the Bay because Kelly had made all the reservations for their trip, but I think he might have told Cheron. He did mention that he and Kelly were going to be hiking in the backcountry."

Clay grunted. "The Great Smoky Mountains is a big park. There's a lot of backcountry in it."

She nodded, then stared down at her phone. A smile played around the edges of her mouth. "That's true enough, but you can only camp at designated sites, and all the sites are numbered."

"Thirty," Clay muttered as he leaned in closer when Ricki held up her phone. "Where the hell is that?"

"About eight miles in, and depending on which route you take, it isn't the usual hike you'd choose for a casual day out enjoying mother nature." Ricki tapped a slim finger against the side of her phone.

Clay leaned closer to study the map. "Good place to kill someone, but an odd place to have witnesses." When he straightened up, his mouth flattened into a thin line as he reached into his pocket for his own cell phone. "Assuming that's where he was, and someone was stupid enough to arrest him way out there, do you know where they would have taken him to be booked?"

Ricki started tapping her screen again. "Gatlinburg would be the most likely place they'd exit the park. The Sugarlands Visitor Center is closest to there." She pointed at the town marked on the map. "And that's in Sevier County, as I recall." She found what she was looking for and once again held the device out for Clay to see the phone number on the screen. "He told Cheron he was on his way to a county jail, and that would be in Sevierville, about a half hour north of Gatlinburg."

Clay punched the number displayed on Ricki's screen into his phone. As he moved off, she heard him say, "I'm Clayton Thomas, chief of police for the Bay in the state of Washington. I'm looking for information on one of your bookings."

Silently nodding her approval, Ricki searched for the ranger headquarters for the Great Smoky Mountains National Park. When it came up on her screen, she entered the number and impatiently listened as it connected and rang on the other end. One of her boots tapped against the floor as the phone kept ringing. She glanced at her watch. She knew the park was in the eastern time zone, which put it three hours ahead of her hometown on the other side of the country. It also meant it was after 5 p.m. there, and likely no one was in the office.

Not willing to wait until morning, she slipped her phone into her back pocket again and plucked out Cheron's phone in its place. Navigating to the recent calls list, she tapped on the last one, which had a Tennessee area code in front of it. It only rang once before a deep voice answered.

"I'm assuming this is Ricki James, or someone who knows her."

Ricki's eyebrows shot up, then immediately slammed down again as she scowled. "You assume correctly. I'm Special Agent Ricki James. And exactly why did you assume that?"

"The same way I imagine you knew to call me. The area code. Hang on a minute. I need to get to a place where we can talk."

There were a long two minutes when there were only muffled sounds she couldn't quite make out. Her foot had started tapping against the linoleum of the kitchen floor once more before the disembodied voice spoke again.

"Okay. I'm outside. Sorry for the delay. I had to put on my jacket. It's still a little cold here."

"Which is where, exactly?"

"I'm standing in front of the county jail, in Sevierville, Tennessee."

"You said you knew me?" Ricki persisted.

The distinctly male voice on the other end rolled into a short laugh. "You and I first met when you were simply Ranger Ricki James, newly assigned to the law enforcement unit. That was a few years before you became a special agent in the ISB. We ran into each other then, too. You probably don't remember me, but I'm still in the Law Enforcement Unit. I'm Supervising Ranger Jerome Johnson."

The image of a tall Black man with a friendly smile and piercing brown eyes flashed into Ricki's mind. "You were stationed at the Mall in Washington, DC." She paused as her thoughts reached back in time. "You walked the Mall with Eddie and me about a week after I was first stationed there."

His laugh was deeper and quieter than a moment earlier. "That's right. But I got tired of the city with all its traffic and bad air, so I transferred out here to Tennessee and have never regretted it." His voice kept an amused note as the laughter faded away. "The last time I saw you and your son, you still had the shine on your new badge with the Investigative Services Branch."

The phone went silent, and Ricki waited, slowly counting to ten in her head, letting him set the speed and tone of the conversation.

"A lot of us follow your cases," Jerome finally said. "They've been good for morale all over the park service. And entertaining, since rumor has it you've had help from none other than a police chief and a former Marine sniper." There was a significant pause before he slowly added, "Who prefers to be called by his military handle of Anchorman."

"That's right," Ricki said quietly, becoming mute again while she waited for him to continue.

Jerome cleared his throat. "Funny thing, I've recently run into that friend of yours."

"I heard about that." Ricki's tone was as dry as dust before she flatly stated, "You let him use your phone."

"Not my work phone," Jerome put in quickly. "I keep one for my private use. I'm sure you understand what I'm saying?"

That you don't want your superiors to know you let Anchorman make an unauthorized call, she thought. "Yeah. I understand."

"We were on our way to the county facility in Sevierville, and being a former Marine myself, I thought he was in need of a small favor."

"That was good thinking, and I appreciate it." She waited a beat. "I was told Anchorman has been arrested."

"He was in handcuffs."

When nothing else was said, she decided it was time to test a more direct route. "Supervisor Johnson, can you tell me why he was arrested?"

There was the sound of a long breath being sucked in.

"No," Jerome said, drawing the word out. "I've been ordered not to talk about Sergeant Kelly Dorman, who was found dead near campsite number twenty-four. Or about the suspect in his murder, or the witnesses who overheard an argument between Sergeant Dorman and the suspect. I also am not to discuss having a weapon sent out for a ballistics test."

"I see." As he kept confirming everything Cheron had said, Ricki looked over at Clay. His face was set in grim lines as he gave her a brief nod, letting her know that Anchorman was indeed in the county lockup. Her grip tightened on her phone as she forced herself to put the sudden jolt of fear aside and concentrate on getting whatever information she could. "Are you allowed to tell me if you've been contacted yet by any other ISB special agent?"

"Now that you mention it, that particular thing wasn't on my list of 'don't talk about this' that I got from the district director. But unfortunately, there isn't anything to tell on that one either. I haven't heard from anyone in the ISB. Maybe someone over my head has, but I haven't heard anything about it."

More alarm bells went off in Ricki's head. An ISB agent in that district should have been assigned within an hour of being notified of a major crime. Two hours at most. Especially when it involved a dead body. And that agent would have made immediate contact with the supervising ranger.

"Who's the agent in your district?" She barely got the question out when the ranger on the other end abruptly cut her off.

"I have to go. My advice to you, Special Agent Ricki James, is to get your butt out here before your friend finds himself shuffled off to a federal prison."

Ricki opened her mouth, closing it once she realized Jerome had disconnected the call. Frustrated, she plucked her phone from her back pocket once again and entered the supervising ranger's number into her own contact list before deleting it from Cheron's. The last thing she needed was the doctor making phone calls on her own, or to get Supervisor Johnson into trouble for letting Anchorman make the call in the first place.

She walked back to where Cheron was still sitting. Sam had deserted his place by the stove and was keeping a quiet watch beside Cheron. He took a half step back when Ricki handed the doctor's phone back.

Answering the questioning look in Cheron's eyes with yet another reassuring pat on the arm, Ricki made her way back to Clay who had stopped just inside the back door. He put a hand over the end of his phone to block out any sound from the kitchen as he leaned closer to Ricki's ear.

"Anchorman is in the Sevier County jail, booked in on suspicion of murder. They wouldn't give me the name of the victim, or much else, other than to confirm that Anchorman was there."

"Kelly Dorman," Ricki said, matching her low tone to his while shooting a worried gaze at Cheron. The doctor was slumped over, head bent, hands clasped firmly together in her lap. "The dead guy's name is Sergeant Kelly Dorman."

Clay's eyebrows immediately snapped together. "Kelly? Didn't you just tell me that's the name of the guy Anchorman went camping with?"

Ricki nodded. She'd never met Kelly, but she'd certainly heard a lot about him. She closed her eyes, calling up the image of Anchorman's compact apartment.

In his entire living space, he only had three pictures on display. One was in an old-fashioned frame, kept meticulously polished, with Anchorman's long-deceased parents dressed in their wedding attire and beaming out from the photo inside it. The second picture was surrounded by a more traditional frame. It showed a tall, dark-haired woman and a young boy who looked to be around ten years old. Ricki had asked him about it once, and Anchorman had said it was his aunt and cousin, back in his hometown in New Jersey.

Both pictures stood side by side on a shelf over his TV, while the remaining picture was in a prominent spot on the other side of the room. Anchorman had placed it on one of the end tables that flanked a fold-out couch, which doubled as his bed.

The photo had been taken during one of his deployments. Kelly was standing in front of an open tent, holding an M16 rifle. Anchorman's arm was slung around his much shorter friend's shoulders as they struck a casual pose and mugged for the camera. Both men were dressed in full combat gear, minus their helmets. Afghanistan, she remembered. Anchorman had told her the photo had been taken on their first tour together in Afghanistan.

"Yeah." She opened her eyes and stared at Clay. "His name was Kelly."

Chapter 3

THE DOUBLE DOORS to the kitchen flew open and Marcie walked in, followed closely by Bill. While the waitress continued her march into the center of the room, the VFW post commander stopped just a few feet in, his hands shoved inside the back pockets of his faded jeans.

Marcie didn't waste any time with small talk, or wringing her hands over the dramatic scene Cheron had created in the dining room as she quickly faced Ricki and Clay. Her hands were placed firmly on her hips, and her mouth was pulled down into a fierce frown.

"It's turned into a circus out there. Everyone heard what Cheron said." When a loud sob came from the doctor, Marcie turned on her heels and walked over to slide a protective arm around Cheron's shoulders. "I've assured anyone who wasn't busy on their phones spreading the news about Anchorman that we did not believe a word of it, and this will all be straightened out in no time." She glared at Ricki before turning that same angry stare on Clay. "And it will be, won't it?"

Ricki didn't need any help to decipher Marcie's look as "it had better be," but before she could even nod, Bill stepped forward. He continued to keep his hands in his pockets as his gaze also moved between Ricki and Clay.

"By the looks on your faces, I'm thinking it's true that Anchorman's been arrested for murder?" He waited out the stares from two pairs of eyes before Ricki finally gave a brief nod. "Okay. Then I'll get things rolling here." He lifted an eyebrow at Clay. "You know the mayor is former army. He and I are regular drinking buddies. Our bar over at the VFW is his favorite place to spend an evening. Now, if you wait a few minutes and let me call him first, I guarantee you'll get as much time away as you need."

Clay nodded his thanks as Ricki blinked in surprise. She was used to neighbors helping out neighbors, but this was beyond what she'd expected.

"And we've already started a fund to get Anchorman a good lawyer," Bill went on. "One that will get him back here where he belongs. And for bond money, too, if it turns out he needs it. We aren't having one of us sit in a jail cell when he shouldn't be there." He turned his bald head, causing the overhead light to give it an extra gleam. He nodded at Cheron, who managed a watery smile back at him. "You heard what I said? He shouldn't be in any jail cell, because he didn't do anything unless it needed to be done. Ricki and Clay are going to bring him home." He shifted his gaze to the pair and gave them the same look Marcie had. "Won't you?"

Clay's frown was back in place when he met Ricki's troubled eyes. "Doesn't sound like we have much choice."

"You don't," Bill declared. "I can also guarantee that the fund is going to be a goodly amount. I've already sent word out to plan some events and raise even more. When you need to get at it, or if you have any problems with the mayor, you just call the post. If I'm not there, whoever is hanging around will find me quick enough." He slowly stretched his back and took his hands out of his pockets. Lifting one until his straightened-out fingers hovered close to the side of his forehead, he executed a crisp salute. Lowering his arm again, he turned on his heels and marched out of the kitchen.

Ricki smiled at the dumbfounded look on Clay's face. He'd been the Bay's police chief for five years now, ever since he'd left his job as a homicide detective in Los Angeles. She knew he'd spent most of his life in big cities and had that hard edge of suspicion and cynicism that often came out of urban environments with their every-man-for-himself mentality.

But she had grown up in the Bay. They might not have had the convenience of being on one of Amazon's daily delivery routes, and the gossip mill could be brutal, but no one was better at circling the wagons around one of their own than the three small towns dotting the shore of Dabob Bay.

I should have known. Her smile grew at the thought. Everyone in town practically doted on Anchorman, so there was no way they would let the man sit in a jail somewhere in Tennessee. To a fair number of people who called the Bay their home, Tennessee was far enough away it might as well be on another planet.

"The fund is good, but we aren't going to have much time to do any fundraising. Anchorman will need a retainer for a lawyer and bail money before we even get to that county jail. Which will be when?"

Clay's practical voice yanked Ricki back to the enormous problem at hand. They needed to get Anchorman out of that jail. "Tomorrow morning, if I can swing the travel arrangements that fast."

The Bay's chief of police held up his phone and jiggled it slightly. "I'm going to call Andre. I'm pretty sure he can help us find the right attorney in Tennessee and get everything rolling on that end."

Andre Hudson was Clay's boss at his Seattle job, and an impressive attorney in his own right. If anyone would know who to call in Tennessee, it would be District Attorney

Hudson. Knowing Clay would get that under control quickly enough, Ricki nodded and held up her own phone.

"I'll make the travel arrangements. As soon as you're finished talking with Andre, get over to your place and pack your gear. We'll meet back here in an hour and head out."

"Think you can get us a flight before tomorrow morning?"

Her mouth thinned into a grim line. "I'll find us one, even if we have to go camp out at the airport and fly standby." When her phone rang, she glanced at the screen. The caller ID spelled out the name of the senior agent in charge of the Seattle ISB office, who was also her boss.

"It's Hamilton." She touched the connect icon, then covered the phone's speaker with one hand as she glanced back at Clay. "Remember. You have one hour."

They turned in opposite directions, with Clay heading for the dining room, and Ricki yanking open the door leading outside to the back alley. She took an involuntary step backwards when she was faced with a sheet of icy rain pounding down between the brick buildings. Flipping the hood of her coat up over her head, she shoved her hand and phone into her pocket as she stepped out into a drenched world. She jogged down the three steps then sprinted for the lime-green beacon that was her jeep parked at the head of the alley.

It took her less than ten seconds to reach it, but that was enough time for a pool of water to slide off her coat, creating its own mini waterfall onto the floor mat as she plopped into the passenger seat.

Ignoring the minor flood, she lifted the phone to her ear. "Are you still there?"

"I'm here." Hamilton's voice had a layer of grit in it, as if he'd just rolled out of bed, or spent the better part of the day talking. "And I'm guessing you've heard the news?"

A trickle of water found its way underneath her butt, forcing Ricki to shift positions on the seat. "I heard, and I'm hoping you're calling to tell me I've been assigned to the case."

"I'm calling to let you know that you *haven't* been officially assigned to the case."

Not at all happy with that, Ricki frowned as she pulled her hood back. "Why the hell not?"

"Because as of this moment, no one in the ISB has been officially assigned to the case."

Hamilton's even tone had Ricki gritting her teeth in frustration. "Then who's working on it? It happened on federal land, so it can't be the local or state police."

The senior agent grunted his agreement. "No. Not them. But not us either. It happened in a park, but the victim was a Marine on active duty."

"Yeah. So . . .?" She trailed off. NCIS. She gave an inward groan. The case had been given to NCIS.

"The Director has decided that the Naval Criminal Investigative Service has more jurisdiction in this matter than we do, so they'll be taking the lead."

Hamilton verifying it caused a ball of anger mixed with a large dose of fear to form in the pit of her stomach. She needed to work this case. She *had* to be assigned to this case.

"I wasn't too thrilled with that small turn of events when I got the phone call, but I think it will work to our advantage."

His words stopped Ricki's mind from racing off in ten different directions. Their advantage? What advantage could come from someone else taking over the case?

"The director pointed out that we aren't the lead on the case, but he's going to insist that we should have a presence since it involves a national park," Hamilton continued. "He thought an assigned consultant who is kept in the loop on all developments would be appropriate. And he asked if I had any recommendations."

"An assigned consultant," she repeated slowly. She wasn't sure what that meant, exactly, but it was better than being completely shut out.

"That's right. And of course, any subject matter experts

who the consultant needs to confer with can be brought in as well." The sudden note of cheer in Hamilton's voice had Ricki's lips twitching into a shadow of a smile.

"Like a highly regarded forensic pathologist?" Ricki suggested, then tucked her tongue in her cheek. "Or an expert on homicide methods?"

"Sure. Sounds reasonable," her boss agreed. "Of course I had a suggestion for this consultant."

Now Ricki did grin. "Of course you did."

"And that said consultant will need to leave for the scene right away since I expect her to be an on-site consultant. More importantly, the scene has been cordoned off and is being guarded by the law enforcement rangers assigned to the park. The only things removed were Anchorman and his rifle. Everything else is still up there, waiting for NCIS and its forensics team to arrive."

"Even better." Ricki glanced at her wristwatch. "I need to make the travel arrangements for myself and my experts, get my gear together, and be back here in forty-five minutes to meet up with Clay."

"I can save you a good fifteen of those," the senior agent claimed. "I've already made travel arrangements for you and two experts. I made a call, pulled a few strings, and got you on a flight out of SeaTac just before midnight tonight. You'll be getting into Knoxville, Tennessee at ten tomorrow morning. It's a forty-mile drive to Pigeon Forge, so there will be an SUV waiting for you at the airport. You're booked into a motel in Pigeon Forge, which is about halfway between Sevierville, where Anchorman is being held, and the park. It's also the same hotel that the NCIS agent will be staying at. I'll have Dan email you the details as soon as we get off the phone."

Ricki sucked in a quick breath. "They've already assigned an agent to the case?"

"Not yet," Hamilton said. "I suspect they have an agent in mind, but all they're saying at the moment is that it will be the next agent up, and they're still checking on that. They might not be admitting they've assigned an agent, but strangely enough, the travel arrangements have been made. And since the flight is coming out of National Airport near Washington, DC, I'm thinking the agent is coming out of Quantico."

The large Marine base was thirty miles south of the nation's capital and played host to a legion of federal head-quarters and diplomatic agencies, including the FBI and NCIS. Ricki had been there several times herself at the begin-ning of her career as a special agent for the National Park Service, being based out of the nation's capital. Agents who worked from Quantico had to be pretty hot stuff, which could be a good thing if they were crackerjack at their jobs, or a bad thing if their egos didn't let them play nice in the sandbox with other agencies. And since she wasn't the lead on the case, playing ball with a sister agency would be essential if she was going to get to the truth and bring Anchorman home.

"He's going to need an attorney," Hamilton stated bluntly. "And a good one. I was told not to make any inquiries into the specifics surrounding Anchorman's arrest, and that point was not negotiable. But I've already heard some rumors floating around."

"I talked to the arresting officer." Ricki's announcement was met with a beat of silence on the other end of the phone.

"He said that a gag order right from the director's office had been put out on this."

Ricki nodded even though the senior agent couldn't see her. "There is, so the ranger couldn't say much. I'm sure he'd get in an ocean of hot water if it got out that he'd talked to me at all."

"It's a funny thing," Hamilton drawled out. "Lately I haven't been able to remember a damn thing after five minutes."

Ricki stifled a laugh. "Is that so? Then I guess it isn't running much of a risk to tell you the arresting officer was a supervisor in the Law Enforcement Unit by the name of Jerome Johnson."

"Do you know him?" Hamilton interrupted.

She made a small sound in the back of her throat. "I've met him. We were introduced prior to me joining the ISB. He gave Eddie and me a tour of Constitution Hall in Philadelphia. I was just starting out as a ranger, on my first assignment at Shenandoah National Park in western Virginia." She ran her tongue over dry lips. "Johnson managed to get bits of information across without really confirming or denying anything."

"Such as?" Hamilton prompted.

"Anchorman was arrested for Kelly's murder," Ricki said, holding up her hand and raising a finger to tick off each point the ranger had slid into their conversation. "The body was found near Campsite 24, which is just off the Little River Trail, according to the supervisor. But Anchorman told Cheron he'd been camping at site number thirty."

"When did he tell her that?"

"During a phone call Johnson let him make." She hesitated for a moment. "Johnson let him use his private cell to make the call. Not the one he uses for work."

"Smart man," Hamilton half muttered under his breath. "Thinks quick on his feet."

"That was my impression too," Ricki agreed. "I looked both sites up on a trail map. They're just under two miles apart."

"Two miles?" Hamilton choked out. "What do they think Anchorman did? Kill his fellow Marine and then wander off for two miles, set up camp, and roast a hot dog?"

Since that was one of many thoughts that had already occurred to her, Ricki lifted her shoulders in a shrug. "I have no idea."

A long sigh came through the speaker. "Supposedly there are witnesses to the murder."

"Not to the murder, at least according to Supervisor John-son. But to an argument between the two men."

The senior agent barked out a laugh. "So now the story is that Anchorman had an argument with his friend, in front of other people, then killed him when their backs were turned before taking himself down to this other campsite to roast a hot dog?"

Thinking Hamilton's scenario was too absurd to comment on, Ricki moved on to the next point that Johnson had mentioned. "Anchorman's gun has been sent off to Quantico for ballistics testing."

"So our dead Marine was shot?"

"Sergeant Kelly Dorman," Ricki supplied.

"Yes," Hamilton replied quietly. "I apologize. Then we can assume that Sergeant Dorman was shot? And you said that Anchorman's gun is at Quantico for testing?"

"That's right."

"Do you know anyone at Quantico who owes you a favor?"

Hamilton's deceptively casual voice didn't fool her for one second. They both knew who he meant. He was undoubtedly referring to Dr. Jonathan Blake, the number one profiler in the country, who also worked for the FBI. But whenever the secretive doctor doled out favors, it was to promote his own agenda, so she'd already relegated calling him to the "last resort" category.

Instead, the big Irish face of Special Agent Finn Sullivan popped into her mind. He was also with the FBI, and he was stationed at Quantico. At least he had been the last time she'd talked to him. Hoping he still was, she made a mental note to call him as soon as she got on site and could see for herself what was going on. If it turned out she needed FBI help, she'd take the outspoken Finn over the gamesmanship of Blake any day in the week. And she was absolutely positive that Clay would too. There was some history between the chief of police and the profiler over Clay's fugitive brother, Lex. Because of it, Clay could barely tolerate Dr. Blake.

"I'll work on that," she promised with another glance at her watch. "If I'm going to get the team together and make that flight, I need to get going."

"Dan will email you those details. If you need any research or other information to help solve the case, just call him. I'll let him know that your requests are a priority."

"Thanks. I appreciate that." Ricki really was grateful for the help. Dan was a former researcher with the CIA, and if anyone could dig out details on a case, it was him.

"Normally I would wish you good hunting, Special Agent James. But this time I'm ordering you to make it quick and airtight. Let's bring our boy home."

"I won't be leaving Tennessee without him," she promised with more conviction in her voice than she felt in the pit of her stomach. "And sir? Maybe you should see someone about that memory problem of yours." She hung up the phone on Hamilton's "what memory problem?"

The arrangement wasn't ideal. She'd rather be the primary investigator than having to deal with some unknown NCIS agent. But it beat having to resign her position with the ISB in order to help her friend.

Sighing at the water still flooding down the front windshield and off the hood of the jeep, she pocketed her phone and pulled the zipper across the opening. With a philosophical shrug, because this was the Northwest, she flipped the still-wet hood of her jacket back up and stepped out into the rainstorm.

Chapter 4

GETTING onto the flight with rifles handguns, and a case of surgical gear that Cheron insisted on taking with her, had proven to be less of a pain than Ricki had anticipated. Thanks entirely to Hamilton clearing the usual mountain of red tape for them.

Knoxville's airport was a less crowded version of the one they'd just left in Seattle, with long concourses encased in glass leading to a central hub. The promised SUV was waiting, and the forty-minute drive to Sevierville was uneventful. From her position in the front passenger seat, Ricki couldn't see Cheron, who was sitting directly behind her, but she could hear the restless movements as the doctor shifted in her seat every few minutes.

Since there wasn't anything she could say to reassure Cheron that the doctor would actually believe, Ricki kept her silence. She glanced at her phone when it signaled an incoming email. She opened it and found her first partial smile in eight hours.

"Andre just sent a message to both of us." She'd turned her head toward Clay but put enough volume in her voice so Cheron could hear as well. "He says that the best lawyer in the South is headed for the county jail and will wait there to meet us."

A loud sigh of relief came from the back seat while Clay grunted his approval. "Does the best lawyer in the South have a name?"

"Christopher Young." She looked up and her half smile grew into a full one. "Andre says we're going to like him."

Cheron leaned forward and stuck her head in the opening between the two front seats. "But will Norman? He doesn't like lawyers very much." She leaned back again and resettled her glasses on the bridge of her nose. "To be more accurate, he doesn't like them at all. It goes back to when his parents passed away and their diner had to be sold. The lawyers sold it and took most of the profit while Norman was serving overseas."

"That wouldn't go over very well with anyone," Clay observed.

Cheron nodded as she wrapped her long, gangly arms around her middle. "I know. But he took care of it when he got home. His parents had engaged a law firm in the neighborhood to draw up their final arrangements. And according to Norman, it was a very tight-knit community. So when he got home, he put the word out that they had acted less than ethically, and the firm lost so much business it finally had to close its doors."

Clay glanced at her from the rearview mirror. "Being lawyers, I'm surprised they didn't sue him for slander."

Now the doctor laughed. "Oh, they probably would have if they had known where the rumors had come from. But Norman told me he made sure they'd never be able to trace anything back to him. He still enjoys thinking about them stewing over who had ruined them."

Clay laughed. "Sounds like something he'd do."

"Yes it does, doesn't it?" Ricki agreed before leaning back in her seat, her brow wrinkled in thought. It really did sound like him. The thought had her smile returning in full force. Revenge maybe, but not over the top. Feeling a twinge of guilt over the small niggle of doubt she'd been harboring about the murder and Anchorman's role in it, she sat up straighter with renewed purpose and checked her watch. "We have about fifteen more minutes until we reach Sevierville. The county jail is on the west side of town, so it won't take long to get there."

They ran into not one, but two traffic accidents on the remaining stretch of road, so Ricki's fifteen-minute estimate grew to triple that before they finally pulled into the parking lot of the county jail. The stone-and-brick building with smoked-glass double doors at the entrance looked as solid as Fort Knox. After double-checking the doors to the SUV to make sure their weapons and equipment were secure, Ricki stood on the sidewalk and waited for Clay and Cheron to join her.

Leading the way, Ricki stepped into the lobby and took a slow look around. It was a busy place with cops and civilians alike rushing about, most of them clutching a stack of paper-work. Even with all the commotion, it didn't take her long to spot the man who pushed himself out of a straight-backed chair and braced his feet apart as he turned to face them.

He stood ramrod straight, but even so, he only looked to be close to Ricki's height of five feet eight inches. Although if she were pressed about it, she'd guess that she had a solid inch on him. He was also about half as wide as he was tall, with a large midsection protruding well over his kneecaps. His short, neatly trimmed beard and mustache were in the same pure white shade as his thick head of hair. The resemblance to a famous colonel who served up fried chicken was completed by the man's pronounced double chin and bushy eyebrows that capped a pair of bright blue eyes.

He was dressed in an expensive-looking dark suit, complete with a button-down vest that sported a gold chain running from a buttonhole to a pocket, which no doubt had a watch tucked away in it. He exchanged a stare with Ricki for a moment, but instead of making a move to cross the room, he gestured her forward.

Not sure she liked getting a royal command like that, she briefly glanced at the reception desk, silently holding a quick internal debate before deciding not to alienate the man. He'd clearly been waiting for them, which made him the most likely possibility of all the people in the lobby of being Andre Hudson's choice of the best lawyer in the South. And Anchorman's best hope for getting out on bail in the very near future. Which was reason number two, and the best one, for not ignoring his imperious command.

Tamping down her irritation at the expectant look beamed directly at her, Ricki crossed the polished floor and stopped right in front of the man with Clay coming up beside her. The two of them deliberately formed a wall in front of Cheron.

"Dr. Garrison?" The voice had the slow cadence of the South as a shaggy eyebrow lifted with the question.

Ricki shook her head. "I'm Special Agent James with the Investigative Services Branch of the National Park Service. And this is Police Chief Thomas from the Bay in the state of Washington." When the rotund man simply lifted his other eyebrow, she stepped to one side and inclined her head toward Cheron. "This is Dr. Garrison."

Ricki had to give him credit for a poker face. Not by so much as a twitch of a cheek muscle did he give any indication of surprise when he got his first look at Cheron.

"Then I gather you're Mr. Beal's significant other?" When Cheron nodded, he did too. "I'm Christopher Young." He paused and let the name hang in the air as he gave Clay an amused look. "I take it you expected to hear something like Buford or maybe Bubba?"

"Oh no, Mr. Young," Cheron chimed in. "We knew your

name. DA Hudson sent it to Ricki. He also said you were the best lawyer in the South."

The attorney smiled and captured one of Cheron's thin hands, sandwiching it between his two pudgy ones. "Only the South? My. I will have to have a talk with DA Hudson." At Cheron's alarmed look, he chuckled and gave her hand a gentle pat. "But I appreciate the kind words. I surely do." Keeping his gaze on Cheron, he let go of her hand and hooked his thumbs into the lower pockets in his vest, one on each side. "Now, we have successfully sorted out who is the doctor, the special agent, and the police chief, although I still need a formal introduction."

Clay immediately held out his hand, taking the one that Christopher Young extended in a firm grip. "I'm Chief Thomas. I'm sure DA Hudson also explained that it will be my name on the checks you'll be hoping to cash."

The attorney inclined his head in acknowledgment. "A timely reminder of who I should be catering to. I understand that your background is in homicide?"

"That's right."

"Excellent." He gave Clay's hand a vigorous shake before withdrawing his own and extending it toward Ricki. "I've neglected to greet you properly as well. And that is a crime, considering I was told that you are the very best investigative agent in the park service."

Ricki smiled when she shook his hand. "Only in the park service?"

"Touché, Special Agent James." Young took his hand back and tilted his head to one side while he studied her. "Well, then. If we are all through establishing our places in the pecking order here, I prefer to be called Christopher."

"And I'm Ricki." Giving her head a slight shake at the attorney's tactics to uncover who was the leader of the group, Ricki gestured toward the confused-looking Cheron. "Dr. Garrison is one of the top forensic pathologists in the country.

The odds are good that the local medical examiner has heard of her. And she prefers to be called Cheron, unless you are one of her professional colleagues."

Young nodded. "Oh, I should mention that I've already spoken to one of those professional colleagues. Namely, the aforementioned medical examiner in this county. And we all need to have a talk about that. It seems he isn't very keen on sharing his space or his findings directly with the good doctor. I detected a bit of professional jealousy." He paused and glanced at Clay. "Andre told me about Ricki, and I understand that Dr. Garrison is a renowned expert in forensic pathology, but might I get a few more specifics about your background and experience in murder cases? Andre didn't have much time to go into details."

"Okay." Clay slowly drew the word out. "I'm the part-time police chief in the Bay, which is where your client lives, as do the three of us, for that matter. I also work as an investigator for the DA's office in Seattle, and before all of that, I spent ten years as a homicide cop in Los Angeles."

For the first time, surprise flickered in the attorney's eyes. "Los Angeles? I just assumed you'd worked as a homicide detective in Seattle."

"No," Clay stated. "I work on murder cases both in Seattle and in the Bay when necessary, but I was a full-time homicide cop in LA." His lips stretched into a wry grin. "And I prefer to be called Clay."

"Impressive, Clay. Very impressive. As we are exchanging credentials, I received my law degree from the University of Virginia and have been a practicing attorney for thirty-five years now. I've dealt with quite a number of homicide suspects, as both a consultant for the prosecutor on particularly difficult cases, and as a defense attorney." He smiled. "Although those are never the same cases, of course. But having worked on both sides of the courtroom, it makes my résumé unique." He brushed some imaginary lint off the sleeve of his jacket, then straightened his tie. "Since it is clear which side I'll be sitting on for this case, I think it's about time I met my client."

Ricki had taken a step toward the lobby desk but stopped and turned back to face Christopher. "You haven't met Anchorman yet? And if you want to get along with him, you'll need to call him that."

He nodded. "Duly noted, Ricki." He then switched to shaking his head. "And no, I haven't met him yet. But I can assure you all, especially you, Clay, that I've been using your money wisely. I've spoken to the county sheriff, who I have worked with in the past, as well as several of the officers who have been in contact with Mr. Beal. And then, of course, the notably uncooperative medical examiner. Enough to know we are dealing with a very unusual situation here."

Ricki stuck her hands in her jacket pockets and stared back at him. "How so?"

"Well, it seems they all universally admire and respect my client, but everyone here is equally convinced that he did, in fact, murder his friend. And I'm afraid if the ballistics report does not come back in our favor, this is going to be a very steep hill to climb."

Ricki shifted her weight from one foot to the other. "Again. How so?"

Christopher looked over at the desk sergeant, who was watching the group with a suspicious gaze. He gave the burly man a friendly nod before glancing back at Ricki. "From what I've been told, and what I can surmise from what I haven't been told, I think there is something about that ballistics report that is being held back from me at the moment. And that is making me very cranky. I dislike feeling cranky." Instead of pulling out his pocket watch, he lifted his arm, displaying a very expensive wristwatch. Encrusted with diamonds all along its edge, it was the only piece of flash that he was wearing. But it was quite an impressive piece. "I think it's time we moved along and heard what Mr. Be— that is, Anchorman, has to say about all this. And then I have a date in court for a bail hearing." He lifted an eyebrow at Clay. "I trust your checkbook will withstand the blow."

Since she knew just how big the trust fund his grandparents had set up for Clay was, Ricki wasn't surprised when he only shrugged. When Christopher narrowed his eyes in speculation, Ricki quickly pointed at the desk sergeant. "Shall we go? We still have a big to-do list on our plates."

"As do I, Ricki." After one last glance at the silent Clay, Christopher casually strolled over to the desk with the other three trailing after him. "Good morning once again, Deputy Boyer." He settled back on his heels and indulged in his habit of sticking his thumbs into his vest pockets. "I'm ready to speak with my client, Mr. Norman Beal, if you'd be so kind as to have him brought into one of the attorney-client conference rooms."

"I can do that, Mr. Young." Boyer used the pen in his hand to point at the group standing behind the lawyer. "And will they be waiting out here?"

Christopher's eyes crinkled at the corners as his smile slowly spread across his broad face. "No indeed. They must come in as well, since they are my interrogation team."

"Your interrogation team?" The deputy sounded as skeptical as he looked. He leaned back until his chair creaked in protest. "I've never heard of anyone bringing along an interrogation team. Are you going to tell me they're all lawyers?"

"Oh good heavens, no, Deputy Boyer. That's very old-fashioned. Far be it from me to bring in a gang of lawyers instead of trained interrogators. I need candid and honest answers to my questions as much as the prosecutor does. No, what we have here is an experienced homicide detective and a special agent with the Investigative Branch of the National Park Service. I've also brought along a forensics expert." He pointed at Cheron. "That would be Dr. Garrison. I have explained all of this to the sheriff, who has given his permission for the entire interrogation team to be present while I confer with my client." He politely pointed to the phone on the desk in front of the deputy. "Give him a call to confirm that, if you'd like."

Boyer stared at the phone for a long moment before shifting his gaze back to Christopher. "They'll all need to sign in and be searched for weapons."

"That's fine. I'm sure that can be done while you have my client brought up from his holding cell." Christopher's smile didn't dim even as the officer glared at him. But Boyer picked up the phone and barked out the request to whoever was on the other end. Slamming the receiver back into its cradle, he jerked his head to the open hallway behind him. "Okay. Let's get that search out of the way."

Chapter 5

THE MEETING ROOM WAS SMALL, with gray walls, no windows, and just enough space for a compact table and three folding chairs. Christopher took one chair, his enormous body immediately swallowing up the whole thing. Ricki watched in alarm as the entire back and seat sagged in protest. If the chair gave way and Anchorman's crackerjack attorney ended up on his ass, she wasn't at all certain that she and Clay could get him back on his feet again.

Clay guided Cheron to a second chair, then took up a standing position behind her, leaning back against the wall. Ricki joined him, leaving the third seat for Anchorman. When ten more minutes passed without her incarcerated cook making an appearance, her boot began a steady tapping against the tile floor. Christopher leaned slightly over to one side, obviously looking for the source of the noise, straightening up again once he spied the movement of Ricki's foot.

"We take things a little slower here in the South," he remarked to no one in particular. "We find it helps with our digestion."

Ricki took her eyes off the door long enough to glance over at him. "I'll keep that in mind."

Another five minutes passed in silence before the distinct sound of a doorknob being turned pulled everyone's gaze in that direction. The door opened slowly, then much to the collective relief of the three people from his hometown, Anchorman stepped into the room. Cheron let out a sob as she jumped out of her chair, practically jumping over Christopher's large form in her rush to throw her arms around the tall man, who dropped his head to her shoulder and whispered into her ear. She immediately pulled back and frowned at the handcuffs keeping his hands and arms immobile in front of him. She lifted her own hands and cupped his cheeks, then rose on her tiptoes to give him a long kiss.

Ricki wasn't sure about being a witness to this side of the good doctor and looked over at Clay, who was carefully staring at the far wall. She gave him a nudge in the ribs with her elbow, which drew his attention along with a slight shake of his head.

"I think *you* should break them up," he said in an undertone. "He's less likely to take a swing at you."

"I can't take a swing at anyone at the moment." Anchorman held up his hands encased in the metal cuffs before dropping them again as he smiled at Ricki. "Glad to see you." He shifted his gaze to Clay. "Both of you."

Since Christopher had chosen the only chair that was facing the door, he didn't have to swivel around to get a look at his newest client. The lawyer didn't get up but waited until the tall man with the crew cut and built as solidly as a tree trunk, narrowed his eyes on him. "We haven't met, but I'm Christopher Young, your attorney."

Anchorman's eyes narrowed even more as he carefully looked Christopher over. "I don't recall hiring an attorney."

Clay immediately took a small step forward, since that was all the compact room would allow. "You didn't. I did. And Mr. Young came highly recommended by Andre."

"Then I'm sure you're very good, Mr. Young, and very

expensive," Anchorman said evenly.

Knowing the man's pride, and not wanting him to fire his attorney within a minute of meeting him, Ricki quickly cut him off. "Which is something we'll all discuss later. Right now, Mr. Young is your attorney, and he already has a hearing set up to establish bail and get you out of here. Which is the number one priority on our agenda today."

The former Marine opened his mouth, then shut it when Cheron placed a hand on his chest.

"Please. Ricki is right. We shouldn't argue about this right now. Mr. Young is a very nice man, and you need his help."

Ricki sent a silent "thank you" to Cheron when Anchorman finally let out a long sigh.

"Fine." He glanced over at Christopher, who was waiting patiently. "You're my attorney."

Christopher gestured toward the empty chair on the other side of the table. "Now that we agree, please sit down so we can get started on your defense."

"I don't need a defense because I didn't do anything wrong. And I sure as hell did not murder my best friend," Anchorman spit out, but he moved toward the chair and stood next to it, waiting for Cheron to sit down before doing the same.

"First, you must take a different attitude." When Anchorman scowled, Christopher simply clasped his hands together and rested them on the table. "No one in this room believes you killed your friend, but you need a defense. Otherwise, you could easily be in that orange jumpsuit and wearing a pair of handcuffs for the rest of your life."

"Good point." Suddenly looking drained, Anchorman rested his forehead in the palms of his hands. "Where do you want to start?"

"With a blood draw and a urine sample." Cheron's bald declaration left everyone else in the room speechless.

Anchorman jerked his head up and stared at her. "What?"

The doctor rose to her feet, then plowed her way to the door, shoving at any arms and legs that got in her way. She opened the door and yelled down the hall until a deputy stepped into view.

Ricki heard her demand that the satchel she'd brought with her, which had been kept at the front desk, be immediately returned to her possession. She insisted on it so vehemently that the deputy finally had no choice but to send her back down the hallway to retrieve it or lock her up for disturbing the peace. While the doctor was berating the poor deputy who'd pulled the duty of standing guard at the door, Ricki slowly turned her head and studied Anchorman's face. Cheron might have the right idea after all. He did look pale, and his gaze wasn't entirely focused.

"Anchorman? Are you feeling all right?" The sharp note in Ricki's voice had him jerking upright.

"Upset stomach. Probably still feeling the bourbon that Kelly brought along."

Ricki exchanged a worried look with Clay. Anchorman was not only an expert marksman, he was also an expert drinker whenever he chose to indulge in that. She'd seen him put away a bottle of whiskey and not blink an eye. And she sure as hell had never seen him get sick over a night of drinking, and especially not still be feeling any aftereffects two days later.

She was keeping a careful eye on him when Cheron burst back through the door, clutching her large black satchel to her chest. The deputy followed her into the room, making the space even more crowded as the doctor plopped her oversized bag onto the table and dug through it. She pulled out two small vials and one clear-plastic specimen jar, along with a syringe.

"I'm going to take some blood, and then I want you to pee in that jar."

Anchorman scowled at her, then pointedly looked around

the room. "Not in a million years."

Cheron straightened up and put her hands on her hips. "Why not?"

The big Marine stiffened his back and blew out a big breath. "I'm not whipping it out and putting in on display for a roomful of people."

"That's not only unnecessarily crude, it's also ridiculous."

"I don't know, Cheron," Clay cut in. "He has a point."

The doctor's chin stuck out as she sent an annoyed look his way. "Now *you're* being ridiculous. There's nothing sexual or embarrassing about any of this. We're talking about a clinical procedure here. The man is accused of murder, for goodness' sake. This is no time to be prudish."

Christopher loudly cleared his throat before making a show of noisily getting to his feet. "Why don't we all step out? I'm sure Agent James would rather not be here while you perform your, uh, clinical duties." He turned and opened the door, sweeping an arm in front of himself as Ricki's cue to move into the hallway.

Partially amused and partially relieved, Ricki moved through the door, followed closely by Clay. Five seconds later, Cheron also exited the room, leaving Anchorman alone with the deputy.

When Ricki raised an eyebrow at her, Cheron lifted her thin shoulders into a shrug. "He didn't want me in there either while he peed in a cup, and I didn't feel like arguing with him. I assume he'll let me back in to draw the blood, unless he also plans on doing that himself."

Ricki smiled at the thought. When Anchorman got into this kind of stubborn mood, she wouldn't put it past him at all, especially when he wasn't feeling well. It had been well established back home that the battle-tested Marine wasn't the best patient.

Cheron waited ninety seconds before opening the door and marching back inside, closing it behind her with a sharp click. Less than a minute later, the deputy exited the room, indicating with a wave of his hand that they could go back in, and muttering a "good luck" as he passed them.

Anchorman was still seated at the table, his expression mutinous as Cheron calmly sat beside him, tucking the blood vials, wrapped in a layer of Kleenex, into her case. While Ricki and Clay silently took up their posts against the wall, Christopher slowly lowered himself into a chair and faced his client.

"If you're ready to begin?" he asked politely, smiling at Anchorman's short, quick nod. He pulled out a cell phone, tapped a few buttons, then laid it on the table in front of Anchorman. A red light glowed on the screen as Christopher wagged a finger at the big man sitting opposite him. "Now, I'm going to record our whole conversation because I'm too old, and make way too much money, to sit here and scribble down notes like a first-year law student." He tilted his head to one side and studied the silent Anchorman. "I also won't be asking the questions." When that caused the Marine's head to jerk back in surprise, Christopher nodded in satisfaction. "Why should I do that when there's a homicide detective and a park service investigator in the room? Now since they're your friends, as well as a big part of your defense team"—he paused after emphasizing that last word— "I expect you to answer them truthfully so we can get on with the business at hand." The attorney leaned forward as much as his large girth would allow and stared his reluctant client right in the eye. "Do I have your agreement on that point?"

Anchorman's gaze flicked to Ricki's before he looked back at the attorney. "You have it."

"Good." Christopher settled more comfortably in his chair before lifting a pudgy hand into the air and waving it back and forth at the two people standing behind him. "Go ahead, then."

Ricki straightened away from the wall and pulled her own

cell phone out of her pocket. Setting it to record, she laid it down next to the one already in front of Anchorman, before taking a half step back and crossing her arms over her chest. "Start with arriving at the park. How did you get there and where did you start hiking in?"

"Kelly drove," Anchorman began slowly. "He keeps a small truck here year-round. He already had the parking tags and the campsite permits, so we drove straight to the trailhead he'd picked out." Anchorman paused for a moment, a frown playing around the corners of his mouth. "We left the truck in a parking lot near a place called Laurel Falls. Got our gear out of the truck and started hiking in. It was maybe a nine- or ten-mile hike to our campsite." He closed his eyes and kept talking. "Not what you'd call great views, but it was really pretty underneath the trees. A lot of green, and a lot of water. It was a good trail for us. Different from what we'd been used to on our tours. We stopped at a couple of places along the way just to sit and enjoy all that green and the quiet. We reached our campsite around 1400 hours. It was early, so we took our time setting up our shelters, collecting some wood, then breaking out our fishing gear." He opened his eyes and his mouth curved into a smile. "Took Kelly a while to catch enough fish for us to make a meal along with some dehydrated food we'd brought with us. I didn't catch a damn thing, so he stayed on my ass about that. The sun was setting by the time we got around to frying those fish up. Then we cracked open the bottle of bourbon that Kelly had brought and sat around talking until we hit our sleeping bags." He looked down at his bound hands that were resting on the tabletop. "The next thing I know, I wake up and there's no Kelly. I went looking for him down by the river, but he wasn't there. When I got back to camp, four guys were waiting, and they all had rifles pointed at me. They put me in cuffs, and we marched out of there and drove straight here." He stopped and shrugged. "That's about all I know."

"How long had you and Kelly been planning on taking this camping trip?" Ricki said, circling back to the beginning.

Anchorman's brow furrowed. "About six months, maybe more."

"Who else knew about the trip?"

A flash of amusement crossed Anchorman's face. "Besides you?" When she only stared back at him, his smile faded and he shrugged. "I don't know. It wasn't a secret."

"Whose idea was it to go on this trip?"

He quirked an eyebrow. "No one's. We've been taking an annual camping trip together for over a decade."

"Did Kelly pick the location and the campsite?"

He nodded. "Yeah. He lives here when he isn't deployed, so he knew the area better than I did."

Ricki kept up a steady stream of questions, walking him through the planning and the travel arrangements before moving on to the day the two men went to the park. "The first day of the trip, how did you get to the campsite?"

"Like I said. We parked in a small lot near this Laurel Falls trailhead and started hiking into the backcountry from there."

She pulled out the trail map of the park, opened it up, and put it in front of him. "Show me how you got there."

He leaned over to peer at the map, then used an index finger and ran it along the line of one of the major roads through the park. "We took this road, stopped here, on the right. Unloaded our gear and hit the trail going south." He paused and frowned. "I remember going past a sign for Fighting Creek Gap, but we stuck to the main trail."

"Were there a lot of cars in the parking lot?"

"Nah." He leaned back in the chair and dropped his shackled hands into his lap. "It was early. Around 0600 when we started out. The sun hadn't been up long."

Ricki hesitated as she thought that over. "Were there any other cars at all in the parking lot?"

Anchorman's eyebrows drew together as he stared at the

top of the table. "No cars that I remember, and just a couple of trucks. I remember making a joke that it wasn't the most popular place in the park, and Kelly said April was too early for most of the tourists, and that hour in the morning was too early for whoever was left over." He glanced across at her. "We didn't meet anyone on the trail until we were a good five miles in, and that was near a campsite. Looked like they'd been set up for a day or two." He lifted a hand to stop her next question. "The sign on the trail said it was campsite number twenty-four."

"Did you talk to these people?"

"Not really. They looked pretty settled in. I think Kelly might have waved a hand, said a couple of words when the woman yelled out at us, us, but nothing much more than that."

"Did you see or talk to anyone else on the trail?"

"Nope."

"After the rangers showed up and took you out of there, did you go back the same way you came in?"

He blinked at the sudden shift in the timeline but shook his head. "No. We came out somewhere else. I don't know where, exactly, but the trip back was a lot rougher than the trip in."

Or you didn't feel well, so it just seemed that way. Ricki kept the thought to herself as another one popped into her head. With Kelly dead, and Anchorman in custody, Kelly's truck had to still be in that parking lot. She filed that away and continued, guiding him through the rest of the hike and setting up camp. When he described putting up their shelters, the first faint alarm bell went off in her head.

"You didn't have tents? You each put up a tarp shelter?"

"That's right." Anchorman lifted his hands and used one finger to scratch the top of his nose. "Tarps have more uses than a tent."

"Were they open sided? Could you and Kelly see each other?"

The big Marine's voice dropped a notch as he shook his head. "The front was open, but otherwise, no. The tarps were large enough to reach the ground when we put up the standard triangle. We both had our shelters facing the fire."

She breathed a small sigh of relief. At least the prosecution couldn't claim that there was no way Anchorman couldn't have seen someone sneaking into Kelly's tent, or Kelly walking off in the middle of the night. She spent another hour taking her cook and business partner through every step of his day and the evening leading up to the murder. Then she turned it over to Clay, who took another hour going relentlessly over the same ground.

When Christopher caught her eye, he tapped his wristwatch. Anchorman had a date in court to set bail, and they didn't want to make him late for that. Ricki moved closer to Clay and nudged him in the side. He didn't look at her but did give a quick nod.

"I'm going with you to the bail hearing, so we need to be on our way soon," Clay told the beleaguered man sitting at the table. Anchorman's shoulders were slumped forward, and by the stony look on his face, he was reaching his limit of being interrogated. "But I have one last question."

"As long as it's the last one, I'm all ears," Anchorman snapped. "What is it?"

Unfazed, Clay cocked his head to the side and stared back at the former Marine. "You said Kelly lives here when he isn't deployed. Does he own a house, or rent a place nearby?"

Anchorman stretched his back and rolled his shoulders to work out the kinks. "He owns a place with some land around it. His girlfriend and her son live there, too, and look after it when he's away."

"Where is it?"

"Over near Pigeon Forge." Anchorman rattled off an address, then stood up. "That's the last question." He looked over at Christopher Young. "What's next?"

The attorney pushed himself out of the chair with a grimace, sighing. "Not getting any younger, I'm afraid." He straightened the sleeves of his suit jacket before leaning over to scoop his phone off the table. Tucking it into an inside pocket of his jacket, he looked back at Anchorman. "As Chief Thomas said, we have an appearance in front of the judge. Your excellent military service record will weigh heavily in your favor. The fact you aren't from around here will not. Still, I'm hopeful we'll have you out of here tonight." He turned his head and looked at Ricki. "Where will you be staying?"

Ricki named the hotel, which was also located in Pigeon Forge. Convenient, since Kelly's house would be close by, which made her wonder if the unknown NCIS agent thought the same thing.

"I will be staying here in Sevierville, since there are more questions I'd like to ask the authorities." Christopher looked at Anchorman. "We will also need to schedule several meetings between now and whenever the preliminary hearing is set up."

Anchorman scowled back at him. "How many meetings?"

"Now that depends on what your investigative team finds out." Christopher turned back toward Ricki and handed her a card with the name of a hotel already written in pen on the back. "This is how, and if necessary, where, you can contact me." He patted his jacket pocket. "I already have your contact information. I will arrange transportation for my client and the chief after the hearing. I will also look for a proper space for the good doctor to work." He sent Ricki a questioning look. "Might I ask what you and Dr. Garrison will be doing in the meantime?"

"I'll get Cheron settled in, and then I'm going to track down an NCIS agent who has been assigned to this case. I'm supposed to be his expert area consultant, and while I'm consulting, I'll be keeping an eye on him."

Christopher smiled. "Excellent."

Chapter 6

THE FIRST FIVE minutes of the drive from the county jail to the hotel in Pigeon Forge went by in silence. Ricki split her attention between the road, her dejected passenger, and the rearview mirror. She was keeping an eye on a black truck behind them when Cheron half turned in her seat and cleared her throat.

"I don't know what to look for."

Not sure what the doctor was talking about, Ricki cast her a sideways glance. "What do you mean?"

Cheron clasped her hands together in her lap. With her body still facing Ricki, she turned her head to stare straight out the front windshield. "Norman was drugged," she stated flatly. "All the physical signs point to it. And I can tell he's still feeling the aftereffects. His face is pale, he told me he feels nauseous, and he's having a hard time concentrating." Her expression had turned fierce by the time she looked at Ricki again. "And did you hear his account of the night Kelly was murdered? He couldn't remember a thing from approximately an hour after dinner until he woke up the next morning. And very late the next morning, too. Which isn't like him at all."

"I heard him." Ricki checked the rearview mirror again,

noting that the black truck was still trailing two cars behind them. "But he admitted to going through a bottle of bourbon with Kelly the night before."

"You've seen him drink. There is no way even an entire bottle of bourbon would do that to him, much less half a bottle, since I'm assuming Kelly drank his share of it," Cheron argued, her voice growing more strident with each word. "He was drugged. But I don't know how to prove it."

Ricki gave her a hard look before returning her gaze to the road. "Why can't you? You took samples and all."

Cheron's long fingers picked restlessly at the cloth of her overalls. "There are hundreds of drugs. I'd need to have some idea what to test for." Her chin trembled as she continued to stare out the windshield. "And then, how was it administered? It's not as if Norman would allow a total stranger to stick a needle in his arm."

Another quick glance in the mirror showed the black truck was still hanging back, but was right behind them. Ricki slowed the SUV down and then sped up again, watching the black truck match each change in their speed. There was no doubt they were being followed. Maybe they had been from the moment they'd stepped off the plane, but certainly since they'd left the county jail.

She did manage to get them a full car-length closer. Close enough to realize a layer of mud covered the front license plate, while the heavily tinted windows effectively concealed the driver and any passenger in the vehicle. Since Cheron was in the car with her, she wasn't going to try any sneaky maneuvers to get a better look at the truck, so she had to settle for driving while keeping an eye on their shadow.

"Ricki? What do you think?"

The pointed question had Ricki's attention snapping back to Cheron. Drugs. Cheron had been talking about Anchorman being drugged. "I don't know how Anchorman could have gotten anything into his system," she admitted. "But if you think he did, that's good enough for me to go on."

"I know he did. I just don't know what to test for," the doctor repeated on a sigh.

"Then go on what you do know," Ricki said in a calm, logical voice. The same tone Cheron would be using if she weren't so worried about Anchorman. "We agree he wasn't injected. So, eliminating that, how else could he have been drugged?"

"In his food or water."

Ricki considered that for a moment. "How long would it take for a drug that causes nausea and memory loss to take effect? Hours? Minutes?"

Cheron slowly unfolded her hands and spread her fingers out, rubbing them against the tops of her legs. "Well, if it wasn't injected, anywhere from a few minutes to maybe an hour or two, depending on the drug."

"Okay, okay. We might be getting somewhere." Ricki spied the sign announcing their arrival in Pigeon Forge. "Let's think on it for a while. At least until we get into our hotel rooms."

It only took her ten minutes to locate their hotel. It looked plain but solid, with a brick facade outside and most of the surrounding land taken up by a parking lot. She pulled the SUV into an empty space, then wrestled gear and Clay's rifle case, along with her own, out of the car and into the lobby. The desk clerk didn't blink at the amount of firepower she was carrying around as she handed Ricki two sets of keys, a sunny smile on her face.

"You're next door to each other on the third floor. The elevators are to the right. Enjoy your stay," the young woman chirped.

Ricki smiled back at her and turned toward the elevators, ushering along Cheron, who was carrying her large satchel and dragging a small suitcase on a wobbly pair of built-in wheels. Like the lobby, the elevator and the long hallway leading to their rooms were deserted. Ricki opened her door and stepped back to give Cheron enough room to slide past her.

"Why don't you drop your gear in this room for the moment?"

Cheron peered into the empty room. "Why?"

"Because if his attorney can't spring Anchorman tonight, you'll be staying in here with Clay and me." When Cheron protested, Ricki gave her a light shove with the back of her elbow. "We can argue about it inside. Hopefully over a cup of coffee."

Giving in, Cheron stepped over the threshold and headed for the small shelf intended to hold a suitcase. "Maybe we can call room service and have something sent up. I'm starving."

Ricki looked around the clean but sparsely furnished room, glad to see the small coffee maker sitting on a counter in between the tiny closet and the bathroom. "I don't think the place has a restaurant, much less room service." *Or a bar.* She knew that wouldn't go over very well with either Clay or Anchorman. She wouldn't have minded a cold beer herself, but right now, food was more a priority. The bagel she'd bought at the airport in Knoxville had long since worn off.

She dropped her backpack onto the bed, then walked to the closet to stow the rifles. "Maybe there's a takeout menu for someplace that delivers," she said over her shoulder. "Why don't you have a look around?"

When she was done securing the rifles, she pulled her head out of the closet and heard Cheron talking to someone on her cell phone. Stripping off her jacket, Ricki hung it up, then headed back toward the bed, intending to sit down and take off her boots. She'd unlaced one when the doctor hung up and nodded at her phone.

"I found a deli-kind-of-fast-food place that delivers. Our food will arrive in the lobby in thirty minutes." She smiled at

Ricki. "I ordered enough for five or six people, since I'm sure both Norman and Clay will be hungry."

Despite everything, Ricki grinned back at her. "Do you think you'll ever break down and call your boyfriend Anchorman?"

"I guess Norman could be my boyfriend, couldn't he?"

Ricki couldn't help but grin at the astonished look on Cheron's face. Considering how relaxed Anchorman had been since their return from her last case in Crater Lake, she was certain he'd finally talked the good doctor into his bed. Which qualified him as a boyfriend, and well on his way to being a lot more if he had anything to say about it.

"Anchorman?" Cheron repeated, trying out the word before she pursed her lips and shook her head. "No. I don't believe so. He's simply Norman to me."

Ricki laughed. If Cheron really thought that, then she was one of one because, as far as Ricki knew, no one else on the planet thought Anchorman was simply a "Norman."

"I've been giving your advice some thought." When Ricki tilted her head in a silent question, Cheron wet her lips. "About the drugs? To consider what I do know? Since it absolutely was not given by injection, then he must have ingested it somehow."

Having unlaced both boots, Ricki toed them off, stretching out on the bed, plumping two pillows behind her head and back. "That's what I thought. But here's the mystery. They spent hours hiking, and then fishing without really talking to anyone in all that time. So if Anchorman had to have unknowingly swallowed a drug just an hour or two before he passed out, how did he do it?"

Cheron frowned. "It must have already been with them. So whoever packed their food laced it with a drug."

"Yeah, that's what I've been thinking, too. Food, water, or maybe a bottle of bourbon." Ricki lifted her arms and entwined her fingers behind her head. "All the perishable kind of things would have been at Kelly's house. It wouldn't make any sense for Anchorman to haul it across the country."

The doctor's eyes got wide behind the thick lenses of her glasses. "He said that Kelly brought the bottle of bourbon. Remember? Do you remember Norman saying that?"

"I remember," Ricki said quietly. "Which makes Kelly's girlfriend the first name to go on our suspect list." Along with Kelly. She couldn't rule out that Anchorman's friend might have deliberately drugged him, so he could meet someone or do something he didn't want Anchorman knowing about. Although she wasn't going to let Cheron in on that. She loved the doctor's naive candor, but the last thing she needed was to have that particular theory repeated to Anchorman. He'd never believe it of his close friend and fellow Marine and might walk out if he heard it. She'd need some very solid proof before laying that one at his feet.

When her cell phone rang, she picked it up from the side table where she'd set it and saw Dan's name flash up on the screen. Hoping the researcher had found out who the mysterious NCIS agent was, she quickly hit the connect icon.

"Hey, Dan. What's up?"

"I think I should be asking you that."

"We've seen Anchorman," she told him without preamble. "He's holding up. His lawyer is trying to get him out on bail."

"Did he say anything about what happened?"

"Not much." Feeling a sudden wave of fatigue, Ricki rubbed a hand along her cheek. "He doesn't remember much about that night. Cheron took some blood and urine samples as soon as we saw him. She thinks he was drugged."

"Drugged?" The shock was apparent in Dan's voice. "By whom? Wasn't he out there alone with the victim?"

"That's the million-dollar question, and yeah, he and Kelly were camping alone." The sudden silence on the other end of the phone was deafening. "Are you still there?"

"I'm here," Dan said quietly. "How's Christopher Young? I've heard good things about him."

"Scary smart," Ricki admitted, since that was the only accurate way she could think of to describe the man. "He's getting everything he can out of the county guys, which leaves the local interviews and the NCIS agent to Clay and me. So I'm hoping you have some news for me?"

"I do. Quite a bit, as a matter of fact."

Feeling that was a solid step forward at last, some of the tension drained out of Ricki's neck and shoulders. "I'll take whatever you've got. Go ahead."

"Let's start with the NCIS agent. His name is Treynor Robard. And from what I've read, his friends call him Trey and his enemies call him sir."

"Cute," she said dryly. "Maybe I'll stick with 'hey you.'"

Dan's chuckle echoed through the phone. "That might be a good idea. Anyway, he's very well educated, having graduated from Berkeley with a degree in anthropology."

Ricki broke into a cough. "In what?"

"Anthropology," Dan helpfully repeated. "It seems he has a fascination with indigenous people. An interest he most likely developed from his grandmother on his father's side. She was a member of the Yurok tribe."

"What did you do? Run a complete family history on the guy?" While Dan sputtered out a defense of his research methods, Ricki's eyes narrowed. Yurok. She'd heard that name before. "They have land near Redwood National Park," Ricki said out loud, recalling several park bulletins she'd read about the tribe. "There was a joint project between the government and the Yurok to reintroduce the condor along that stretch of California coastline."

"Yes, well, I didn't see that Treynor Robard, or his grandmother, were involved with that project, but he has quite a résumé."

"How does a guy go from studying anthropology to being an NCIS agent?" Ricki wondered.

"I imagine his father being a career cop helped. He retired from the San Francisco Police Department about five years ago."

She sighed. Again with the family history, when she was more interested in the present. Somewhere in the background, Ricki could hear a phone ringing. She glanced at her watch and did a quick calculation of the time difference. "I guess you're in the office?"

"Yeah, I am. Anyway, this Robard guy has only been with NCIS for a couple of years. Before that he spent a decade with the Wranglers based at Lemoore Naval Air Station."

Ricki frowned. The Wranglers? "Is that some kind of cowboy outfit inside the navy? What do they wrangle?"

Dan laughed. "Lost people mostly. It's an elite search and rescue unit. It seems Treynor Robard was one of their helicopter pilots."

Ricki blinked in surprise. "He flew helicopters? Why isn't he still flying helicopters?"

"According to his military record, he asked for a transfer to NCIS. Some strings were pulled from what looks like very high up, and his request was granted."

"Why did he ask for a transfer?"

"No reason was cited in the record," Dan said. "Just that the request was made and approved. Funny thing though, there's an NCIS office at Lemoore, but Robard asked to be stationed at Quantico."

"And he was? Just like that?" When Dan made a confirming noise, she wondered just who this guy was. It wasn't everybody who got to handpick their assignments in the military. "What did he do? Rescue a general or save the President?"

"No idea," Dan replied. "I'm just letting you know what

was in his file. From his reviews, he doesn't mind taking chances and has nerves of steel."

"Yeah. I'll bet he does." Ricki sighed. Whatever else he was, Treynor Robard was career military, so the odds were good he put a lot of stock in going by the book. Which wouldn't bode well for Anchorman. She used two fingers to gently rub her temples. There was a headache brewing just behind her eyes, and she figured it had a name that sounded like Treynor Robard. "Do you have any other good news?"

"That's about it. Oh, and that question you sent me a few hours ago about Kelly Dorman's next of kin? His medical records list his mother in North Carolina, along with a Sondra Lewis and Norman Beal. Strangely enough, Anchorman is first on the list."

"Kelly listed Anchorman as his closest next of kin?"

"Yes. Right before his mother. And then Sondra Lewis, who is showing the same residence as Sergeant Dorman's, along with a Dilbert Lewis, age twenty-three. The house is just outside of Pigeon Forge. I can send you directions."

"No need. Anchorman gave us the address. I'm going to be heading over there in the morning, provided Treynor Robard doesn't show up between now and then."

"You never know about that kind of thing," Dan said. "I'll email you a copy of all my notes. And you keep us up-to-date on what's going on with Anchorman."

"I'll do that. Did you get my message to Finn?"

"I've been trying." Dan's voice took on an apologetic note. "I've left messages everywhere I can think of for him to call me back, but so far I haven't heard from him."

"Okay, thanks. We'll keep in touch." She disconnected the call and winced at a sharp stab of pain. The headache had begun to pound a little stronger. Closing her eyes in defense, she wondered if she'd remembered to pack any aspirin. As she was reaching for the backpack she'd moved to the floor,

Cheron walked over, two white capsules in her outstretched hand.

"Here. You look like you could use these."

Surprised and grateful, Ricki reached for the pills and then the glass of water Cheron thrust at her.

"You need to drink that whole glass. Water is good for a headache."

Ricki nodded her thanks and wasted no time in downing the aspirin, along with the entire glass of water. "How did you know I had a headache?"

Cheron's smile had a wispy quality to it as she gingerly sat down on the bed next to Ricki. "I'm a doctor, and I've known you for more than a year now. It's obvious when you have a headache. Your face gets all scrunched up." Cheron proceeded to wrinkle her nose, making Ricki laugh.

"That's good to know. I'll try not to do that."

The doctor shrugged. "It's fine. Everyone has something they do when they're in pain or under a great deal of stress. It's simply human nature." She relaxed a little more and absently pushed her glasses farther up the bridge of her nose. "While you were speaking to Dan, Christopher Young called. The judge did grant bail, so Norman and Clay will be here as soon as all the paperwork is processed." Cheron smiled despite the worry that lingered in her eyes. "Since the ballistics report hasn't come back yet, they didn't have much to hold him on. Other than two witnesses who claim they heard Norman and Kelly arguing but didn't describe them very well, other than them being male and wearing heavy jackets. And, of course, there was the fact the two men were on a camping trip together. I have no idea how Mr. Young got around that."

Smart. The man was both smart and tricky. Ricki looked down at the phone she still held in her hand. "Why did Young call you?"

"Oh, he wanted to let me know he's found a surgical suite with an attached lab I can use. It's forty minutes away in

Knoxville, but since the county medical examiner isn't willing to share his facilities, I'm happy to have a proper space. Now all I need is a body to autopsy and permission to perform one." She glanced over at her satchel. "At least I have something to test."

Ricki slowly rolled her shoulders back and forth. "Permission to see Kelly's autopsy results shouldn't be a problem. According to Dan, Anchorman is listed as Kelly's closest next of kin. A Sondra Lewis, who is his live-in girlfriend, also made the list."

"Just one signature should be enough," Cheron said. "And how did Dan find that out so quickly?"

With the headache backing off as the aspirin kicked in, Ricki relaxed against the pillows. "I make it a habit to never ask Dan that question." A loud knock on the door had her glancing down the short hallway.

"Maybe that's our food. The desk clerk said he would have it sent up." Cheron started to rise, but Ricki shot out a hand and grabbed her wrist, keeping her in place.

"I'll get it. You scoot back a bit and stay out of sight." Ricki swung her long legs over the edge of the bed and carefully stood up. She walked down the hall, removing her gun from her shoulder holster before putting her eye next to the peephole. The distorted image of a man with jet-black hair and light brown eyes came into view. He was looking directly at the peephole, a smile on his face as he held up two large bags, one in each hand.

"Food delivery."

Ricki kept her Glock down at her side and firmly planted her feet on the thin carpet. Turning her body so that her shoulder would block any attempt the man might make to barge his way into the room, she slowly opened the door a crack. "Just set the bags down. I'll get them in a minute."

"The food isn't the only reason I'm here. I just commandeered it from the delivery guy. And gave him his tip." The voice was deep, with a slight note of amusement in it, which, for some reason, grated on her nerves. "Are you Special Agent Ricki James?"

Not wasting her breath on how he knew that, she kept her answer short and to the point. "Yes."

"Then that would make you my local area expert." He gave a quick nod. "I'm Special Agent Treynor Robard, with NCIS."

Chapter 7

RICKI MADE no move to open the door wider. Instead, she kept an eye on him through the peephole. "Hold your credentials up, Special Agent Robard."

He disappeared from her narrow view for a moment, and when he straightened up again, the food bags were gone. Lifting one empty hand, he carefully removed a small black leather case from his shirt pocket, then held it up high enough so she could plainly see his official NCIS ID. He politely waited a beat before saying, "My badge is attached to my belt."

Ricki pursed her lips in exasperation. She had expected to have to go looking for the guy, not have him show up on her doorstep with bags of food. Pulling the door open the rest of the way, she stood in the entrance and slowly holstered her gun.

Agent Robard bent over and retrieved the two large food bags. When he straightened up, he didn't move forward but stayed in place as he studied her face. He finally leaned slightly to one side and looked past her down the short hallway toward the bed at its far end.

"Any particular reason for that kind of caution?"

Thinking of the black truck which she had no intention of telling him about, Ricki shook her head. She hadn't decided yet how much she was going to share. Technically, she was supposed to be an expert on the area, which was a stretch since she'd only visited the park once and that was a good ten years earlier. But she was a quick study, and if he wanted to know about the trails and the local plants, she would accommodate him.

Shrugging in answer to his question, she stepped to the side. "I've got a civilian with me." Letting that serve as the only answer he was going to get, she waited until he passed her, before shutting the door and following him into the room.

Cheron was standing near the night table, her hands clasped in front of herself as she gave the agent a wary look. While the NCIS agent set the bags down next to the small TV, Ricki walked over to join Cheron, giving her a reassuring smile before refocusing her gaze on the agent who had turned to face the two women.

Now that she got a good look at him, Ricki guessed he was just a hair under six feet tall, with broad shoulders and a piercing gaze from those light brown eyes. It wasn't hard to picture him in a jumpsuit and helmet as he sat at the controls of a helicopter. Except for his hair. The thick, dark mane was longer than the usual military style, almost brushing his collar, with one wayward strand curling across his forehead. In his jeans, wool shirt, and heavy hiking boots, he fit right into the area, and with his background in search and rescue, she doubted he needed an expert consultant on how to navigate the backcountry. Which made her wonder why he'd agreed to having one in the first place. He didn't look like a man who would be happy about dragging around someone he probably considered extra baggage.

When his gaze shifted pointedly from herself to Cheron,

Ricki tilted her head toward the doctor. "Cheron, this is Special Agent Robard from NCIS. And this is Cheron Garrison."

"Agent Robard," Cheron said politely, but she didn't move to extend a hand, staying glued to Ricki's side.

"Dr. Garrison, it's a pleasure to meet you."

The agent's use of Cheron's professional title had Ricki tensing. She saw it in his eyes. He'd known she wasn't coming alone, and very likely was fully briefed on all three of them.

"We just got word that Norman has been released on bail," Cheron said carefully. "He'll be joining us as soon as he's out."

The agent rolled his eyes to the ceiling. "I was told I'd likely have the prime suspect as a member of the team, so I guess I'm going to have to live with that." He lowered his gaze again and pinned it on Ricki's face. "Won't I?"

"Yes, you will." Ricki crossed her arms over her chest. "Who told you that?"

He strolled over to the small desk and pulled out the chair. Sitting, he propped one ankle on top of the opposite knee. "It isn't unusual for one agency to brief another."

Since Hamilton was the only one who could have done that, and she knew damn good and well that he hadn't, Ricki's answering smile held a layer of frost in it. If Agent Robard wanted to play "I've got a secret," that was fine with her. She had work to do, with or without his cooperation.

"Anchorman was let out on bail because the prosecution didn't have any evidence to hold him, since the ballistics report isn't back yet." She shook her head. "Your forensics lab seems a little slow."

"Does it?" Looking right at home, Robard slowly glanced around the room before returning his attention to Ricki. "I'd agree with you, except it isn't our lab that's slow. The FBI is testing the rifle against the bullet found in the body, which had to wait until after the autopsy. I haven't heard yet if it's been completed, but I was told it would be done first thing this morning."

Thinking she'd better take advantage of the man's chatty mood, Ricki sat on the edge of the bed, pulling Cheron down with her. "You said 'the bullet'? As in one?"

Robard leaned back and, dropping his boot to the floor, stretched out both legs. "Do you think a retired Marine sniper would need more than one to hit his target?" When Ricki remained silent, he frowned. "Actually, it was two bullets, fired directly into Sergeant Dorman's back."

Quickly losing her frosty composure, Ricki gaped at him. "In the back? You're telling me that Kelly was shot in the back?"

He nodded at her. "That's what the preliminary report from the field said." When Ricki bit her lip, he nodded again. "Now tell me why you don't think it's weird that there isn't any other evidence against Sergeant Beal?"

"I might think it's weird," she said, her mind still racing about how Kelly was killed.

"You might, but you don't. You're probably not a bad poker player, Agent James, because it doesn't show in your face, but it does in your voice. And that tells me that you already know the only thing removed from the scene beside the body was the rifle."

Wanting to tread lightly, Ricki considered what to say. "I heard that. And that the response team was told to leave everything 'as is' for NCIS. So I gather your forensics team hasn't arrived yet?"

"And won't until tomorrow afternoon," Robard said.

Ricki went still. It was a small opening, but an opening, nevertheless. A chance for her to get up there and see the campsite and crime scene for herself. Before the place was crawling with NCIS forensic techs. "So you want me to arrange for someone assigned to the park to guide you and your team to the crime scene once they arrive?"

"I'm sure you can get hold of a map and manage it just fine, Agent James."

"No problem." Ricki smiled. If the forensic techs didn't arrive until the next afternoon, the hike would be delayed until the following day. With an early start, she could slip in and out of there tomorrow without Agent Robard being any the wiser. Especially since she already had the route Anchorman and Kelly had taken.

It was an eight-mile hike in, which meant double that to get there and back. If she wanted to have enough time to look around and get back before Robard missed her, she'd have to make a start before sunup. Now all she had to do was figure out how to explain her absence for the entire day to the NCIS agent. As it happened, she had the perfect excuse sitting right next to her.

"While you're getting ready for your team, I can get Cheron settled into her medical suite tomorrow."

Robard's gaze grew sharper as he looked from her to Cheron. "Medical suite?"

"Yes," Cheron said with a decisive nod. "I need a space to do some drug testing and possibly conduct an autopsy of my own. Especially if we can't get access to the medical examiner's report."

The NCIS agent shoved the thick lock of hair that had slipped farther down his forehead back into place, never taking his eyes off Cheron. "I can guarantee that the primary investigator on the case, which is me, will get a copy of that report as soon as it can be printed. And I'll be happy to share it with you. But why the drug testing?"

Ricki had to grit her teeth in order not to give Cheron's leg a solid kick to keep her quiet. But since that would never go unnoticed, she simply shut her eyes, then quickly opened them again to give the doctor a hard glare.

"Thank you," the doctor chirped, oblivious to the dagger-eyed message Ricki was trying to send her. "I'm interested in any food or drink at the campsite, and especially in the bottle of bourbon that is still up there."

Robard's head didn't move, but his gaze shifted over to Ricki. He said nothing, just sat waiting.

Thinking Cheron had already let the cat out of the bag, and that maybe a little transparency would gain her a small slice of trust, Ricki kept her expression blank as she nodded. "Cheron thinks that Anchorman might have been slipped something that knocked him out."

"Drugged?" He frowned. "How could that have happened? They were out in the middle of nowhere."

Ricki saw the possibility of Kelly drugging his friend flicker over Robard's face as his eyes opened slightly in surprise.

"I wouldn't mention that out loud within earshot of Anchorman," Ricki said, easily reading his expression. "Not if you want to stay conscious yourself."

"What are you two talking about?" Cheron stretched her neck, peering around Ricki to stare at the agent sitting in the small chair next to the desk. "Whoever prepared that food, or maybe tampered with the bourbon before Norman and Kelly left for that trip, is clearly the main suspect in the murder."

"Didn't they bring their own food?" Robard asked.

"Not Anchorman," Ricki said. "He would have had to either buy it here or drag it across the country. I'm betting Kelly arranged for all the food and camping gear."

"And the liquor?" he asked softly.

She nodded. "Kelly brought the bourbon. In any event, Cheron has a way to test it all, thanks to Anchorman's lawyer. He's getting Cheron set up in her own medical space in Knoxville."

"And that would be Christopher Young?"

"Yeah. That's him."

Robard displayed a rare smile. "Nice choice for a defense attorney. I've heard good things."

"Hasn't everybody?" Ricki muttered under her breath.

There was a drawn-out moment of silence while Robard pulled his legs in and stretched his back. "I don't suppose there's an extra sandwich in one of those bags?"

Cheron immediately stood and moved toward the counter where Robard had set down the two large paper bags bulging with food. "Of course there is, but we'll need to settle for drinking water. I never buy soda, and the deli didn't have any beer."

"That's fine with me." Robard rose from the chair in one effortless movement. He walked over to the coffee maker and picked up the small ice bucket sitting next to it. He smiled as he held it out to Cheron. "Dr. Garrison, would you mind getting us some ice for those glasses of water? I'd like a private word with Agent James."

"Um . . ." Cheron cast an uncertain look toward Ricki. "I'm not sure about . . ."

Ricki waved her hand to cut the doctor off. "It's fine, Cheron. The ice machine is over near the elevator."

Still looking uncomfortable, Cheron reluctantly took the offered ice bucket and plodded toward the door. Once it had closed behind her, Robard turned and faced Ricki.

"I'd appreciate it if you wouldn't sneak out of here and visit that campsite on your own," he said quietly. "Especially since I plan on going up there myself tomorrow."

Now that did surprise her. "You want to hike in, take a look around, then hike out and do it all again with your team the next day?"

He shook his head. "Not exactly. I thought I'd take you up on that offer to find a ranger to guide the forensic team in, and I'd spend the night up there. I'd like to get a feel for the area, especially at night, which was when the murder took place. There are some things about the response team's report that I'm not clearly understanding."

"Such as?" Ricki asked.

He took out his cell phone and tapped several times on the screen. "This report states that the body was found approximately a mile and a half from the campsite where Anchorman was picked up. They had reservations for that specific site." He glanced over at Ricki. "I stopped by the Sugarlands' headquarters and checked on that before coming here. The reservation was made months ago."

"Yeah, that would fit. They had to time the trip for when Kelly was back in the States," Ricki supplied. "Anchorman was looking forward to it all winter."

This time when Robard smiled, there was a layer of genuine warmth in it. "Was that before or after you all were tracking down that serial killer out west? The Traveler, wasn't it?" He let out a low whistle. "That sounded like one nasty piece of work, if the newspapers are to be believed."

Ricki thought of Tim Martin and the wide path of destruction he'd left behind before he'd been caught. "You can't believe everything you read in the papers, but yeah, in this case, he was definitely a nasty piece of work."

Robard watched her for a moment and then glanced back down at his phone. "Okay. Back to our problem. Why so far from their camp? Was he chasing the man down?"

"Not according to Anchorman," she stated flatly. "And he never would have shot his friend in the back. Not two days ago, or a million years ago."

The NCIS agent shrugged, then tucked his phone away. "It must have been pitch-black out there unless you're going to tell me there were lights set up along the trail. So if he didn't have a nightscope with him, he might not have had much choice."

Ricki's expression hardened to stone. "He wouldn't have done that, and he didn't do it."

"Which is why I want to get up there and see for myself." Robard paused. "And if you can't be more objective than that, you won't be much help to me."

"I *am* being objective," she insisted. "You'll see for yourself once you've met Anchorman."

"I'm looking forward to it." Robard smiled, then opened the nearest bag of food. He carefully lifted out sandwiches and set them on the counter. "If you want to wait for him to make his appearance, I hope you don't mind watching me eat. I'm starving."

Ricki walked over to stand next to Robard so she could unpack the second bag of food. She held up a sandwich with a large *V* printed in black marker on the outside wrapper. "This must be the vegetarian. That's for Cheron."

She looked over when the door to the room opened and Cheron herself appeared, clutching the ice bucket to her chest, a huge smile on her face. Ricki's mouth curved up when she spotted Anchorman walking in right behind her, with Clay coming in last. As Clay closed the door, the retired Marine's gaze lasered in on Robard.

"Who are you?" Anchorman demanded, wrapping a hand around Cheron's upper arm to keep her from going any farther into the room.

Robard slowly put the sandwich he was holding down on the counter before turning to face the big Marine. "You must be Anchorman."

Anchorman stepped in front of Cheron and crossed his arms over his wide chest. "Yeah, I must be."

"That would be Sergeant Norman Beal, Scout Sniper, US Marine Corps?" Robard inquired politely.

"You forgot retired," Anchorman stated. "Now it's your turn." He half growled at Clay when the chief gave his shoulder a light shove, then pushed past him.

"Relax," Clay stated. "Treynor Robard here must be the NCIS agent Ricki went looking for."

She smiled, handing Clay a ham sandwich after he'd bent down and kissed her cheek. "He is, only I didn't find him, he found me. He just showed up at the door, so no searching was required."

"Lucky." Clay shifted the sandwich to his left hand and held out his right. "Clay Thomas, part-time police chief out in the Bay, and part-time investigator for the Seattle DA's office."

The other man nodded as he shook Clay's hand. "Special Agent Treynor Robard, NCIS."

Clay shrugged out of his jacket and tossed it onto the bed before grinning at Anchorman. "See? He's Special Agent Treynor Robard."

"Yeah, I heard him," Anchorman grouched, making a face. He looked over his shoulder at Cheron. "Why are you poking me in the back?"

"Would you please move, Norman? I want to set this ice down."

Anchorman plucked the bucket from her hands and took two steps forward. He dropped it onto the counter next to the sandwich bag. "There."

Cheron put her hands on her hips and gave him an exasperated look before glancing over at Ricki. "He's in a bad mood."

The retired Marine snorted out his annoyance. "You're expecting me to be all excited at finding the guy who wants to put me back in jail calmly eating a sandwich in my room?"

"I'm expecting you to be polite," Cheron stated. "And this is not our room."

Robard stepped around Clay to face Anchorman. "How about thinking of me as the guy who is here to find out the truth about what went on in the park the night your friend was killed? And if you didn't kill him, we could use your help."

Anchorman's eyebrows beetled together. "We?"

The NCIS agent pointed at Ricki. "Me and my expert area consultant over here."

"Fine." Anchorman walked over to the desk chair, spun it around, and straddled it. "What do you want to know?"

Chapter 8

Robard leaned back against the counter and crossed one booted foot over the other. "Let's start with the obvious question. Did you kill Sergeant Kelly Dorman?"

Anchorman's hands closed into fists and then slowly relaxed, opening again and hanging over the back of the chair.

Cheron moved to stand next to him, putting a hand on his shoulder. "Maybe he shouldn't be talking to you unless his lawyer is present." When Anchorman looked up at her and made a sound of protest, she laid a hand on his cheek. "We aren't home, and we don't know any of these people. More importantly, they don't know you. They have the power to put you back in jail in a blink of an eye, and maybe we wouldn't be able to get you out a second time." When she looked at Robard, her back was stiff and her usual polite smile nonexistent. "His lawyer needs to be here."

When the agent pulled his mouth into a thin line, Ricki took a step forward. She really didn't need this to deteriorate into a standoff. Cheron was right when she said that Robard could toss Anchorman back in jail. And this time maybe not the local county facility, but a federal one several states away.

"Why don't we start with what you know about Kelly's life here in Tennessee?" She subtly positioned herself directly in front of the couple, blocking their view of the NCIS agent. Once they'd both centered their attention on her, she sat on the edge of the bed closest to them and took out her cell phone.

"I'll record this for Christopher Young, and for the time being, we'll stay away from what went on up at the camp." When Robard voiced his disagreement, she glanced over at him. "Anchorman's statement regarding the events up at the camp is on record, and I'm sure you have a copy. It's the victim we don't know much about."

"Why do you need to know about Kelly's life?" Anchorman demanded. "Some asshole is wandering around with a loaded gun at night and thinks Kelly is a deer or bear, or some shit like that. What does his personal life have to do with anything?"

Robard's expression went blank as he stared at his prime suspect. "What makes you think Sergeant Dorman was accidentally killed by a hunter?"

Anchorman met and held the agent's gaze with his own. "A couple of the deputies at the county lockup were talking to me about it. They said that was probably what happened." His lip lifted into a sneer. "You should be out looking for that hunter, not hanging around the hotel scarfing down a ham sandwich."

Ricki immediately held up a hand to stop Robard from blurting out anything that might send Anchorman into shock. "I'll tell him," she said quietly, nodding her thanks when Robard leaned back and folded his arms over his chest.

"Tell me what?"

Now Anchorman was glaring at her, but she simply returned a calm gaze as she slowly took a deep breath. "Kelly was shot in the back. It might have been a hunter, but we have to assume it wasn't."

The big Marine's head jerked so hard it looked like he'd taken a heavy hit to his jaw. When he refocused on Ricki, the look in his eyes promised violence. It chilled her blood, and she knew down to her bones that all Anchorman wanted to do was get his hands on whoever had shot Kelly. A friend so close, his fellow Marine was considered a brother in every way except blood.

And she couldn't allow that. Then he *would* be guilty of murder. Right at the moment, he might consider the price of spending the rest of his life in prison a fair one in exchange for avenging Kelly, but she did not. He needed to get past it. And quickly.

Both Robard and Clay stood up in an instinctive reaction to the sudden tension in the room. When Clay stepped closer to Ricki and put a hand on her shoulder, Anchorman blinked.

He stared at Clay's hand for a moment before lifting his gaze to Ricki's. "I'd never hurt you." His breathing slowed when she smiled at him. He nodded and took another deep breath before shaking his head at Clay, then turning to look at Robard, who was poised to tackle him to the ground. "You can stand down. I'd never hurt any of them." He hesitated before adding in a dry voice, "You maybe, but not them."

Robard relaxed his stance and returned to leaning back against the counter. "Duly noted."

Cheron's nails dug into Anchorman's shoulders hard enough to make him wince. "He's joking, Agent Robard." She looked down at Anchorman, her frown fierce. "Tell him you were joking."

Despite the anger still lingering in his eyes, Anchorman had to purse his lips to keep them from turning into a nasty grin. "Sure I was, Special Agent Robard. Sorry."

The NCIS agent responded to the sarcasm in the Marine's tone with an I-bet-you-are grin of his own. "Thanks. I feel much better." He ran a hand through his thick, dark hair. "From what I read in the preliminary report from the rangers' response team, the hit looked close enough for it to be a deliberate kill. And I'm truly sorry to have to tell you that. But it means one of two things. Either he was mistaken for you in the dark, or he was the target all along."

Anchorman shook his head. "I'm a good half foot taller than Kelly, and a lot bigger across the shoulders. There is no way anyone would mistake us as the same guy, not even from a distance."

"Okay. Let's assume Kelly was the target. That would make you a suspect." He quickly held up his hand when Anchorman's eyes were back to shooting daggers at him. "Or someone who had a hard-ass grudge against Kelly. Did he ever mention a problem like that to you?"

"No." Anchorman paused, then shook his head. "No, he didn't, but I'm not sure he would have unless it had come to blows. Kelly tended to ignore that kind of noise around him. But if he had noticed anything like that at all, he would have told me." He paused again before his voice dropped to just above a whisper. "That's what made him such a good shooter and spotter."

"Spotter?" Robard blinked. "Kelly was your spotter?"

"Well, I spotted more for him, since I was the better shot."

Robard nodded. "Yeah. I understand that's the way it works. The better marksman spots the target, then calls out the distance, angle, wind speed, and whatever else might affect the shot. Then the shooter makes those adjustments and pulls the trigger."

"That about sums it up. We always worked in pairs, and for my last three tours, whenever we were hunting a target outside a city, Kelly and I were a team. I did the spotting and watched his back, and he took down the target." Anchorman dropped his gaze to the ground. "The two of us got in and out of some very tight places, too. I knew he'd never leave me behind, and he was just as sure I'd always have his back, no matter what." He looked up again. "Like I just told you, if he was aware of trouble dogging him, he would have said something."

Robard said nothing as he pushed away from the counter and ambled over to the window that looked out on the parking lot, his back to the room.

When he remained silent, Ricki took that as her cue to continue asking questions. "How long has Kelly been living in Pigeon Forge?"

Anchorman tore his gaze from the silent Robard. "Seven, maybe eight years. He liked this area, so he regularly got assigned to the recruiting station in Knoxville in between deployments. Having a scout sniper as a recruiter always increased the enlistment numbers. That's why he bought a place here. He was planning on retiring from the Corps at the end of this year and starting a business here."

"What kind of business?" Ricki asked.

A reluctant smile had the corners of Anchorman's mouth sliding up. "An Airbnb, of all the damn things. And he wanted to expand into a chain of them. He talked about having two here, two in Gatlinburg, and then eventually including a couple over in Nashville. It would have been a helluva a thing, if the guy could cook any kind of edible meal for his guests." His smile bordered on a smirk. "Or clean. The Corps and tight circumstances forced him to be neat, but on his own? He was fine with living in a disaster zone."

Since she ran a diner but wasn't anything to talk about in the kitchen either, Ricki could easily relate to that. She knew how she'd solved the problem and assumed Kelly would have had to have done the same thing—hire someone else to do it. "Okay. Then who was he going to get to manage that piece of the day-to-day operation?"

Anchorman shrugged. "His girlfriend, I suppose. We never talked about that end much."

Ricki sighed in exasperation. "Are you going to make me drag every little thing out of you? I know the girlfriend's name, and that she and Kelly lived together at the same address, along with her son. I got that much from Dan. What else can you tell me about her? And don't be polite about it."

"She's pushy and loud, but Kelly always liked that kind of woman." Anchorman rolled his eyes in obvious disapproval. "I don't know why."

"Doesn't sound like someone who would do well at playing hostess to complete strangers," Ricki observed.

He nodded his agreement. "Yeah. I thought the same thing. And I'm not too sure how much handyman kind of help the couch warmer would have been."

"The couch warmer?" Ricki repeated. "Are you talking about the son?"

"Yeah, that's what Kelly called him. Dill the couch warmer."

"Dill? The child's name is Dill?" Cheron looked horrified. "Didn't his mother like him at all?"

"He's not a child anymore. He's twenty-three," Anchorman pointed out. "But yeah, I guess it was some kind of family name, and the kid's old man insisted on it. But I don't think he stuck around long enough to see what his son had to put up with because of it. I know Kelly had to straighten out a couple of guys who kept calling the kid 'dill pickle.' And I'm sure he heard that more than once before Kelly came along and made the locals think twice about saying it out loud."

"Poor guy," Cheron murmured.

Anchorman waved that off. "When he was little, yeah. But like I said, he's twenty-three. Old enough to earn his own respect and to pull his own weight."

"As in, not spend his days warming a couch?" *And old enough to carry a secret resentment toward someone like Kelly*, Ricki thought. She mentally added the son to her "possible" list, right after his loud and pushy mother. And she wasn't ruling out the possibility of a scheme hatched between the two of them. Which statistics showed would likely involve money.

"How was Kelly going to finance this Airbnb plan of his?"

"He had the money to start out with one or maybe two," Anchorman stated flatly. "And there was some guy who was trying to convince him to go in as partners, but Kelly was leaning toward trying it on his own."

Ricki sat up a little straighter. "What guy?"

"Another vet who lives in the area." When Ricki's boot tapped on the floor, he smiled and shook his head. "Kelly said that he'd been in the army for a couple of six-year stints before opting out. And he claimed to be some kind of sharp-shooter. Kelly used to laugh at how hard the guy was always trying to impress him."

Ricki returned his grin. "I take it Kelly never mentioned he was a scout sniper?"

"Nah. He told people I was, but he never fessed up to being part of that group himself. Not even to his girlfriend. He just didn't want to put up with that kind of attention. But I think he got a kick out of this other guy's bragging about his skill with a rifle. And Kelly had respect for anyone who spent time in hot zones."

"But he didn't want him for a business partner?"

Anchorman let out a short laugh. "I don't think he wanted to listen to the bragging that much."

"Did this guy have a name?"

"Stu Landers," Anchorman said. "Kelly mentioned that he already had some kind of business here in town."

Making another mental note to track this wannabe business partner down, Ricki moved on. "Did Kelly mention anyone else? A relative, or maybe a former girlfriend and her now-current husband?"

"He didn't have a former girlfriend, as far as I know. Except in high school. And he left her behind when he joined the Corps." Anchorman rolled his eyes to the ceiling. "I got the impression she might have been the reason he joined the Corps in the first place."

"But he found a home here," Ricki stated, waiting for Anchorman's slow nod. "And where is Kelly's family?"

"They're all in the same place as that old high school girl-friend of his. In Waycross, Georgia. His mom ran what Kelly always called an old-fashioned, short-term boarding house, mostly for hunters. Kelly grew up hunting in the Okefenokee Swamp."

Ricki blinked in surprise. "That's quite a place, from what I hear. It's a national refuge, and a one-of-a-kind 'must-see' that's still on my bucket list."

Anchorman grinned. "You have a bucket list at your age?"

"Every age has a bucket list," Ricki informed him. "Kelly must have honed his shooting skills there if he spent any kind of significant time wandering around that swamp."

"Yeah. He was great at hunting just about anything on four legs, or two for that matter," Anchorman stated, his eyes suddenly taking on a fierce gleam. "The very best. One of the best in the Corps, and I would swear to that."

"I know. You've told me that before," Ricki said quietly. "So Kelly's entire family is still in Georgia? None of them live in Tennessee? Or have maybe visited recently?"

"There's just his mom and his brother, and Kelly always went to see them. I made the drive with him once. It's only about eight hours from here, so it isn't a big deal."

"Why didn't they ever come to see Kelly?"

Anchorman tilted his head to the side and considered the question for a moment. "His brother, Kevin, has a family and they're just getting by, so he didn't have the time or the money. And his mom has never left Waycross. The idea made her too nervous to make the trip." He gave Ricki a direct stare. "I never heard Kelly complain about it."

She nodded, smiling. "He doesn't sound like the complaining type. Kind of like his good friend." Her smile grew when a pale red tinged Anchorman's cheeks. In the years she'd known him, he still hadn't mastered how to react to a personal compliment. "Now don't get all hot and bothered by this, but it has to be asked." She drew in a slow breath. "You said Kelly has money stashed away for his Airbnb plans, but how about anything else? Did Kelly have life insurance through the corps?"

"Yeah." Anchorman's voice took on a sharper edge. "Through the Veterans' Affairs program, like a lot of guys who spend time in combat zones. So?"

"You know what the 'so' is," Ricki said evenly. "How much was it, and who was the beneficiary?"

Anchorman shot a quick glance at Robard, who was still staring out the window. "It was a quarter million, and I'm the beneficiary."

Shocked into silence, Ricki could only stare back at him. She'd expected to hear the mom's name, or maybe his live-in girlfriend. Anchorman had just baldly stated the reason that catapulted him right back into being the number one suspect. And damn, she'd asked the question right in front of the agent responsible for investigating the murder. The sudden weight of Clay's hand on her shoulder reminded her to breathe again.

"Why did Kelly make you the beneficiary?" Clay asked, breaking the silence that had dropped into the room like a brick falling from the sky.

"He knew I'd see that his mom and brother got the money, and that it was invested so it could provide them a lifetime income. He's listed as my beneficiary for the same reason. To make sure my half million goes exactly where it's supposed to. We trusted each other."

"Shit, Anchorman." Ricki jumped to her feet and paced to the start of the short hallway leading past the bathroom, then turned and faced the seated Marine, her hands on her hips. "Did anyone else know that Kelly was planning on retiring from the Marines?"

"I don't know. He hadn't submitted his papers yet. He said he'd get around to it in the next couple of months with a January first retirement date." Anchorman clasped and then unclasped his hands that were resting on the back of the chair he was straddling. "As far as I know, I'm the only one he told."

"When did he tell you?" Ricki snapped out. "On this trip?" When he shook his head, she closed her eyes in frustration. "Okay. Then when?"

"He was home last fall and met me in New Jersey when I went to visit my aunt." He leveled a look at her. "It wasn't too long after we had that encounter with the Hermit in Cascades National Park. Remember?"

She opened her eyes and glared back at him. "Thanks for the reminder. So you went to see your aunt, and Kelly was there. And the two of you had a nice cozy chat about his plans to retire."

"Friends do that," Anchorman said evenly. "I bought him a bottle of his favorite brand of bourbon, and we chopped it up for a couple of hours in my aunt's living room."

Ricki threw up her hands. "Of course you did. Please tell me someone else was there?"

"Like whom? Aunt Sally was out for the evening playing some regular card game with her friends, so it was just Kelly and me staying at the house."

While Ricki's boot started tapping a rapid staccato against the thin carpet, and Clay rested his forehead in the palm of one hand, Robard finally turned around and braced his feet apart.

"I think I've heard enough to get a good start on the investigation. And I have a proposition on where to go from here."

Yeah, I'll bet, Ricki thought as she stared back at him. She hoped this proposition of his didn't include marching Anchorman to a jail cell.

"What do you have in mind?" Clay asked, once again breaking the silence.

"A reenactment of sorts. I'd like to get Anchorman back to the crime scene. It might jog his memory."

"I was never at the crime scene," Anchorman snapped. "Except to hike past it with Kelly on our way into the campsite, and then I passed it again when I was marched back out by a squad of rangers with badges."

Robard's only reaction to Anchorman's outburst was a shrug. "All right. Then back at your campsite, since it's the last place you claim you saw Kelly."

"It *is* the last place I saw him." Now the big Marine was almost snarling at the NCIS agent. "If I'm asked a question, I give an honest answer."

Robard lifted an eyebrow and cocked his head to the side. "Yeah. I've noticed that." When that seemed to calm Anchorman down a notch, the agent addressed Ricki. "I'll call two of my colleagues to provide an escort for Dr. Garrison to that medical space in Knoxville, and have them stay there to keep an eye on her." He cut Ricki off with a wave of his hand. "As a guard for her safety, not because she's a suspect or untrustworthy." He switched his attention back to Anchorman. "I'm assuming that's a requirement in order for you to agree to the rest of the plan?"

Anchorman's head moved once up and down in a sharp nod. "You assume correctly."

"Fine." Robard returned his gaze to Ricki. "If we take Anchorman with us, it's up to you to arrange that he'll be watched at all times. And that arrangement has to satisfy my boss." He smiled at Cheron, who was giving him a wide-eyed stare. "And someone will need to get permission from his attorney."

Ricki chewed her lower lip as she considered the possibilities. It was a risk. There was no doubt about that. Anchorman could easily say something else that could dig the enormous hole he was standing in even deeper. But she might also get a very big lead. And another plausible explanation of what could have happened that night in the park besides Anchorman shooting his best friend in the back.

And right now, they desperately needed something.

A spurned potential business partner was weak. And so was a girlfriend who might be a coconspirator with a twenty-three-year-old who spent most of his time on a couch. Certain there was another explanation that they just needed time to find, taking Anchorman back to the camp to hopefully jog his memory was worth the risk. She also didn't see any other options at this point.

She looked over at Clay, who gave a barely perceptible nod, before carefully clearing her throat. "I think we should do it." When Anchorman and Cheron both looked doubtful, she added a bit more force to her voice. "Anchorman is innocent, and we have to prove it. Right now we haven't got much to go on. And you," she said directly to Anchorman, "are the only one who was there, so you're going to have to be the one to give us that something else to track down."

Anchorman lifted a hand and placed it on the one Cheron still had lying on his shoulder. "Okay. Let's do it."

Ricki exchanged a look of solidarity with him, then squarely faced Robard. "Will the arresting officer satisfy your boss as a babysitter for Anchorman?"

Robard smiled his approval. "I can sell him on that."

"Okay," Ricki said. "Let's make our calls."

Chapter 9

AFTER A RESTLESS NIGHT, Ricki still felt heavy-eyed and a little groggy. She slid a strap of her backpack over one shoulder, using her right hand to hold it in place as she picked up her rifle with her left hand. "Ready?" she called to the man behind her. Not waiting for an answer, she made sure her backpack was balanced before withdrawing her hand and opening the door to step out into the narrow hallway leading to the elevator. She started down the corridor, hearing Clay pull the door shut behind them. At 0700, they were the only ones waiting for the elevator. As it made a slow ascent toward them on the first floor, she let out a sigh.

"How do you think Robard will want to play this?"

Clay turned to face her rather than the elevator door. "I think he'll split us up into two cars. Anchorman, his two guards, and one of us in the first vehicle. And that will most likely be me, because that would give him a chance for some one-on-one conversation with you. Anyway, that's what I'd do. No weapons in the first car, and you, him, and all the guns in the second car."

Ricki considered that for a moment. "Why would he put

you in the first car? He seemed pretty interested in your homicide background."

Clay smiled. "Because I'm not the prime suspect's business partner, and I haven't come right out and declared him innocent." He gave her a wry grin. "I'm also almost as big as Anchorman. There's safety in numbers and size."

"So you're saying I'm relegated to riding with Robard because I'm shorter, lighter, and wear my feelings on my sleeve?"

"Something like that." When the elevator bell dinged, announcing its arrival, Clay followed Ricki into the compact car. "I hope there's coffee in the lobby."

"There is," Ricki laughed. "Starting at 7 a.m. Last night I read the hotel brochure that listed all the amenities."

"Which are what besides morning coffee?" Clay groused.

"Well, free parking, free Wi-Fi when it's working, plus coffee, and a continental breakfast. Starting at 8 a.m." As the elevator doors opened into the compact lobby area, Ricki grinned. "Oh. And, of course, there's a TV in every room, and housekeeping service on request."

"Funny," he said, giving her a hard poke in the arm. "If the coffee isn't ready, I'm telling Robard we have to stop for some, or this whole overnight trip is off."

"It's not a bad idea, you know." Ricki looked around the deserted lobby and frowned. Not even the desk clerk was anywhere to be seen. For all their sakes, she hoped he was somewhere close, making the coffee.

Clay shifted his backpack off his shoulder and set it at his feet. "What's not a bad idea?"

"This scheme of his," Ricki said as she followed his example and slid her backpack to the floor. "We hike in with a small group, get a look at the scene, hear what Anchorman has to say, and then tomorrow we take him back out while Robard hangs around in the woods and waits for his forensics team. That should give a good day, maybe two, to interview the girlfriend and her son, and track down that army vet."

She turned when the front lobby doors opened and a man with skin the color of dark bronze and wearing a wide smile, stepped across the threshold. He was tall, with a good amount of gray peppered into his black hair, and she recognized him immediately.

Law Enforcement Ranger Jerome Johnson. No, Supervisor Johnson now, she silently corrected herself as she stepped forward and held out her hand.

"Supervisor Johnson? I'm Special Agent Ricki James."

He took her hand in one of his large ones and gave it a quick shake. "Since we've already met, there's no need to be formal. I'm Jerome, and you're Ricki." He turned and pointed to the sturdy woman behind him who looked to have about ten years on Ricki. Her smile was as wide as Jerome's, and her blue eyes beamed out a welcome from beneath a short cap of blond hair. She was wearing the olive-green jacket and brown trousers of the park service, along with the badge that put her in the law enforcement unit.

"I'm Ranger Nora Thorne," she said, without waiting for Jerome to introduce her. "And I'm a big fan."

Not altogether comfortable with that, Ricki quickly pointed at Clay. "This is Police Chief Clay Thomas, from the Bay in Washington. That's near Olympic Park."

Nora grinned. "Yeah. I've been there, along with my four kids and the hubby. It's a magnificent park." She looked almost giddy when she turned to Clay. "And I have to say, you certainly live up to the hype. I'll have to be sure Mr. Thorne gets a look at you. He'll be pea-green with jealousy. After twenty-five years of marriage, it will do him some good."

Clay's polite smile looked pained around the edges, and his eyes narrowed when a noise that sounded like suppressed laughter came from Ricki.

"Everyone back in the Bay, not to mention the greater

metropolitan area of Seattle, would agree with you," Ricki got out with a straight face.

"Nora will be the second officer that NCIS requested to accompany Norman Beal on this overnight hike, and we'll both be accompanying him back here, along with the two of you," Jerome said, ignoring the look of glee exchanged between the two women that promised Clay would be ganged up on. Instead, he took a pair of zip tie handcuffs out of his coat pocket. "I'm under orders to keep these on him at all times. How do you think he's going to take that news?"

"Badly, but he'll wear them," Ricki promised, mentally crossing her fingers.

The entire group turned as the elevator doors opened, and Robard stepped out with Anchorman and Cheron. The agent nodded at Ricki and shook Jerome's hand and then Nora's when she introduced them.

Stepping back, he glanced around the lobby. "I just talked to my two guys, and they're waiting in the car. It's the first parking stall to the right of the door. If the officers will accompany us, I'll walk Anchorman and Dr. Garrison out and make the introductions. Then Dr. Garrison can be on her way with her escort, as promised." He looked around the lobby again. "Duane is on the lobby desk this morning, and he promised to have coffee and pastries ready to take with us."

"Thank you." Ricki cast a sideways glance at Clay. "That will save a lot of complaining."

Robard smiled. "It was a self-serving arrangement, I can assure you."

As they moved off, Clay watched them, a thoughtful look on his face. "You know, you should give Robard a break and a little trust here. It might go a long way."

"Why?" Ricki followed the direction of his gaze. "Do you know something I don't?"

"I know he's on Anchorman's side," Clay said, nodding

when Ricki shot him a skeptical look. "He's bending over backwards to give the man a chance to clear himself."

"Do you think so?" She still wasn't sure she believed that, but she had to admit, so far, the NCIS agent hadn't put up any major roadblocks to Anchorman trailing along with them. And he could have. Probably even should have.

When a skinny kid who looked to be barely eighteen walked in clutching three large thermos jugs to his chest, both Clay and Ricki hurried over to help him. It didn't take long to transfer everything from the night clerk's arms into theirs, and they were soon going through the double doors into the cool morning air, the smell of fresh coffee chasing after them. Jerome was already helping a handcuffed Anchorman into a large SUV with the park service logo on its side.

"Chief, you'll take the shotgun position next to Ranger Thorne." When Clay scowled, Robard gave him a sympathetic smile. "Supervisor Johnson will ride in back with Anchorman." He held out his hand. "If you'll give your rifle to Agent James, I'll take your handgun."

Not the least put off by the request, Clay handed his rifle over to Ricki and his Glock to the NCIS agent. "I should warn you. She's a better shot than I am, and I'm pretty good."

Robard nodded. "So I've heard. But not as good as Anchorman, so there can't be any weapons in the car he's riding in. That was the deal I made with my boss and the director of the National Park Service on our call last night."

Clay shrugged. "It's fine with me. I know Anchorman better than you do. He won't make any trouble, especially not with a woman in the car." Clay's smile was a little crooked. "He has his own code that won't bend on that."

"Not surprised." Robard glanced at Ricki. "Shall we get going? Ranger Thorne told me it's a twelve-mile drive to the parking lot at the trailhead."

As Clay peeled off, Ricki fell into step beside Robard. While they walked in silence toward a small dark-blue SUV, she thought over what Clay had said. A bit of trust might go a long way, and it was Anchorman's life they were talking about. She waited until they were on their way to make that first step, following the ranger's SUV as it turned onto the main highway that led straight to the park.

"I think it would be easier if you called me Ricki."

"No problem," Robard said easily. "I'm Trey. Or you can call me Boa."

"Boa?" Well aware of how pilots got their call signs, she couldn't keep back the smile. "As in the snake, or the feathered scarf favored by strippers?"

Robard gave her a quick glance. "Well, I wasn't wrestling with anything in in South America,, so yeah, it leans more toward the stripper. I made the mistake of going out to a club with some guys from my new unit the first time we got passes to leave the base."

"And?" Ricki prompted when he went silent.

"One of the ladies there, um, gifted me her scarf."

"Now, why would she do that?" Ricki asked, her expression and tone all innocence. But she grinned when the agent's shoulders hunched in a little.

"That's not the point. The guys saw her give it to me, and that was the call sign they voted on. Boa." He let out a snort. "If it were like the movies and you got to pick your own, I'd have a call name like 'Maverick' or 'Iceman' too, but it doesn't work that way. The squad gets to pick it, and then you're stuck with it the rest of your career. End of story."

Ricki laughed at the half-annoyed, half-embarrassed look on the agent's face. When she wound down, she took pity on him as she settled back into her seat. "Okay. Would you prefer to be called Trey or Boa?"

"I don't fly much anymore, and when I do, it's not for the navy, so Trey is fine."

"Trey it is then." She relaxed and enjoyed the passing

scenery. "So, Trey. I know you flew helicopters for the Wranglers out of Lemoore."

"Not just any old helicopter. Knighthawks," he said easily. "We flew Knighthawks. And if you're going to ask me why I gave it up, save your breath. I don't talk about it." He sent her a pointed look. "Like you probably don't talk about what happened to your first partner."

Nice shot. And now I know you researched me as much as I looked into you, Ricki thought. "You've got me there." She shot him a curious look. "So what's it like flying helicopters?"

He visibly relaxed. Clearly she'd hit on a subject he enjoyed.

"It's noisy, mostly. But the feeling of floating on air is really addicting." He grinned. "Until someone starts shooting at you."

"I guess you were shot at quite a bit until you got into search and rescue."

He nodded. "Yeah. The pilot was always the enemy's favorite target, too. Or the rear rotors. Take either of those out and the bird will probably go down." He draped an arm over the top of the steering wheel and glanced over at her. "How long have you been with the park service?"

"Since I got out of college." Feeling more comfortable, she returned his smile. "One marriage, one son, a divorce, and a dozen years later, and here I am."

He laughed. "That's boiling your life down to the basics. So what's Ricki short for?"

Taken by surprise, her mouth dropped open before she could remember to keep it shut. Strangely enough, she wasn't asked that question very often. "Richelle. It was my grandmother's name. My dad came up with the shortened version of Ricki."

"Okay. Now we're even. I know how you got your name, and you know how I got my call sign. Is there anything else I need to know?"

Making up her mind, Ricki nodded. "Yeah. After we checked on Anchorman at the county jail, Cheron and I drove over to the hotel in Pigeon Forge. Clay stayed behind to arrange for Anchorman's bail."

Trey kept his eyes on the road as he maneuvered around a slow-moving semitruck. "Okay."

"We were followed all the way from the jail to the hotel," she stated bluntly.

Trey's head swiveled around, and his light brown eyes turned a shade darker. "Followed? You and the doctor? Who followed you?"

"Well, if I knew that, I'd have already had a chat with him." Ricki rolled her shoulders back before a boot started tapping against the SUV's floor mat. "Black truck, looked like a Ford F-150. Heavily tinted windows and what looked like mud was smeared all over the front plate."

"Convenient." Trey's attention returned to the road in front of them. "I'm assuming Clay knows about this?"

"Yeah."

"How about Anchorman? Did you tell him?"

Ricki shook her head. "No. And I'm sure I'll catch grief for that later on, but at the moment it doesn't sound like a good idea."

"Have to agree with you there." A full minute of silence passed before Trey said, "Thanks for letting me know. I appreciate it."

"No problem." She smiled, glad she'd followed Clay's advice and given the agent a little trust. "I didn't want you to think I'd taken a leap off the deep end when you see me wandering around parking lots looking for a black truck."

"It would have to be a black truck," Trey complained. "I happen to own one of those." When he caught her suspicious look, he grinned. "It wasn't me. Mine is sitting in a lot behind the guarded gates of Quantico."

She shrugged. "It must be a guy thing because Clay has one too. And it's sitting in the parking lot at SeaTac."

"So what do female agents drive?"

"A jeep." She thought of the bright green vehicle currently parked in the alley behind the Sunny Side Up. Her son had dubbed it "the lime-cicle" the minute he'd seen it, and like nicknames that became call signs, the name had stuck. "The trailhead parking areas tend toward the smaller side. It shouldn't be any trouble to spot a black truck."

"Well, it wasn't anyone in NCIS, and if it was from the FBI it would have been a dark gray sedan, not a truck. I also doubt if whoever is following you would leave that truck somewhere you could easily spot it," Trey said.

"Me either," she agreed. "But they might try to sneak in behind us, park in the lot, and then get back out before we do, so we need to stay alert."

It wasn't long before the SUV they were following drove past a sign perched on a wall of native stone, welcoming visitors to the park. Trey stayed close behind the vehicle. When Ranger Thorne kept the SUV on the main road, rather than make the right-hand turn onto Little River Road, Ricki nodded her approval.

"It looks like we're headed for the Huskey Gap trailhead. It's just a few miles ahead, on the right." She leaned forward to keep an eye out for the parking lot. "I'm betting it's the same way they brought Anchorman out. It's not a bad hike. More importantly, it's not a crowded trail. The only thing we might see along the way is bears."

"Bears? Great."

When the SUV in front of them pulled into a small parking lot carved out of the trees alongside the road, Trey did the same. Ranger Thorne selected a spot to park, and Trey pulled in right next to her. Ricki reached over and grabbed her backpack from the floor of the backseat, then hopped out of the vehicle and headed for the rear hatchback.

Trey popped it open, and they both gathered up the rifles and handguns stashed there.

Clay climbed out of the larger vehicle and walked back to where Ricki was standing, leaving it to the two rangers to get a handcuffed Anchorman out of the car. While they were seeing to that, he holstered his Glock and walked the other two handguns and a rifle back to the rangers. Since there was only one other vehicle in the lot, and it was a bright-colored sedan, there wasn't anything for Ricki to check out, so she sprinted across the road to join the rest of the group standing in front of the small sign that marked the start of the trailhead.

Trey eyed the narrow path before putting his hands on his hips and turning to the two rangers. "Tell me about this hike?"

Jerome nodded at Nora, who started by clearing her throat, then taking a wide stance with her hands behind her back as if she was about to give a nature lecture to a flock of tourists. "Well, it's a steep climb for the first couple of miles, and then it's all downhill from there to the fork at the Little River Trail. From that point, it's fairly flat and easy going." She gestured to the path behind her. "It doesn't get much wider than this, and there's a couple of downed trees, but not so big that we can't get around them. Overall, it's a nice hike. Not much for the grand scenery except for an occasional peek here and there, but some beautiful clusters of wildflowers. And the streams are running high with the melt off, so they're also an impressive sight to take in. There are a lot better views from some of the other trails, but this one isn't well traveled. The odds are good that at this hour, and this early in the season, we'll have it to ourselves."

Trey looked toward the path and frowned. "So it's an uphill climb for two miles or so?"

"That's right," Nora confirmed. "I don't think it's something anyone here can't handle, if that's what you're worried about."

He nodded but looked over at Jerome. "How many pairs of those zip tie handcuffs did you bring?"

"I have four more, and Nora has about the same."

"Five," Nora piped up. "I have five pairs with me."

The NCIS agent blew out a breath and turned back to consider the trail that disappeared into the trees. "Ricki told me there are bears. Which I'd expect this time of year."

Jerome lifted his shoulders in a casual shrug. "And you expect right. It's spring. Mama bear and her cubs usually wander around looking for food as she has multiple mouths to feed. We'll have to be careful to avoid them." He pointed to the rifle Trey was holding. "I'd remind you that we don't shoot things in the park, Agent Robard. Not unless there's no other recourse."

"Understood." The agent pointed to Anchorman's hands. "For his own safety, we need to remove those." While Jerome gaped at him with a dumbfounded look on his face, Trey stared Anchorman right in the eye. "I'm Boa. Captain, US Navy, but no longer on active duty. And I'm asking you, Sergeant, if you intend to cause any trouble."

Anchorman stood up straighter and didn't flinch at the hard stare. "No, sir. You have my word."

"I'll take the word of a decorated Marine," Trey said. "Supervisor Johnson, if you'd remove those zip ties? We'll put them back on once we reach the Little River Trail. Until then, I don't want him falling flat on his face, or getting mauled by a bear so we'd have to carry him back."

While Jerome took out a heavy utility knife and cut through the zip ties binding Anchorman's wrists together, the former sniper looked over the supervisor's head and nodded at Trey. "I appreciate this, but you need to remember that I'm retired from the Corps, and you aren't on active duty anymore. So don't expect me to be saluting your navy ass every time I turn around."

Trey laughed. "I'll consider myself warned."

Chapter 10

THE UPHILL CLIMB was exactly what Ricki had expected, with the reward being a descent to the Little River Trail. It took the group two hours to make the trip, walking single file along the narrow track.

A light wind danced through the treetops, breathing life into the forest. Surrounded by the lush green of new growth, they were treated to a visual reminder that spring was well on its way. Patches of wildflowers lined the path in the clusters that Ranger Thorne had promised. The splashes of color randomly gave way to small clearings with an explosion of flowers in full bloom, only to taper out as the trail was again encased in the trees and the green carpet of ferns that covered the forest floor.

The air was cool and crisp, with the dappling of light flickering through the leafy canopy above, giving the path just a touch of magic. It would have been a perfect day if it hadn't been for Anchorman walking along between the two rangers, no rifle strapped to his back, and his head down.

Since they were following the only visible trail, there was no chance of making a wrong turn, so Trey was in front. He set a brisk pace on the uphill climb and then a more careful one on the descent down the backside toward the river. When they reached the intersection with the Little River Trail, Nora called out to turn south. Now that the path was much wider, Clay moved up to walk beside Ricki. They were behind Anchorman, his hands again confined with a zip tie handcuff now that they'd reached more level ground. Since his two human watchdogs had kept to the single-file arrangement, Ricki tried not to feel as if they were walking the big Marine to a secret gallows somewhere deep in the forest.

The spooky image had her taking a firmer grip on her rifle and making an effort to concentrate on their surroundings. They still hadn't come across any other hikers, or any other signs of human activity by the time they passed Campsite 21.

Ricki's mood lightened considerably when they reached the sturdy, picturesque wooden bridge that crossed the river. The sound of the rushing water yielded its own kind of tranquility. Even Anchorman perked up, managing a smile as he watched the river beneath them tumbling along its way.

The path followed the water for another mile, the soothing sounds of the forest and water mingling in an uninterrupted harmony that lasted right up until the group rounded a gentle curve and were confronted with the jarring bright orange of crime scene tape. It stretched across the trail, blocking anyone from passing that point. And just to make sure of it, a ranger sat in a fold-out chair just beyond the tape.

Spotting them, he jumped to his feet and stood with his legs braced apart, ready to stop anyone from taking another step. Trey's hand flashed out as he held up his credentials less than a foot from the man's face.

"Special Agent Robard, with NCIS."

Trey had barely announced himself when Jerome stepped up beside him. "Hi there, Mike."

Mike did a quick duck of his head as he continued to frown at Trey. "Sir."

"I'm sure you were told about the group I'd be bringing up here today?"

The ranger leaned slightly to one side, his eyes growing wider when he spotted the handcuffs on Anchorman. "Um. Yes, sir. Charlie, that is Ranger Stubben, and I got the call last night." He made a gesture for the supervisor to step off the trail and around the tape. "We're set up just a little ways down at camp two-four, if y'all want to take a breather. I think Charlie has some coffee going."

When Trey nodded, Jerome smiled at Mike. "That would be great. Thanks. And you and Charlie can pack up and head back. We'll be keeping an eye on the site until the forensic team gets here."

Jerome skirted the crime scene tape, with Anchorman following and Nora maintaining her guard at the rear. When Nora passed the bemused Mike, she said in a loud whisper, "That's Agent Ricki James and Chief Clay Thomas behind me, if you can believe that."

"You don't say?" Mike breathed, and his eyes got wide again.

Ricki tried not to grit her teeth, and barely managed a polite smile as she stepped past the gaping ranger and continued the short walk to Campsite 24. It was little more than a clearing next to the trail and the river, with a firepit surrounded by flat stones large enough to sit on. Two small single-man tents were set up, one on either side of the firepit, and deeper into the trees there was a bear bag hung on a line slung over a hidden branch high overhead.

Ricki had seen, and occupied, the same kind of setup hundreds of times before, so she didn't bother to look around like Trey was, but followed Anchorman, sitting next to him on one of the longer, flat rocks. From the sideways look he shot her, it was clear he didn't want any company. But that was just too bad. He was getting some, whether or not he liked it.

She carefully leaned her gun on the side farthest away

from him to keep from getting any worried looks from Jerome or Nora. "How are you doing?"

"I'm good."

He sounded far from it, but she didn't argue with him. "Do you remember being here?"

"I wasn't," he snapped. "We walked right past this place."

Ignoring his bad mood, Ricki gave him a light, friendly bump with her shoulder. "Did you notice anyone here?"

He was quiet for a moment, then slowly nodded. "Yeah. An older couple. It looked like they were breaking camp, but they still had their fire going."

"Do you remember anything else about them? Like what they were wearing?" When he remained silent, she tried something else. "You know food smells. Were they cooking something over the fire?"

Now Anchorman closed his eyes and slowly breathed in and out. "He had on a dark jacket, but hers was a bright yellow. And there was coffee. I remember smelling it right before Kelly called out a hello."

Ricki's heart rate picked up a notch. "Kelly talked to them?"

He shook his head. "No. He just yelled a hello, and we kept walking."

"Did they yell a hello back to Kelly?"

He paused and then smiled. "Yeah. The woman did. She told us to be careful and have a good hike."

"Anything else?"

"No." He opened his eyes again and looked at her. "Like I said, we just kept walking. We still had another couple of miles to get to our site."

"Did you see or pass by anyone else after that?"

"No. It was quiet. Just the wind and the sound of the water. We followed the river all the way to the camp." He scuffed a boot in the dirt, then looked off into the distance. "We had to cross it a couple of times. Kelly almost fell on his ass. He did manage to get soaked up to his kneecaps. He was getting pissed off because I couldn't stop laughing and calling him an old man who couldn't keep his balance on a couple of rocks."

"Oh yeah?" Ricki kept her tone light. "Did he try to push you in so you'd be soaked, too?"

Anchorman gave a dismissive sniff at the idea. "That would have been a girly thing to do. A good punch would have settled it if he'd been that pissed off."

Ricki rolled her eyes. "A girly thing? Really? So what did he do?"

"Nothing. Once we got to the other side, his pants and boots would have dried out after we got a fire going. So it was a no harm, no foul kind of deal. Happens all the time."

Now Ricki laughed. "And I suppose you're going to tell me that's a guy thing."

"It was," Anchorman stated with an annoying amount of conviction. "He evened the score when he caught all the fish for our dinner, and I came up with zip."

"Yeah, that would have done it," she agreed, keeping her voice mild. But she filed every bit of information away. You never knew what might come in handy later.

It was less than five minutes later when Trey gave the signal to leave. This time Clay took point while the two rangers, with Anchorman between them, fell in behind the chief. Trey walked next to Ricki, gradually slowing his pace until they were out of hearing range of the rest of the group.

"Did Anchorman say anything helpful?"

She didn't bother to pretend not to know what he was talking about. "He remembered seeing an older couple there at two-four. The woman was wearing a yellow jacket, and she told them to be careful and have a good hike."

Trey came to an abrupt stop. "They talked to this older couple?"

Puzzled at his reaction, Ricki stopped too. "No, not

exactly. Kelly had yelled out a greeting, and the woman yelled back at them. The man with her was wearing a dark jacket, and she had on a bright yellow one. That's about it. Oh, and they were breaking camp but still had a fire going and were brewing some coffee."

"Anchorman remembered the coffee?"

Ricki shrugged. "He's a cook. He'd remember the smell of the coffee more than the people." When Trey started walking again, so did Ricki. "You seem pretty interested in this non-encounter with the elderly couple. What aren't you telling me?"

"Did Anchorman mention if he and Kelly were having an argument when they passed by this campsite?"

Now Ricki stopped and reached out to grab Trey's arm, forcing him to stop as well. "An argument? What makes you think they were having an argument while they were near that campsite?" She dropped her hand, releasing his arm as she narrowed her eyes on Trey's face. "Cheron mentioned that Anchorman told her there were witnesses. It couldn't be to the murder. So, did that older couple say they heard Kelly and Anchorman arguing?"

Trey's expression remained blank as he stared back at her. "What makes you think they couldn't have witnessed the murder?"

Her upper lip curled in disgust. "Oh, come on, Robard. You were a search and rescue pilot, so I know you spent a fair amount of time in the backcountry. Like you said before, there aren't any streetlights out here and it would have been pitch-black at night. Unless you're going to tell me these witnesses just happened to be wandering around trying out some night vision goggles, there is no way they saw anyone being murdered." She dug the heels of her boots into the dirt and lifted her chin. "I've been trying to be straight with you. How about you return the favor?"

"Maybe they didn't see it, but perhaps they heard the

murder going down." He was silent a moment, his brown-eyed gaze boring into hers before he finally nodded. "But okay, point taken." His feet shuffled in a restless motion as he looked off into the distance. "One thing that's been bothering me is that the witnesses didn't hear anything that night, just the two men arguing earlier in the day. At least according to the report I received. I haven't had a chance yet to talk to them myself to find out why they slept through a gunshot, since that's how Kelly was killed." He ran a hand through his hair and then sighed. "From their location at Campsite 24, and the description of one Mr. Marvin Packer and his wife Susan, right down to the yellow jacket, I'd say they're the same older couple that Anchorman just told you about."

"Marvin and Susan Packer," Ricki repeated under her breath before raising her voice so Trey could hear her. "Where do they live?"

"Knoxville. They came out here for a few days of relax-ation. I put an inquiry into the park service headquarters at Sugarlands, and their story checks out. They've had multiple trips to the park in the last year, and most of them included a reservation for Campsite 24." He hesitated before continuing. "I'm going to be tied up here with the forensic team for a day or two. As my expert area consultant, maybe you could take a drive up to Knoxville and drop in on the Packers. Get some clarification on what they saw and heard." He gave her a sharp look. "And record it. I can email you their information, along with a copy of the statement they gave to Supervisor Johnson as head of the response team. It would also give you a chance to check up on Cheron."

Ricki's whole body relaxed. This was good. Very good. "Yeah. Yeah, I can do that. Anchorman said it looked like they were breaking camp when he and Kelly passed by. That could be why they didn't hear or see anything, since they'd already left. I can get verification of that."

"Okay." Trey gestured toward the now-empty trail ahead

of them. "If we're square, maybe we should catch up with the others?"

She smiled. "No problems here. Let's pick it up."

Chapter 11

WITH THE PATH toward Campsite 30 again narrowing, Ricki took the lead as they followed the river. It didn't take long to spot the rest of the group ahead. Thinking they'd stopped to wait for her and Trey to catch up, her pace slowed when she saw Anchorman, down on one knee, his head bowed. But he wasn't waiting, he was grieving. The area opposite the river was cordoned off with the familiar bright orange tape.

As she quietly drew closer, Ricki caught Clay's eye. He inclined his head slightly toward the blocked-off area before shifting his gaze to the ground. Jerome and Nora took another step down the path to make room for Ricki when she came up beside Anchorman and laid a gentle hand on his shoulder. He didn't move at her touch, just kept his head down as he stared at the small dark patch barely showing in the dirt in front of him. There was a thin white line of paint sprayed onto the ground around it. Ricki glanced over at Jerome, who nodded in return.

"I had them do that in case it rained before the forensic people got here. I wanted to preserve the size of the blood-stain." He winced, casting an apologetic look at Anchorman's bowed head.

Ricki didn't say anything but shifted her gaze back to the area inside the white outline. Beyond it the bright green of young ferns poked out from the dirt and rocks in random spots.

"Has it?" she asked, still studying the slightly darkened patch of dirt and the foliage around it. "I mean, has it rained since Kelly was found?"

"It would be typical for this time of year, but no, it hasn't," Jerome said. "Would you corroborate that, Nora?"

Nora shifted her weight from one foot to the other. "No rain," she confirmed. "A touch of frost here and there in the lower spots of the park, but no rain."

"Hmm." Ricki's tone was noncommittal. From the corner of her eye, she saw Clay lean over the edge of the crime scene tape that marked-off the area.

"Not much blood spatter around the chalk mark. Or inside it either," he said.

When Anchorman's shoulder tensed underneath her hand, Ricki gave it a firm squeeze before turning to face Jerome. "Would you and Nora take Anchorman farther down the path?"

The big Marine didn't protest. He simply braced his bound hands on his raised knee and, in one fluid motion, easily pushed himself into a standing position. Still not saying anything, he took up his position between the two rangers and walked off.

When he was out of earshot, Ricki's boot started tapping against the packed dirt of the path. "There isn't any blood spatter that I can see." She glanced over at Trey. "How about you? Do you see any blood spatter outside of that white paint?"

"No," Trey said. "But maybe we just can't see it. The forensic team needs to do more extensive testing before I can confirm or refute that conclusion."

Ricki put her hands on her hips and shrugged. "I'm not

concluding anything. I'm simply noting the lack of blood spatter on any of the rocks or plants near the spot where the body was found. And since he probably died from a gunshot wound to the back, then judging by how the body was likely positioned, I'd say most of it was lying across the path."

Clay straightened up and studied the area of the trail where the body must have lain. "Anyone coming this way would have had to have tripped over the guy." He glanced at Trey. "Who found the body?"

"A lone hiker who'd spent the night at Campsite 23, according to the report," Trey said.

"Where's that?" Clay asked.

Ricki took a step back and looked down the stretch of trail they'd already covered. "About three and a half miles from two-four. Down Goshen Prong Trail. It forks off this one, heading to the southwest." Her boot went back to its tapping. "Did this lone hiker mention why he came down this way, or if he saw the Packers still camped at two-four?"

Trey opened his mouth and then shut it again, taking a minute before he answered. "He wanted to check out Campsite 30 for a future spot to stay since he'd heard it was a nice site. And no, he didn't see the Packers. He stated that two-four was empty."

"And is that in the report?" Ricki's voice was dry, and her frown didn't change when Trey shot her an annoyed look.

"No. It's in my notes," he finally said. "The county sheriff didn't see any reason to detain him, so he got his information and let him fly home to Chicago. I called him last night."

"And may I also have a copy of your notes?" Ricki asked without looking at him. She didn't expect a "yes," so wasn't surprised when she didn't get one.

"Sure. Once I get them written up in a report."

She sent him a cool look, then turned on her heel and walked past Clay. "Let's get going," she called over her shoulder. When she reached Anchorman and his guards, she sidled past them on the narrow trail and took the lead. She was going to have to get the name of that solo hiker out of Trey, or maybe, if she was lucky, Jerome had it. And she was due for a little luck.

Twenty minutes later, she came to a river crossing. It was spring, so the water was high, rushing past with enough force that it was going to take some effort to stay upright while slogging through it. She looked at the larger rocks poking out at intervals. They were far enough apart she didn't even try to use them as an improvised bridge. Instead she waded in, hearing the splash behind her as Jerome did the same, with the others following behind.

The water swirled halfway up her shins as she plowed through it before scrambling up the bank on the other side. She didn't look behind to see how the rest of the group was faring. Even with his hands bound, she doubted it would be a problem for Anchorman, and everyone else was an experienced hiker. She had other things on her mind besides playing lifeguard while they ferried their way across the fast but fairly shallow river.

She was still brooding when they reached a second river crossing. Here more stones were visible that could be used as a foothold, but it would be tricky. The water seemed faster and more violent as it found its own way through the rocky barrier.

Since she was already wet, she didn't worry about whether her boot landed in water or on a rock, concentrating more on keeping upright than dry. Just beyond the crossing was a peninsula of land, bounded by the river on either side so there was no escaping the sound of rushing water. In the cleared-off area between the rivers was a firepit, built with wood and stones, Old logs, complete with splinters, were placed randomly around it for the usual seating that was typical in the backcountry.

Ricki walked into the site, making her way to the firepit.

She leaned her rifle against one of the logs, then slipped her backpack off her shoulders, letting it drop to the ground as her gaze roamed the area. Both tarp shelters were still standing, with the edge of a sleeping bag poking out from one. There was a tin cup balanced on top of a log near the firepit, and she could see a second cup lying in the dirt next to a log on the opposite side. Besides those two things, the site was spotless, with everything in its place. Even the bear bag was still hung high in the trees.

Ricki walked over to where Anchorman was standing, flanked by Nora and Jerome. She grabbed her cell phone and held it out to Nora. "Would you mind following us around and recording what Anchorman says? It's a request from his lawyer." Which was putting it politely. It was actually a nonnegotiable condition that Christopher Young had demanded before he would consent to his client making this trip.

She hadn't remembered to do that when they had stopped at Campsite 24, but she figured better late than never. Hoping the attorney would see it the same way, she handed her phone to a bemused Nora and showed her how to navigate to the record button on the screen.

With that chore taken care of, Ricki turned to face Anchorman.

"Which of the shelters was yours, and which was Kelly's?" she started off.

Anchorman pointed to the one with the sleeping bag. "That one was mine. Kelly put up the other one."

She mentally gauged the distance between the two. Since they were on opposite sides of the campfire, they wouldn't have intruded on each other's privacy. But still, it would be tough to argue that Anchorman wouldn't have noticed Kelly leaving camp, or being forcibly removed from it. Especially since the single, wide-open sides on both shelters were facing each other. "Okay. Walk us through what happened after you got your shelters up." She reached over and gave him a quick poke in the back. "And I mean that literally. Walk us through it."

With a jerky nod, Anchorman crossed the short distance to his shelter. "I finished first." He turned and walked to the firepit. "I came over here to check for wood. Sometimes the previous campers leave a small pile as a courtesy to the next person who comes along." He pointed to a spot near the firepit and a small stack of branches of various sizes. "There was some there, and I went looking to add to the stock." He waved a hand back toward the trail. "I started looking out that way and made a sweep around the campsite. I found enough dry wood to keep us going through a good part of the night and reheat up more coffee in the morning. By the time I got back, Kelly was over here. He'd boiled a pail of water to sterilize it, so we would have some clean drinking water." He walked to stand by one of the logs near the pit. "He'd also changed into his spare jeans and was working on attaching hooks to a couple of lines."

"So he had on dry clothes?" Ricki clarified. She was keeping close to Anchorman's heels as she and Nora followed him around the firepit.

"Yeah. He wasn't wearing any socks, though. I remember when I went to change into some dry clothes, he told me not to wear any either because they'd only get wet when I put my boots back on." He stopped his pacing and smiled. "I told him I wasn't a green recruit just starting basic training, and to save his advice for fishing." He glanced at Ricki. "I'm not much good at it."

A smile tugged at the corners of her mouth. "I've been out on Dabob Bay with you back home, so yeah, I know."

"We took up a place on the river over there." Anchorman started to put his hands in his pockets, belatedly remembered they were tied together, then held them up at waist level. "Want to walk over there too?"

Ricki nodded and followed as he walked to one of the rivers that ran along the border of the campsite. He braced his feet apart before making an up and then outward motion with his arms, as if he were casting a line into the water. "Damn if Kelly didn't catch two right off the bat. Then we kept at it for a good hour before he got another bite. By the time we had enough to make a decent meal, the sun was starting to set." He turned and slowly walked back to the camp. "I carried the fish, since I was going to cook them, and Kelly carried the hooks and lines." He stopped by the firepit, then started walking straight to his shelter. "I went to get my pack because my knife was attached to the side, and I'd brought along a couple of spices in case we caught anything." He stuck his head into the shelter, then immediately pulled it out again. He turned a frown on Ricki. "My pack is gone."

"We have it," Trey said. He and Clay had been following behind Ricki, keeping their distance so they wouldn't bother Anchorman, but close enough to hear what he was saying.

"Kelly's too?" Ricki asked.

"No. His should still be here. Sorry I didn't mention Anchorman's backpack before,, but yeah, it came back with the rangers. along with his rifle. Everything else was to be left for my forensic team," Trey said. "And once they've finished their job, I will be very happy to forward you a list of the contents."

Ricki lifted an eyebrow when Clay gave Trey a hard smack on the shoulder. "Stop aggravating her."

"Why?" Trey asked as he gingerly rubbed his shoulder. "She aggravates me."

Turning her back on both of them, Ricki nodded at Anchorman to continue. "You got your backpack, and then what?"

"Since Kelly was carrying all the food packets, I had the cooking gear. We've always split the weight up between us. Anyway, we met back at the firepit." He walked over that way and sat down on a log, next to the abandoned tin mug. "We both started cleaning the fish, and then I cooked them. It was dark by the time we finished dinner, had our coffee, and got everything stowed away again."

"Do you know what time that was?" Trey asked, earning him a mildly amused look from Anchorman.

"I never look at my watch when I'm out here. There's no point."

After delivering that bit of philosophy, Anchorman fell silent. Ricki took several steps forward and sat down next to him. "What did you and Kelly do after dinner?"

For the first time, he hesitated. "I think we took our boots off and dried them out next to the fire."

"What else?" she prompted. "Did the two of you finish that argument you had earlier when you were hiking in?"

Anchorman's head whipped around. "What argument? The only words we had were about him slipping off those rocks when we were crossing the river. And that wasn't an argument, it was just a little trash talk."

"Okay, then what did you talk about?" she asked smoothly. "Sports? Your time together in the Marines?"

"I guess it must have been the usual stuff. And probably about what Kelly wanted to do after he left the Corps at the end of the year." Anchorman sighed. "That whole Airbnb thing."

"And the vet who wanted to go in on it with him?"

"Yeah," he said. "Maybe that too. I don't really remember. Except before we ate, he did ask if I was going to take Fitz up on his offer to invest in his company."

Now that surprised her. She knew Fitz was Anchorman's brother-in-law, but he rarely talked about him or his sister. The only family member he regularly mentioned was his Aunt Sally. "Are you going to make the investment?"

"Nah. I'm not into making that custom furniture stuff that Fitz does." Anchorman relaxed, leaning his forearms on his knees. "And while we were cleaning the fish, Kelly complained a bit about his girlfriend's son. He said he'd been pushing the kid hard to get off his butt and do something, like join the service." His forehead furrowed in thought. "I don't remember how long we talked. Right after we finished cleaning up, we started in on making a pretty good dent in that bottle of bourbon that Kelly had brought along."

Clay caught her eye as he casually made a circle around the firepit. He picked up a long stick and poked through the ashes, then tossed it aside and straightened up. Putting his hands in his pockets, he turned to face Anchorman. "Did you finish it off?"

"The bourbon?" A crease formed between Anchorman's eyebrows. "I don't remember. It must have hit me hard, because I don't remember going back to the tent to sack out for the night." The crease deepened and his lips thinned out. "One of the last things I remember is Kelly laughing about having trouble getting the bottle open." He shook his head. "I don't know. It's all kind of a blank."

"Do you remember if he took the bottle back to his shelter?" Clay asked.

While Anchorman lifted his hands, palms up in a "who knows" gesture, Trey stepped over to the second shelter and ducked inside. He was back out in less than five seconds. Walking rapidly toward the firepit, he stopped in front of Jerome. Crossing his arms over his chest, he gave the supervisor a hard stare.

"There's nothing in the shelter."

Jerome glanced over his shoulder toward the tarp Kelly had put up. "You mean there's no bourbon bottle?"

"I mean, there's nothing," Trey stated flatly. "No bourbon bottle, no sleeping bag, no backpack. Nothing."

The supervisor crossed his own arms, mimicking Trey's stance. "Yeah. I noticed there wasn't a sleeping bag. I don't recall noticing the backpack one way or the other, and didn't know about the bottle of bourbon."

"It wasn't mentioned in the report."

"And so?" Jerome shot back. "I didn't have an inventory sheet of what the man brought with him. Anchorman's backpack was in the other shelter. That was in the report. I had no way of knowing if anything else was missing."

"So you thought the victim came out here and slept on the ground?" Trey snapped.

Ricki got to her feet and waved a hand between the two men. "Hey. A sleeping bag isn't the only thing that's missing. Where's the backpack and the bourbon?" She looked down at Anchorman, who was still seated on the log. "And did Kelly bring a gun with him?"

"We both did. Rifles," Anchorman said. "I guess I carried mine back to the shelter along with my boots since it was there when I woke up the next morning, and sometime during the night I must have put my boots on." He shrugged. "And I'm sure I would have set my rifle in its usual position against my backpack before I crawled into my sleep . . ." His voice trailed off, then he slowly turned and stared at his shelter. "My rifle was there, but it was on my left." His head moved back around as if it were on a string being manipulated by someone above him. "When I woke up the next morning, I automatically reached out for it, and it wasn't there on the right side, leaning against my backpack. It was on the ground, on my left."

Ricki nodded. That would fit what she thought had happened that night. "And what about Kelly? You said he had a rifle too?"

The Marine blinked, then slowly got to his feet. "Yeah. A brand-new Weatherby. He picked it up a week after he got back into the country, and it cost him over three grand. He treated that thing like a baby." Anchorman narrowed his gaze on Kelly's shelter. "If it wasn't with him, it would be in his shelter."

Ricki aimed a questioning look at Trey, who shook his head.

"Not with the body."

"And I'm assuming Kelly also had a sleeping bag?" Ricki asked a stone-faced Anchorman.

"Yeah. He did." He met Trey's gaze head-on. "And there was a bottle of bourbon."

"Okay, okay," Trey relented. "It's reasonable to assume that all three of those things made it to the camp. So where are they now?"

Chapter 12

"Excuse me, Agent Robard." Ricki inclined her head toward Clay. "Can we talk to you a minute?"

The NCIS agent turned on his heel and walked over to the far edge of the campsite. Ricki knew the other three still standing near the firepit would hear the entire exchange, but at least she could keep them at her back and pretend that they couldn't.

"You can't believe that Kelly was killed where he was found," she said in a flat tone. "You said he was murdered with a bullet to the back. And by Anchorman. Which means he was shot with a rifle. And yet, there wasn't any sign of blood spatter around the body."

"What makes you think he was killed with a rifle?" Trey said.

"Besides the fact you took Anchorman's rifle for testing?" Ricki ground out. "Because that's all there was to test since Anchorman doesn't carry a handgun. Just his rifle. In the backcountry, that's all a former sniper needs. A rifle and a very big knife."

"I'll keep that in mind." Trey heaved a long breath, then ran a hand over the top of his head. "And no. I don't think

Sergeant Kelly was killed where his body was found. But I'm still going to wait for the forensic guys to confirm that before I rule it out completely."

"Then what? He was carried there in his missing sleeping bag for a mile and a half?" Ricki's boot started tapping as she kept her stare pinned on Trey.

Trey shrugged. "Sergeant Dorman wasn't a big guy. Given the physical differences between the two men, I think Anchorman could have managed it with a basic fireman's carry. Even over that distance."

"One guy, hauling dead weight in a fireman's carry over two river crossings?" She shook her head. "That's really stretching it, Robard. And what happened to the sleeping bag, the backpack, and the missing bottle of bourbon, not to mention Kelly's brand-new gun?"

"He could have ditched all those somewhere in the forest. The odds were good that we'd never find them."

Ricki wanted to pull her hair out in frustration. She settled for shoving a long stray lock behind one ear. "You cannot believe that Anchorman would toss a three-thousand-dollar rifle into the trees and leave it there to rot?"

Trey stuck his hands into the back pockets of his jeans, an uncomfortable look on his face as he stared into the distance. When he looked back at her, there was a speculative gleam in his eyes. "Then what do you think happened here?"

"I think Cheron was right and both men were drugged. At least Anchorman was. His account of how he felt that following morning, plus Supervisor Johnson's observations, support that. And whatever he took was likely in that missing bottle of bourbon."

"You mean the one the victim brought?"

Ricki ignored the sarcasm in Trey's tone and continued to lay out her own interpretation of events. "Once Anchorman was out, the killers took his rifle, shot Kelly, and then carried the body to a place where it could be easily found. And how convenient that that's exactly what happened before Anchorman could look for his friend himself?"

Trey's hand shot up to stop her. "Hang on. Are you thinking someone took Anchorman's gun, and then put it back into his shelter without Anchorman knowing it? Because that's where it was found. Right next to his sleeping bag."

The choking sound behind her had Ricki turning her head. She caught the skeptical look on Anchorman's face before he shifted his gaze away. It was the same as the one in Trey's eyes. Even to her own ears it sounded like a stretch. For all she knew, the man slept with one hand on his rifle.

"What I don't think," she said, raising her voice a couple of notches, "is that Anchorman put his gun on his left side when he's right-handed." Her head bobbed in a decisive nod when the snorting noises behind her were suddenly cut short.

Trey paced a few feet, shaking his head and muttering to himself. He was standing, looking out into the trees, when Anchorman's voice suddenly cut through the air like a knife through butter.

"Hit the dirt."

It was the urgency in the tone as much as the words that had both Ricki and Clay immediately diving for the ground barely a split second before the crack of gunfire bounced through the trees. There was a scream from the direction of the firepit, closely followed by a second shot that had Trey collapsing right where he stood.

Clay immediately started to crawl toward the agent, who was clutching his leg. Ricki could see the red oozing between his fingers even as she unzipped her jacket and drew out her Glock. A muzzle flashed, followed by a bullet hitting the dirt just six inches from Clay's foot. She swung her gun around, getting off several quick shots, then keeping up a steady stream as Clay reached the wounded NCIS agent and dragged him four feet by the collar of his jacket to take cover behind a tree. Another bullet hit the log near the firepit where

Anchorman and the two rangers were, along with both her rifle and Clay's.

Clay opened up with his sidearm, laying down his own curtain of fire to give her time to reach a safer position than lying out in the open. She made a quick crawl for the trees, pulling herself up into a crouch behind one of the thicker trunks.

"Two."

Anchorman's strong shout was music to her ears. Whoever had let out that scream of pain, it hadn't been him.

"Who's hit?" she yelled just before another barrage of bullets slammed into the firepit logs. She ducked back behind the tree as Clay reached into his jacket pocket. She aimed toward the point where she'd seen the flash and fired off more rounds, giving Clay time to reload.

"Jerome." Nora's voice rose over the gunfire. Ricki was thankful to hear that while it was shrill, it wasn't hysterical. "In the shoulder. I've got a bandage on it."

As another bullet pounded into the tree trunk, small shards of wood flew out, pelting Ricki's jeans. While Clay took up the bullet exchange again, Ricki reloaded her own gun, switching her attention back to the group only partially hidden behind the very short logs. "Nora, listen to me. You've got to cut Anchorman loose. Do you understand me?"

There was movement behind the logs and then a long minute of silence. On the other side of the firepit, a flash of motion in the woods caught her eye. Taking aim, she shot off five rounds in that direction. The minute she squeezed the trigger, Anchorman emerged from behind the logs and did a quick crawl toward her rifle, using her fire as cover. A second later, the barrel of her rifle disappeared.

"Two o'clock," she yelled, then shot off several more rounds, tracking the slight movement she could only catch glimpses of between the trees. While she kept the shooter busy, Anchorman slid around the far end of the log and headed for the trees. Once he was out of sight, Ricki swiveled around and watched for anything that would help her spot the second shooter, who was steadily harassing Clay. There was gunfire behind her, but no bullets came in their direction. Praying that meant Anchorman had flushed out his guy, she kept her gun moving in a slow sweep across the line of trees in front of her. Both she and Clay waited and watched as the forest fell into a silence that was only broken by the sound of rushing water.

She kept still, straining her senses, all too aware of the minutes ticking by and the blood being lost by both Trey and Jerome. Despite the cool air, a trickle of sweat slowly trailed from her forehead to her cheek. Not daring to take a hand off her Glock, Ricki gritted her teeth and kept up the slow quartering of the woods.

Come on, Anchorman. Say something. The desperate thought was met with more silence. She'd count off one more minute and then she'd have to move. Hoping Nora was taking care of Jerome, she knew Trey would need some kind of bandage on that leg soon, which meant either she or Clay would have to put down their gun. While she was a better shot with a rifle in her hands, Clay had the edge when it came to their respective Glocks.

Just as she reached the end of her count, Anchorman emerged from the trees separating her from Clay.

"Clear," he called out, then started toward her.

She quickly waved him off. "You and Clay help Trey. He's hit in the leg. I'm going to look at Jerome."

As Anchorman switched directions, Ricki holstered her gun, then sprinted toward the firepit. She skirted the nearest log and knelt down beside Jerome. "How bad is it?"

Nora was kneeling on the other side of her supervisor. Her head was bowed as she used both hands to press on what looked like a folded-up sock that she was using to stanch the flow of blood from a wound in his shoulder. "I don't know. He passed out a few minutes ago, but it seems like the bleeding is slowing down. At least I hope so. I've run out of socks."

Ricki nodded and rose to her feet. "I have a first aid kit in my backpack. I'll dig it out and then we'll get to work."

It took another fifteen minutes to fashion a makeshift bandage that looked like it would keep the blood in check, at least for a while. Ricki was just finishing up, with a sock-less Nora gone to the river to wash her hands, when Clay and Anchorman appeared, supporting Trey between them as the agent slowly hopped his way toward the firepit. His face was drained of all color, but he didn't utter a sound as his two human crutches slowly lowered him until he was sitting on the ground, his back against a log and his awkwardly bandaged leg out in front of him.

"How does it look?" Ricki asked when Clay walked over and sank to his knees next to her.

"It looks like the bullet went clean through, so it could be worse. That's not to say it won't go south if he doesn't get some help." Clay glanced down at Jerome. "How's he doing?"

"About the same. I think he's stable for now, but that's not going to last forever."

When Anchorman moved in their direction, they both stood in tandem, and the three of them stepped a few feet away.

"I don't suppose either of you has any cell service out here?" the former sniper asked.

Ricki made a face at him. "Funny. And we don't have a SAT phone either. But Jerome said that the two rangers camped out at two-four do."

"I can call them." Nora's voice sounded behind Ricki, and all three of them turned to stare at her. "We brought our walkie-talkies and Mike has one too. They're powerful enough that two-four should be in range with any luck. Their campsite isn't even two miles away. If they're still there."

"Then give Mike a call," Ricki said with a relieved smile.

Maybe help was closer than she thought. But that hope didn't last long as Nora tried to raise one of the rangers at camp two-four on the walkie-talkie.

After a few minutes, she looked over at Ricki and shook her head. "They aren't answering." Alarm crossed her face. "You don't think those guys who were shooting at us got to them first, do you?"

"I don't know. But it's just as possible they packed up and left since Jerome gave them the okay to head back," Ricki said. "But either way, it's not likely the shooters are still hanging around."

"They might be," Clay put in. "Waiting for us to make a break for it so they can catch us out on the trail."

Anchorman shook his head. "I don't think so. We aren't the only ones needing medical help. I clipped one of them."

Knowing that was about as big a piece of luck as they were going to get, Ricki nodded her agreement. "Then I'd say they're probably hightailing it back to one of the main roads. Or wherever they left their truck."

Clay rocked back on his heels. "Do you think it's the same guys who were following you and Cheron?"

"What?" Anchorman scowled as he pointed an accusing finger at Ricki. "You were followed and didn't say a word to me?"

"Now's not the time." There was just enough snap in Ricki's voice to have Anchorman holding back any argument, but annoyance was still written all over his face. If he was mad at her for not telling him about the black truck, that was too bad. They could argue about it later. Right now, they needed to get Trey and Jerome some help.

"One of us is going to have to go for help. If the two rangers simply didn't hear the walkie-talkie, that's great. We get to them, make a call on the SAT phone, and help is on its way. Otherwise, we need to make sure they've simply broken camp and weren't attacked themselves. Either way, someone is going to have to hike out."

Clay's gaze narrowed on her face. "And by someone you're talking about yourself?"

She didn't flinch under his hard stare. "That's right."

"Why is that?" Anchorman drawled. "If the two shooters are still in the area, I'm the best one to handle them, and you know it."

"And if it comes to having to hike out to get help, then I'm the one who is best in the backcountry, and *you* know that," she fired back. "Not to mention the fact that if those two rangers just aren't answering the walkie-talkie and they spot you hoofing it down the trail alone and armed, they're likely to shoot first and ask questions later."

Anchorman switched his glare to Clay. "How about some help here?"

"I don't like it," Clay stated quietly. "If those guys are still in the area, then having the two best shots stay here for defense is the best move. And that would be you two. I should do the hike out."

Ricki blew out a breath hard enough that it whistled between her teeth. "You're the least experienced in the backcountry of the three of us, and you've made the trip out here exactly once. That Huskey Gap Trail is hard enough to see in broad daylight, much less at night." She waved a hand at the two men. "We're wasting time here." She turned to Nora. "You've got the smallest pack. Start unloading it. I want to travel as light as possible. All I'll need is some spare cartridges, a water bottle, and an extra flashlight."

The ranger hesitated for a brief second before straightening her spine. "I know the backcountry, too, and this one better than you do, Ricki. And all of you are better shots than I am. I should make the hike out."

Ricki turned back to smile briefly at the woman before shaking her head. "I'm faster, and right now, speed is important." Her gaze swept across the three pairs of eyes staring at her. "This discussion is done."

There was a charged silence before Clay crossed over and put his hands on her shoulders. "I still don't like it, but this is your world out here, so yeah. The discussion is done." He looked over his shoulder, directing his gaze at Anchorman. "It's done."

"I'll unload my pack," Nora offered, while the two men continued to stare at each other.

"I hope we don't regret this," Anchorman said quietly, before turning away. He walked over to the edge of the clearing and stood looking out into the trees, his back to the group.

It was only a couple of minutes before Nora returned, but she wasn't carrying her backpack. Instead, she held up several small carabiners. "When we were at the hotel, I noticed you had on a hiking belt, so it should support these with no problem." Taking a step closer, Nora used the small clips to secure a flashlight on one side of Ricki's belt and a canteen in its carrier to the other side. "The flashlight looks small," she said in a conversational voice, "but it's the best one on the market. It has an emergency beacon that can light up like a miniature sun." She then reached into her pocket and held out a headlamp. "I know you have one, but take mine as a spare. Oh, and these." She reached into another pocket and pulled out four triple-A batteries. "Take these, too. They're for the flashlight, just in case. I figure cartridges in one jacket pocket, the extra headlamp and batteries in the other." Nora glanced up at the sky. "The sun's already going down. It's going to be a lot darker in another hour. The last thing you need to happen is for your batteries to give out."

"Thanks. I appreciate that." Ricki tucked the items away and picked up her rifle.

"Take one of the walkie-talkies," Clay said. "I tried calling Mike and Charlie, but they aren't answering. It could be they haven't left yet and are still busy packing up, but if they've already taken off, give us a call and let us know you're heading on."

"And be on the lookout for the four-legged variety of predators, not just ones with two legs," Nora chimed in. When Clay scowled at her, the ranger shrugged. "It's spring, Chief. The mama bears have cubs to feed, and the male bears haven't been out of hibernation that long. They're all hungry, and that means they'll hunt at night if their stomachs drive them to it. And the coyotes and foxes usually hunt at night too. But in this section of the park, I'd worry more about the bears."

"That's great," Anchorman called out. "I really needed to hear that."

"I'll be careful. I know what to look and listen for," Ricki reassured Clay. "I'll be very careful," she repeated, her raised voice, aiming it at Anchorman's back.

Clay's jaw hardened for a moment before he relaxed and cupped her face in his hands.

She closed her eyes when he leaned down for a kiss, savoring the warmth of his mouth. When he drew back, Nora clapped her hands together.

"Yeah. I thought that was the way of it." She chuckled as she hooked the walkie-talkie to the back of Ricki's belt. "Hard to miss the way you two look at each other. I'm thinking there will be wedding bells soon."

"I've already asked." Clay's mouth curved into a crooked smile when Ricki rolled her eyes at him. "She told me to think about it some more."

Nora laughed, and Ricki did too, before lifting on her toes and placing another quick kiss on Clay's mouth. She stepped back and grinned at him. "You keep thinking, and I'll be back before you know it."

Chapter 13

RICKI KEPT her rifle in one hand as she left Campsite 30 at a brisk trot. She jogged in the mornings whenever she could, and always did when she was at home, so she knew she could cover the two-mile distance in good time, even over the rough ground. Especially without the additional weight of her backpack. But her heavy hiking boots weren't running shoes, and it cost her extra energy to keep up the fast pace.

Mindful of the hidden hazards along the trail, she took a longer step to avoid the hard tip of a rock protruding upward in the middle of the path. As she kept up her speed, eating away at the distance at a steady clip, her gaze swung from the ground in front of her to the surrounding trees, since trouble could come from either place.

Forty minutes later, she spotted the post for site two-four. When it came squarely into view, she didn't need to step off the trail to see that it was deserted. Gone were the two tents, along with both the rangers who'd set them up. And so was the SAT phone.

Ricki bent over and braced her hands against her knees as she looked farther up the trail. No one was in sight. Of course, someone else might come along, but with the reservations still blocked off for Campsites 24 and 30, it wasn't likely. And those were the only campsites past the intersection with the Huskey Gap Trail. She reached around and unhooked the walkie-talkie as she moved toward the same flat rock she and Anchorman had occupied earlier that afternoon. She pressed the push-to-talk button and waited for the count of three. When she was sure the airway was clear, she called out to Campsite 30. There were a few seconds of static before a broken rendition of Nora's voice came through the speaker.

"Campsite 30 is receiving. Go ahead."

"Nora, I'm at two-four. Both rangers and their equipment are gone. Repeat. They are gone. I'm heading up Huskey Gap. Over."

She released the talk button and listened, but what came back was garbled, and she didn't have time to mess with it. The light was disappearing fast, and she needed to cover as much of the trail as possible while she could still see it without a flashlight. Hoping her message had gone through, she took the extra minute to hide the walkie-talkie in some ferns growing around the base of a tree. It wouldn't do her any good on the trail with the uneven, and at some points high, elevations between her and the campsite where everyone was waiting.

Picking up her rifle again, she set off on the mile trek to the intersection with the Huskey Gap Trail. Since the path was wide and flat, she kept to her slow jog, wanting to cover the ground but conserve her energy at the same time. Once she reached the junction, it was a solid four miles back to the main road. Even though it was an uphill climb on the first leg of the trail, the bad news was that she'd be approaching the steepest part in the dark, and that might prove to be a prob-lem. The odds were much greater that she'd take a tumble going downhill, especially if the trail was hard to see.

Putting the hazards ahead out of her mind, Ricki concentrated on the path in front of her. The wind had died down, leaving the forest around her eerily silent. The only sounds were her own footsteps and the steady churning of the river next to the trail. It was fifteen minutes before she came upon the last campsite she'd pass before she needed to veer off toward Huskey Gap.

As the sun struggled to hold on before losing its battle and dipping down below the horizon, she jogged past the empty campsite and kept going. There were no signs or sounds of activity anywhere, and most telling was the lack of a glow from any fire. A few minutes later, she came upon the sign pointing east. Without hesitation she made the turn, slowing her pace to a quick walk. She was barely a few tenths of a mile in when the sun disappeared, leaving her and the forest in a silvery twilight. Even that small amount of light would be gone in an hour, so Ricki turned on her headlamp and kept going.

She kept to her fast walk for over an hour, sometimes having to slow down when the trail narrowed to little more than an animal track. Stepping carefully to avoid tripping on any hidden rocks, she trained her flashlight on the ground and followed the narrow strip of dirt that wound its way through the forest. She was halfway back to the road when she caught the faint sound of a large breath being exhaled in one short burst. It repeated itself, only louder, causing Ricki's heart rate to kick into high gear. She knew that sound.

Huffing. There was a bear nearby, close enough for her to hear it. But since sound carried so well at night, especially out where there was no other city noise to mask it, it could be much farther off than it seemed. Keeping to her steady pace, Ricki curled her fingers until they had a death grip on her rifle, tightening them even more at the sound of the crack of small branches being crushed under a large weight. She pulled her mouth into a grim line—that bear just might be as close as it sounded.

When the huffing noises changed pitch to a low, deep-throated pulse, she knew she was in trouble. That was an aggressive signal in bear speak, and the odds were the big animal was now tracking her. Without slowing her step, Ricki swung her rifle up and pointed the barrel into the air. She shot off three rounds, the noise ripping through the night like a sudden crack of thunder. When the sound faded away, she carefully listened again. She caught the same faint crack of twigs and small branches, but it was farther away, and moving in the opposite direction of the trail.

Hoping that was all she had to deal with from the native inhabitants in the park, she went on her way. Hearing a clock tick in her head, she pushed herself until her lungs were burning and the muscles in her legs and back were screaming in protest. She couldn't hold back a small cry of relief when the trail suddenly opened up onto the road.

Stumbling across the blacktop toward the SUV, she managed to get the door open and slid into the front seat before collapsing forward, resting her arms and forehead against the steering wheel. She slowly counted to ten, then forced herself to sit up.

She started the engine, letting it idle as she dug her cell phone out of her pocket. Opening the compartment between the seats, she took the charger out and plugged it into one of the USB ports. She had to wait until a charge registered on her phone, but the second it did, she punched in 9-1-1.

The operator was both calm and efficient, and within minutes, help was on its way. Ricki leaned back in the driver's seat, still holding the phone and staying on the line as the operator had told her to do. But she closed her eyes, wincing at the cramping in her legs as she tried to stretch them out to ease the pain.

She knew she should get out of the car and walk around to allow her muscles to gradually cool down, but she wasn't about to leave her barely charged phone. So she let the pain wash over her in waves as she waited for what seemed like an eternity before she finally heard the wail of sirens.

The first vehicles to come down the road with their lights flashing and sirens blaring were big trucks with the National Park logo on their sides. One pulled right up next to her and a thin man with long legs opened the passenger side door even before the vehicle came to a complete stop. He took one large step, then leaned over to look Ricki in the face.

"I'm Supervising Ranger Phil Renning. Are you all right, Agent James?" When she turned her head and simply stared at him, he curled a hand around her shoulder and gave it a gentle shake. "Ricki? Are you all right?"

"I am now." Ricki winced as she automatically shifted her weight in the seat. "Have you got medical people coming? There are two injured up at the camp."

"On their way. And a helicopter is ready to take off as soon as they know where they're going."

"Campsite 30, but I can't guarantee they'll have a fire built to mark their position." Ricki finished swiveling around to face Renning, letting her legs dangle over the side of the seat.

"There's a powerful spotlight on board," Renning said. "They'll find them. Do you think Agent Robard can read Morse code? I was told he served in the navy."

Ricki managed a weak smile. "He was a captain with a search and rescue unit, so he probably can."

Renning nodded. "Well then, he's going to get to experience what it's like to be on the other end of a rescue operation." The supervisor stepped away and climbed back into the big truck.

Ricki heard him giving orders over the two-way radio and assumed he was talking to the helicopter pilot. When several other vehicles careened into the small parking lot, one of them an ambulance, she gingerly lowered herself off the car's seat and onto the pavement. She was standing by the open door, holding on to it to keep herself upright, when two men with paramedic written in bright yellow across their jumpsuits came running over.

"Are you Agent James?"

When Ricki nodded, the one closest to her bobbed his head as well. "I'm assigned to the group who will be doing the hike to get to your guys. We're waiting for a doctor. She's about ten minutes out. Can you tell us what the injuries are?"

"Gunshot wounds," Ricki stated without any preamble. "First victim is a park employee. He's a Black male, in his late fifties or early sixties, with a gunshot wound in his shoulder. The second victim is a white male, in his mid-thirties, and he took a bullet in his leg. It looks like it went straight through. We stopped the bleeding, but I doubt if those makeshift bandages will hold too long." When Renning returned and stood behind the paramedics, Ricki leaned to the side to catch his attention. "There are other complications."

Catching her hint to speak with him alone, the supervisor asked the paramedics to check on the rest of the team and then took hold of Ricki's arm. "Can you make it over to the curb so you can sit down before you fall on your face?"

Ricki nodded and, using his arm for support, hobbled to the curb and sat. She would have given a month's pay to take her boots off, but the minute she did, her feet would swell up like balloons and she'd never get them on again. Instead, she stretched her legs out in front of herself and settled for wiggling her toes.

Renning sat down beside her and pulled his long legs up in front of himself. He set a battery-run lantern down on the curb between them, then leaned forward and rested his forearms on his thighs. "Before we get to the complications, tell me who was shot. From your description, I gather Supervisor Johnson was hit in the shoulder."

"Yes, that's right. And Special Agent Robard was shot in the leg." Ricki carefully rolled her shoulders back and forth, breathing a sigh of relief at the low level of pain. A couple of aspirin would take care of that.

"All right. Now, about those other complications?"

She drew in a long breath. "We weren't out there shooting each other. There were two guys hiding in the trees who started shooting at us."

"So it wasn't Anchorman trying to make a break for it?"

Annoyed that the gossip mill seemed to be working overtime, Ricki vehemently shook her head, sending her long, dark ponytail whipping across her back. "No. It wasn't Anchorman. If it wasn't for him, I'm not sure Clay and I could have held the shooters off. They had us pinned down at the campsite. Anchorman was able to slip into the trees, and he thinks he got a piece of one of them. But at any rate, they turned tail and ran."

"Your suspect had a gun?"

Her back stiffened at the question, and her voice turned to frost. "He's a suspect, not a convicted felon on his way to prison. And he's out on bail that was set by a duly appointed judge." She paused just long enough to suck in a breath. "He's no killer any more than I am. And he's pulled my rear end out of the fire more than once. Believe me, if you're ever in that kind of situation, Anchorman is the guy you'll want watching your back." She paused again, intending to go on, but caught the smile on Renning's face. She stared at him, baffled. Crossing her arms over her chest, she glared at the man. "You don't think he shot his friend either."

The supervisor's smile grew several inches. "No. And neither does anyone else on staff. That theory seems to be solely owned by the guys over at County." He looked away for a moment. "And maybe NCIS."

Ricki drew her legs up and then stretched them out again as she thought it over. "I don't think Agent Robard believes it either, but none of the evidence so far is on Anchorman's side. Except this shooting is a pretty good indication there's something else going on here."

"Such as?" Renning prompted.

"I don't know. I'm still thinking it through. But the first shot hit Jerome."

"Jerome?" Renning sounded genuinely shocked. "Why would they shoot Jerome first?"

She sighed. "Because he didn't duck as fast as Anchorman."

The ranger's brow puckered into deep lines, and his eyebrows snapped together. "What the hell does that mean?"

"I don't know," Ricki admitted. "Or rather, I'm not sure. Like I said, I'm still thinking it over."

Renning watched her for a full minute before he pushed himself to his feet. He shook his head when she started to get up too. "No. You stay put. I'll send some medical help over this way to have a look at you. Now, back to those complications. I gather you think we should send some of the law enforcement unit, and their rifles, along with the rescue team?"

"As a precaution," Ricki said. "I think it's unlikely the shooters are still in the area, especially if one of them needs some medical attention."

"All right. I'll let the team leader know and assign some more guys to go along. You stay right here, and I'll send someone over. And now that I know who's injured, I'll give the height and weight estimates to the team as well. If it's going to have to be a carry-out rather than a helicopter lift, it's going to be a long night."

Ricki nodded and watched Renning move off toward the large group gathered at the far end of the parking lot. While the supervisor was busy organizing the rescue party, she got back to her feet and gingerly made her way to the SUV, where her cell phone was still lying in the middle console. She wiggled up into the driver's seat and reached for the phone to look up the number for the county sheriff's office in Sevierville.

When the front desk answered, she identified herself and asked for the shift supervisor. The phone went silent long enough that her boot began tapping against the floorboard until a sharp pain went from one of her toes straight up her shin. She was still wincing when a deep voice came onto the line.

"Sergeant Danks. I hear you had some excitement out at the park tonight."

Since she wanted a favor from the man, Ricki gave him a short version of the shooting, then listened to the sergeant whistle softly.

"That is some serious shit going down. And you say there were two shooters out there? And they took two of you down?"

"We weren't expecting that kind of company," Ricki said.

"But you ran them off?"

"*They* weren't expecting our kind of response." Feeling that should be enough to give the sergeant something juicy to report to his fellow officers, Ricki switched the phone to her other ear. "I have a favor to ask, Sergeant."

"Okay. I'm listening."

"We think we might have wounded one shooter, and he'll need to get some medical help."

There was a brief silence. "And you want me to keep my ears open for any reports of a gunshot wound?"

Ricki nodded even though she was alone in the SUV. "I'd appreciate it."

"I can go you one better than that, Agent James. I'll make some calls. See if I can shake some information loose for you." He listened to Ricki's thanks and then chuckled. "It's not a problem, but I'd sure like to know who winged the guy. Was it you?"

"Nope. It was Anchorman."

Another louder whistle came through the phone. "Anchorman? You don't say. Well, that's really something."

"Yeah." Ricki smiled in satisfaction. "It was something all right."

Chapter 14

Ricki stretched her legs out, grimacing at the twinges and aches that insisted on making themselves known. Against the advice of the paramedics, she'd spent the night in the SUV, declining a ride in the waiting ambulance in favor of a restless night scrunched up on the backseat of the rental vehicle. With daybreak finally making an appearance, she pushed her way out of the SUV and walked over to stand next to Supervisor Renning's command vehicle.

He was already on the radio, listening to the shout coming out the other end over the pounding beat of rotor blades. Less than a minute later, a helicopter flew overhead.

Ricki tilted her head back and tracked its progress until it disappeared over the treetops. Turning her attention back to Renning and the radio, she listened as the helicopter crew and the ground team that had hiked in the night before, coordinated the airlift of the two wounded men.

She held her breath, hanging on every word coming from the radio. When the second, all clear was given and the pilot radioed they were on their way to the trauma center in Knoxville, her knees went weak with relief. She sat on the ground, nodding when Renning reached down and gave her a quick pat on her shoulder.

"Six of my men will be staying to wait for the NCIS forensic team, and the rest will be making the hike out with Ranger Thorne and the others." He looked at his watch. "I'd give them until noon to make the trip back."

Ricki looked up at the supervisor, inclining her head in acknowledgment, before she pushed herself to her feet and went back to the SUV to wait. Much to her extreme relief, everyone had shown up exhausted but safe and sound, just after 11 a.m. Despite the interested audience, Ricki went straight to Clay, wrapping her arms around him for that extra minute, too tired and happy to protest the long kiss that drew a few quiet chuckles from the rest of the team as they stepped around the couple.

Once she'd reluctantly let go of him, she turned and gave Nora a firm hug, and then gave a harder one to Anchorman, who was still holding a rifle that no one seemed to notice. Leaving the rescue team and their support group to finish packing up in the parking lot, she, Clay, and Anchorman drove Trey's vehicle back to the hotel. They didn't bother to stop in the lobby but headed straight for their respective rooms. Ricki had collapsed on the bed, feeling the slight bounce when Clay did the same. They were both asleep the minute they shut their eyes.

Hours later, the loud blare of an alarm had Ricki opening one bleary eye. It took her a moment to pinpoint the source of the noise as coming from the bedside clock. She bolted upright when she saw it read 3:36 p.m., throwing an arm out to the side only to have it land on an empty space. Wondering where Clay had gotten himself off to, she spied the note lying on his pillow.

Went for coffee and food. Be back soon.

Smiling, and looking forward to both the coffee and something to eat, Ricki headed for the shower. The steamy heat washed away the bulk of the aches in her muscles, and she was already dressed and drying her long hair when the door opened and Clay walked in. He was balancing a tray supporting three tall cardboard cups with steam pouring out of their tops in one hand, and holding a very large white paper bag in the other.

Ricki eyed the size of the bag as she pulled her almost-dry hair back, using an elastic band to secure it at the nape of her neck. "Are you planning on inviting some people over?"

He grinned at her as he set the tray on the desk. "Just Anchorman. He'll be along in a minute." He kept the bag in one hand as he crossed the room, bending down to give her a long, tender kiss that had her looping her arms around his neck and pressing in closer.

When he lifted his head, she answered his smile with one of her own. "What was that for?"

"A good afternoon and a thank you."

Puzzled, she drew back a little. "For what?"

"That greeting when we finally made it back to the parking lot." His smile turned into a teasing grin. "A long, heated kiss from Ricki James while she was on duty? I'd never thought that would happen."

She placed a hand in the center of his chest and gave him a shove. "I'd already worked enough overtime yesterday, so wasn't on the clock when you showed up." She sniffed when he continued to grin at her. "Which means you still haven't seen it happen, because I wasn't on duty."

Clay's "uh-huh" was interrupted by a sharp knock on the door. Ricki strode down the short hallway and answered it, caught by surprise at the mutinous expression on Anchorman's face.

"I need to get to Knoxville," he declared.

Ricki took a quick step to the side to keep from getting plowed over as the big Marine stomped into the room. "And what's the big rush?"

"I called Cheron, and she's not happy about what happened yesterday, so I need to get there and calm her down." He stopped next to the bed and planted his feet in a wide fighting stance before accepting the cardboard cup Clay held out to him. "So, when can we go?" He took a sip of coffee, then spied the white bag Clay was still holding. "Is that food? Pass it over here."

Clay held the bag out to the side and shook his head. "Ricki gets first choice." He glanced over at her. "They're all sandwiches piled with meat. I wasn't in the mood for anything healthy or carb free."

She laughed and stuck out her hand. "Well, I'm not feeling picky. Hand one over, and the two of you can fight for the rest."

Clay did as she asked before passing the bag to Anchorman. "One measly sandwich after that feat you did yesterday isn't going to cut it, Ricki."

She took a big bite of what turned out to be sourdough bread around thick slices of chicken breast, and then pointed at the coffee. She'd finished chewing by the time Clay handed her one of the remaining cups. "What feat?"

"Supervisor Renning told me the time the call went in to 9-1-1. You must have run all the way back."

"Yeah, well, the bear helped." She shook her head when his mouth dropped open, turning her attention to Anchorman. "As it happens, we can leave for Knoxville whenever you're through eating. We'll drop you off at Cheron's on the way to the hospital. I want to check in on Jerome, and hopefully have a talk with Trey. Now that he's laid up, we need to get going on this case."

Anchorman stuffed the last of his roast beef sandwich into his mouth before he nodded his agreement.

"I'll eat on the way," Clay grumbled. He took the bag Anchorman handed him and grabbed the last cup of coffee. "That way I can hear all about this bear."

"Nothing to tell," Ricki claimed. She scooped up her backpack and rifle on her way to the door. "I never saw it."

THE THIRTY-MILE RIDE to Cheron's temporary lab in Knoxville went by quickly, with Ricki and Clay passing the time laying out plans for what to do next. When Anchorman vehemently protested his role, or lack of one, Ricki glared at him over the back of her seat.

"You will stay with Cheron and keep out of trouble."

"That's not what you were saying yesterday," Anchorman complained.

Ricki threw him an exasperated look. "Fine. If someone shoots at you, then you can shoot back."

"I'd have to find a rifle first." He crossed his arms over his chest and stared out the side window. "Renning made me give up mine, which was technically Jerome's, before he'd let me come back to the hotel."

Before Ricki could think of an appropriate response, her cell phone rang. Plucking it from her jacket pocket, she held up a finger to stop Anchorman's grousing, then touched the connect icon. "This is Special Agent Ricki James."

"Agent James, this is Sergeant Danks from the county sheriff's office. We spoke last night?"

Ricki nodded and raised a thumbs-up to Clay. "Yes, Sergeant. I hope you have some information for me?"

"Yes, ma'am, I surely do. And didn't have to work too hard for it. I made those phone calls last night like I promised, and this morning there was a message waiting for me from the sheriff's office up in Sullivan County. It seems they did get a call from a doc working in the emergency room at the hospital up in Bristol. That's about a hundred miles north of here, right on our border with Virginia."

Picturing a rough map in her head, Ricki got a fair idea of

where Bristol, Tennessee, was located. "All right. What did this ER doc have to say?"

"Well, the story was a bit strange. According to the deputy I talked to, the doc called because he treated a gunshot wound on a patient he saw last night."

She frowned. "Is that within the usual window of time that an ER reports a gunshot wound to the authorities?"

Danks grunted something that resembled a negative response. "We usually get a call while the patient is still in the ER. But the doc said this guy claimed he'd already reported it himself and even had a paper with an official report number to prove it." The sound of creaking leather came through the speaker as the sergeant shifted in his chair. "The doc put the number into the chart and clocked out of his shift. But when he came back today, he had a change of heart. It seems there was a lot about this guy that struck him as odd."

"Oh? Like what?" Ricki's boot started tapping, making Clay smile.

"Well, his birth date made him out to be about thirty-eight, but the doc would have pegged him closer to thirty, if that. And then he listed his height as a good four inches shorter, and the doc said he'd swear to that one. He claimed he'd seen enough guys stretched out on an examination table to know when someone is over six feet tall. So thinking about all that overnight, the doc decided to report it. This guy claimed he'd been in a hunting accident over in Henderson County. At least that's what was stated in the report the patient had on him. I guess the guy bandaged his arm up himself and got as far as Bristol before he was forced to get it looked at. Now since the forested area where this accident supposedly happened is an unincorporated area, the doc had to report it to the county sheriff's office instead of a city police department up there."

"Did this doctor give you a description of the patient?"

"Hospital took a picture of the guy's ID, but the doc said it isn't him. I can have it sent over to you, but I wouldn't give two cents for it being legitimate."

"Me either," Ricki said. "But I'd like to see it anyway. How about that report he flashed at the doctor?"

Danks laughed. "It seems the deputy up in Sullivan County checked on that, and it was as fake as a bill of sale for the Brooklyn Bridge. So that deputy made the drive to Bristol, because it's only ten miles up the road, and took a look-see at the cameras in the emergency room and out in the parking lot."

Ricki's eyes grew wide, and the grip on her phone got tighter. "Did he spot anything interesting?"

"Not in the emergency room." Danks didn't bother to hide the disgust in his voice. "That asshole kept the hood of his jacket up, wore a ball cap, and kept his face turned away from the cameras. Right offhand, I'd say he didn't want there to be any pictures of him. But he couldn't drive out of that parking lot without going right past a camera. I don't know if he was alone because the windows on that truck were so heavily tinted, but I'm assuming he wasn't driving himself so he must have had help. At least we've got the plate."

"Black Ford F-150 truck?"

"That's right. You've tangled with this truck before?"

"I've seen it," Ricki said. "But I couldn't get the plate."

There was more creaking leather, followed by Danks's smug tone. "Well, you've got it now, Agent James. Give me your email, and I'll shoot it to you along with the doc's description of the guy, and a copy of the guy's ID. Fake or not, it might be some help."

"Sergeant Danks? You made my day," Ricki replied. "Thank you."

"Happy to be of service. It's all over the station that you hiked out of that park in record time to get your guys some help. And by yourself in the dark, no less. That takes guts, Agent James. You need anything else, you give us a call."

Before Ricki could thank him again, the call disconnected. Shrugging, she twisted in her seat and had begun to fill Clay in when her cell phone beeped with an incoming email. She immediately opened it, taking a long look at the ID before scrolling down to the truck's license plate number. "Got you, you sonofabitch." She forwarded the information to Clay's phone, then pulled up Dan's number in her contact list. He picked up on the first ring.

"Dan, it's Ricki," she said, effectively cutting him off in the middle of reciting his name. "I need you to track down the owner of a license plate. It's from Pennsylvania." She rattled off the two numbers and five digits, just as Clay was pulling up in front of a low, modern-looking brick building. She asked Dan to text her the information and tucked her phone away.

Clay had barely turned off the engine when Cheron came bursting out the door. She looked dwarfed in the oversized wool coat she had on, and the too-big boots on her feet made her legs move in more of a shuffle than a walk. As soon as Anchorman exited the car, Cheron threw her arms around his waist and hugged him tight enough and long enough that he finally had to pry her away and hold her at arm's length.

"Are you all right?" He frowned over her head, his gaze scanning the front of the building. "Did something happen? Where are those two guards that NCIS agent was supposed to put on you?"

She gave him an incredulous look, then propped her hands on her hips. "You got shot at, Norman. Isn't that enough to happen? And those two guards went out to get a bite to eat. I promised them I would stay inside and keep the door locked."

He turned his frown on her. "All the shooting was yesterday. Today I'm wondering why both those guards left you here instead of just one of them going to pick up some food? Especially after that whole thing with the black truck."

Ricki's head whipped around. Since Cheron had her back

to her, she waved both hands in the air to get Anchorman's attention, and then rapidly shook her head back and forth.

"What black truck?" the doctor demanded.

Anchorman's gaze flicked over to Ricki and then back to Cheron. "Um . . . We thought we saw a black truck hanging around the parking lot at the hotel."

Cheron's eyes narrowed on his face. "There are black trucks all over the place. What's so special about this one?"

He snaked an arm around her shoulders and pulled her to his side. "I'll let Ricki explain."

Ricki sent him an annoyed glare that promised retribution, then forced her lips into a smile. "Let's talk about it inside. It's a bit chilly out here."

Relenting, Cheron linked an arm through one of Anchorman's and urged him toward the door. "I wish you'd take getting shot at a little more seriously."

Anchorman bent his head and whispered something into Cheron's ear. Following them with Clay, Ricki couldn't hear what the man said, but she heard Cheron's giggle as she waited for Anchorman to open the door so she could lead the small group inside.

The tiny lobby was deserted. Cheron walked past the reception desk and through the door leading into the back. Since the absent-minded doctor had completely forgotten to lock the entrance, Ricki stopped to take care of that pesky chore before trailing after everyone into the back room.

There was a compact lab set up with a long counter, several microscopes, and other equipment that Ricki wasn't familiar with, and in the center of the room was a stainless-steel autopsy table. The room wasn't silent, not with the constant hum of a large refrigerator and three other machines that were all lined up against the back wall. There wasn't much by way of decoration, but the place looked spotless.

"Christopher Young did a nice job of finding you a workspace," Clay said. "I hope you've uncovered some new information for us. We've got a few theories on what might have happened, but nothing concrete so far."

Cheron's eyes lit up with interest. "Oh? What theories?"

Anchorman pulled a tall stool out from under the long counter and perched on it. "Ricki thinks somehow there was a drug in the bourbon that Kelly brought, which automatically makes him the prime suspect for putting it there. But overlooking that glaring problem, because Kelly didn't do that, then this unknown someone came into our camp, took my rifle, shot Kelly with it, then put it back in my tent without me knowing a thing about it. Which would take a damn miracle." He shook his head and braced a hand against one knee. "Then this supposed miracle guy carried Kelly for a mile and a half, maybe in his sleeping bag, and dumped his body on the trail." Anchorman ended his explanation on a shrug. "Agent Robard is willing to go along with that, except for someone swiping my weapon and me not realizing it. He also likes the idea of me being the one who carried Kelly out of camp because Kelly was smaller than I am, and he thinks I could have managed it." He shrugged again. "I'm hoping you can come up with something better."

The doctor turned wide eyes on Ricki and adjusted her glasses farther up her nose. "Did you really come up with that theory?"

Ricki lifted an eyebrow. "It fits everything we've heard." She jerked her head toward Anchorman. "How he was still groggy and kind of disoriented when the rangers found him the next day. And that his gun was on the wrong side of his sleeping bag, not to mention the mysteriously missing bourbon bottle."

"There's also the fact that both Kelly's sleeping bag and his brand-new, very expensive gun are missing," Clay put in. "Not to mention that two guys were taking potshots at us."

"And," Ricki finished off, "there wasn't any blood spatter where the body was found, which means he wasn't shot there.

Kelly was carried from wherever he was killed and dumped alongside the trail."

The doctor clapped her hands together, beaming at Ricki. "That's brilliant. Simply brilliant, and I absolutely agree about the body being moved. The place it was discovered is not the same place where Sergeant Dorman was killed." She paused to turn and face Anchorman. "And the reason you didn't notice anyone taking your rifle was because you were most definitely drugged."

When everyone stared at her, she practically skipped over to the far end of the counter and picked up a piece of paper. "These are the findings of several tests I ran on Norman's urine and blood sample. It didn't show up in his blood because too much time had passed." She paused again and said in a more dramatic voice, "At least for Norman. However, it did show up in his urine sample, and there you have it."

When she stopped talking and simply waved the paper in the air, Ricki took several steps forward. "That's great, Cheron. Now exactly what is it that we have?"

"Ketamine," the doctor said, her voice as excited as if she'd won the lottery.

Anchorman slowly stood up, then walked over and plucked the paper from Cheron's hand. He stared at it before shifting his gaze to her. "Ketamine. What is it?"

Cheron smiled. "Basically, it's an anesthetic. It will disorient you to the point you won't know or remember what happened for some period of time. At least several hours if you ingest enough of it, which, if you were working through a bottle of bourbon, I imagine you did." She reached over and gave his arm a gentle pat. "It's more commonly known as the date-rape drug."

"What?" The word came out on an explosion of breath as Anchorman's face flushed red with fury. "I've never used anything like that."

Now the doctor grabbed his arm and gave it a hard shake.

"Norman Beal, calm down. *You* didn't use the drug. Someone used it on you." She looked over at Ricki. "And that's not all. I called that arrogant ME, told him what I found, and demanded he run the same test on Kelly. He sounded much more reasonable when he called back just an hour ago and told me that Kelly's blood had indeed tested positive for ketamine. Barely traces of it, but it was definitely there. And there was a much higher concentration in the urine he extracted from Kelly's urethral tract. He also sent over copies of his autopsy photos, and we both agree. The victim was most likely lying flat on the ground and shot in the back from twelve to fourteen inches away." She looked over at a stone-faced Anchorman. "Something you would never do in a million years."

"No he wouldn't." Ricki had been holding her breath long enough that she was starting to feel dizzy and was forced to suck in a column of air. "They were both drugged." Relief at finding an answer flooded through her, making her knees go weak enough she had to lock them in place.

So now she was certain how Kelly had been murdered without Anchorman knowing about it. She was even ninety percent sure that the two men who had followed them, and taken shots at them in the park, were the ones responsible for delivering the drug and killing the sergeant. What she needed to do now was catch them and find out why they had murdered Kelly Dorman. And done their best to set Anchorman up to take the fall.

Chapter 15

THE ARGUMENT with Anchorman about him staying put and keeping Cheron company had been thankfully short. The fact that her two supposed bodyguards were still out enjoying their early dinner had a lot to do with the Marine finally giving in.

Glad she wasn't in those bodyguards' shoes with Anchorman waiting for them to make an appearance, Ricki took off with Clay at the wheel. The GPS on Clay's phone chirped out directions to the hospital, and while he was busy navigating the streets of Knoxville, she called Christopher Young. When he picked up the phone, his first words surprised her.

"Well, Agent Ricki James. I was just getting ready to give you a call."

"Why?"

Ricki's blunt response had the attorney chuckling. "Because there's been a development I just learned about that we need to discuss. Preferably without my client present. When do you think we can arrange that?"

"Clay and I are on our way to the hospital in Knoxville. Where are you?"

"As it happens, I've heard bits and pieces about your little escapade in the park yesterday, including that a ranger and the NCIS agent assigned to this case were wounded and taken to the hospital in Knoxville. I thought you would make your way there sometime today, so I am here in this lovely city waiting for you."

Just as she'd thought, Christopher Young was one smart attorney. And a well-informed one. "We'll be at the hospital in about ten minutes. We can meet in the lobby and find a quiet place to talk."

There was a humming noise on the other end, a sure indication that the attorney was thinking it over. "Actually, am I correct in assuming you intend to drop in on both of the wounded men?"

"Yes," Ricki said cautiously. "There are some things I want to go over with Trey after I've filled you in on what our investigation has uncovered."

"Excellent. Let's kill two birds with one stone, so to speak, and you can fill me in at the same time as Trey, who I am assuming is Special Agent Treynor Robard?"

"That's right."

"Excellent. Then I'll meet you in the hospital lobby shortly, and we'll proceed from there."

Young ended the call before Ricki could ask him anything else. All she could do was hold out the phone and shake her head when Clay glanced over at her.

"Anchorman's attorney said there's been a new development, which he wants to discuss with Trey present. And he wants to hear what we've uncovered."

Clay's eyebrows shot to the top of his forehead. "He wants to talk over the case with the lead investigator for the prosecution?" He snorted as he turned the SUV into a large parking lot. "That's a new one on me. I'm not even sure he can ethically do that."

"Me either," Ricki agreed. "But, apparently, Mr. Christopher Young is going to do just that."

It took several minutes to find a free space in the visitors' section of the parking lot, and then just as long to walk to the front of the hospital and make their way across the entire length of the lobby. Christopher Young was already there, standing with his hands clasped behind his back as he studied a bronze plaque on the wall. When Ricki walked up behind him, he didn't turn around but continued to study the plaque.

"It's an amazing thing, the kind of tributes human beings put up to each other. Give money to a hospital, and we'll engrave your name onto a piece of metal and hang it on the wall." The attorney turned around and smiled at Ricki. "Do you think you'll have your name on a plaque hanging on some wall one day?"

"I don't know and really don't care." She gestured toward the elevators. "Trey is on the tenth floor. We'll need to take those elevators over there."

The ride up was silent as people got on and off. Ricki exited on the tenth floor with the two men close behind her. She walked over to the nurses' station, showed her badge, and was directed down a corridor. Trey's room was halfway along, opposite another nurses' station. The door was only partially closed, so Ricki knocked, stepping inside when Trey called out, "Come in. I'm decent."

She peeked around the curtain drawn partway across the room and grinned at him. "That's good to hear."

"Well, it's a good thing you called and warned me you were on your way, or you might have seen more of me than you intended to." Trey nodded at Clay, his gaze only skimming over Young before returning to Ricki. His face was pale, and his leg was raised on a pillow, but otherwise he didn't look half bad for a guy who had been shot and then airlifted to a trauma center.

"How was the trip here?" Ricki asked. "A little different being on the other side of things?"

Trey shrugged, then stacked his hands behind his head

despite the IV tube in his arm. "I had to take a ride in the basket as part of my training, so I've been there before. The pilot did a good job holding the craft steady. I'll have to remember to thank him." He looked over at Young, who had made himself comfortable in the only visitor's chair in the room. "Who are you?"

"He's Christopher Young," Ricki said, taking on the introductions. "He's Anchorman's attorney. And he already knows who you are."

The NCIS agent's gaze stayed on Young. "Anchorman's attorney? Then I guess you've already heard?"

Ricki frowned and shot a look at Young. "Heard what?"

"I believe Agent Robard is talking about those new developments I mentioned," Christopher said. He directed a smile at the man lying in the bed. "I'll let you explain."

Trey looked pained and let out a long sigh. "The ballistics on Anchorman's rifle came back. And it's not good."

Christopher raised a shaggy eyebrow at Trey's choice of words but remained silent.

"His rifle is a match for the bullet that killed Kelly," Ricki stated flatly. "We already expected that."

"But there's more, isn't there, Agent Robard?" Christopher's smile never wavered, even when Trey scowled back at him.

Since the NCIS agent didn't say anything else, Ricki leaned over and tapped him on the shoulder. "What more?"

"It seems," Christopher interjected, "that there was only one set of prints on the rifle. And those did indeed belong to Anchorman. However, they were also only in one place. Near the top of the barrel."

Ricki blinked. Taking a step back, she turned to face the attorney. "What do you mean there were prints only in one place? It was Anchorman's rifle. His prints should have been all over the stock and the barrel. Not to mention the trigger."

"No, no, and again, no, is my understanding." Christopher

leaned to the side to peer around Ricki. "Is that correct, Agent Robard?"

Trey had brought his arms back down to lie on the bed. "That's right."

"It was wiped clean?" Clay moved to lean against the wall, crossing one heavily booted foot over the other. "The gun that was used to kill Kelly was wiped clean, and then returned to Anchorman's shelter? According to what he told us, the only time he touched it after that, was to be sure it was there when he woke up the next morning."

"And it was replaced on his left side, not his right, where he always places it," Ricki added. Her brow furrowed and her foot started tapping. *He's not used to murder*, she thought, then focused her gaze on Clay when he loudly cleared his throat.

"Who isn't used to murder?" Clay smiled, accurately reading the annoyance on Ricki's face.

Not really surprised she'd voiced her thought out loud, Ricki shrugged. "The killer isn't used to committing murder. Or at least one of them isn't. Taking a shot at us was a mistake, and forgetting to bring along some latex gloves so the rifle had to be wiped down to get rid of his prints, was another."

"And not putting the rifle back exactly where he found it was a third," Clay reminded her before zeroing his attention in on Trey. "Which should buy us some time."

Deep lines creased down Trey's cheeks. "We have the rifle that has been verified as the murder weapon, and the only prints on it belong to Anchorman. That alone means he should be under arrest and heading toward a federal facility under guard."

"What about the drugs in his system, and in Kelly's?" Ricki argued. "That's hard proof that they were both drugged."

Trey's mouth dropped open before he shut it again. "What are you talking about?"

"Dr. Garrison discovered a powerful drug in Anchorman's urine," Christopher intervened smoothly. "Of course she immediately contacted the county medical examiner, who then ran the same test on Kelly, and came out with the same result." His blue eyes swung back to Ricki. "Ketamine wasn't it? Commonly known as Special K on the streets, and as the date-rape drug in the press."

Trey was silent for a moment. "Ketamine?"

"That's right," Ricki said. "They were both drugged."

The NCIS agent went silent again, his gaze focused on the blanket covering him from the waist down. "You have proof the drug was present in both men, but you can't prove the order the ketamine was taken," he finally responded, his voice low. "A good prosecutor would argue that Anchorman drugged Kelly, shot him, and then ingested some of the drug himself in order to cover his tracks."

"That's idiotic," Ricki snapped.

"Agreed," Trey shot back. "But it's still a possible explanation. And a better plan than him simply going on the run."

Feeling the walls closing around Anchorman, the fight instinct kicked in and her mouth formed into a smirk. "Oh really? Why is that? Anchorman could have vanished into the forest and come out anywhere along the Eastern Seaboard, and then disappeared for good."

Trey shrugged. "He would have been caught eventually. Disappearing for good isn't as easy as it sounds, especially when several federal bureaus are searching for you, not to mention that the entire US military was also told to keep an eye out for you. Even worse, he would have been cut off from most of his contacts and couldn't have used his passport to get out of the country, which he didn't have with him anyway. At least it wasn't in his backpack. Maybe he thought it would be a better plan to try for a cover-up, and if that didn't work, send out a call for help to his close friend, the investigative agent with the park service. She'd come running to his rescue." He gave her a hard stare. "Which you did." He turned that same look on Clay. "Along with her favorite partner, a police chief with homicide experience."

Clay matched his shrug. "The fact Anchorman has friends in law enforcement who would move mountains to help him still doesn't make him guilty, Trey." Clay's mouth twitched into a wry smile. "It only means he has good taste in friends."

"What about the missing bourbon bottle?" Ricki demanded. "Or the fact he ran those two shooters off yesterday instead of joining with them?"

"If there ever was a bourbon bottle. And if Kelly brought it with him, the way Anchorman is claiming, then who put the drug in the bottle? Kelly? How does that fit with your whole, they-were-drugged explanation?"

"And chasing off the two shooters?"

"Friendship runs both ways," Trey stated in a voice devoid of any emotion. "And again, a good prosecutor is going to point out they could have been military friends of Anchorman, especially since none of you got hit. Only the two guys who would have stopped him from running."

"Nora wasn't wounded," Ricki stated.

"It's unlikely that two military guys would have seen her as the biggest threat. That's what we're trained to do. Take out the biggest threat first."

She stared at him in disbelief. "You cannot believe any of the crap that just came out of your mouth."

Suddenly looking tired, Trey rubbed two fingers over his eyes. "It's what a jury would believe that's important." He dropped his hands again and stared at her. "And off the record, no, I don't believe any of it. And our boss doesn't like any of this either. But it isn't our job to pass judgment on whoever killed Sergeant Kelly Dorman, just to catch the bastard. And right now, that's looking like Anchorman."

While the charged silence hung heavily in the room, Christopher made a big show of shifting his weight in his chair. "Well, now that we have things out in the open, perhaps we could move on. Besides the news about the two victims being drugged." He paused and tilted his head down to stare at Trey from beneath bushy eyebrows. "And I want to put on record here that there were indeed two victims. Ricki, was there anything else to report?"

"The black truck," Ricki said slowly, her narrow-eyed gaze still on Trey. "We've got a plate on a truck that was exiting the parking lot of a hospital up near the Tennessee-Virginia border. The driver stopped at the emergency room to get treatment for a gunshot wound."

Trey's head snapped up. "Tell me you aren't joking?"

"Not joking. One of my guys is tracking down the owner of the truck registered with that plate right now."

For the first time since his visitors had arrived, Trey smiled. "Now I can use that to buy us some time. Get my boss to slow-walk the paperwork for Anchorman's arrest."

Clay straightened away from the wall. "How much time?"

"Maybe forty-eight hours, possibly a little more. Like I said, my boss isn't keen on Anchorman being a killer either, and his service record puts a lot of points on the board in his favor." His fingers moved restlessly on the blanket. "If I can get you the time, you'll need to find enough substantial evidence to point away from Anchorman, and he can continue to stay a free man until this whole thing is cleared up."

"Is that all?" Ricki's tone was drier than the Sahara, and she was about to add another snippy comment when she caught the warning look in Clay's gaze, clearly reminding her that two days to work the case was better than nothing.

Belatedly remembering the enormous pressure Trey had to be under to arrest the owner of that murder weapon, she summoned up a smile. "Sorry. I appreciate any amount of time you can give us." She glanced at Clay. "We're on a tight clock, so I guess we'd better get started."

"It will take me some time to get hold of my boss and talk him into this, so your clock starts ticking tomorrow morning." Trey's smile faded as he added a warning of his own. "Two days, Ricki. That's what we've got. Two days."

"Then I suggest we make the most of it." Christopher briefly struggled to push himself out of the low-standing visitor's chair. Once he was on his feet, he tucked his thumbs into his vest pocket. "One critical area we must address is to break the testimony of the couple who claim they overheard Anchorman and Kelly arguing."

"The Packers?" Ricki asked. When the attorney nodded, so did she. "They live here in Knoxville, so I thought we'd head over that way now."

Christopher removed one thumb from its pocket long enough to wave his hand in the air. "I've already taken the liberty of contacting them. Unfortunately, they are not in town at the moment, but they will be back the day after tomorrow, so I made an appointment for you to speak with them in their home." He reached into the outer pocket of his suit and withdrew a folded piece of paper. "Here are the details. In reading over their statement, I did notice that other than their clothing, and the fact they were carrying rifles, a physical description of the two men was missing. I suggest you start there." He handed the paper over and then stood, studying Ricki. "What else will you be doing?"

"We have other people we need to talk to," she said absently, tucking the paper safely into her own pocket. "Kelly's live-in girlfriend and her grown son to start. From what Anchorman said, there might have been some animosity between Kelly and his girlfriend's kid. There's also a veteran we need to track down. Apparently he wanted to go into the Airbnb business with Kelly, and Kelly wasn't so keen on the idea."

"An Airbnb business?" The thought made Christopher chuckle. "Having looked over Sergeant Dorman's military record, I wouldn't have pictured him as doing something so, shall we say placid, as running an Airbnb. What about the victim's family?" Christopher asked. "I understand he had life insurance, and surely they would benefit from his death?"

When both Ricki and Clay only shrugged, Trey's loud sigh bounced around the room. "Anchorman is listed as the beneficiary on Sergeant Dorman's policy." He rolled his eyes to the ceiling. "Did you think I wouldn't check?"

Christopher slowly shook his head. "Oh my. This case really is a messy one, isn't it?"

Chapter 16

RICKI AND CLAY pulled out of the hospital parking lot and headed back to the medical building, intending to pick up Anchorman. Expecting him to have Cheron in tow, they were surprised when he stood on the curb alone, waiting for them. Once he'd climbed into the SUV and buckled his seatbelt, he leaned back and closed his eyes.

Bracing a hand against the center console, Ricki twisted around so she could see him. "Where's Cheron?"

The former Marine didn't open his eyes as he settled more comfortably into the seat. "She should be at the airport right now, waiting for her plane."

It didn't take Ricki long to connect the dots. "You sent her home?"

He opened one eye. "She decided to go home after we discussed it. If I get tossed into prison, we agreed she can come back."

"How did you talk her into that?" Ricki asked. Cheron might have looked fragile enough to get blown over in a stiff wind, but she usually did exactly what she wanted, and it was hard to believe that the doctor had wanted to leave.

"I told her that there were still two shooters out there and it was dangerous for her to be here, which made her a distraction for me. And if I'm distracted, I can't guarantee I'll duck so fast next time."

Clay reached up to adjust the rearview mirror, both his eyes meeting the one Anchorman had open. "And she bought that?"

Ricki used two fingers to pinch the bridge of her nose. "That's because he told Cheron that the first bullet was aimed at him, and because he dove for the ground so fast, it hit Jerome instead."

"Is that what you think?" Clay asked.

She nodded. "Yeah. Pretty much. How about you?"

"The thought had crossed my mind." Clay maneuvered their vehicle onto US Highway 441 and headed south. The ride back to Pigeon Forge had an underlying sense of urgency for the two people occupying the front seat. Their backseat passenger, however, slept most of the way home.

Halfway through the hour-long drive, Ricki gave up trying to follow Anchorman's example. She stared out the side window for a few minutes before shifting in her seat for the third time.

"Something bothering you?" Clay asked, keeping his voice low.

"This whole case bothers me."

He smiled. "Anything specific?"

She stared out the front windshield. "Why try to kill Anchorman now?"

Clay rested one wrist on top of the steering wheel. "I have to agree. If they were shooting at him, they were trying to kill him. But if that was their intent, why wouldn't they have done that at the same time they killed Kelly? Anchorman drank the bourbon, too, or whatever was laced with ketamine. He would have been just as easy a target as Kelly."

"But not as easy to carry. Even if there were two of them." Ricki pondered that as she continued to stare at the country-side passing the window. "Maybe there was some significance to where Kelly was found?"

Clay snorted at that. "Lying across the trail where anyone who came along would trip over him?"

Silently conceding the point, Ricki slumped in her seat. "Yeah. They had to have taken Anchorman's gun, and then hiked back to the campsite if they used it to kill Kelly somewhere besides there to return it to his tent. It looks more like they were trying to set him up than kill him. At least at that point. So what changed?" She sighed and stretched her legs out. "What changed?" she muttered again under her breath.

She was still brooding over the question when they turned into the parking lot of their hotel in Pigeon Forge. The second the car's engine was switched off, Anchorman's eyes popped opened. He yawned and then sat up and looked around.

"Nice ride," he commented as he unsnapped his seatbelt and opened the car door.

"Yeah, I appreciate all the help with the driving," Clay said as he waited for Ricki to come around the front of the SUV and join them.

Anchorman gave him a friendly slap on the back of his shoulder. "You didn't need any help, and if you had, last time I checked, your copilot over there has a license."

Ricki smiled as she joined them on the sidewalk. "Yes, I do. But right now I'd like something to eat and a cold beer before we do anything else."

Clay threw an arm over her shoulder as they walked toward the lobby door. "That sounds like a solid plan to me."

He and Ricki led the way into the hotel. They'd only taken three steps inside when a tall woman with light brown hair leaped up from the lobby sofa and came rushing toward them. In pure self-defense, Ricki and Clay split apart to keep from being plowed right over. The woman didn't slow down a step, running past them and hurling herself at Anchorman. The big man had the good sense to brace his legs against the impact, which saved him from being knocked on his butt right there in the lobby.

"NB! We came as soon as we heard." She leaned back and cupped his face with her hands. "Are you all right? This whole thing is nonsense, and we'll get it straightened out and then you can come right home with us. Fitz will help you. He'll know what to do."

A man with dark hair and an apologetic smile tapped Ricki on the shoulder. "I'm sorry. You'll have to forgive my wife. She's been worried sick about her brother."

Ricki stared at him as if he had two heads. Brother? She and Clay turned in tandem to get a good look at the woman, who was still clinging to Anchorman and talking a mile a minute.

"Dina?" Anchorman caught his sister's wrists and managed to peel her hands off his neck. "What are you doing here?"

"We came to rescue you, and take you home, of course." Dina stepped to the side. When she turned around, she already had a firm hold on one of Anchorman's arms. Having the same brown color in her hair and eyes as her brother, she boasted a good portion of his height as well. Which she used to her advantage as she gave Clay and then Ricki a good once-over. "You must be Ricki." Her gaze skipped over to Clay. "And you are?"

"That's Clay," Anchorman cut in. "He's police chief in the Bay, where I live. And yeah, that's Ricki." When he looked at his two friends, Ricki could have sworn Anchorman was gritting his teeth. "This is my sister, Nadine Pollack." He lifted his free arm and pointed to the man who was now standing between Ricki and Clay. "And that poor guy is Fitz, her husband."

"And his brother-in-law," Fitz added as he held out his hand to Ricki and then Clay. "Fitzgerald Pollack, but I don't

171

hear Fitzgerald much. It's too long and sounds too snotty for a kid from the neighborhood. Everyone calls me Fitz."

Fitz had dark hair with a liberal amount of gray at the temples, and broad shoulders on top of a body that was at least two inches shorter than his wife's.

Anchorman's sister suddenly remembered her manners and let go of her brother's arm long enough to step forward and offer her hand as well. "And everyone calls me Dina. As I'm sure you can tell, no one from the neighborhood ever goes by their formal names."

Ricki shook the woman's hand, then looked from her to Anchorman and back again. The family resemblance was unmistakable. It was funny that Anchorman never talked about her much. Ricki gave that thought a mental headshake. She couldn't recall the last time he'd mentioned his sister. And she wasn't sure how she felt about Dina suddenly popping up out of nowhere. She'd always taken it for granted that the role of sister in Anchorman's life belonged to her. Up until a minute ago, she'd conveniently forgotten that someone else was already occupying that position.

She looked over at Fitz and smiled. "So, you all grew up together in the same neighborhood?"

"Yes," Dina answered for him, making Ricki wonder if that was normal for Fitz. "My husband and I were high school sweethearts. We got married right before Norman went off to join the Marines, along with our cousin, Ryan."

Anchorman quickly stepped forward, his face flushed a deep red. "We grew up together," he said abruptly. "But that was a long time ago. What I'd like to know is what you're doing here now?"

Dina faced him, her fists dug into her hips. "Now what would *you* have done if the police had shown up on your doorstep claiming I had killed someone? Just said 'thank you very much' and gone on with your day like nothing had happened? And that was several days ago. Strangely enough, I don't remember getting a call from you. The only time I know anything about what's going on in your life is when I make my monthly call to our Aunt Sally. But this? This is way beyond a family-duty call. And I had to read about it in the papers." She lifted both hands and pretended to be framing a headline. "Marine murdered in the Great Smoky Mountains National Park."

"I thought you learned it from the police," Anchorman said dryly.

"Same difference, NB," Dina slapped back. "Either way, I certainly didn't hear it from you."

Getting an up-close-and-personal inkling of why Anchorman didn't talk about his sister, Ricki stepped forward and tapped the annoyed woman on the shoulder. "Excuse me." When the woman whirled around, Ricki smiled. "Exactly who showed up at your door with news about your brother? Was that the local police?"

"Certainly not. They were military police. At least they were dressed in military uniforms. I'm not sure what branch of the service they were from." She looked at her husband. "I was dealing with that charity project I'm in charge of when they simply showed up. So they mostly talked to you. Where did they say they were from?"

"Um, Naval Criminal something or other." Fitz looked a little sheepish. "I'm sorry. I was in shock, so I really wasn't listening too much after they said that NB had killed his friend. I was sure the two of them were pretty tight." He glanced at Anchorman. "Didn't you serve together overseas? I remember you said something about him being your team member?"

"Yeah. He was." Anchorman's voice had a layer of steel in it. "And I didn't kill him."

"I never thought you did," Fitz declared. "Never. I just couldn't believe anyone else thought you did either. Not if they'd ever served in the military, anyway. Then they would have known better and looked for some other suspect. I mean, you wouldn't have killed another Marine. You were highly decorated. A hero, for god's sake."

"You kill some people and you're a hero. You kill others and get tossed in jail for it," Dina sniffed. "But I never believed it either," she hastily assured her brother. "Not for one minute."

Anchorman crossed his arms over his chest and stared back at his sister. "If you didn't believe it, then what are you doing here?"

Dina's mouth pulled down at the corners. "To get you out of this mess, of course. I thought we might have to bail you out of jail first, but I can plainly see that isn't necessary. So I'm assuming they haven't arrested you yet?"

"They arrested me." Anchorman nodded, and his words were clipped.

"Well then, who bailed you out? Or did you have enough money to do that on your own?"

Anchorman exchanged a pained look with Ricki before blowing out a soft breath. "That really isn't any of your business, Dina. The relevant thing is that I'm not in jail and intend to stay that way with the help of my friends here."

"Which brings us back to my question," Ricki said in a voice loud enough to override Dina's protests about family being first. "Exactly when did these NCIS guys show up on your doorstep?"

Dina gave her a slightly superior look before finally saying in an irritated tone, "I told you. Several days ago."

"Several days can cover a lot of territory," Ricki said evenly. "Can you remember the exact date?"

"I don't know." She looked at Fitz. "Well?"

"Um . . . Two days ago? We would have come sooner, but I didn't think to ask where you were. I'm not sure those two guys would have known anyway, if you'd already been bailed out of jail."

"All right. There's your answer. We're going to stay until we can get this cleared up," Dina declared.

Anchorman looked genuinely horrified. "Stay where? Here?"

"Of course." Dina stood on tiptoe to look over Ricki's head toward the front desk. "This isn't our usual choice for hotels, but it will have to do since this is where you're staying, and we need to be close by." She held out her hand and waited impatiently. Fitz had been holding her purse by his side and now lifted it and handed it to her. She thanked him with a quick pat on the cheek, then strode across the lobby, taking a direct line to the registration desk.

Fitz's gaze followed her movements before swinging back to his dumbfounded brother-in-law. "Look, man. I'm sorry about this. I'll see what I can do to persuade her to go home and let the professionals handle this." He added a smile to the nod he directed at Ricki and Clay. "If you need us to stay around, I can swing a few days. There's a lot going on at the business, so I need to get back, but I can run things from here for a short while anyway. Whatever you need." Fitz held up a fist and waited with a hopeful look in his eyes.

Anchorman sighed, then gave his sister's husband the fist bump he was obviously waiting for. "Look. I appreciate the offer, and it's getting late to drive back to High Point tonight, but if you could get Dina out of here tomorrow, I'd owe you a big return favor. And you can count on me paying up."

His brother-in-law laughed as he shook his head. "I've thought the same thing myself a time or two over the last thirty years, so no favor required." His smile faded. "I'm really sorry about this, but she got it into her head that we had to come. I would have settled for a phone call, but she wasn't having any of that." He looked toward the desk where his wife was still talking a mile a minute with the beleaguered clerk. "Look, if you could have dinner with us tonight, I think that would pretty much satisfy her sense of family duty, and it will make it easier for me to talk her into going home." His expression turned sour as he continued to watch his wife. "If that doesn't work, I can always threaten to cut off her credit cards."

Anchorman looked uncomfortable, but there was real concern in his eyes. "Are you and Dina having problems?"

Fitz's smile was immediately back in place. "Nothing out of the ordinary. The last argument we had was about coming here."

"Dinner would be fine," Anchorman agreed.

"Great." Fitz turned his smile on Ricki. "We'd be happy and, frankly, very flattered if the two of you would join us?"

Clay subtly landed his big boot on Ricki's toe. "We appreciate the invitation. But Ricki and I still have work to do tonight, and we should be heading out."

"Yes. Work." Ricki quickly added her agreement. "Lots to do if we're going to get old NB off the hook."

Fitz poked Anchorman in the arm. "Yeah, NB here was lucky to get away with his initials as his nickname." His eyes crinkled at the corners in amusement. "He had a good friend who went by the name of Moldy."

"That would be a tough one," Ricki said. "We just need old NB to walk with us out to the car, and then he'll be all yours."

Nodding his understanding, Fitz backed off a few steps. "I hope we have a chance to see you again, Agent James." He smiled at Clay. "Chief Thomas."

When he headed for the front desk, Ricki made a beeline for the lobby doors with Anchorman close enough to breathe down her neck.

"Work?" he hissed the minute the doors closed behind them. "You're pleading work and leaving me here with Dina?"

"And Fitz," Ricki reminded him. "He seems like a nice guy."

"What does he do?" Clay asked, cutting across Anchorman's sputtering.

"He owns a custom-made furniture factory in High Point. Built the business up from scratch, with the help of what little they got from the sale of Dad and Mom's diner."

"So Dina didn't want to run the diner herself?" Ricki asked, curious about the family that Anchorman very rarely mentioned.

He shrugged. "She was just finishing up college and wasn't interested in running the diner, and had no time to deal with those thugs who called themselves lawyers and picked the estate clean." He ran a large hand over the top of his buzz cut. "It doesn't make any difference. It was a long time ago."

Ricki wondered if that was the reason Anchorman had chosen to stay in the service. His parents were gone, and so was the diner he'd probably thought he'd be coming home to run after his enlistment was up. And Dina certainly wasn't that big of a draw to come home to. Not to mention she would have already been married. Letting it brew in her mind, she reached over and gave him a quick hug. When she stepped back, she grinned at the surprised look on his face.

"Spend some time with your sister and then get a good night's rest. There's a lot to do in the next forty-eight hours."

As Ricki walked off, Clay winked at Anchorman. "Yeah, NB. You have a nice dinner."

"You call me that again, and you're going to find yourself flat on the ground with a swollen jaw," Anchorman said without any real heat in his voice.

Clay grinned and gave him a half salute. "I'll keep that in mind."

Chapter 17

THEY PULLED into the parking lot of the first bar that looked reasonable. Its neon lights, only half of them lit, advertised food as well as various brands of beer.

Clay stood with Ricki on the small sidewalk leading past the front door. "The Wooden Nick. Interesting name for a bar."

Ricki grinned. "If you include the letters that aren't lit, it says Wooden Nickel."

Clay shrugged and walked over to the red door with its layer of chipped paint. "Looks like the place could use a good handyman."

When they stepped inside, a TV over the bar was calling out the latest basketball game, with a dozen or so patrons scattered around the room, and half that many occupying stools at the bar. No one gave the newcomers more than a cursory glance as they claimed an unoccupied table pushed up against a wall. They shrugged out of their jackets and laid them across a couple of the empty seats at the table. Leaning back in her chair, Ricki looked around the place with interest.

It was a decent size—not too large, but not cramped either, with enough room to move freely between the tables.

The place didn't run to very much decor, settling for the head of a large buck mounted on one wall, and pictures of the town back in its earliest days scattered randomly around the remaining space. There might not have been much to it, but she liked the place. It had the comfortable feel of not trying to be anything but what it was—a small hometown watering hole. The kind favored by the locals.

She looked over at the bar where the menu was scrawled on a blackboard nailed to a post. It only listed fries, wings, and a burger, which certainly cut down on the decision-making time. Since she had come in wanting a beer and a burger, she was happy with the limited offering. What more could you want from the local beer joint?

"If you want something to eat or drink, we don't have no table service for another thirty minutes," the huge man behind the bar yelled. "So unless you're willing to wait, you're gonna have to walk back to the kitchen and give Cook your food order, then come up here and I'll pour your drink."

Clay grinned at Ricki from across the table. "Burger and a beer?"

She nodded. "I'll get the beers." Clay gave her a thumbs-up, then scooted his chair back. Once he got to his feet, he headed straight for the open door in the back of the room with a painted sign over it spelling out KITCHEN.

As he crossed the room, the noise level dropped. Ricki didn't have to look around to see what had caused that. She was pretty sure it sprung from the rest of the bar's patrons getting a clear glimpse of the badge attached to Clay's belt. Knowing she'd get exactly the same reaction, she got up and walked slowly to the bar, trying not to grin when the room went completely silent.

She sat down on a stool at the end of the long counter and turned her head enough to flash a smile out at the room. The bartender put down the glass he was drying and took a sideways step to stand in front of her. He looked over her shoulder and scowled at the nearest table.

"What's the matter? Haven't you seen a lady cop before? She's in here to have a drink and some food, not arrest anyone." When the noise level in the room rose again, he leaned over the bar and stared Ricki in the eye. "That's right, ain't it? You're not in here to arrest anyone, are you?"

Ricki shook her head. "I don't have the authority to do that, but I'll be happy to call the local deputies if there's someone you think needs arresting."

He snorted a laugh. Straightening again to his considerable height, his mouth parted in a smile, displaying gaps where several teeth should have been. "So what can I get you and your partner?"

"Two beers. Whatever you recommend that's on tap is fine."

His grin widened. "You know, I'm liking you more and more. I'm Trip. Been called that since I was a kid because I was always tripping over my own big feet. And you'd be Officer . . .?" He let the question hang in the air, waiting for her to fill in the blank.

Ricki ducked her head in a friendly nod. "Well, Trip, I'm Ricki. And it isn't Officer anything. It's Special Agent Ricki James." When Clay emerged from the kitchen and strolled back to their table, Ricki jerked a thumb at him. "And that's Chief Clay Thomas."

Trip rubbed the back of his neck as he shook his head. "A special agent and a police chief? Now, you wouldn't be from one of those states way out west, would you?"

"Washington," Ricki confirmed. "Why do you ask?"

Trip's face lit up. "Yeah, yeah. That's the one. Ain't you friends with that Marine? The one who shot Kelly?"

Ricki rolled her eyes to the ceiling. "He's a Marine vet, actually, and he didn't kill anyone. But yeah. We're his friends."

"Well don't that beat all that you just walked right in here like this? That's a real piece of luck for Sondra."

"Glad I could help." Ricki watched as he expertly filled an ice-cold mug with beer, leaving the perfect amount of foam on top. She'd heard the name. Sondra was Kelly's live-in girlfriend, but Ricki played along. "Who's Sondra?"

"My waitress, who should be reporting for her shift in about twenty minutes. She's also Kelly's girlfriend," Trip stated, confirming what Ricki already knew. "You know. That dead guy your Marine friend didn't kill? She and her kid live in his house, and she's been wanting to talk to that Marine real bad. Something to do with her living situation. Maybe you could fix her up?" His eyes took on a sly gleam. "I'll front you those beers if you'll help her out. I'd be real happy not to have to hear her talk about where she and that lazy kid of hers are going to live."

Thinking it was more her lucky day than it was Sondra's, Ricki shot Trip a big smile. "We'll pay for the beers, but sure. I'll talk to her. When she comes in, send her over to our table." Adding another smile for good measure, Ricki picked up the two beers and headed back to where Clay was waiting. When she set the mugs down in front of him, he glanced at his watch.

"Good timing. The food should be ready in about five minutes."

Ricki slid into her seat and drew one of the mugs closer to her side of the table. "That's great. We should have about fifteen minutes to eat before our first interview gets here."

Clay took a sip of the ice-cold brew, gazing back at Ricki over the rim of the thick glass. "Oh? Who would that be?"

"Sondra. Kelly's girlfriend. It seems she's a waitress at this bar."

His eyebrows lifted in surprise. "Now there's a piece of unexpected luck." He cocked his head to one side and narrowed his gaze on her face. "It was a piece of luck, right? Dan didn't tell you she worked at this bar, did he?"

"Nope. All he said was that she's a cocktail waitress." Ricki looked around at the wood-plank walls, with the faded pictures and single deer's head. "Cocktail lounge isn't exactly the way I would describe this place, but if the word works for her, I'm fine with it."

A few minutes passed in companionable silence before the cook walked out of the kitchen, balancing two plates in one hand, and carrying a bowl heaped to a peak with a mountain of fries in the other. He marched over and set the food down on their table, turning and stomping back to the kitchen without saying a word.

"He's not much for conversation," Clay observed, making Ricki laugh before they both dug into their food.

They ate like it was their first meal of the day, which it was, managing to finish their burgers before a short, petite Black woman blew through the front door. Her coat was already half off as she sprinted past the bar.

"I'm not late. I'm not late," she shouted at Trip before expertly tossing her coat onto a hook on the wall. She whirled around to scoop up a red apron from a stack perched on the end of the bar. Picking up a tray and balancing it on one hand, she scanned the crowd, nodding at a few of the regulars before her gaze stopped on Ricki and Clay. Trip walked over to where she stood and leaned over the bar, saying something to her in a low voice that had her nodding. She lowered the tray and tucked it against her side before strolling across the room. Pulling out the last empty chair at the table, she sat down without waiting for an invitation, and shifted her gaze from Ricki to Clay.

"Trip tells me you're friends with Anchorman. He's that Marine who everyone is saying murdered Kelly. Is that right?"

Ricki turned a hard-eyed stare on Trip for leaving out the part about Anchorman being innocent, while Clay smiled at the woman with the fierce look in her eyes, sitting across from him.

"He's right about us being that Marine's friends, and wrong about him murdering Kelly." He held out a hand. "I'm Clay Thomas, chief of police for a town in the state of Washington."

She took his hand and gave it a quick shake. "Sondra Lewis. I'm, or I was, Kelly's girlfriend. Me and my son were living with him going on two years now."

Having made her silent point with Trip, who was now looking very busy wiping the bar, Ricki met Sondra's steady gaze. "I'm Special Agent Ricki James with the National Park Service's investigative unit. We're attached to the team of the prime investigator looking into Sergeant Kelly Dorman's murder," she said smoothly. She didn't see any need to mention that Clay wasn't officially attached to the case at all, and, technically, it was a "team" made up of one NCIS agent. Unless another investigator from that agency was on the way since Trey was now laid up with a bullet in his leg. "Trip mentioned that you wanted to talk to us?"

"Yeah. It's about Kelly's, I don't know, I guess you'd call it his estate." She tapped a nail painted in a bright green against the wooden tabletop. "Not the money from his life insurance policy, you understand. I know that all goes to his mama and his brother living down in Georgia, which it should, because Kelly and me? We weren't married or nothin', and his kin needs that money. I could see that for myself when we visited them last year. I'm only interested in the house here in Pigeon Forge. Like I said, my son and me have been living there for a couple of years now, and I'd like to stay if we can come to an understanding about the rent. But if we can't do that, then I'm going to need some time to make other arrangements."

Ricki carefully studied Sondra's face, and all she saw was an earnest kind of desperation. What she didn't see was someone trying to wiggle their way into an inheritance. "And why do you want to talk to Anchorman about this?"

Relief washed over the woman's face. "That's right, that's right. Kelly always called him Anchorman. Something about him being a rock when it came to having his team's back." She visibly relaxed in her chair. "He's a big White guy. His people are from New Jersey, I think. He's been to the house a couple of times, and I'm remembering he talked about a friend of his from home. Called him Ricky. I thought it was short for Richard." She slowly perused Ricki's face and long, slender form. "But I guess not."

"It's short for Richelle." Ricki stacked her hands on the tabletop in front of her. "And I think a meet with Anchorman can be arranged. But first, I need some information from you."

In the blink of an eye, Sondra's smile vanished, and a wariness crept into her gaze. "What kind of information?"

"Did Kelly have any enemies, or maybe someone he had an argument or disagreement with?"

Sondra shook her head. "Not Kelly. He wasn't the disagreeable sort. He was real good at listening to everybody." She pointed at Clay. "He said Anchorman didn't kill him. Is that why you're asking that question?"

"Yes." When Sondra looked taken aback by her blunt response, Ricki only shrugged. "Anchorman didn't do it, so someone else did. We're trying to find out if anyone had a reason to murder Kelly."

"Now that's going to be a problem," Sondra baldly stated. "Because everyone like Kelly, including his best bud, Anchorman. Those two were as tight as a knotted rope, so it was hard for me to believe he hurt Kelly. But from what I hear, there wasn't anyone else up at that campsite except those two, so who else could have done it?"

"There was someone else up there," Ricki flatly stated.

The petite woman leaned forward and carefully studied

Ricki's face. "Yeah. I can see you believe that. But who else was up there? Can you tell me that?" When Ricki stayed silent, Sondra flopped back against the chair and crossed thin arms over her chest. "You're his friend, and you want to believe he'd never shoot Kelly, but that don't make it so."

Painfully aware of that small nugget of truth, Ricki still rejected it. She absolutely knew two other people had been up there, but she wasn't prepared to explain how she knew it to Sondra, and by extension, everyone else in the bar.

"If that's all you were interested in, then can I get that meet with Anchorman?"

Ricki took a sip of beer as she considered the other woman for a moment. "I've been told that Kelly intended to retire and start his own business here in Pigeon Forge. An Airbnb."

Sondra shrugged. "Yeah. He'd been saving his money and had his eye on a couple of places. So what?"

"And there was someone wanting to go in with him as a partner in the venture?" Ricki went on, ignoring Sondra's belligerent tone. "Another local veteran, wasn't he?"

"Stu Landers," Sondra supplied. She crossed one leg over the other and lounged back in her chair. "Again, so what? Kelly wasn't interested, and he was working up to telling Stu that. But even if he had, it wasn't something to kill anyone over." She turned her head and looked around the room. "If Stu were here, he'd tell you that himself."

Ricki could feel several pairs of eyes from the tables around them boring into her as she kept her own gaze on Sondra. "Does Stu come in here often?"

"He lives on Forest Drive in that development just down the road, so yeah, he comes in here pretty regular. And so did Kelly. These guys here"—Sondra reached out an arm and swung it in a wide arc—"they're all Stu's friends. And Kelly's too. And none of them are taking the news of my Kelly's murder very well. You might want to keep that in mind, Miss

Special Agent of whatever. Now have you got anything else to ask, or can I start my shift?"

"How about bourbon?" Ricki threw out. "Did Kelly like bourbon?"

"Bourbon?" Sondra made a dismissive noise in the back of her throat. "What's bourbon got to do with anything? And yeah, it was his favorite drink. Besides beer."

"Did he take a bottle with him on the camping trip with Anchorman?"

Sondra threw her hands up in the air. "Now how would I know that? I was at work when he got to packing for that trip. I don't know what all he took with him besides that new gun of his." She shot a glance at Clay. "I don't know why men have to spend so much money on a gun."

"Rifle," Ricki corrected, then had to fight a smile when Sondra muttered "whatever" under her breath. "Okay, you didn't see Kelly get his backpack together, but how about in general. Did he keep a bottle of bourbon in the house?"

Kelly's girlfriend looked exasperated and more than a little mutinous. "Again with the bourbon."

When Sondra turned her head and looked away, pointedly ignoring the question, Ricki quietly reminded her, "Remember that meet you want."

Sending a dagger-eyed look across the table, Sondra clenched her jaw into a firm line. "No. My grandpa was a mean drunk, so I don't allow liquor to be kept in my house. It's fine at work, but not in my house. And you don't walk into my house, or sit at my table, drunk either. A couple of bottles of beer in the fridge, and that's it. Kelly might have stashed some bourbon out in the garage, but I can guaran-damn-tee you that there wasn't any in my house."

Ricki blew out a breath and leaned back, making the wooden slats of the chair creak in protest. If there wasn't any liquor in the house, and he had it hidden in the garage, or bought it while on his way to meet up with Anchorman for their camping trip, there wasn't any opportunity for someone to have slipped the drug into the bottle. Feeling a dead end, she looked over at Clay, who wore the same expression of frustration that was undoubtedly on her own face.

"One last thing, Miss Lewis," Ricki began again. "You mentioned a son who also lives in the house?"

"Yeah, Dilbert. He's my boy. He goes by Bert, and he doesn't keep any alcohol in my house either. Not if he knows what's good for him."

"How old is Bert?"

Sondra's upper lip pulled back into a sneer. "Now why are you asking about my boy? He didn't do anything wrong."

"But he was one of the last people to see Kelly, so I need to talk to him." Ricki reached into her pocket and pulled out one of her cards. "Have him give me a call to set up a time for us to come by the house tomorrow." When Sondra made no move to take the card, Ricki quirked an eyebrow at her. She needed to talk to Dilbert Lewis and, fortunately, still had a chip to negotiate with. "He makes the call and keeps the meet, and then I'll set up something with you and Anchorman." She stretched out the hand holding her business card a bit farther. "Deal?"

"Deal," Sondra declared at the same time she reached out and snatched up the card, tucking it away in the top pocket of her collared shirt. The shirt looked big on her, and Ricki wondered if it had belonged to Kelly.

"Then I'll wait to hear from him, and after that, you'll hear from me." Ricki picked up her mug of beer and took a long sip.

Sondra's dagger look was back in full force as she pushed away from the table and stood up. "I'd better, or I'll come looking for you. You can count on that."

Knowing the woman meant every word, Ricki lifted her mug in a salute. "That's also a deal."

Chapter 18

"WHAT DO YOU THINK?" Clay asked as Sondra retreated to the bar with her tray firmly grasped in one hand.

Ricki stared after the waitress. "I think she knew Kelly very well. More than someone who was just looking for a free place to live." She glanced at Clay as she raised her beer mug to her lips. "I think she really cared about him."

Clay leaned back in his chair and stretched his long legs out underneath the table. "That's the vibe I got from her too. And she's not trying to rip anyone off either. She asked about renting the house, not having it given to her as a payment for the time she looked after it whenever he was deployed."

"I wonder what . . ." Ricki stopped mid-sentence when an older man, with a gray beard reaching to his chest, sat down in the chair vacated by Sondra. He wore a baggy plaid shirt and an equally baggy pair of jeans with the hems stuffed into a pair of tall army boots that looked like they'd been around since the Second World War.

"Don't mind Sondra," he stated right off. "She's still grieving hard for Kelly. We all are." He nodded toward the bar. "Trip says you two are investigating Kelly's murder."

Ricki's eyes narrowed slightly, but she pasted on a polite

smile. "That's right. I'm Special Agent Ricki James, and this is Chief Thomas."

The elderly man wiggled his eyebrows at Clay. "What are you chief of?"

Clay hesitated just long enough to clearly convey the message that he was reserving judgment on the man before he smiled. "A city near Olympic Park in the state of Washington."

"Olympic Park," the man repeated slowly, drawing a gnarled hand down the length of his beard. "And now here you are, sitting in a bar close to another park. Is that part of your chief duties? To look into murders in any park?"

Clay's smile stayed put, but his gaze grew harder as he stared back at the man. "No. That's her job. I came along as part of her team."

"Kind of like a posse." The elderly man's watery blue eyes slid across to meet Ricki's gaze. "Is that what you have, Agent James? A posse?"

Ricki didn't rise to his bait but settled more comfortably in her chair. "Right now, what I have is a team member sitting across from me, a beer sitting in front of me, and someone I don't know asking questions."

The uninvited guest smiled, revealing several gaps in his bottom teeth. "Didn't mean to be rude. I'm Herbert Twain, but I go by Herb."

"Well, Mr. Twain," Ricki drawled, deliberately ignoring his hint to call him by his given name. "What can we do for you?"

"I'm wondering what you do with this posse of yours, missy? And what kind of agent are you? Like a spy or something?"

Ricki let the dismissive way he'd addressed her pass and simply shook her head. "Not a spy. I work for the investigation branch of the National Park Service." When he gave her a blank look, she smiled. "We investigate any major crimes that happen in the parks."

Understanding dawned on Herb's face. "You mean like someone getting murdered? Is that why Trip said you're investigating Kelly's murder?"

Ricki nodded. It didn't bother her to stretch the truth a bit. "Along with NCIS, since Kelly was in the active military." She took a sip of her beer and studied the elderly man. "And I ask you again, Mr. Twain, what can we do for you?"

Herb pursed his lips and leaned his forearms against the table. "It's more like, what can I do for you? I overheard you asking about Stu Landers. I'm thinking you might want to know where he lives."

Ricki shrugged and ran a slender finger up and then down the side of her beer mug. "I already have that information." *Or at least the street he lives on*, she thought. "But thank you for offering it."

"You might have it, but you aren't going to find him there.'"

From the corner of her eye, she saw Clay shift in his seat so he was squarely facing the open room. When she heard a chair squeak, she automatically rolled her shoulders backwards to be sure she felt the presence of her gun at the small of her back. Like Clay, she had moved it there from her shoulder holster before they'd entered the bar. A precaution that was shaping up to be a necessary one.

"Since you know he isn't home, maybe you could tell me where Mr. Landers is at the moment?"

The old man leaned back, threaded his fingers together, and rested them on the small bulge of his stomach. "Camping out in the park. At least he said that's where he was going when he was in here four days ago. Said he needed some quiet time to think something over."

"And I don't suppose he happened to mention what that something was?" Ricki asked the question out of habit. She didn't expect an answer, so it was no great surprise when she didn't get one.

"Nope. He kept it his business, and out here we respect that."

"Then maybe he talked about going to a particular place in the park?"

Herb lifted his shoulders in an exaggerated shrug. "Can't really say. He camps in a lot of places there." He stared down at his hands. "He didn't mention any place in particular."

"Well, it's very civic minded of you to offer that information, Mr. Twain." Ricki conjured up a polite smile. "We appreciate that."

The elderly man's head jerked up, and he stared at Ricki for a moment, his teeth cutting into his lower lip. "No problem. You know all those campsites in the park require reservations, don't you?"

"Is that so?" She held her smile in place as she kept an eye on the burly man who got up from one of the back tables he was occupying with three other guys, then slowly walked over to the bar.

Herb braced his hands against the table and pushed himself to his feet. "Well, I wish you luck in your investigation, although we heard the guy had already been caught and hauled off to the county jail."

Wondering just how many people were included in that "we" Herb had used, Ricki deliberately picked up her mug and took a slow sip. "Thanks again, Mr. Twain."

"You're welcome, missy. You take care now."

"I will," she said to his back as he walked off. Letting her gaze sweep slowly across the room, Ricki didn't look at Clay when she murmured, "Are you finished with your beer?"

"Yeah," he said before pushing back from the table and getting his long legs underneath him. "Let's find someplace else to be."

Thinking that was an excellent suggestion, Ricki also got

to her feet. Scooping up Clay's jacket, she handed it to him before retrieving her own. She deliberately took her time to shrug into it, and then slowly stuck her hands into the pockets as she strolled across the room with Clay. She smiled to herself when he used his larger body to block her back from the dozen pairs of eyes following them as they crossed the room.

As soon as they stepped outside, he turned around and stared at the closed door leading into the bar. "Now that was something straight out of *Deliverance*."

Ricki laughed as she pulled on her gloves. "I think you'd better watch the movie again, city boy. They were just putting on a show for the northerners." She stepped off the narrow porch and headed for the SUV. "Herb's worried about his friend, so I'm guessing Mr. Landers has been gone longer than his buddies in the bar expected him to be. Herb got no grief about talking to the cops, so I'm thinking they all knew he intended to tell us where Landers went and how to find him." She took out her phone and punched in a number as she opened the car door.

"Good thing you speak the language then, because I didn't pick up on any of that." Clay skirted around the front of the car and slid behind the wheel. "Who are you calling?"

"Nora, since Herb wanted us to check the park reservation system. I'm hoping Nora has access to it and can tell me where Stu Landers has set up his tent."

A few minutes later, Ricki hung up the phone with a satisfied smile. "Nora's on her way back from visiting Jerome in the hospital up in Knoxville. She's still on administrative leave, but said she'd stop by their headquarters and get the information for us." Ricki tucked her phone away and crossed her feet at the ankles. "She'll call back in an hour or so and let us know what campsite Landers reserved."

Their hotel loomed into view a minute later, and Clay pulled into the half-full lot, right behind a cream-colored Mercedes.

Clay gave the sleek vehicle a long look. "I saw the North Carolina plates. What do you want to bet that's the sister and her cowering husband's car, and they're still here?"

"Anchorman's problem," Ricki said absently before exiting the SUV. If the hike to wherever Landers was camping couldn't be done in one day, she'd have to ask Nora to send some rangers up there for a wellness check. She didn't want the guys at the bar stewing and worrying over their friend. Of course, she'd only met Trip and Herb, but that was enough for her to gauge the temperature of the place. A different kind of band of brothers, but a band nevertheless. Formed over beer from a tap. Like a beer brotherhood.

She was still grinning at the thought as she walked into the lobby. When she felt a soft poke in her arm, she looked up at Clay.

"I think our helpful desk clerk wants to tell us something."

She glanced in that direction, where the young man standing behind the tall counter was waving at them. Hoping she wasn't going to hear about another missing friend, she and Clay switched directions and crossed the shag rug that covered most of the lobby floor.

Clay stopped and rested a forearm on top of the counter. "What can we do for you?" When the young man opened his mouth but nothing came out, Clay added a smile. "Is there a problem with the credit card?"

The clerk audibly swallowed as he shook his head. "No, sir. It's fine." He lowered his voice to a whisper. "I just thought you might be looking for your prisoner?"

Exasperated with the built-in drama of a small-town gossip mill, Ricki leaned over the counter and looked the shorter clerk directly in the eye. "He's not our prisoner. Even the justice system said he was free to walk around."

When the clerk took an involuntary step back, Ricki straightened up again. "Now. Where is he?"

"Outside, by the pool. He's been out there for a while

now." The young man lifted his hands and nervously cracked several knuckles before he realized what he was doing and dropped his arms by his side. "We just put the chairs out yesterday, but the pool itself isn't open yet, so there aren't any lights on back there. I thought you might want to check on him."

Ricki looked at the narrow back hallway that led to the pool. "Did he go out there with anyone else?" she asked, thinking of Dina and her husband.

"No. He got on the elevator with the couple he had dinner with, then he came right back down alone and headed out that way." It was clear from the clerk's tone that he thought Anchorman had made a run for it.

Not bothering to correct him, Ricki simply turned and headed for the dingy hallway, with Clay keeping pace right behind her. Just as the kid at the desk had said, the pool area was dark. It took a moment for her eyes to adjust to the moon-light, but it didn't take long to spy the big figure sitting side-ways on a lounge chair. His hands were clasped in front of him, and his head was down.

Worry clouded her gaze as she walked across the cement deck surrounding the pool. Grabbing a chair from the nearest table, she set it down close to Anchorman's knee and took a seat with Clay following suit. The three of them sat silently together. The only sounds were from a tree branch moving in the soft night breeze and the occasional car passing by on the road beyond the brick wall that separated the back area of the hotel from the parking lot.

Five minutes passed before Anchorman finally stirred, lifting his head. In the moonlight, Ricki could see the glitter of tears in his eyes. She instinctively reached out and gently placed a hand on his bent knee.

"What is it?"

"Kelly's gone." His voice broke, and it took another full minute before he got it under control. "He wasn't just a brother. I also owed him my life a dozen times over." His hands were clasped together so hard his fingers and knuckles were white, and those broad shoulders began to tremble. "And what if I did it? What if I shot him? In the back." His voice broke again, and there was no hiding the indrawn breath and the underlying sob that went with it.

Ricki fought to control her own tears. She'd never seen him like this. Never thought she would. He was Anchorman, with everything that word implied. And now he was breaking apart. *Over nothing*, was her sudden, fierce thought. Nothing.

"You didn't hurt Kelly, man."

Clay's voice had the same tinge of anger in it that was in her head. But right now, anger wasn't going to help them. Or Anchorman. She shook her head at Clay, then gave the big Marine's knee a soft squeeze. "What makes you think you might have shot Kelly?"

Anchorman unclasped his hands and picked up his cell phone that was lying next to him on the chaise lounge. He used both hands to turn it over and over as he stared at it. "I needed some fresh air after spending almost an hour at dinner with Dina. When I sat down, I thought I'd look up this ketamine shit that Cheron said was in my system." He set the phone down again and looked over at Ricki. "This disas-sociation thing Cheron talked about. It can make you do things and stop you from remembering that you did them." He bent his head back down and clasped his hands together again. "What if that stuff triggered some kind of flashback and I heard Kelly moving around? Maybe he came over to check on me, or was just going to take a leak?" He drew in a ragged breath. "Maybe I thought he was the enemy, sneaking up on me. And I grabbed my rifle and shot him." He moved his broad shoulders in a quick shrug. "With my training, it would have been automatic for me. Pulling that trigger would have been pure instinct if I thought I was about to be ambushed."

"Oh my god," Ricki breathed out, while next to her Clay swore under his breath.

Anchorman gave them both a sideways glance, the corners of his mouth pulled all the way down to his chin. "Yeah. It could be that bad."

She removed her hand from his knee, straightened, and held one hand up, palm out, as she moved it in a circle. "What's bad is that whole explanation." Her brisk tone had Anchorman's shoulders slumping even more.

"It's possible," he mumbled.

Ricki shook her head hard enough to send her ponytail whipping around to slap the side of her face. "It is not possible. Did you stop listening to Cheron once she said the word ketamine? Or maybe it was when she called it the date-rape drug, and you got all tangled up in that." She crossed her arms over her chest. "Maybe you should leave the detective work to us. Like fishing, it doesn't seem to be a strong point of yours." Just as she'd hoped, his head snapped up and a glint of anger replaced the sheen of moisture in his eyes.

"I'm saying it could have happened."

Clay lounged back in his chair and stretched his legs out in front of him. "No, man, it couldn't."

Anchorman's hands dropped and he balled them into fists. "Why the hell not?"

Clay was trying to bait the Marine into taking a swing at him to shake him out of the pit of guilt he was wallowing in, but Ricki didn't want to have to patch either of them up. Waving a hand between the two men to break their eye contact with each other, she swung a heavy boot out and gave her cook a hard kick in the shins.

He immediately shifted his attention away from Clay to glare at her. The bad news was he looked madder than a poked bear. But on the flip side, she knew that no matter how pissed off Anchorman got, he would never haul off and hit her. "What the hell was that for?"

"That's how you get a stubborn jerk's attention." She pointed at Clay. "An experienced homicide cop just stated that you shooting Kelly couldn't have happened. And that's because Cheron plainly said the evidence showed that from the angle of the entry wound, Kelly was lying on the ground when he was shot." She stood, forcing him to look up at her as she shook a finger at him. "Is that what you think you did? In a drug-induced fog, you wrestled your friend to the ground and decided to shoot him? And then what? You wrapped him up in his sleeping bag, carried him a mile and a half to dump him right on the trail? That's what you do in your flashbacks? Wrap bodies up in sleeping bags and carry them a couple of miles?"

"Don't forget that he hiked back to camp, got rid of the bourbon bottle, crawled back into his sleeping bag, and then went against all that training and instinct of his and put his gun down on the wrong side, where it would be harder to grab while, as far as he was concerned, he was deep in enemy territory due to his flashback." The layer of amusement in Clay's voice had Anchorman's jaw hardening in response.

Relieved when the anger finally drained right out of Anchorman's gaze, Ricki sat down again. "You didn't kill your friend. Those two guys who shot at us murdered Kelly and wanted to frame you for it. Get that into your head."

Anchorman sighed and lifted a hand, scrubbing it across one cheek. "Which we can't prove."

"Yet," she corrected. "But there might be a guy who knows something about that." When the former Marine's eyes widened in surprise, Ricki nodded. "Remember that vet who wanted to invest in Kelly's Airbnb business venture? Well, it seems he decided to go on a last-minute camping trip to think something over."

Anchorman's face scrunched up. "So?"

"He left the day that . . ." She hesitated, searching for something to say besides "the day Kelly's body was found."

"The day that you were arrested. When news about the murder would have started to circulate in town. I think we should pay him a visit and find out what it was that was bothering him so much he had to get away, not only from his house, but completely out of town."

"If he isn't home, how are we going to do that?" Anchorman asked.

Right on cue, Ricki's phone rang. She pulled it out and saw Nora's name on the screen. Holding up one finger to keep Anchorman quiet, she tapped the connect icon. "This is Ricki." She listened, a smile creeping across her lips. "Thanks, Nora." When she hung up, she grinned at Clay. "Campsite 42. It's accessible from the other side of the park, so it will take us around two, maybe two and a half hours to get there from the hotel, but it's just over a mile hike in."

Clay nodded. "We can do that in a day easily enough."

Anchorman looked from one to the other, then got to his feet. "I'm going with you."

Chapter 19

WITH A TWO-HOUR DRIVE in front of them, the alarm went off very early the next morning. Ricki forced her feet out of bed and into the shower before she talked herself into rolling over and getting another hour of sleep.

Clay gave her butt a friendly slap as she stood in front of the mirror in her underwear, impatiently dragging a brush through her long hair. She didn't bother with the hair dryer—didn't have time for it. Opting to put her locks into her usual ponytail while they were still wet, she pulled on the rest of her clothes and then wiggled her feet into her boots.

By the time she was checking her rifle and dropping spare cartridges into her jacket pocket, Clay was already dressed. He looked completely relaxed, undoubtedly using some magic trick she had yet to master, and that made her cross her eyes at him. He only grinned as he slung his backpack over one shoulder and held the door open for her.

"One of these days you're going to have to teach me that trick you use to get showered and dressed so fast," she muttered as she passed him.

As they stood together, waiting for the elevator, he leaned down closer to her ear. "Easy. Shave your head bald. Then you won't have to mess around so much with your hair." He reached over and tweaked the end of her ponytail. "Although I'd really miss it."

Suppressing a shudder at the thought, Ricki stepped into the elevator and jabbed the button for the ground floor. "Uh-uh. Not going to happen."

The short ride to the lobby ended on Clay's laugh. As soon as the doors opened, Ricki spotted Anchorman, leaning against the wall opposite the elevator, arms crossed over his chest.

"There won't be any coffee for another hour."

His announcement brought out a grunt of annoyance from Clay. "That's the first thing I'm going to be checking the next time we have to stay in a hotel."

"I'm sure the coffee kiosk down the street is open," Ricki said. She walked past Anchorman and through the lobby, barely sparing a nod for the sleepy-eyed desk clerk before heading out the door. On the way to the SUV, she held her hand out and wiggled her fingers. "I'll drive."

Clay handed the keys over with a curious look. "Any particular reason why?"

"We're picking Nora up at the Sugarlands Visitor Center. She's coming with us."

They were all settled into the car and headed for the highway before Clay turned in his seat to look at her. "I thought Nora was still on administrative leave from the shooting at the campsite?"

"Why would she be?" Anchorman demanded. "She never got off a shot because she was busy trying to keep Jerome from bleeding out. You'd think they'd give her a pat on the back instead of a suspension."

Amused, Ricki glanced at him in the rearview mirror. "She probably will end up getting a commendation for that. She got the suspension for turning you lose."

Anchorman rolled his eyes, then stared out the rear

passenger window. "Figures. Sometimes I think law enforcement takes that no-good-deed-will-go-unpunished thing way too far."

"If that were true, then you'd be spending the day with your sister and her husband instead of hiking through the mountains with us."

"I wouldn't call a mile or so a hike." Anchorman's sour tone matched his scowl. "And if I had to spend an entire day with Dina, you'd end up arresting me for a murder I actually did commit."

Clay looked over his shoulder at the man sprawled across half the back seat. "That bad, huh?"

"We spent most of our dinner listening to her latest shopping trips and charity projects. Then there was her speech on the new car she wants, and how she was thinking of redecorating everything in her five-bedroom, four-bath house, except the in-ground pool. They never had any kids so what do they need a house that big for, anyway? The whole dinner was a detailed lesson on how to become rich and useless." He lifted his hands in a helpless gesture. "My sister and I could be from different planets, and sometimes I think we are. Our parents didn't live like that, so I don't know where Dina's urge to be one of the idle rich came from."

"Fitz's business must be doing very well for him to afford all that," Clay observed.

The former Marine only shrugged. "I don't know. He has to sell a whole bunch of rocking chairs and wooden bed frames to keep Dina in the lifestyle she thinks she's entitled to."

Ricki chuckled. "If his business is doing that well, maybe you should have taken him up on that offer to invest in it."

Anchorman pretended to gag at the suggestion. "And be forced to spend more time with Dina and Fitz because my money was tied up in their factory? Not gonna happen in this lifetime. I have enough money, thank you very much."

Clay's laugh joined Ricki's, and the rest of the ride passed in comfortable small talk about their lives back in the Bay, and Eddie's latest exploits in building what he'd loudly declared to his mom as "his best robot yet."

Fifteen minutes later, Clay took one of many long looks into the side-view mirror. "We have company. Picked up that small white truck a couple of minutes outside the hotel parking lot, and it's been tailing us ever since." He looked over at Ricki and grinned. "I think that's Herb in the driver's seat. Not sure about the passenger, but if I had to guess, I'd say he's the bartender from last night."

Ricki leaned over as her gaze cut over to the rearview mirror, quickly studying the reflection of the vehicle behind them. The large figure, slightly hunched over in the passenger seat as if there wasn't enough headroom for him in the small truck's cab, was definitely Trip. "Yeah, that's him." She returned Clay's grin. "I guess they wanted to be sure we'd check things out."

"Who are those guys?" Anchorman asked. "Do I need to literally ride shotgun on this one?"

Ricki shook her head. "They're harmless and it's a free country. They can drive along the same road if they want to."

For the rest of the ride she occasionally looked in the mirror, smiling when she saw the little white truck with Herb bent over the wheel, doggedly following in their tracks. When they reached the deserted parking lot at the Sugarlands Visitor Center, which also served as one of the main entrances to the park, Nora was sitting on the curb, waiting for them. Clay opened the passenger side door and held it for her, shutting it behind her after she'd joined Anchorman in the back seat.

"Hey, good morning!" Nora said in a greeting meant to encompass everyone in the car. "Should be a nice day for a hike."

"Do you live around here?" Ricki asked as she pulled the

SUV onto the main road that cut across the entire width of the park.

"Close enough. About twenty-five miles west of here, in Wears Valley." She smiled at Ricki, then turned to wink at Anchorman. "You should stop by. We have some of the best views of the Smoky Mountains that you'll ever be lucky enough to see."

"I've been to Wears Valley," Anchorman said with a shadow of a smile. "Kelly took me through on our way to go camping south of there. I remember it was a pretty place."

Nora let out a hoot of laughter. Still sporting a wide smile, she tapped Ricki on the shoulder. "Your boy back here has a real knack for the understatement. When I tried to congratulate him on the sterling effort at getting rid of those two guys who were shooting at us? He said, 'It got the job done.' And now he's calling Wears Valley a pretty place? I swear to you, it's a lot more than just a pretty place. It's a slice of heaven."

"Saying it was pretty is a big compliment from him," Ricki stated. "Trust me on that one." She waited while the ranger's laughter died down. "Since you're still on admin leave, are you going to get in trouble going on this hike with us? I don't want to cause any problems for you."

"You aren't," Nora declared. "Besides, you never asked me to come along. I asked you. And an off-duty ranger can hike anywhere in the park, just like every tourist who visits. If we happened to be going along the same trail, well, that's just the way it is."

Having made her decision clear, Nora settled back and began pointing out landmarks and interesting sights along the way. The last leg, Heintooga Round Bottom Road, was little more than a dirt track through the forest. It was a rough and beautiful ride that led them right up to the Spruce Mountain Trailhead, which was marked by a slight indentation in the road and a small sign perched at the bottom of a hillside.

Ricki parked the car, and within a minute, everyone was out of the SUV with their rifles strapped to the side of their packs.

Ricki held up a hand so Nora wouldn't start up the trail. "Let's wait for Herb and Trip. They should be here in a minute or two."

Nora leaned to the side and stared down the one-way road. "Who are Herb and Trip?"

"They gave us the tip about Landers being up here," Ricki said. "Clay spotted them following us from Pigeon Forge, and I think they want to come along. I'd rather have them walk with us than try to sneak around and follow us from behind."

Nora frowned. "Friend or foe?"

"Neither," Clay said. "They're just persistent."

He turned and walked out onto the road as the little truck came chugging along. Herb managed to squeeze it into the space left in the pullout by the SUV. The engine sputtered before shutting down and was followed by Herb's spindly leg appearing under the open driver's side door.

He stepped onto the ground and waved at Clay. "Hi there, Chief. It's a nice day for a hike. And how'd you know this is one of my favorite spots?"

Clay raised a skeptical eyebrow. "You hike up here much?"

"All the time." Herb glanced at his companion, who was standing on the other side of the truck. "Don't we, Trip?"

The large man rubbed his hands on the sides of his well-worn jeans and gave Ricki a sheepish grin. "Sometimes. But Stu comes here a lot."

Herb shot his passenger a disgusted look. "But we didn't come here to find Stu. We came to get in some hiking."

Without taking his gaze off Ricki, Trip sighed. "I think they know we were following them, Herb." He walked forward until he was standing a few feet from Ricki. "We'd like to tag along, if you don't mind?"

Clay walked up in time to hear Trip's question. He frowned at the bartender. "And if we do mind?"

Trip stuck his hands in his coat pockets and rocked back on his heels. "Then we'll just wait right here."

Ricki silently debated it for a moment and then gave in. "Fine. It's a public trail. Come along if you want to."

"That's exactly what I was thinking, missy," Herb declared, then blinked when Ricki turned a cold eye on him.

"If you want to come along, it's Agent James, or Ricki."

Herb held his hands up in a sign of surrender. "Okay. Don't get your skirts blown up."

Deciding the old man was a lost cause, Ricki pointed at him and then Trip. "This is Herb, and that's Trip. They're part of some kind of Beer Brotherhood that gathers at one of the local watering holes in Pigeon Forge." She switched the direction of her finger and aimed it at Nora. "She's Ranger Thorne. And the big guy standing next to her is Anchorman."

"I knew you were the sniper," Herb said with a cackle in his voice. "Son, you sure look the part." He turned his head and grinned at Ricki. "Sondra told us last night after you left. She also wanted me to tell you she might've let you think she believes Anchorman shot Kelly, just to be spiteful, but she don't. She said she doesn't know who did, just that she's sure it weren't him." He jerked a thumb at Anchorman before facing him again. "Are you really a sniper?"

"Retired," Anchorman said. "And I'd be careful how I addressed Agent James if I were you. She's as good a shot as I am."

When Herb turned an astonished look on Ricki, she smiled. "Almost," she hedged. "I'm almost as good." She nodded at Nora. "We'll keep these two between Clay and me if you'll lead the way. Anchorman prefers to take the rear position." She gave Herb a stony look. "There will be no talking on the trail."

While Herb and Trip both gaped at her, Nora started off, and Clay herded the two civilians into their position between Ricki and himself. Satisfied they'd have peace for at least the next 1.2 miles, Ricki marched along the trail. She followed Nora, enjoying the solitude of what Nora had claimed was one of the more remote and least-traveled routes in the park.

Once again it was a steady climb up to the campsite. They passed a small waterfall and had an occasional glimpse of the mountains around them, but for most of the hike, they were surrounded by a world of green, wrapped in a cocoon of quiet. Ricki glanced back more than once at Anchorman. After he'd come close to a meltdown the night before, she was glad to see the contented look on his face.

They were thirty-five minutes out when they approached the edge of the campsite. A small tent occupied one of the few spaces that was clear enough to set up a camp. Ricki's gaze quartered the area. Except for the tent and backpack that was visible inside it, the place was completely deserted.

She took a long step and reached out a hand, latching on to Nora's arm to stop the ranger's forward progress.

"Hang on a moment." Ricki's voice was barely above a whisper. "Is there any other trail out of here?"

The ranger shook her head. "No. This is the end of the Spruce Mountain Trail. It's the only way in or out. The only intersecting trail has been closed for a while."

Nodding her understanding, Ricki put one finger against her lips as Clay moved up beside her. The group stood in silence, with only the ever-present breeze making any noise. After a few moments, Ricki heard a steady sound beneath the more erratic one made by wind passing through the treetops high above. It was the kind of buzz made by hundreds of tiny wings beating against the air.

"Shit."

Clay's low-voiced curse only added to the sinking feeling in the pit of her stomach. She took a small step to the side and caught Anchorman's eye as she slipped off her backpack, removed her rifle, and then set the pack on the ground, Clay doing the same before handing his rifle to Anchorman than pulling out his Glock. "Make sure they all stay here, and keep a sharp lookout," Ricki said quietly.

She didn't wait for Anchorman's agreement, but slowly started forward. Clay fanned out to the side so they were flanking the small tent as they followed the unknown sound. He stopped to look inside the mostly empty tent while Ricki continued to walk its length. Once she reached the back, she didn't have to go far to find the source of the noise.

A body lay sprawled on top of a young growth of ferns, it's head turned to the side showing a sunken cheek and one eye. Hundreds of flies buzzed all around the dead man. She got close enough to see the single, open eye, staring at nothing, and the two holes in his back. The man's parka was soaked in dried blood that had run down his side and saturated the ground beneath him. From the splayed-out position of his arms, she thought he might have been trying to run for his life. But he hadn't made it more than fifteen feet from his tent.

Ricki looked around. His killers had probably come in the same way she and her small group had, cutting off the man's access to the only escape route from the camp. Clay walked over and handed her a worn leather wallet.

"His ID says he's Stuart Landers. Fifty-two years old. Five feet ten inches. Brown hair, brown eyes, and he lives in Pigeon Forge."

Ricki took the wallet and flipped it open. A man stared back at her from a photo on the driver's license. She took several steps closer to the dead body and held up the license, comparing the picture to the face of the man on the ground. It was a perfect match. Sighing, she slipped the wallet into her pocket and walked backwards to the tent where Clay was waiting, his Glock raised and ready.

"Like you've pointed out before, this is your world, Ricki. What do you think?"

She took another moment to stare at the body sprawled

out on the ground. "I think he's been dead at least a day or two, and whoever shot him is long gone."

"It doesn't look like they went through his backpack," Clay said.

"Yeah. I would have been surprised if he'd been robbed, and this definitely wasn't an accident."

Clay nodded. "Agreed. Is it looking like our two shooters?"

"Well, he was shot in the back." But since Anchorman's gun was still in police custody, the ballistics wouldn't match what was found in Kelly's murder. Which meant, once again, they were hitting a sure hunch with no proof. But at least if Stu Landers had been killed sometime between today and when Kelly was shot, it gave Anchorman a rock-solid alibi. With a sigh, she patted the pocket containing Landers's ID. "Let's show the driver's license to Trip and Herb so they can make a positive identification of the deceased. And then we'll need to report it."

Chapter 20

"HE'S DEAD?" Trip's ruddy complexion faded to a chalky white as he pointed a beefy finger at the small tent. "Right over there. His body is right over there?"

Ricki nodded and tucked Stu Landers's wallet into her coat pocket, then looked at Herb. "Why don't you start back to the trailhead? Anchorman will go with you."

Now Trip began to wring his hands together, his gaze still on the tent. "I don't think we should just leave Stu here. It doesn't seem right."

"How long you figure he's been dead?" Herb asked.

"I would guess at least two days," Ricki said.

"You hear that?" Herb asked his friend. "Stu's been lying out here for at least two days. That's what Agent James thinks, and I'm betting she's seen a lot of bodies." He looked back at Ricki. "You said you investigate major crimes that happen in the park, didn't you?" He took a slow, exaggerated look around. "Well, this is a park, and I'd say someone being murdered is a major crime, so you're the one who's going to be figuring this out. Isn't that right?"

Ricki looked past him, toward Anchorman. "Can you

walk out with these two and wait with them by the cars until we get there? We won't be far behind you."

"Sure." Anchorman walked forward, stepping in between Herb and Ricki. "We'd better get started." He gave Trip a solemn look. "You never know who might still be hanging around."

Trip made a high-pitched squeaking noise before doing a one-hundred-and-eighty-degree turn to head back down the path, his long legs propelling him forward at a fast clip. Herb ran after him, breaking into an awkward gait to keep up with Trip's much longer stride.

"You'd better go and get them under control before Herb falls flat on his face and breaks something," Clay said.

Anchorman started to shoot up his middle finger but caught sight of Nora staring at him, so turned the motion into a wiggling of all his fingers before trotting down the trail after the two who had already fled the scene.

Ricki left Anchorman to it and immediately turned toward Nora. "What are the chances an animal will get to the remains in the next several hours? Because I'm thinking it will take that long for us to get some help up here to remove the body and process this scene."

"There have never been many reported animal sightings along this trail," Nora said. "At least not that I'm aware of." She swept an arm out to the side. "You can see for yourself that we're at one of the higher points in the park and fairly remote. Plus there's no intersecting trails. At least none that are open, so there isn't a lot of foot traffic back here." She shrugged. "Given all of that, I'd say the body has a slim chance of being eaten or mutilated by four-legged creatures or disturbed by two legged ones before we can get it out of here." She sighed and rubbed a hand across her forehead. "It doesn't sound like anything has gotten to it yet, and you think it's been lying out here for two days?"

"Yes." Ricki looked back at the trail. "Okay then, where's the nearest ranger station?"

Nora sighed and switched her hand from her forehead to run several fingers through her short brown hair. "Now that's a little harder. I think our best bet is to head over to the Ocanaluftee station. It's about thirty minutes west once we hit the Blue Ridge Parkway."

Ricki frowned. That was at least a forty-minute drive when the distance to the parkway itself was factored in. She walked over to her abandoned pack and opened the flap to one of the side pockets, drawing out a map of the park, which also showed the areas around the boundaries. She studied it for a moment, then walked back to Nora. "What's this?" She pointed to a place near the bottom of the map.

Nora bent her head to take a closer look. "That's a private campground on Cherokee land." She lifted her head and met Ricki's questioning gaze. "I've been there. It has an office that's usually staffed with at least one person. And it's close to where the road at the trailhead crosses the parkway."

"It's also outside of the park," Ricki said, waiting briefly for Nora's confirming nod. "Which means there will be cell towers and cell service." She looked over at Clay. "I need you to take Nora back to the SUV, and . . ."

Clay's hand shot out in a "stop right there" motion. "Hang on. I'm not leaving you up here alone."

Her frown deepened as she shook her head at him. "It won't be for long. Take Nora back to the SUV," she repeated. "And have Anchorman drive her to that campground." She returned her attention to Nora. "You call this in as soon as you have cell service, and have some rangers meet you at that campground. Once you have some help, bring them, and Anchorman, back here." She leaned forward until her nose was within an inch of Nora's. "Don't let Anchorman out of your sight. I don't want him up here alone with us, or to give someone any way to twist this all around and try to pin this murder on him." She paused and thought it over for a moment. "As a matter of fact, I don't want him back up at this campsite at all. He's to wait down at the trailhead."

"Okay." Nora barely breathed until Ricki stepped back, and then she froze again under Ricki's hard stare.

"He's never to be out of your sight, Nora," Ricki repeated.

The ranger nodded. "I heard you. I'll stick to him like glue."

Ricki took the car keys out of her pocket and tossed them to Clay. "Once you get Nora and Anchorman on their way, I'd appreciate it if you'd hike back in and keep me company."

Clay caught the keys in midair. "I still don't like it, but I'll double-time it there and back."

Ricki found her first smile since they'd stepped into Campsite 42. "I'm counting on it. And before I forget, you tell Trip and Herb to hightail it back to Pigeon Forge and keep their mouths shut. I don't want a word of this to get out. And we'll see them later tonight at the bar, just as soon as we're done here and can get back. You also tell them no excuses. I expect them to be at the bar when we walk in."

Clay grinned. "Now that will be my pleasure. Mind if I ask why?"

She looked back down the trail. "One of them knows something about why Stuart Landers got out of town and picked one of the more remote sites to camp. I'd like to hear the reason he did that, and my money is on Trip. I think Herb is the Beer Brotherhood's gossip, but it's Trip who Stu talked to."

"Wouldn't surprise me," Clay said as he pocketed the keys and waited for Nora to adjust her backpack. "Everyone talks to the bartender."

Ricki watched them walk off, keeping her gaze on Clay until his tall form disappeared into the trees. She continued to stand and listen, absorbing the sounds around her, becoming familiar with the natural rhythm and movement of the forest. It was a ritual her uncle had taught her—to feel her surroundings, not just see them. If something changed, she would know, even before the threat became visible. It was a practice that had saved her life on more than one occasion.

When she was satisfied she knew what to listen for, she crossed over to the small tent. There was a sleeping bag in the corner, still rolled up. And a backpack lying on its side near the front opening into the small space. Laying her rifle on the ground, she took out a pair of the latex gloves that she always carried with her and considered her options. Not wanting to walk on the tent floor, in case the killer had left any shoe prints inside, Ricki finally sank to her knees and rested her hands on her thighs.

Once she'd pulled on the gloves, she reached in and managed to get two fingers around one of the straps of the backpack. Struggling to lean forward without toppling onto her face, her arm muscles tightened into hard knots as she strained to lift the pack up and over the tent floor. Despite her precarious hold on the single strap, she managed to get the heavy bag out of the tent and into the sunlight.

As soon as she set it down next to her, she sat back on her heels, her knees digging into the ground. Concentrating on slowing her breathing, she listened for a moment. Hearing nothing out of place, she stood in one fluid motion, then lifted the backpack by the strap before bending over to pick up her rifle.

It only took a few moments to walk around the tent and duck down behind it, making her invisible to anyone coming up the trail. She wasn't expecting any company, at least not the two-legged variety, but there wasn't any point in advertising her presence either.

The flies were still buzzing around the body. It looked like a physical obscenity, completely at odds with such a beautiful setting. Stu Landers had met a bad end, but there wasn't a damn thing she could do about it, so she shut out the sight of the single eye that appeared to be staring right at her, along with the ugly image of busy insects covering him, and turned her attention to the backpack.

Ricki carefully picked through it, gently moving items aside to reveal the ones underneath them. In the main compartments, she found nothing but the usual gear and meal packs someone would take on a camping trip. She counted the packs, then continued with her search.

She'd gone through all the side pockets and was about to stop looking through the pack in favor of quartering the area, when her fingertips brushed over something at the very bottom of a deep pocket. Carefully drawing it out, she held a small, dog-eared notebook up to the light. It had a yellow cardboard cover on the front and rectangles of lined paper inside—all held together by a spiraled piece of wire. The same kind of notebook that occupied the office supply shelves in any retail store, and was made to fit into a shirt pocket.

Opening it, Ricki carefully flipped through the pages. Most of them were covered with phone numbers, dates, and reminder notes written in some kind of shorthand that Landers had come up with. Nothing struck her as unusual until she came to the last page. At the top, Stu had written BEAR COUNTRY CLUB, followed by an exclamation point. Underneath it was a drawing of a hunting knife with a lightning bolt behind it, and both were encased in an upside-down triangle. Next to the odd picture were three question marks.

Ricki took a seat in the dirt, bending her legs at the knees and crossing them over each other while she studied the picture. She didn't know if there were any golf courses or country clubs in the area, and she sure didn't recognize that picture. It could mean something, or nothing at all. But it was the last entry Landers had made in his little notebook, and he'd thought it was important enough to bring along with him when he'd tried to make a run for it, out of Pigeon Forge.

She glanced over at the body and shook her head. "Should have kept going, Stu. Or better yet, planted yourself in the county lockup and told someone what you knew."

Shifting her gaze, she looked up to the treetops and then back down to the forest surrounding the campsite. There wasn't much she could do except wait. Wishing she had cell service so she could contact Dan, or do some poking around the Internet herself, she tucked the notebook into an inside pocket of her coat and zipped the opening shut. Deciding she'd find some other place to be invisible besides behind the tent with a dead body, she got to her feet.

Toting the backpack and her rifle, she returned the pack to its place inside the tent and was about to look around for a tree large enough to hide behind when she heard her name called out. Clay, giving her a warning that he was approaching the camp. She looked at her watch and smiled. He must have run a good part of the way, because barely an hour had passed since he and Nora had left to hike back to the road. She stood where she was, waving when he broke through the trees, his chest visibly heaving. She walked over to her backpack and took out a water bottle.

When he plopped down on the nearest log around the firepit, she crossed over and handed him the water. He took it with a grateful nod and downed half its contents in one continuous gulp. Lowering the bottle, he wiped a hand across the sweat on his brow while his gaze swept the immediate area.

"Anything happen?"

Ricki looked around the quiet campsite, then smiled. "Besides you yelling like a banshee?" she teased. "Nope."

He took a deep breath and held it before letting it out slowly. "I didn't want to get shot." He sent a quick look toward the tent. "Did you go through Landers's pack?"

Since she was still wearing her gloves, Ricki unzipped her jacket and withdrew the small notebook. She opened it to the last page and held it out so Clay could see it without touching the paper.

He squinted at the page before looking up at her. "Do you recognize the name of that country club?" When she shook her head, his gaze returned to the notebook. "How about that symbol? Have you ever seen it before?"

She turned the notebook around so the page was facing her. "No. Doesn't ring any bells."

"Not for me either." With his breathing rapidly returning to normal, Clay stood and took off his own pack, setting it down next to Ricki's. "Nora said she was going to call for help as soon as Anchorman got them out of the park and within range of a cell tower." He glanced at his watch. "Which should be around now. She said to expect someone to be coming up that trail within two hours."

"Given how remote this campsite is, that's a pretty good response time," Ricki said before looking him over. His face had returned to its usual healthy color with a hint of tan, and he wasn't sucking in great gulps of air, which was a good thing. "I guess we can either do some work and quarter the area, or sit around and relax until the cavalry arrives."

"Are we going to stay on scene until the body is removed?" Clay asked. "Because that could take a while and we might want to let Anchorman go back to the hotel instead of hanging out in the SUV." He grinned. "I think his sister is still in town. It would give him a chance to spend more time with her."

Making a face at his bad joke, Ricki looked off into the distance. When her boot began to tap against the ground, Clay laughed.

"Okay. What are you thinking?" he demanded. "Something is going on in that complicated mind of yours."

"This new case we just stumbled across," she admitted.

"Or more specifically, who is going to be the lead on this case." Her boot stopped tapping, and she rocked back on her heels. "I need to give Hamilton a call. See what he can swing from his end."

"Do you think your boss can talk NCIS off the case?"

"Not the one involving Kelly. He was active military, so they have a solid claim to that one. But here?" She pointed at the tent. "NCIS doesn't investigate the murder of non-active personnel and Stu Landers was a vet. So, he wasn't in the active military." Warming up to her argument, she began to pace. "This is a murder, given the bullet holes in the guy's back. A murder that happened in a national park. Which makes it our jurisdiction and our case."

"Ah." Clay reached out and snagged her arm when she passed him. Putting his hands on her shoulders to hold her still, he smiled. "And there's no reason to mention that the two cases are related."

"They might be, but at the moment we can't swear to it," Ricki was quick to point out, not wanting to concede any point. "All we can say is we have a suspicion the two cases are connected, but we don't have any hard evidence."

Getting control of this case was essential. Not only because it needed to be solved to get justice for Landers and his family, but also to give her a more official way to keep tabs on what was going on in Kelly's murder investigation. If another NCIS agent did show up to take Agent Robard's place, then there was no guarantee he or she would be as cooperative as Trey. And besides that, everything she'd stated to Clay was true. Stu Landers was murdered in a national park. The case should belong to them.

She was distracted from her racing thoughts when Clay leaned down and gave her a quick kiss on the lips. "Now all Hamilton has to do is get you assigned to the case, since this isn't your district. But you're already here, and have some familiarity with the park itself, so it would be reasonable to have you lead this investigation."

"Exactly," Ricki declared. She wiggled out from beneath his hands and took two steps backwards to pick up her rifle. Cradling it in one arm, she grinned. "I can sell it. In the meantime, let's quarter the area and see what we can find."

Chapter 21

It was late afternoon when Ricki and Clay returned to the SUV, tired and hungry since they'd only had a couple of energy bars stowed away in their backpacks. They'd left a small gang of rangers and rescue workers up at the site to secure it, take photographs, and deal with the body.

They were met with an annoyed "what took you so long?" stare from a very bored Anchorman, as he helped them stow their rifles and gear. He loudly declared that he would be doing the driving before sliding behind the wheel. Ricki gladly gave up the front seat to Clay.

"Where to next? Or are we headed back to the hotel?" Anchorman asked.

"I am," Clay stated flatly. "So just point the SUV in that direction. I need a shower and some serious food."

"Me too," Ricki agreed. "And I need to make some calls. Let's get through the park at the speed limit." She leaned forward and tapped Anchorman on the shoulder. "Not over the speed limit. The last thing I want to do is have a conversation with another law enforcement ranger."

Anchorman met her gaze in the rearview mirror and grinned. "Getting tired of your own kind?"

Ricki rolled her shoulders and then leaned back against the seat. "No. Just tired, period. Too tired to explain why you're playing chauffeur, and we still have work to do. So we need to get out of the park."

"Who are you calling besides Hamilton?" Clay asked. "Trey? He should get an update." He frowned. "And probably Christopher Young, since there's a high probability that the two cases are linked."

"I'll leave Young for last," Ricki said. "It's Dan I'm wondering about. I haven't heard from him since yesterday, and he owes me the names of the registered owners of that black truck."

Clay turned completely around in his seat to look at her, the lines on his forehead deepening with a scowl. "He hasn't sent you the info on a simple run on a plate?"

"No, he hasn't." Ricki pursed her lips. And for Dan, that was just plain weird. "Which is why he'll be my first call."

The next two hours were spent crossing the park. In the back seat, Ricki dozed on and off while Clay did the same in the front. Anchorman kept the pace steady, but right at the speed limit since the traffic was light. It was almost sundown when they reached the northern end of the park and passed the Sugarlands Visitor Center. Several minutes later, they drove by the exit sign, signaling that they were on the last leg of the trip to Pigeon Forge. Ricki held her phone up, checking on the service bars, but it was Clay's phone that immediately rang.

"It's Jules," he said, reading off the name of his longest-serving deputy back in the Bay.

As urgent as her own calls were, Ricki lowered her phone, and both she and Anchorman brazenly eavesdropped as Clay greeted Jules, and then fell silent. He listened intently, adding an occasional "uh-huh," and with each one, Ricki scooted closer to the edge of her seat.

"Okay. Now, this doesn't sound like kids. I want you to

send me a list of the places that have been hit, and those photos you took. I should be back at the hotel in less than fifteen minutes. I'll pull everything up on my laptop as soon as I get there, and together we'll go over what you've found along with the photos. In the meantime, call over to the PDs in both Olympia and Tacoma. And maybe the one up in Port Jefferson, too. Find out if they've had any similar incidents." He listened for another minute before saying a terse goodbye. Dropping his phone into the opening in the center console, he draped an arm over the back of the seat and looked at Ricki. "There have been four break-ins in the last three days, and this morning, Christie was robbed at gunpoint in her shop."

Ricki's eyes flew open as she teetered on the edge of the seat. Christie owned a small clothing shop a block away from the Sunny Side Up. "Is she all right?"

"Shaken up but fine." Clay's expression was grim as he glanced at Anchorman. "They also broke into your truck that you left parked behind your apartment. At least Jules is assuming it's the same perpetrators."

"Perpetrators? As in plural?" Ricki's mouth thinned to a straight line. "How many does Jules think there are?"

"At least two, but he has a witness that swears he saw four men looking into the windows of a house that was also robbed. He called the station, but by the time the deputies arrived, the burglars had disappeared."

"Wonderful." Ricki shifted enough to look at Anchorman in the mirror. "Christie's place is close to the Sunny Side Up, and I don't like that Marcie and Sam are there, closing up by themselves at night."

Anchorman scowled out the front windshield as the SUV shot forward, blowing right past the speed limit. "Maybe you should go home. Both of you." When Ricki and Clay shook their heads, he ignored them. "I've got that fancy lawyer, not to mention the truth is on my side here. Not to mention that I sure as hell didn't kill that Landers fellow. And this time I have a great alibi to back that up since I was either surrounded by agents and a cop, or was in the county jail."

"We're not going home," Ricki stated firmly before giving Clay a questioning look. "Or at least I'm not. Anchorman might have a point about you flying back, though. The Bay is your responsibility, and you should be putting that first."

"Amen," Anchorman said.

"Not jumping to any decisions here until I read the report, see those photos, and have a three-way call with my two deputies." Clay ran a hand down the side of his face. "And talk to the mayor," he added reluctantly. "He could order me back, which wouldn't give me much choice in the matter." He blew out a long breath. "But assuming that doesn't happen, I have an idea of what you can do at the Sunny Side Up to keep it from becoming a target."

He was interrupted by the staccato ring of Ricki's phone. She almost declined the call until she saw the name that had popped up on the screen. "It's Dan," she said quietly.

"Take the call," Clay told her. "Anchorman and I will go over my idea while you talk to Dan and find out what the holdup is on that license plate."

Going along with Clay's suggestion, Ricki connected the call. "Hey, Dan. Have you got the names attached to that plate number for me?"

"No names, but there's a reason for that. Also, Hamilton is on his way to a meeting with his boss in San Francisco, but he gave me a message to pass along to you, and he wants that done ASAP."

Shifting the phone to her other ear, Ricki sat back against the seat. "Okay. What's the message?"

"Hamilton got a call today about another murder there in the Great Smoky Mountains park. The senior agent in charge of that district of the ISB told Hamilton that they're spread thin, so he requested that you be assigned to that case. Since you're already on scene. Hamilton agreed with the request."

He paused, letting out a soft chuckle. "And that's when your boss was told that you're the one who found the body? He wanted me to confirm that."

If it weren't for the bad news coming from the Bay, Ricki would have laughed. At least being assigned to the Landers case was one thing off her to-do list. And the fact that it hadn't required any arguing on her part was simply icing on the cake. "Yeah. That's right," she said in answer to his question. "I was just getting ready to call him about it. I was up there most of the afternoon helping on scene, which was on the opposite side of the park from our hotel. And that meant a two-hour drive home before we got any cell service again."

"No bars at all in the park?"

"No towers, no bars," she replied. "I'll send Hamilton a quick text, letting him know I'm already working the case."

"And you'll send in a report on it tonight," Dan prompted. "He wasn't happy about being blindsided by the news that not only was there another murder, but it was his agent who discovered the body."

Knowing she'd been up at the crack of dawn, and now was looking at a late night to boot, Ricki's tone strayed into annoyance. "How about that license plate?"

"Yeah. That plate. You're sure about the numbers?"

"Got them right off the security tape of a hospital. Why?"

"Well," Dan said, dragging the word out. "Then this is a new one on me, because as far as the great state of Pennsylvania is concerned, that plate doesn't exist."

"What?" Ricki was stunned. It was a new one on her, too. "The plate on the truck was fake?"

Dan's voice held a note of apology. "Right down to the renewal tags, if those were on display, too. Ricki, I swear to you, I tried every combination I could come up with, in case the plate had been altered. But there wasn't a black truck registered to any of them. I'd sure like to see that security footage from the hospital, because all I can tell you right now is that the number you gave me simply doesn't exist."

"Which means I'm no closer to finding those shooters than I was two days ago." She looked up and found Clay staring at her over the back of the seat. She lifted her shoulders in a helpless shrug as she turned this latest stumbling block over in her mind. "I need an alternate source for security footage, or some kind of video showing a clear view of those guys' faces." They had just reached the outskirts of Pigeon Forge when she looked out the front windshield and sat straight up in her seat. "I'll call you back," she told Dan before abruptly hanging up on him. She reached over and tapped Anchorman on the shoulder. "See that neon sign up ahead?"

"The Wooden Nick?" he asked.

"Yeah. Let me off there. Trip is the bartender, and I need to have a talk with him. You and Clay go back to the hotel and pick me up later." She glanced at Clay. "After you find out what's going on in the Bay."

Anchorman slowed as the entrance to the parking lot loomed ahead. "How about you and I get dropped off at that bar, and Clay takes the SUV to the hotel, sees to his business, and then comes and picks up both of us?"

Clay nodded his approval. "I vote for that plan."

"Fine." Ricki gave him a light poke in the arm. "As long as you can take care of your business, I'm good with that plan. Also, I get to grill Trip." She watched them as they drew closer to the turn-in for the parking lot. "He knows something about Landers's murder, and he's going to tell me if I have to stay in his face all night."

Anchorman made the turn into the crowded parking lot and double-parked behind the cars next to the curb at the entrance. He and Ricki hopped out and waited while Clay came around the front of the car and got behind the wheel.

"Keep your phones on," he told them. "I'll text when I'm on the way to pick you up."

As Clay put the SUV into gear and maneuvered his way back to the street, Ricki and Anchorman headed for the front door of The Wooden Nickel. It was just as dim inside as it had been the previous time she'd walked into the place. Ricki pointed toward the same table that she and Clay had occupied before, and which, by some miracle, was empty while all the rest of the tables in the place were taken. "Grab that one, and order burgers for us while I have a word with Trip."

"Come on. I'll walk you over." Sondra sauntered up, holding a tray in one hand. "Trip told me you'd be stopping by, so I put a reserved sign on it."

Ricki smiled her thanks before strolling over to the bar. She stood with her foot hooked on the lower rung of one of the stools while she waited for Trip to make his way down to her end. The big man finished pouring a beer, and once he'd handed it to the customer warming another barstool, he made his way over to Ricki.

"Agent James." He ducked his head in a quick greeting, then stood, wringing his hands.

"We need to have a talk, Trip."

The bartender shot a look over her shoulder. She didn't need to turn around to know that Herb was sitting at the closest table. She'd spotted him the second they'd walked into the bar. And right now she'd bet that he was trying to send the bartender all kinds of messages behind her back.

"I need to figure out who'll tend the bar while I'm sitting down with you."

"Okay. I'll be waiting right there for you to join me." She pointed at the tap that dispensed beer. "And I'll take two of those along with me."

While Trip held a thick mug underneath the tap, Ricki quickly spun around and raised an eyebrow at Herb. The elderly man immediately looked down at the plate of food in front of him and squirmed in his chair. Satisfied that Herb would stay put while she talked to Trip, Ricki picked up the two mugs of beer and joined Anchorman at the table.

Setting one mug in front of him, she took a seat and lifted her own beer for a long sip. It tasted like heaven and hit her empty stomach with a stronger impact than usual. What she needed was some food.

"I hope you ordered the burgers?" When Anchorman nodded, Ricki settled more comfortably in her chair.

Since it looked like Trip intended to take his own sweet time before leaving the safety of his bar, Ricki took out her phone and smiled at the indicator that appeared at the top. Service. And strong enough to do an Internet search. She typed in Bear Country Club, Pigeon Forge, Tennessee, and a close match popped onto the screen. She stared at it, then put her phone on the table, screen-side down.

"Did Kelly like to go to shooting ranges?"

Anchorman paused with his mug in midair. "Yeah. He liked to beat the local scores. He got a kick out of it. Why?"

She flipped her phone over and used a single finger to slide it across the table. "How about the Bear Country Rod & Gun Club? Did he ever mention that one?"

The former Marine shrugged. "He might have."

Ricki grinned. "I'm betting he did. And that he used to go there with his fellow vet, Stu Landers."

"Sounds right. Landers was pursuing Kelly hard. Like I told you before, he wanted to invest in the Airbnb scheme." Anchorman paused to take a sip of his beer. "Kelly said the guy wanted to diversify his income streams, or something like that."

"What other kind of income streams did he have?" she asked absently as she watched several customers gather up their jackets and head for the door, along with a good deal of slaps on the back and a few friendly arm punches. They'd barely exited the room when another group of men stepped inside.

"Kelly said he had some kind of framing business, so he worked mostly on construction jobs. But with all the forest fires that have been happening the last few summers, milled wood has gotten a lot harder to come by, and so expensive Kelly said it was tough for Landers to make a profit." Anchorman gave Sondra a big smile when she came up to the table and set a plate with a big, juicy hamburger and a mound of fries in the space in front of him.

Ricki watched him dig into the fries as Sondra set the second plate she was carrying in front of Ricki. The aroma wafting upward from the plate had her mouthwatering in anticipation. "So that's why he wanted to diversify his income?" She took a big bite of her burger while she looked expectantly across at Anchorman.

"What? Oh, yeah." He nodded as he lifted his burger off its plate. "The price of wood got to be a problem. Yeah. I think Kelly wanted to help him out, but he wasn't any more interested in taking on a partner in his business than Kelly was for his Airbnb."

She nodded. "I remember you saying something along those lines."

"Agent James?"

When Ricki looked up at the sound of her name, Trip was standing by the table, still wearing his bar apron. She pointed to the empty chair and smiled. "Have a seat, Trip."

He carefully lowered his large frame onto the wooden chair, then sat with his back stiff and his hands holding on to the edges of the seat. After several tries, he managed to look Ricki in the eye.

"I'm not a hero, Agent James."

When he took a sideways glance at Anchorman, the former Marine cocked his head to the side and smiled. "No one sets out to be a hero, Trip. You just do what you think needs to be done, and sometimes other people slap that label on it, and sometimes they don't. It depends on the mood they're in, I guess."

Trip blinked and then his shoulders relaxed. Letting go of his chair seat, he folded his hands and rested them on the table. "People tell a bartender things, and if you want them to keep coming back and buying your beer, then you keep your mouth shut about whatever you've heard." His shoulders lifted in a quick shrug. "That's the job."

Ricki considered him for a moment. "I can understand that, Trip. But sometimes you can't keep silent. Especially if people are going to get hurt." When his gaze dropped to his hands, Ricki softened her voice. "Or did get hurt. Stu Landers made his own decision to go out on his own rather than go to the police, and he paid a heavy price for that. But it also means that whoever killed him is still walking around, free to hurt someone else. I think Stu would want you to help keep that from happening."

Trip raised his head, and his mouth quirked up into a wry smile. "Yeah. That's what Herb said." He let out a heavy sigh. "Stu was afraid. He came in the day we heard about Kelly and said he had to get out of town for a while. That his gear was all packed up, and he was headed out to a campsite in the park, and that he might be gone for a week. Maybe more." Trip only hesitated a second, and his voice grew steadier. "He said he needed the time to think, and he gave me that look. The one that says he wants you to ask him about it. So I did. I asked him what he needed to think about for a whole week. And he said Kelly told him he thought two guys had been following him around for a couple of days. He even pointed them out to Stu. You know, without being really obvious about it, so those guys wouldn't know Kelly was watching them too. They were shooting at the station at the end of the row, and when Stu and Kelly left, they did too." Trip took another deep breath and then went silent.

"You said they were at a station?" Ricki quickly asked, wanting to keep Trip talking. "Were they at a shooting range?"

The bartender nodded. "Oh yeah. I'm not sure which one. There were a couple that Stu liked to go."

"And did Stu say anything about what happened after he and Kelly checked out of the shooting range?"

"Yeah." Trip added a slow nod. "He said Kelly left and pretended to go to the john, but instead he walked past this black truck with a big decal on the passenger side of the windshield. Kelly memorized the license plate and told Stu he was going to have it checked out." The big man shrugged. "I don't know if he did or not, because the next day he let to go camping and I didn't see him again." Trip glanced at Anchorman. "I guess Kelly went camping with you. And then we heard he'd been killed." He shifted in his seat as he gave Ricki a pleading look. "I don't know if that meeting at the gun range had anything to do with all of this, and I couldn't say so one way or another if I was questioned by a hundred cops. But I would swear on a stack of Bibles that Stu was afraid that last time he came in and said he had to get out of town. And I think it was about those two men Kelly said were following him."

Chapter 22

RICKI DIDN'T SAY anything as Trip pushed himself to his feet and retreated to the bar. She started to ask Anchorman what he thought, but the words caught in her throat. His expression was completely blank, and not a muscle moved as the former Marine stared at Trip's back. Even his chest didn't rise and fall, as if he was holding his breath.

Regretting that she hadn't insisted he go back to the hotel with Clay, Ricki reached out and laid a hand over the one he had resting on the table. "Anchorman, are you all right?"

Whatever thought or memory had him in its grip, her voice seemed to break the hold. He blinked and then slowly turned his head to look at her.

"He never said a word. Kelly didn't tell me anything about being followed." His voice had started out confused but ended up angry. His eyes narrowed to slits, and his jawline went rock hard. "Why would he do that? Why didn't he say anything? We told each other everything that was going on in our lives." He stabbed his index finger against the wooden table. "He knew about you and Eddie, Clay, Marcie, and everyone else at the diner. I even told him the latest gossip making the rounds in the Bay. It made him laugh. And I heard about Sondra and her couch-potato son that he liked more than he let on. And the missions." Anchorman stomped a heavy boot on the ground, drawing several pairs of eyes from the tables closest to them. "What was going on in his unit. Stuff he shouldn't have been telling me, but he did anyway." Anchorman paused to jab his finger into the air in front of Ricki's nose. "He damn well knew he could trust me. So why not this? Why didn't he tell me this? It cost the little shit his life."

Ricki didn't interrupt or try to calm him down. From the corner of her eye, she saw Sondra's wide eyes staring over the hand that was covering her mouth. If the woman was frightened, she'd get over it. And if the fierce expression on Anchorman's face was scaring anyone else in the bar, that was just too bad. He needed to get it out, had needed to for days. Picking up her beer, she took a long sip, not flinching at all when Anchorman's boot hit the ground again.

"Do you think we wouldn't have had our guard up on that trip if I had known?" He glared at Ricki, who dutifully shook her head. "Do you think we would have been drinking that booze if there might have been a threat waiting somewhere out there? Do you think . . .?" He sputtered to a halt and simply stared at her. And for the first time since she'd met him, there was a helpless look in his eyes.

She couldn't stop the tears glistening in her own eyes, or the hoarse scratch in her throat. But she could put the right intensity into the words he needed to hear. "I think you feel like you failed to protect his back, and guilty because that was always your job."

A bolt of anger flew from Anchorman's eyes. He beamed it at her for a long moment before it disappeared, as if a light switch had suddenly shut it off. He kept a dull gaze on her as he slowly leaned back in his chair.

"It was my job," he said in a low, flat voice. "It was always my job."

Ricki shook her head. "The guilt you're feeling isn't yours

to carry. Any more than it would be if Kelly had died in a traffic accident because of faulty brakes. You can't fix something, or stop something, you don't know about." When he looked away, she gave his hand a gentle squeeze. "Kelly messed up this time. Not you. He should have told you." She leaned back, waiting until he looked at her again. "But I can understand why he didn't."

He scowled and picked up his beer. "You mean why he didn't trust me enough to let me know what was going on?"

"I mean why he valued your friendship and the time he spent with you so much, he didn't want to give it up for nothing."

"What do you mean for nothing? Getting killed like that was for nothing."

"What I mean is," Ricki said, holding on to her patience as he continued to spit and snarl. "He knew exactly what you would have done if he had told you. You would have gone hunting for them, all over the county and the surrounding states, if that's what it took."

"Damn straight."

"And it might have taken that, because Kelly didn't know where to look for them," she continued. "He had a bogus license plate from their truck and wouldn't have had any more luck tracking it down than Dan did. So why shouldn't he enjoy the camping trip the two of you had been planning for months? There was no reason to think those guys would follow you into the park. Or even know exactly what campsite you were going to."

Some of the anger drained from Anchorman's eyes. "Kelly never tells anyone our exact routes, and only a few people ever know his destination. I do the same." He sighed and scrubbed a hand down the side of his face. "Habit."

When he met her gaze, she was relieved to see his was clear again. The storm had been rough, and it might hit him again in the coming weeks and months, but it had passed for the moment. She watched, half in amusement, as he lifted his beer mug and drained it, setting it back on the table with a solid thump.

"I need some air." He stood up, reached into the pocket of his jeans, and threw three twenty-dollar bills onto the table. More than double what their tab was for the burgers and beer. He looked around, and ignoring the stealthy glances from all around the room, he nodded at Sondra. "Sorry for the noise."

Ricki gave a mournful look at her half-full mug and barely eaten burger and sighed, but she got to her feet and followed him out the door. Anchorman stood on the edge of the narrow porch, his hands jammed into the back pockets of his jeans, staring up at a night sky lit with stars.

"This is a nice place, but Kelly would want to go home. I told his mama I would call her and let her know when she can make arrangements to bury her son." He scuffed a boot against the worn and stained boards of the porch floor. "Would you call the county medical examiner and ask when they'll be releasing his body?"

She moved to stand beside him to also look out into the night. "I can do that."

He removed his hands from his pockets and draped one arm around her shoulders. "It's a good place. But as soon as we catch the bastards who shot Kelly in the back, we're going home." His voice dropped a notch as he gave her shoulders a brotherly squeeze. "And thanks. I owe you."

For the first time in an hour, Ricki smiled. "Well, that's good to know." She gave him a quick jab in the side with her elbow. "In that case, why don't you give me the names of all the people you did tell about this camping trip, even if you left out any specific information about it?"

He dropped his arm and shook his head. "Back in the Bay? Who didn't I tell I was going camping would make a shorter list."

"Okay. Who did you tell that doesn't live in the Bay?"

"What makes the difference? They shot Kelly, not me. And they could have, given the condition I was in. But it was Kelly they were after."

Ricki frowned. That was right. They were obviously after Kelly, but why not shoot them both? Especially since they tried to finish off the job a couple of days later? She set aside an idea that popped into her mind, more to let it brew than dismiss it, and got back to her question. "So humor me. After all, you do owe me one, remember?"

Anchorman made a grumpy sound in the back of his throat. "Fine. Um. We were going to hop up to New Jersey and stay a few days with my Aunt Sally, so she knew about the trip and when we'd be showing up at her place. I also talked to a buddy who retired to Colorado, and another one in Chicago, and mentioned it to them. Then there was Twister. He's on leave and hanging around Camp Lejeune. He's got a girlfriend down there. He's been with her off and on since basic."

"How far is Camp Lejeune from here?" Ricki asked.

Anchorman shrugged. "I don't know. I never drove it." He scratched his head. "I made the trip to Charlotte once during basic training. It was about a four-hour drive, I think."

And another couple of hours from Charlotte to here, Ricki said to herself. "What about Finn?" The outspoken FBI agent who'd tagged along on several of her cases had formed enough of a friendship with Clay and Anchorman for them to keep in touch.

"Talked to him a couple of months ago, and I might have mentioned it," Anchorman said. "That's about it." He frowned. "I'm surprised he hasn't called. I'm sure this whole mess made the rounds at Quantico."

"It has, and I called him," Ricki said. "He's on a joint task force with Border Patrol. They're tracking a major drug shipment coming up from Central America and heading this way.

He was going to try to get cut loose but didn't think he'd be able to."

The big Marine frowned. "I don't want him to stop what he's doing to hightail it back here. We have it under control."

I wish, Ricki thought. "What about Dina?" she asked, getting back to who Anchorman had told about the camping trip. "After all, she is your sister. Maybe you mentioned the trip to her?"

He snorted a laugh. "Maybe if I would have if I ever talked to her. But I don't. And we're both happier living on opposite sides of the country."

"Well, she's here now, trying to support you in her own way." At the sour look on his face, Ricki gave up on the subject of his sister. Instead, she pulled out the latex gloves still stuck in her back pocket and snapped them into place. Once her hands were covered, she reached inside her parka and retrieved the small notebook that she'd found in Landers's backpack. Flipping to the last page, she held it up in front of Anchorman at eye level.

"Don't touch this, but take a look. Have you ever seen that symbol before?"

Anchorman leaned forward to get a closer look, then shook his head. "Nope. What is it?"

"Remember Trip saying that Landers told him the black truck had a decal of some kind on the passenger side of the windshield? I think he drew a picture of it, right next to the name of the firing range where he and Kelly spotted the owners of that black truck." The night air had cooled down enough to make her shiver. A stark reminder from mother nature that it was early spring in the mountains, not summer. She looked down the road. In the distance, she could see the lit-up sign of their hotel. "It's about a twenty-minute walk back to our rooms. Rather than interrupt Clay, what do you say we hoof it?"

"Sounds good. That should clear the last of the cobwebs

out of my brain." He fell into step beside her, moving to the side closest to the road.

She smiled but didn't comment on it. Despite his rough exterior, Anchorman was always a gentleman. Wishing she could have met his parents, Ricki refocused her attention on the case. "At least we have a couple of leads to work on to track our shooters down."

Anchorman raised a skeptical eyebrow. "Like what? The license plate was a bust, so now all we have is a black truck with tinted windows."

"And the name of a gun range where we know they were, and some kind of logo that might have been on their truck." When he didn't look impressed, Ricki grinned. "Do you know what gun ranges usually have?"

"Targets? Protective glasses?" he guessed.

"Uh-huh. And security cameras."

Anchorman stopped, a grin spreading across his face. "That's right. Maybe we can get a picture of those bastards."

Since "those bastards" had been very good at avoiding looking into any camera at the hospital, it would be no surprise if they had known exactly where the cameras were at the shooting range. While the odds were against them finding any clear shot of their faces, they might get height and build, and that would be a start.

The two of them walked along, making good time. They entered the lobby and went straight toward the elevators, only to be cornered by Dina, who popped up from a wingback chair and took a quick hop to the side to block their path.

"We've been waiting here all day, and now half the night too," she said, her voice bordering on a whine. "Where have you been?"

Anchorman nodded at Fitz, who was standing off to the side, before giving Dina a bored look. "Finding dead bodies and having a beer. How did you spend your day? Shopping?"

"Here?" Her upper lip curled in disgust. "I'm sure there's

nothing here we need. I was hoping we could have dinner together?"

Her brother lifted broad shoulders into a shrug. "I already ate, thanks. But if you're hungry, there's a place down the street that serves a decent burger."

She gritted her teeth. "Then how about a drink? There's something we need to tell you."

"I had a beer with my dinner." Anchorman turned his head and glared at Ricki when she stepped hard on his foot with the heel of her boot. Giving in to the reprimand in her gaze, he drummed up a smile. "Look, Dina. There's a problem back in the Bay that Clay's having to deal with, and he might need our help."

His sister didn't look at all pleased as she waved a hand in Ricki's direction. "Well, she's the secret agent, or whatever, so that's her job. But you're a cook in a diner. Why do you have to help?"

"Because I live in the Bay. It's my home," Anchorman stated. "So, if you have something to tell me, go ahead. Otherwise, I'm going upstairs."

"First it was the Marines, now it's your job." She added a poke in the chest with her manicured finger to the accusation in her voice. "But it's never your family."

"They are my family. And so was Kelly. That's why I'm here. If that's all you wanted to say, then I've heard your complaint, and now I have to go." He pushed past her and headed for the bank of two elevators.

"We need to go home tomorrow."

Dina's bald statement had Anchorman turning back around. "Is there anything wrong?"

Looking satisfied that she'd finally gotten his attention, Dina slowly nodded, while behind her, Fitz shook his head.

"It's something to do with the day-to-day business. It's more of a one-off kind of emergency," Dina declared.

"Not an emergency," Fitz countered. When his wife glared

at him, he stood his ground. "I handle the business, and you don't. So I'd be the one to know what's an emergency and what isn't." He looked away from her, meeting his brother-in-law's grin. "But it does need to be taken care of in person, I'm afraid."

Trying not to look annoyed, and not quite pulling it off, Dina walked over to her brother, rose on her toes, and placed a quick peck on his cheek, then looked over at Ricki. "I know Norman will never call me to tell me the outcome of the trial. But I'm sure I can count on you to do so."

Not bothering to mention that the trial, if it came to that, was probably months, if not a year away, Ricki pasted a smile on her face and nodded. "Of course."

"Wonderful." Dina took several steps back until she was standing next to her husband. She stared at her brother, looking like she had something else she wanted to say. But after ten seconds of silence had passed between them, she sighed. "Let's go find a decent place to get something to eat." With barely a glance at her husband, she scooped up her coat from the back of the chair she'd draped it over, and briskly walked across the lobby and out the door. Fitz gave his brother-in-law and Ricki an apologetic smile before trailing after his wife.

"One less thing to worry about," Anchorman muttered under his breath.

Deciding he'd have to deal with his own messy family issues, Ricki covered the short distance to the elevator in three long strides and pushed the button.

Chapter 23

"NEXT TIME *you* can go back to the hotel and have a deli sandwich, and *I'll* get a burger at the local bar."

Ricki smiled. "Okay. But I don't think I could have solved the crime spree in the Bay in less than eight hours." She buckled her seatbelt as Clay put the SUV into gear.

The morning was clear, and the bright sunshine had already chased away any lingering night chill. Ricki's jacket was already off and folded up next to her on the front seat. They were once again taking the forty-five-minute drive to Knoxville, this time to keep an appointment with the Packers. She wanted to hear for herself their story about the supposed argument between Anchorman and Kelly.

Anchorman was in his spot in the rear passenger seat, his arms folded over his chest. "So what happened back in the Bay? Was it kids after all?"

Clay made a scoffing noise. "Do you think it was some local kids that robbed Christie at gunpoint?"

"Probably not," Anchorman conceded. "So, some guys who drove up from Olympia or something?"

"More or less." Clay settled back as they cruised along the highway at a steady speed. "But the pictures the deputies took of the crime scene screamed that it was an amateur job, and done by more than one guy. And then Jules sent along the security footage from Christie's shop. That was a one-man job, but when the robber walked away, he had a distinct hitch in his step. I'd seen that particular limp before, on a fisherman who occasionally parks his RV up at Quinlan. I've watched him walking around the bait shops up there, and once we had a short chat and I asked him about it, and then asked around about him. I was told that he shows up every few months, stays a couple of weeks, and then heads somewhere else. It seems this trip to the Bay, he brought some of his buddies. Jules and Ryan picked them all up last night, with some backup from the county sheriff." Clay grinned. "Jules said that they hadn't been in custody for more than ten minutes when the other guys were claiming the RV owner did the robbery at gunpoint on his own. Which means Mr. RV is going to be spending a few years in a state prison."

"Why were you asking around about Mr. RV in the first place?" Anchorman asked.

Clay shrugged. "He set my radar off. That's all."

Ricki smiled. Some instincts you were born with, and some were learned. Either way, Clay was meant to be a cop. The role suited him perfectly.

Anchorman cracked a laugh. "So, you have no blind spot, huh?"

"Everyone has a blind spot," Clay maintained. "It's knowing what it is that can be the hard part, because ignoring it can be hazardous to your health."

The former Marine grunted his agreement. "True enough. Out in the field, that kind of thing will get you killed."

As the two went off into a discussion on military tactics versus police actions, Ricki let their voices flow around her as she reread the report Trey had sent on the ranger's initial interview with Marvin and Susan Packer. There were some glaring blanks in their account that needed to be questioned, and she began to mentally line up her approach to the couple. But their first stop was going to be the hospital. Ricki looked up from her phone when Clay pulled up to the entrance.

"I don't see why I can't come along," Anchorman complained. "I have a right to confront my accuser, don't I?"

Ricki turned around in her seat with an exasperated sigh. "First off, they haven't accused you of anything. The federal government, along with the state of Tennessee, did that. All the Packers did was report an argument between two people that someone along the chain assumed were you and Kelly. And the last thing we need is for you to show up and the prosecution claim that you scared them into changing their stories."

He looked offended as he stared back at her. "I don't scare old people."

"That you're aware of," Ricki said before she made a shooing motion with her hand. "Now get out of the car. Your attorney is going to meet you in the lobby so you can wait for him there."

When Anchorman climbed out of the car, shutting the door hard behind him, Clay rolled down his window. "And stay out of trouble."

Anchorman didn't bother to look around but stuck his hands in his jacket pockets and strode away at a rapid clip.

"I think he's a little put off," Ricki commented with a straight face. A moment later, she broke out into a laugh. Clay chuckled as he steered the SUV back to the street and toward the Packers' residence. He had already put their address into the GPS on his phone and followed the directions leading to Oakwood, a small residential enclave three miles from downtown Knoxville.

The house proved to be a mixture of the old South and the Midwest, with a large, covered porch and a windowed dormer on the roof. They were approaching the three steps that led up to the porch when the front door swung open and a short woman with gray hair and a sunny smile stood in the entrance, waving at them.

"Y'all must be that special agent and her team." Her smile grew even wider. "I can't tell you how thrilled I was to hear those nice rangers were sending a female FBI agent."

Ricki gave a mental sigh even as she smiled back at the woman. "I'm Special Agent Ricki James, with the Investigative Services Branch of the National Park Service."

"Oh." Susan Packer looked disappointed. "I thought that nice man on the phone said you were from the FBI. Do you investigate murders too?"

"Yes, I do," Ricki said, keeping her expression solemn. "And this is Police Chief Clay Thomas, from Washington. He also investigates homicides."

Susan perked right up. A slight blush tinged her cheeks as she stared at Clay. "My. This is just like something you'd see on TV, isn't it? A sinfully handsome police chief and his faithful female partner?" She rubbed her hands together as she stepped to one side, holding the front door open. "Please do come in." She half turned her head and yelled for her husband. "Marvin? They're here."

There wasn't any kind of front foyer, so Ricki stepped right into the living room. The decor had a more modern look to it than she'd expected, given the quainter appearance of the outside of the house. A leather sofa and matching dual recliners were clustered around a brick fireplace. In the space beyond them was a mid-sized dining room table with a china cabinet crammed full of a mishmash of plates, wine glasses, and vases.

A tall man walked through the open door that led into the kitchen, a dishtowel over one shoulder. Mr. Packer was a good half foot taller than his petite wife, with a thin build and a thick head of hair that had gone pure white.

His smile was friendly as he walked forward and draped an arm around his wife's shoulders.

She tilted her head back and smiled up at him. "This is Special Agent Ricki James. She works for the National Park Service, not the FBI. And that nice-looking gentleman is Police Chief Clay Thomas. He's here all the way from the state of Washington." She frowned as she glanced back at Clay. "Or was that Washington, DC?"

"No, ma'am," Clay said. "We're both from the state, not the capitol."

Marvin stepped forward and shook their hands, then pointed toward the brown leather sofa. "Have a seat." He helped his wife into one of the recliners, and then sat on the edge of the second one, his forearms resting on his upper thighs while he studied Ricki. "You're a long way from home. I heard you tell my wife that you both investigate homicides. Have we run out of murder cops here in Tennessee?"

Ricki smiled. "No, sir. I'm sure you have quite a few right here in Knoxville. But I investigate murders that happen in the national parks, and Chief Thomas is part of my team."

"Oh?" Marvin settled himself more comfortably in his chair. "You partner up with police departments? So you don't work with the FBI?"

"Not unless we have to." While both Packers laughed, Ricki took out her phone. "Is it all right if I record our talk?"

The couple both stared at the phone Ricki was holding up, then slowly nodded together.

"That's fine," Marvin said. "That will keep everybody honest, won't it?"

She set the phone down on the small coffee table in front of her. "Yes, sir, it will." She recited the date and time, and where the recording was taking place, then asked the couple to each state their name. Once that was taken care of, she looked at Susan. "Can you tell me why you were at the park five days ago?"

"Oh dear." She sent a helpless look toward her husband. "Is that when we were there? I don't remember exactly when it was."

He reached over and gave her hand a gentle pat. "Agent James is right, dear. That's the day we broke camp at site twenty-four and headed for Jakes Creek Trail." He glanced at Ricki. "We had reservations to spend two nights there, and then we were heading home."

Ricki blinked. "So you weren't at the campsite the night of the murder?"

"Oh no." Susan wagged a finger back and forth. "We most certainly were not. I don't know if anyone was camped at twenty-four that night, but we certainly weren't."

So Anchorman was right. They were breaking camp, which explained why the couple didn't report seeing or hearing anything the night Kelly was murdered. Ricki moved on to what they had witnessed before they'd left the site. "You told the rangers that you had heard an argument between two men?"

"Yes, we did." Marvin's voice was firm, as if he expected some pushback from Ricki. When she gave him an encouraging smile, he relaxed into his chair. "It was the day before the body was found. And believe me, when it was, the news spread all over the park like wildfire. As soon as we heard, we remembered the argument between those two men. So we broke camp that very same day and went right to the ranger station, where we had a talk with Ranger Johnson."

Susan nodded. "Such a nice man," she put in. "Took our statement and said someone might be in touch later on." She smiled at Ricki and then at Clay. "And here you are."

Crossing one ankle over the other, Ricki returned the smile. "Yes, and we appreciate you talking with us. Now, what did you hear that day?"

"Well," Susan began. "Like Marvin said, we were at twenty-four, enjoying a last cup of coffee before we had to break camp and move over to site twenty-seven on Jakes Creek. We heard the argument before we saw the two men come up the trail." She looked at her husband. "Or at least I did."

"Me too," Marvin volunteered. "One minute it was all peace and quiet, the next we heard these voices practically shouting at each other. When they finally came into sight, they were still arguing, and kept it up until we couldn't see them anymore."

"And what happened when you couldn't see them anymore?" Clay asked, making Susan's face flush red as she stared at him in confusion. "Did their voices fade away or just stop?"

Marvin lifted a hand and stroked his chin. "Now that you mention it, they just stopped. I guess they were through arguing."

"What direction did they come from, and where did it look like they were headed?"

The older man chuckled. "Only one way to come and go on that trail, Agent James. Those two came from the north and headed south down the trail. There isn't anything else down there except Campsite 30."

"What did they look like?" Ricki asked. Her heart sank a little when Marvin shrugged.

"Ranger Johnson asked us the same thing, but we couldn't really say. We were relaxing at the time, and neither one of us had our glasses on. All I can say is they had on heavy jackets, and both of them had their hoods up, so I didn't get a look at their faces. Not that I was trying very hard. It's not a good idea to draw the attention of anyone who is already angry."

"I only got a glimpse of them," Susan admitted. "I didn't want to make any eye contact, so I stared at the ground until they'd passed by."

Ricki frowned. It would be useless to ask if they talked to the two men, since both Packers apparently had done their best to avoid them. "Did you hear them say anything specific? Maybe what they were arguing about?"

"Guns, I think," Marvin said slowly. "I heard the word Springfield, anyway. The only other thing I could understand were their names. They kept shouting out each other's names. Usually followed by a curse word or two."

Susan was vigorously nodding, her short gray hair bouncing around her head. "That's right. It was 'shit, Anchorman, this,' or 'screw you, Dorman, that.' They said it several times. To be honest, it was a little frightening, and I was very glad we were moving to another site. Later, I remember thinking that I hoped they wouldn't spoil the evening for the others."

Ricki froze in place. "Others?" she repeated slowly. "What others are you talking about, Mrs. Packer?"

"Oh goodness. The other two men who came by about an hour later." She wrinkled her nose at her husband. "You remember them, don't you, Marvin? Much friendlier than those first two." She covered her mouth with one hand and giggled. "They looked so opposite, too. Kind of like a Mutt and Jeff sort of thing."

"Mutt and Jeff?" Ricki's heart rate bumped up a level. "What do you mean?"

"Maybe you're too young to have read that old comic strip." Susan giggled again. "You know, where Jeff is very short, and Mutt is very tall? That's who those two men reminded me of."

"That second pair of hikers you saw were different heights?" Ricki chose her words carefully, not wanting to have anyone listen to the recording and claim she was trying to shape what Susan Packer was saying. "Did you get a good look at them?"

"Certainly good enough to notice that height difference. And that they had very short haircuts. The kind the boys wear in the military," Marvin chimed in before giving his wife an indulgent smile. "Didn't you talk to them?"

"Yes. I waved when the shorter man called out a hello, and when they waved back, I told them to have a nice hike." She paused to sigh. "I so hope they were just going down to take a peek at site thirty and weren't intending to camp there with those other two."

Ricki took a slow breath in and out. "That second pair of hikers you saw were headed south, toward Campsite 30?"

Susan nodded. "Yes. But I don't know if any of those men stayed there overnight. We left shortly after that."

"All right." Ricki shot a sideways glance at Clay, who was clearly fighting not to smile. She couldn't blame him. It was all she could do not to jump up and pump her fist into the air. "Just to be clear, you saw two pairs of hikers that day? One that was arguing, and calling each other Anchorman and Dorman, and a second pair where one was very tall and the other much shorter? Is that right?"

"Yes, dear." Susan looked at her husband, who added his nod. "I hope we were helpful?"

Unable to hold back any longer, Ricki's lips curled into a big smile. "Very helpful. Thank you so much."

Chapter 24

RICKI WALKED into the hospital lobby. The large, open space had overstuffed chairs and love seats clustered together in small groups. Potted plants added pops of color to a decorating scheme that heavily favored pale salmon and beige. She carefully scanned the room, looking for Anchorman and his attorney, but neither of them was anywhere in sight. Thinking they might be upstairs talking to Trey, she and Clay headed for the elevator.

The tenth floor was moderately busy as they strode down the hall. The door to Trey's room was open, so Ricki stepped inside, stopping so suddenly Clay barely kept from plowing into her back. A man she'd never seen before was sitting in a chair next to Trey's bed.

He looked up, his blue eyes meeting hers with the same flat look every cop had mastered. She didn't need a formal introduction or a crystal ball to know who he was. When her gaze shifted to Trey, she could see by the warning look in his eyes that her suspicion was right. She was staring at Trey's replacement from NCIS.

When Clay crowded in behind her, she stepped to the side to give him enough room to get a look at the guy himself.

From the corner of her eye, she saw the moment's hesitation and then the slight stiffening in Clay's shoulders.

The silence in the room drew out until Trey belatedly pushed himself higher up on the mound of pillows at his back. He lifted a hand toward his visitor. "This is Special Agent Mark Edwards, out of Quantico." He dropped his hand back to the top of the bed. "Those two are Special Agent Ricki James with the ISB, and Police Chief Clay Thomas from Washington."

Edwards stood up and walked around the end of the bed. He shook hands with both Ricki and Clay, then took a step back, hands clasped behind his back. It was such a classic military stance that it didn't leave a lot of doubt about his background. And while Trey had proven to be more than flexible in how he approached the investigation, it would be a wild piece of luck if the very uptight-looking Edwards was cut from the same bolt of cloth.

Carefully sizing the man up, Ricki decided she wasn't feeling that lucky.

"I've been briefed on the reason for your attachment to this investigation, Agent James," Edwards said. His tone was mild, but the look in his eyes held a strong hint of disapproval. "I understand that you were assigned as an expert on the area?"

Ricki felt her temper start a slow burn. "The murder of Sergeant Dorman took place in a national park, Agent Edwards." She looked down at his pressed trousers and leather shoes which were a stark contrast to her worn jeans and scuffed boots. "How much time have you spent in the backcountry?"

"Not much."

His overly polite tone had her gritting her teeth. "Which is why I was assigned to the case."

His smile did nothing to soften his features or convey any kind of warmth. "Understandable." He paused. "To a point since the agent who was initially assigned to the case has a great deal of experience in wilderness conditions. But since the forensics team arrived as scheduled, and the crime scene has now been processed, there isn't any reason to spend more time in the park." He gave her a sharp look. "Unless, of course, the primary suspect somehow ends up lost in the forest, at which point I'm sure your services would be needed." He walked over and picked up a leather case that was lying on a seat built in underneath the window. When he turned to face her again, that cold smile of his was still in place. "Until that time, I have requested that you be removed from the case, since your backcountry expertise is no longer required." He gave her a curt nod and literally marched out the door.

Ricki waited until the sound of his footsteps had faded away before tapping her boot against the linoleum floor. When Clay moved the visitor's chair close and gave her a light push, she turned on him with a glare. "What was that for?"

"I thought you'd like to sit down before you explode."

"I'm perfectly fine," she gritted out, then walked over to stand near the bed and threw her hands in the air. "What was that?"

Trey looked from Ricki to the empty doorway. "Sorry. Edwards borders on brilliant in analyzing evidence, but he wouldn't have been my first choice. The guy isn't so great at coloring outside the lines, which is what's needed here. But my boss didn't ask for my opinion." His hands balled into fists. "Since Edwards has seniority, he also thought it was his job to deliver a dressing down for not keeping a closer eye on Anchorman."

Clay laughed. "How the hell were you supposed to do that from a hospital bed?"

The NCIS agent opened his hands and turned them palms up. "No idea. But he found out that Anchorman not only went along on our trip to the murder scene, but ended up with a gun to boot."

Ricki's mouth dropped open in disbelief. "Did he also know that we were being shot at, and two of us were down?"

"I don't know, and he didn't express any interest in hearing about it," Trey said with a shrug. "But since I'm now officially on leave, none of us will know what's going on with the investigation."

Ignoring the bad taste in her mouth that Edwards had left, Ricki sat in the chair he'd vacated. "Not necessarily. But we need to call Anchorman. He and his attorney are somewhere in the hospital, and they should both hear this."

"I'll give him a call," Clay offered before moving off to the far corner of the room.

Trey's eyes lit up with interest. "What did you mean by not necessarily?"

"We have another dead body, and this one has been assigned to me." While Clay tracked down Anchorman, Ricki ran an astonished Trey through the events of the prior twenty-four hours, ending with their stop at The Wooden Nickel and her talk with Trip.

When she finished, Trey slowly shook his head. "So Kelly was being followed? And probably by the same two guys who were following you, and are also likely the same two who shot at us?"

"That's right," Ricki said. "Stu Landers is the only person who knew that Kelly was being followed, and he ended up just as dead."

"That is one helluva coincidence." The agent whistled softly between his teeth just as Anchorman and Christopher Young walked into the room.

"What coincidence?" Anchorman asked.

"I just filled Trey in about Stu Landers," Ricki said before glancing over at Christopher. "But didn't bother to do the same with the tight ass who replaced him and wants to see your client put away for Kelly's murder." She stood up and walked over to the window, leaving the only chair in the room for the attorney.

Christopher inclined his head in thanks and sat down. "Yes, I was informed of the change in investigators myself just this morning and again just now by Chief Thomas. It seems Agent Edwards chose to stop by the county sheriff's office and present his credentials before coming to the hospital. Unfortunately, he didn't leave the best impression on either the desk sergeant or the sheriff."

Clay grinned. "So, of course, they immediately informed you about the new agent in town."

"Very kind of them," Christopher said in a polite, formal tone. "It never pays to piss off the local authorities. A lesson Agent Edwards has not yet learned, apparently." He lifted a hand and waved it at Ricki. "Anchorman told me all about Stu Landers, and the probability of a surveillance tape at this gun range he and Sergeant Dorman frequented. Very promising. Especially if it provides us with an alternative suspect, or in this case, two other suspects, to my client." He leaned back and tucked his thumbs into his vest pockets. "And I also understand that this Stu Landers wrote something in a notebook that might help you track down the current location of these alternate suspects?"

"That's right," Ricki said. "It's a symbol of some kind." She took out her phone and pulled up the image she'd scanned from Stu's notebook. "Does anyone recognize this image?" She walked over to the bed and held it up for Trey, who shook his head, and then got the same reaction from Christopher Young. Not surprised no one knew what the symbol stood for, she tucked her phone away. "I'm going to send it to a colleague of mine, who is a top-notch researcher, and put him on it."

"Excellent," Christopher said. "And because it was found while investigating Mr. Landers's murder, which at this time is not officially connected with the case involving Sergeant Dorman, there is no obligation to turn that little notebook with the symbol in it over to the prosecution in our case." His lips formed into a smug pout. "What a shame for them. Now, about your interview with the Packers? I'm hoping that yielded the same good results?"

Ricki laughed. "Better than good. To use one of your favorite expressions, it was excellent. It turned out there was also more to their story than the prosecution knows." She patted her jacket pocket. "And I got every word on record."

"Which I'm sure we're all eager to listen to," Christopher said. "But it would be very helpful if you could tell us the highlights right now, and we'll get into the details later."

While Clay propped himself up against a wall, the attorney, Anchorman, and Trey all leaned forward as Ricki gathered her thoughts. "What the Packers didn't say in their interview with Ranger Johnson was that they saw not one, but two sets of hikers that day." She paused at the collective intake of breath all around the room. "The first pair they saw, or rather heard, were the two who were arguing. An argument that started just before the pair came into view of Campsite 24, and abruptly ended when they were out of sight. They didn't get a good look at them because both men had their hoods up, and the Packers didn't want to draw any attention to themselves and then possibly become a target for two angry men." She smiled at Anchorman. "But the Packers had a very good description of you and Kelly. She said, unlike the first pair, you and Kelly looked like Mutt and Jeff."

Anchorman's eyebrows snapped together. "You mean like that old comic strip with the short guy and his really tall friend?"

She grinned at him while Trey laughed and Christopher slapped a beefy hand on one knee.

The attorney rubbed his hands together as if he already sensed victory was headed his way. "Just to be clear, are you saying if we parade Anchorman in front of the Packers, they'd recognize him as one of the men in that second pair of hikers? The pair that was not arguing?"

"I'm sure of it," Ricki said. "And their story matched the one Anchorman told me. That the Packers were breaking camp and told Kelly to have a nice hike. When the first pair came by, they were relaxing with a cup of coffee and never said a word to them."

Trey made a low humming noise. "So they weren't at the campsite the night of the murder?"

"No," Ricki said. "I need to have a ranger take a look at the reservations for that night, but I'm betting that Campsite 24 was empty."

Christopher struggled to get out of the chair. After a few moments, he managed to lumber to his feet. He straightened his vest and nodded at his client. "This is indeed good news, and very timely. The prosecutor has been making some noise about having Anchorman's bail revoked, due to the unfortunate shooting incident that put Agent Robard and Supervisor Johnson into hospital beds. I think I need to pay the prosecutor a call and let him know about this turn of events." He crossed the room, but when he reached the door, he looked back at them. "You will keep me informed of any other new developments? We still have the ballistics evidence that needs to be explained."

As soon as he left, Ricki looked up, right into Anchorman's sober stare.

"The Packers said Kelly and I were the second pair of hikers they saw that day?"

Feeling a tingle of warning along her nerves, Ricki slowly nodded. "That's right."

Anchorman shifted his weight so he stood with his legs braced apart. "Then the shooters were ahead of us on the trail? They were already at the campsite waiting for us?"

She knew by the suddenly stricken look in his eyes that he

was again feeling a heavy weight of guilt. "It wasn't your fault. You know that."

"She's right." Trey's strong voice bounced off the walls. "It was an ambush, pure and simple. You had no way of knowing someone was out there, hunting you."

The retired Marine slowly paced to the far side of the room and then back again. He drew in a long breath through his nose, closing his eyes as he let it out. "I know." He opened his eyes again and nodded at Trey. "I know. But it's going to take some time to adjust to the fact I couldn't protect Kelly's back." He sucked in a long breath. "Or my own, for that matter."

"Those shooters getting to the campsite first also means something else," Ricki put in. When Anchorman faced her, she folded her arms over her chest. "They knew where you were going. And I doubt if they followed Stu Landers all the way across the park to that remote site. Unlike you, he did know someone might be hunting him, so he would have been on the lookout for any kind of tail."

"Which means they also knew where he was headed," Clay said.

"Yeah." Ricki's boot did a fast tap-tap-tap against the floor as she stared at Anchorman. "You told me that neither you nor Kelly ever told anyone what your final destination was. It was a habit of yours not to. And Landers didn't mention his exact destination to Trip. But the killers knew exactly where to go. Now, how did they manage that?"

"And why?" Trey's quiet question dropped like a rock into a lake, creating ripples outward. "This wasn't a random stalking and shooting. So why Kelly?"

Anchorman stared out the window. "Revenge maybe? Over something that happened during one of his deployments?"

"Possible," Trey agreed. He shifted restlessly in the bed. "But I went over Sergeant Dorman's record with a fine-tooth comb, and nothing jumped out at me that would rise to this level. At least not with anyone in the military."

"Money or jealousy," Clay stated. "If we rule out revenge, those are the two most common motivations behind a homicide."

"Maybe Sondra had an ex-husband or boyfriend who didn't like being an ex," Anchorman suggested.

Trey glanced at Ricki. "What about her son? Maybe he had beef with Kelly?"

She shook her head. "I can't see someone Kelly called a couch warmer sneaking around in the forest." She shrugged. "I might need to talk to him, and he's still on the list, but at the very bottom. The kid just doesn't ring any bells with me."

"Me either," Clay said, seconding her assessment of what they'd heard about Dilbert Lewis.

"Which leaves money," Trey continued. "I finally received Kelly's bank records, and he did have a reasonable sum saved up. People have killed for less than fifty thousand dollars."

"Which is a lot less than the quarter of a million he had in life insurance." Ricki's boot started tapping.

Anchorman scoffed at that. "Kelly's money goes to his mom and brother, and they sure didn't come up here, sneak around in the woods, and then shoot him in the back." When he caught Ricki staring at him, he lifted a questioning eyebrow, but she only shook her head.

"What about the other guy? Landers?" Trey asked. "Did he have any money problems?"

Ricki's boot stilled, and she put her hands on her hips. "According to Trip, Landers owned a framing business that wasn't doing so well. But if he was trying to scam money out of Kelly, why kill him?"

"It's a loose end that should be checked out," Trey said. "So where does all this leave us?"

"Catching the killers," Ricki stated, before giving

Anchorman a hard look. "Alive. Then they can tell us why they went after Kelly."

Clay pushed away from the wall. "In that case, I guess we're headed back to Pigeon Forge and a date with a security camera."

Chapter 25

Ricki was already taking out her phone as she climbed into the passenger seat of the SUV. She punched in Dan's number and waited for him to pick up. It was only a few seconds before she heard his greeting.

"Hey, Ricki. How's the case going?"

"Things are starting to break our way, and we just might get Anchorman completely in the clear," she said. She knew she should fill him in on the details, but the ride back to Pigeon Forge wasn't that long and she had other calls to make before they got there. Silently promising to fill Dan in on every detail as soon as she could, she switched the phone to speaker so she could still hear him while she pulled up Stu's drawing. "I'm sending you a picture of some kind of logo, and I need you to track it down and let me know who or what it stands for." She forwarded it to his email.

"Hang on a minute," Dan said. "It's coming through now."

She patiently waited out the silence, with nothing but the click of a keyboard coming from her phone's speaker.

"Okay." She could hear the frown in Dan's voice. "It looks like some kind of big-ass knife with a lightning bolt behind it.

Is it supposed to be from one of the drug cartels, or maybe a local survivalist group?"

"I don't know. I wish I did because we're pretty sure it's going to lead us to our killers. "

"Then I'll get right on this. I don't recognize it at all, so it might take me a while to get through all the possibilities on the various law enforcement databases. But I might get lucky and it just pops up. Either way, I'll get the information for you. Is there anything else you need?"

Making her mind up quickly, she barely hesitated before making another request. "Yeah. I'll also email you the name of a company. I need some background information on it, particularly their current financial position."

"That one should be easy to do. Send me the name and I'll look it up," he said.

"Okay, will do. Sorry, but I'm pressed for time here. I need to make another call."

"No problem," Dan assured her. "And I'll get that information to you as soon as I can."

She thanked him and had started to hang up when she raised the phone to her ear again. "Dan, Dan? Are you still there?"

A second later, he came back on the line. "I'm here. What's up?"

"We're trying to figure something out about the campsites at the park," she said. "How hard would it be to hack into the reservation system? Could *you* do it?"

He laughed. "Into a federal database? Probably not, but I appreciate your confidence in my abilities. However, since it isn't the Department of Defense, I could possibly find someone through the dark web who could do it. Why? What are you trying to find out?"

"What campsite someone made a reservation at," she said.

"You're a park investigator. Why don't you just call and ask?"

"Because our suspects wouldn't be able to do that," she replied.

"Oh." When he fell silent, she could almost hear him thinking through the phone. "That reservation system acts like any other. Anyone who makes a reservation gets a confirming email. If you know the name of the person who made a reservation, then you don't have to hack into the federal database. You just need to hack into that person's email and read the confirmation notice. It should have the dates and the campsite the reservation was for."

"If we can get hold of one of the computers used to make a reservation, could the hacker be identified and traced back to a physical location?" she asked, thinking that Sondra might give her access to Kelly's computer.

"I'm sorry to say it isn't as easy as they make it look in the movies or on TV. Even the service provider probably couldn't do more than give you an IP address, but where is it located? That could have a very wide error factor, easily into the hundreds of miles."

"But someone could get into a personal computer and read the emails?"

"Yeah, sure," Dan said with a shrug in his voice. "But you don't have to get into his personal computer, just the server for his online email account. It's not a walk in the park, but it can be done a lot easier than getting into a federal system with multiple fail-safes and firewalls."

Dumbstruck that she hadn't thought of that herself, she again thanked Dan for his help. Disconnecting the call, she sent Clay a rueful smile. "Well. I'm guessing that's how our killers knew where to track Kelly and Landers down."

"Do you think they have that kind of skill set?" Clay asked.

She nodded. "Oh, yeah. They can produce fake license plates, so who knows what kind of resources they have at their disposal. They appear to be highly skilled at tracking, staying invisible, and moving in the backcountry. But not at murder. I think this might be their first rodeo."

From behind the wheel, Clay smiled. "Me too."

Anchorman leaned toward them and rested his forearms on the front seats. "Why are you saying that? I mean, two people are dead. That doesn't seem like amateur hour to me."

"Why move Kelly's body?" Clay asked. "You were drugged up enough you wouldn't have reacted to the shot even if they'd made it inside Kelly's shelter."

"So he would be found. That's why the body was moved," Anchorman stated.

"It wasn't necessary to move it in order for it to be found," Clay said, continuing the narrative. "Either you would have come out of your drug-induced stupor and reported it. Or you would have run, and the next campers at site thirty would have discovered it and the manhunt would have been on. Or thirdly, you would have hidden the body and the girlfriend would have reported Kelly missing. Then the manhunt would have been on for both of you, at least until they found Kelly's body and then went looking just for you. It also would have been smarter to move Landers's body and bury it somewhere, then take down his tent and get rid of it, along with anything else that belonged to him. He had no family in the area that we know of, so the only person who knew he was going camping was Trip. And who's saying Landers didn't change his mind and take off for someplace else?"

"And taking Kelly's gun was just plain stupid," Ricki put in. "If he tries to pawn a gun that expensive, it's going to pop on some federal or local database, and then we can trace it right back to them."

Anchorman plopped back against the seat. "Okay. Not too bright with the details. How is that going to help us?"

"It depends on the size of the pool of suspects we might need to narrow down. We're probably looking for well trained and on the younger side without a lot of experience in the civilian world," Clay said.

Anchorman winced. "So you think they're military?"

"Probably former military and recently discharged," Ricki said, remembering the age estimate made by the emergency room doctor. She took out her phone and began a quick Internet search until she came up with the phone number of the Bear Country Rod & Gun Club. It took eight rings before someone picked up on the other end. *They also didn't know Kelly,* she thought silently, mentally counting off the rings on the other end of the phone. If they had, they wouldn't have called him "Dorman" when they were trying to make themselves known to the Parkers. And that put a whol new spin on things.

"You've reached Bear Country." Whoever owned the bored voice didn't sound like they'd been out of their teen years very long.

"This is Special Agent Ricki James." Ricki didn't get any further than that before the voice said "hang on," and the phone went silent as she was put on hold. She listened to a few minutes of the country western version of elevator music before a raspy-sounding woman came on the line.

"Is this the agent who's looking into Stu's murder?" The voice not only had a grit to it but was loud enough that Ricki had to hold the phone six inches away from her ear.

Ricki waited a beat, debating how to answer that question when she had no idea who was asking it. "This is Special Agent Ricki James with the National Park Service," she repeated. "Who am I talking to?"

"Donna Spanner. I own the Bear Country. Trip down at The Wooden Nickel told me this female agent who is chasing after the person who shot Stu would be calling me. So is that you?"

"Yes, it is, Mrs. Spanner . . ." Ricki said, only to be cut off again.

"I'm no Mrs. You can call me Donna or Spanner, which-ever blows your skirt up. What'd you say your name was?"

Drawing on her patience, Ricki tried again. "I'm Special Agent Ricki James, and yes, I'm looking into the murder of Stu Landers. Trip said that Stu Landers and Kelly Dorman were at your shooting range sometime in, say, the last month. Can you confirm that?"

Donna's voice cracked around the edges. "I already checked that after Trip called, and yeah, they were here. Ten days ago. It took me a couple of hours to go through all the disks, but I found them. And I'll bet I know who you're looking for, since they were the only two strangers getting shots off."

"You were there? You saw them?"

The woman's laugh ended in a severe coughing fit. "I gave up smoking a year ago and I'm still hacking out my lungs." She sighed. "A two-pack-a-day habit will do that to you, I guess. But no, I wasn't here. Sophie was, and she's too old to remember much beyond what she had for breakfast. After I talked to Trip, I pulled up the security tapes and had a look." She coughed again. "I call it a tape, but it's somewhere in the cloud. I don't know what to call that kind of recording, so I just stick to tape."

"We'd very much like to get a look at it, no matter what you call it. We're about ten minutes out from Pigeon Forge. Would you be willing to meet us at your facility and let us review that tape?"

"Have you got a warrant?"

Ricki exchanged a pained look with Clay. "No, I don't," she said evenly. "But I can get one."

There was a cackle on the other end and what sounded like an open hand slapping on a knee. "I'm just giving you a hard time, Agent James. But if that big Marine sniper is with you, it would be nice if you could bring him along. He was all the talk down at The Wooden Nickel, and I'd like to get a look at him."

Ricki glanced back at Anchorman just in time to catch him rolling his eyes. She gave him a wicked grin. "Yeah. I can do that. And you might be interested to know that he's single, with a good income."

While Anchorman gaped at her with bulging eyes, Ricki said a quick goodbye to Donna and put the address into the GPS app on her phone.

"According to the GPS, we're seventeen minutes away from the shooting range." When she looked at Anchorman, the stunned look on his face had turned into an annoyed glare. Her lips curved into a sugary smile. "Unless you'd like us to drop you off at the hotel first? I'll explain to Donna why you couldn't come along after all."

"I'm not missing out on getting a look at that tape," he growled. "But you'd better not encourage that female to . . . Do . . ."

Since he seemed to be at a loss for words, it was only polite to help him out. "Do what? Treat that magnificent body of yours like a sex object?"

"Don't be talking about my body," he snapped, then his eyes narrowed when Ricki started to laugh. Folding his arms over his chest, he stared out the window. "I'm not talking to you."

Clay joined in Ricki's laughter. "He's not talking to you? That's a pretty neat trick. Can you teach it to me? I can think of a time or two it would have been nice not to have him talking to me."

"Watch it there, Chief," was Anchorman's ominous warning. "*You*, I know how to deal with."

Clay's smile stayed in place. "I'll keep that in mind."

Ricki spent the rest of the ride catching up on her messages and emails. She sent a text off to her son, and a couple to Marcie, before leaving the rest for later. It took less than five more minutes to reach the gravel-covered parking lot of the Bear Country shooting range. The lot was narrow, holding just two aisles with cars parked on both sides, but it ran half the length of a football field, flanking the road.

The main building was on the well-worn side and the whole structure leaned slightly to the left. The wood walls had turned gray with age, and the entrance was a single door painted a bright red. Before pulling the door open, Ricki noticed the set of cameras tucked under the roof's overhang and pointed at opposite sides of the parking lot. She hadn't expected that kind of coverage on the outside of the building, and it had her walking into Bear Country with a huge smile on her face.

The interior was as shabby looking as the outside and almost bare, with a counter along one wall and two benches bisecting the center of the room. A solidly built woman with short, dark hair and dressed in jeans, heavy boots, and a wool-flannel shirt, stepped out from behind the counter and clomped her way across the room.

"I'm Donna Spanner." The deep lines that crisscrossed her face said she'd spent most of her life in the sun. They deepened when she smiled as she reached out to take Ricki's hand in a hard shake. "Since you're the only female with these two, that would make you Agent James."

"It would." Ricki nodded at Clay. "This is Police Chief Clay Thomas from Washington."

Donna's eyes widened, and she let out a small gasp. She stared at Clay for a moment before turning stunned eyes on Ricki. "How do you get any work done staring at that all day?"

Ricki shrugged. "It's a puzzle."

"If I were thirty years younger, I'd be all over that."

Half amused that Donna talked about Clay as if he couldn't hear her, Ricki pointed a finger at the big man who was trying to hide behind the chief. "And this is Anchorman."

"Now I knew that the minute he walked into the building." The older woman put her hands on her hips and gave the uncomfortable Marine a careful once-over. "You're exactly the way Sondra down at The Wooden Nickel described you. All piss and vinegar and strong as a tree."

Anchorman's head jerked back in surprise. "What? I'm not like that."

"Depends on who is doing the judging, now don't it?" Donna grinned and then latched on to Ricki's arm. "Let's go look at that tape. I have it all ready for you. And the log with the checked-in and checked-out names and signatures too."

On the counter was a yellow legal pad, with each line covered by a name, date, and time. Several pages were already flipped over, and Donna ran a finger along the outer edge of the one currently on top, stopping about halfway down. "See there? That's them. John Jones and Jason Jones. See a few entries above them? That's where Stu and Kelly signed in."

Ricki leaned in closer to get a better look.

"We check everyone's ID, no matter how long we've known them," Donna said over her shoulder. "And Sophie is real good about that. If those are the names they signed in with, then they had IDs to match them."

"I'll bet they did," Ricki muttered under her breath. Fake IDs to go with fake license plates. She got out her phone and snapped a photo of the page. Straightening up, she looked toward the back room where a rickety desk held a flat-screen computer that looked completely at odds with its surroundings. "Let's see what's on that tape."

Chapter 26

DONNA PULLED out the rolling desk chair and pointed at it. "Sit," she told Ricki, then grabbed a straight-backed chair pushed up against the opposite wall and dragged it over to the desk. "I have it all ready to go here." She pushed some buttons and then worked on the keyboard. "We're looking at ten days ago. I'm going to fast-forward it to 1300 hours on the tape." Her shoulders vibrated when she laughed. "I guess I don't have to tell anyone here that's 1 p.m. to most people."

Ricki watched as the tape sped forward. People appeared and then disappeared a second or two later as they were replaced at a shooting station by another patron. She leaned closer to the screen. "This is the rifle range?"

"Yep." Donna pressed a button and the picture froze in place. "Six stations, eight feet apart. We have one for pistols, too, but none of your guys stopped there. So I'm only queueing up the tape for the rifles. We had the one-hundred-yard targets set up that day." She pressed the play button, then grinned at Ricki, revealing slightly yellowed and crooked teeth. "I checked, in case you asked." She squinted at the screen. "Okay. Here we go. See?" She tapped a finger on the screen. "There's Stu. He's heading for station three. And that's Kelly right behind him. He'll take station two."

The room went silent as four sets of eyes watched the two men cross the flat stretch of dirt between the back of the main building and the rifle range. The whole area was under a porch roof, extended to a few feet beyond the edge of the long counter, which was divided into stations. The two men were talking as they approached their positions at the counter, each cradling a rifle in one arm, with the barrel pointing down.

"Kelly had his new gun with him."

Anchorman's quiet voice floated from behind Ricki. She nodded but kept her gaze glued to the screen. Ten minutes passed. The man and woman shooting on either side of Kelly and Stu left and, over the next quarter of an hour, were replaced by two other customers.

When two men entered the frame at the thirty-seven-minute mark, Donna tapped the screen again. "There they are. Those are your two guys."

"How do you know that?" Clay asked.

"After we're done with this tape, I've got another one to show you," Donna said.

Ricki's gaze tracked the two men as they crossed the screen, passing behind Kelly and Stu as they slowly walked to the far end of the counter. She watched, willing one of them to turn his face toward the camera. But they were careful.

"There," Anchorman growled. "Kelly made them." He jabbed a finger toward the screen. "I saw it. Kelly recognizes them."

"Hang on," Ricki said. "We'll reverse and take a closer look when we're finished with this sequence." The images rolled on. At forty-two minutes in, Kelly said something to Stu and then set his rifle down. He exited the frame in the direction of the main building while Stu continued shooting.

"Do you have any cameras inside?" Ricki asked.

"Only on the front counter," Donna said. "And you don't need them."

Anchorman grunted, drawing Ricki's gaze over to him. "He's not going to the head. Kelly made those two. He's out in the parking lot looking for that truck."

When five more minutes passed and Kelly still hadn't returned, the two men at the far end of the counter moved closer together.

"They're talking it over," Ricki said. "Whether to go out together to look for Kelly and take their eyes off Stu, or to split up."

Thirty seconds later, Kelly reappeared in the frame, holding his stomach with two hands. He walked over and picked up his gun, but rather than taking up the target practice again, he cradled it and stepped back three feet. A moment later, Stu turned around. His mouth moved, and then he also picked up his gun, and the two of them exited the picture. Donna reached over and pushed the button to freeze the screen.

"Kelly always was a smart sonofabitch," Anchorman chuckled.

Clay nodded his agreement. "He moved far enough away he had to shout for Stu to hear him at that distance and over the noise from the other shooters." He leaned in closer. "And for the guys at the end to hear him too. Look. The stupid shits took off their ear protectors." He grinned. "I'm betting Kelly just claimed a stomach problem to explain his long absence, and probably threw in where they're going next to boot."

"That's a sure thing," Anchorman said.

Ricki leaned back, looking over at Donna when the older woman nudged her arm.

"Want to go to the next tape?"

"Not yet." Ricki gestured toward the frozen screen. "If they know where Kelly is headed next, those two shouldn't be rushing out the door to follow him. Let's see how much time Kelly bought here."

As the screen came to life again, they all watched the two men take more shots, not leaving much time between rounds.

"They look good," Anchorman muttered. "A lot better than they did a minute ago. And I'll bet they're hitting those targets. Some solid training there."

"They missed you up at the camp," Clay said.

The Marine slowly shook his head. "Yeah. Only because I saw the flash from light hitting a scope. But I wouldn't count on that happening twice. And I'll bet they've got assault rifles stashed somewhere."

"Okay. They're making a move." Ricki's gaze followed the two figures until they disappeared from the screen, never once showing their faces to the camera. Sighing in frustration and annoyance, she leaned back in the chair and tucked a loose strand of her dark hair behind one ear. "Let's go back to the point where the two guys come in behind Kelly and Stu Landers."

Donna put the DVD player into reverse, expertly stopping it as soon as the two men came into the frame.

"Now run it in slow motion," Ricki said, leaning in again as the older woman complied.

A few seconds later, Donna punched the stop button. "There," she cried with a triumphant smile. "I saw it too. See? Right there, Kelly turns his head just enough to get a look at the two guys right after they passed him in single file."

Ricki judged the angle between Kelly and the two men. "I think he got a look at one of their faces, if not both of them." She pointed to the second man. "At least he saw that one."

"And look." Donna repeatedly jabbed her finger against the screen. "Oh shit. Stu's head is turned too. He must have gotten a look at that guy as well."

Which is why he was so scared, Ricki thought. Stu might have been able to identify at least one of the men Kelly claimed were following him. Which would have signed his death warrant. "Let's see what else you have," she said out loud.

Donna reached over to a stack of DVDs sitting next to the computer and plucked two disks off the top. "This is from the cameras out in the parking lot." She quickly jabbed at the keyboard, lifting her hands once the images on the screen began to fast-forward. Her hand hovered over the keys as she watched the position count at the bottom of the screen. She stopped the fast-forward and started the clip again in slow motion.

"Here we go. This is right after Kelly left the range the first time." They watched as Kelly slowly walked the length of the nearest row of cars, his neck craned as he looked beyond them. When he passed out of the frame, Donna hit the stop button again. "No worries. I have him picked up on another camera. The one mounted at the end of the building didn't have a wide enough angle to cover the whole parking lot, and I wanted a visual of the whole space. So I put one up on each of the two lighting poles on either end of the lot. And look what I found?"

She tapped away again, bringing up a clip from a different camera and fast-forwarding the images to the spot where Kelly appeared in the frame. "That lighting pole is near the second row of cars. And take a look. He's headed right for that black truck off to the right."

There weren't any other cars at that end of the lot, so the truck stuck out like a sore thumb. Shaking her head, Ricki watched as Kelly walked around it, pressing his face against the driver's side window, then moving on to the long, flat bed in the rear. He came up again on the passenger's side, and his hand reached out to touch a large patch on the lower corner of the windshield before he moved off, walking quickly toward the main building. When he was no longer visible on the screen, Donna exited the clip and went back to the parking lot camera near the entrance of the building.

"This is where they're leaving. They came in Stu's car and parked out front, so they were caught on the first parking lot camera." The two men appeared on the screen, stopping beside a car in the front row. Stu's back was to the camera, but Kelly was facing it and was saying something to the other man. A moment later, Stu shrugged and reached into his shirt pocket. He handed something to Kelly before they both climbed into the car and it backed out of its parking space. They didn't go to the far end of the lot, but went straight out to the street, turning onto the highway and leaving the screen, causing Donna to hit the stop button again.

"What was that about?" Anchorman asked no one in particular.

Ricki's boot tapped against the floor. "Stu's little notebook. I think Stu handed his notebook to Kelly."

"So Kelly drew that symbol, not Stu," Clay said. "Which makes sense because Stu never got close enough to the truck to see it."

"I agree." Ricki looked at Donna. "Do these cameras zoom in?"

Donna grinned. "And that's the big prize I have for you." She toggled between views again. "I took a look at those two strangers walking out to their truck, and guess what I found?" She waited until they approached the truck and then zoomed in on the man climbing into the passenger seat. He turned his head, just before it disappeared below the frame of the open door. It was only for a second, but it was enough. Donna punched the stop button, and the screen froze. The man's face was caught head-on in the middle of the screen.

A collective yelp went up from the group. Ricki twisted around and lifted a hand for Clay's high-five.

"We've got the stupid shit. Right there. We've got him."

Clay smiled in satisfaction, his eyes lighting up at the sudden scent of the hunt.

Ricki's grin was just as big as his, only sobering when she caught the intense look on Anchorman's face as he leaned over Donna and stared at the screen. Ricki knew that man's face was now burned into Anchorman's memory, so she put a hand flat against his chest and pushed. He didn't look at her, but he did straighten up and move back a step. Realizing she'd need to have a serious talk with him or leave him at the hotel while she and Clay went hunting for the guy, she waved a hand in front of the screen.

"Can we get some prints of that?" she asked. "And then can you zoom in on the lower part of the windshield? I'd like to get a better look at that patch Kelly touched."

Donna smiled and worked the keyboard. It wasn't long before the clack of the printer filled the small room. "I don't know how good an image I can get of that patch. Those are good cameras out there, but that decal, or whatever it is, isn't that big." She used the mouse to isolate the area she wanted and tapped on the keyboard to zoom in closer. She'd been right about the quality of the image, but it was good enough to see that the whole patch was a rectangle, and at the bottom was some writing that wasn't in the picture Kelly had drawn.

"I think you're right, Donna," Clay said. "It's a decal. And if you've lived for years in a city, you'd probably recognize it." He nodded at the screen. "See that writing on the bottom? I think those might be numbers, not letters. This looks like a parking decal to me."

Ricki sat straight up. "So the symbol would be a company logo?"

"Most likely," Clay replied. He looked down at Ricki and grinned. "Which would make it a helluva lot easier to trace."

She almost clapped her hands in excitement. Oh, yeah. And Dan would be able to track it down in no time at all, once he knew exactly where to look. Donna ejected the disk and handed it to Ricki. "That's the original. I kept a copy for myself." She pushed against the desk, scooting her chair back, barely missing Anchorman's foot. She twisted around, the lines on her face deepening as she faced the three looking back at her. "I know you'll catch those guys, but y'all be careful, now. They were real good at shooting those guns."

Chapter 27

RICKI HUNG UP THE PHONE, shaking her head and rolling her eyes at the same time.

Clay pulled the SUV out onto the road, then glanced over at her. "What did Dan say?"

"Something along the lines of 'stand by.'" She gave in to a short laugh. "I guess knowing he's looking for a corporation and not a gang affiliation is really going to speed things up on his end. At least that's what he implied."

"So what's the plan?" Anchorman called from the back seat. "And I hope it involves food."

Ricki set her phone in an empty slot in the side console and stretched her legs out. "We find out what company owns that parking decal, pay them a visit, taking along our picture of the suspect, and get them to tell us everything we need to know about their employee of the year." She rolled her shoulders to work out a kink. "Until then, I could eat. The Wooden Nickel isn't far from here."

"Nope." Clay instantly rejected the idea. "Dive bars and their burgers are fine, but five days of it in a row, along with takeout from a deli, is about all I can stand. I'd like to go someplace with a little more variety."

Anchorman lay back in his seat and folded his hands on his stomach. "I think there was wings on their menu if you're tired of burgers."

"Nope again," Clay stated firmly. "We've got some time while we wait for Dan's call. Let's go someplace decent."

Anchorman lifted a boot and lightly kicked the back of Clay's seat. "I think city boy up there is missing some of his amenities."

Ricki thought so too, but diplomatically kept it to herself. She looked down at her jeans and hiking boots. "Not exactly dressed for a night out."

"It's a small town, just like back home. We don't dress up to go to dinner at the St. Armand," Clay said, referring to the fancy resort on a hill overlooking Brewer, the southernmost town in the Bay. "And that's an upscale restaurant that doesn't get excited about a dress code as long as you have shoes on and are decently covered." He wiggled his eyebrows at her. "Wouldn't you like a glass of wine or something besides a beer to go with a good steak?"

"Tempting." She glanced back at Anchorman. "We're going to catch these guys and then we'll be headed home." She smiled. "All of us. Which means you'll be back in the kitchen. Want to see if a real restaurant can top your cooking?"

"They can't," Anchorman said, his voice infused with confidence. "But I'll go along, providing I get to pick out the place." At Clay's suspicious look, he grinned and added, "Which will have a full food and bar menu, with great appetizers and desserts. And, of course, a steak." When Clay finally nodded, the big Marine gave his seat another solid kick. "I still say you're just missing city life."

Clay looked in the rearview mirror, his gaze narrowing on Anchorman. "And I say if you kick my damn seat again, you'll be spending time with Trey in the hospital."

Anchorman barked out a laugh, and Ricki rolled her eyes

at them before looking away to hide her smile. It was a relief to hear them taking good-natured potshots at each other. It meant they were all relaxing with the feeling there was light at the end of the dark tunnel they'd been in.

Clay followed Anchorman's directions, staying on the highway, then turning onto a road marked by a huge sign, tagging it as the entrance to Margaritaville Island Hotel & Resort.

The colorful center of the resort boasted a fountain surrounded by shops and restaurants. Ricki smiled at Clay's "you're kidding" when he spotted the Ferris wheel. He followed the signs to park the SUV, and when they got out of the car, he shook his head. "I should have known you'd take us to some kind of amusement park. Corn dogs and cotton candy aren't what I had in mind."

Anchorman laughed and slapped him on the back. "Relax. You'll like this place."

The Margaritaville Restaurant was busy but not packed to the rafters the way Ricki imagined it always was at the height of the season. It was still early for dinner, but a respectable enough hour that no one would be faulted for getting a drink with some alcohol in it. And while she had teased Clay about missing his city life, she was secretly looking forward to something besides bar food.

Inside, the decor was all light wood and bright colors, with a giant blender occupying the center of the downstairs restaurant. The large bar area on the second floor was completely open, with a view over wooden railings to the restaurant below.

There wasn't any wait to be seated, and it only took them a few minutes to place their orders, since both Clay and Anchorman opted for a steak with fries. Ricki went for the southwestern salad, because she was pretty sure she hadn't had anything resembling the color green in a week or so, and decided to complete the meal with the house margarita. When it came, she took a sip and closed her eyes in appreciation. Since she wasn't driving, there definitely might be a second one of those showing up at their table.

An hour passed as they enjoyed eating their food and talking about their lives back in the Bay. Ricki had both men laughing at her son's attempt to build a robot with artificial intelligence, something Eddie had described as a complete fail but a great learning experience.

Plans for expanding the Sunny Side Up, and Clay taking on more responsibility in the Seattle DA's office, floated around the table. Ricki was listening to Clay recount one of his cases from his homicide days when he stopped mid-sentence and stared over her shoulder. She looked around, and then wished she hadn't. Special Agent Mark Edwards had entered the restaurant and was headed right for them. Without waiting for an invitation, he scooped up a chair from a recently vacated table nearby and simply sat down next to Ricki.

"I'm surprised to see you here. I thought you were staying at the same hotel that Trey was at."

She gave a mental sigh as Clay furtively looked around for their waiter.

Edwards smiled at Clay. "I don't need a menu, Chief Thomas. I ordered at the hostess station once I spotted you all sitting here. She's going to put the order in and bring it to this table."

"Accommodating of her," Ricki said. "But we were just getting ready to leave."

"We're only waiting on the bill," Clay added.

"No problem. We can chat until it gets here." Edwards thanked the waiter, who stopped at the table long enough to drop off a beer. The short man, who was carrying a tray loaded with more drinks, nodded when Clay asked him to track down their bill.

Edwards's blue-eyed gaze rested on Anchorman. "I take it that you are Norman Beal?"

Anchorman crossed his arms over his chest and stared back at the agent.

After a moment of silence, Edwards slowly exhaled. "And you prefer to be called Anchorman?"

"I do," Anchorman said before baldly stating, "and I'm your main suspect."

"You are the government's main suspect in the murder of Sergeant Kelly Dorman." Edwards's voice was as flat as his gaze. "And I'm the government's primary investigator on the case." He broke off the staring match with Anchorman and glanced at Ricki. "Speaking of investigators, I've been trying to get hold of Trey, but he isn't picking up his calls. Have you talked to him lately?"

Ricki shrugged. "Not since we left his hospital room this morning. And he isn't likely to be back at the hotel."

Clay picked up his beer mug and peered at Edwards over the rim. "Speaking of which, aren't you supposed to be closeted in your room going over the case reports?"

Edwards didn't look at all offended by the question or Clay's tone of voice. "I was, but I needed a break. I'm staying at the hotel here at the resort, so it won't take me long to get back to my review."

"Here?" Ricki slowly looked around. "It's a little pricey for a government employee, isn't it?"

Edwards's eyes crinkled at the corners with amusement. "It would be, but I made a deal long ago with our Accounts Payable department. If they'd pay my hotel bill, within reason, I'd pick up my entire meal tab. We're both happy with that compromise." He settled more comfortably in his chair and took another sip of beer. "There were some things in my case review I was hoping Trey could clear up, but since you're here, maybe you can explain them."

Not sure she wanted to get into this discussion with Edwards, but she remembered what Trey had said about the man's prowess at analyzing evidence, and she did not want to miss anything he might inadvertently let slip about the case. So although she didn't like it, she still reluctantly nodded. "Sure. Ask away."

He rested his elbows on the arms of his chair and steepled his fingers. "I brought the inventory list of everything that was collected from the crime scenes—both the one on the trail and at Campsite 30. In Anchorman's account, he mentioned a bottle of bourbon."

"Yeah. We think it was laced with ketamine." Ricki's forehead furrowed into shallow lines. "Why are you asking about the bourbon? The bottle was never found." Her mouth flattened into a thin line. "Or was it?"

"Found?" Edwards shook his head. "No. It wasn't on the inventory list. But I don't understand why you think it contained ketamine."

"Because that drug was found in the victim's system, and in Anchorman's," Ricki said. "I'm sure that's in one of the ME's reports."

"Yes, it is. And Dr. Garrison was kind enough to forward the results to our lab in Quantico, and, as you pointed out, I already had the county medical examiner's results."

"You talked to Cheron?" Anchorman interrupted him. "I don't want you talking to her. She did her tests and now she's back in the Bay. She isn't involved in this case anymore."

"Understood. But," Edwards raised his voice when Anchorman started to object, "the results were interesting."

Judging by Anchorman's suddenly pained look, Ricki figured Clay must have kicked him under the table. "What was interesting about them?" she asked.

"The levels of the drug. They were very high in the sample taken from Sergeant Dorman." Edwards looked at Anchorman. "And in your sample as well. My lab tech told me that they were dangerously high. Mixed with alcohol, it could have killed you."

"And almost did, if the way I felt when I woke up the next morning is any indication," Anchorman muttered.

"Yes, I'm sure that wasn't pleasant," Edwards said. "But my point is that the level was too high for someone simply trying to establish an alibi."

Ricki went still, not sure what Edwards was saying, or even if she was hearing him correctly. It almost sounded as if he was trying to rule Anchorman out as a suspect.

Their waiter approached and laid a small tray with the bill on it in the middle of the table. "There's no rush," he announced before heading toward another table.

Edwards waited a beat, but when no one moved to pick up the bill, he smiled and kept talking. "The problem is, everyone seems to be convinced that the ketamine was in the bourbon, but the bourbon bottle is missing so there's no way to prove it. There's also the problem of timing."

"Timing?" Ricki frowned. What was Edwards talking about?

"Yes, timing," the agent confirmed. "The reservation was for five days, according to the preliminary report."

Understanding dawned on Ricki's face. "Whoever put that ketamine into the bourbon would have had no way of knowing what night Kelly and Anchorman would drink it."

"Exactly. So you can see the timing problem," Edwards stated. He paused since his food had arrived, staying silent until the server had arranged it in front of him and then walked off. "Now, about that timing. What was the killer's plan? To hang out in the woods until his victims decided to break open the bottle? That alone would be taking a risk. To lace the bourbon with the drug, he would have had to have opened the bottle. What if Sergeant Dorman or Anchorman had noticed that? They might have become suspicious and then decided not to drink it at all."

"Was there a jug half filled with water on that inventory list?" Ricki asked.

Edwards cocked an eyebrow, looking as if he was fighting to keep from smiling. "Yes, there was. White, opaque plastic. Looked like it would hold a gallon."

She looked at Anchorman and tapped a finger on the tabletop in front of him. "Was that your drinking water?"

Anchorman pushed his empty plate to the side, then folded his hands and set them in the cleared space. "Yeah. Kelly boiled water from the stream, and once it cooled down, stored it in that jug." His gaze met Edwards's. "Like Ricki said, it was our drinking water. We were going to use it for our coffee with dinner that night, and in the morning."

"Ah, yes. Your dinner." Edwards sliced off a piece of his steak, then took his time chewing and swallowing. "The fish you caught while sitting at the edge of one of the streams with your back to the campsite. A position, which Special Agent James stated in one of her reports after visiting Campsite 30, that had no clear line of sight to the tents or the firepit, where the jug of water was kept. So naturally, I've requested that the water in that jug be tested for ketamine. I'm sure it will test positive since this killer, or killers don't seem to be too efficient at carrying out murder." He glanced at Ricki and then shifted his gaze to Clay. "If they were, they would have brought gloves to handle the murder weapon instead of wiping all the prints off it. And would not have carried the body so far it became questionable that there was only one man involved in the crime. And of course, they never should have stolen Sergeant Dorman's gun and left Anchorman's. There was no reason for Anchorman to have thrown it away, and if he'd taken it for himself, we would have found it since the entire campsite and the surrounding area were thoroughly searched. So someone else must have taken it, and most likely the undoubtedly expensive bourbon as well, since that would fit the pattern. Which is why I'm having the drinking water tested for ketamine. Something I'm sure would have occurred to both of you if you weren't so distracted by other things. Which is an excellent argument that anyone so close to a suspect shouldn't be on the case at all." He popped another piece of steak into his mouth and chewed while the other three people sitting at the table gaped at him. When he was done chewing, he pointed to the check still lying in the center of the table. "Well, I don't want to keep you. If you see Trey, I'd appreciate it if you told him to give me a call."

"We'll do that." Knowing they'd been summarily dismissed, Ricki slowly pushed her chair back from the table, its legs scraping against the wooden floor. She stood and headed for the front entrance as Clay and Anchorman also got to their feet. When she arrived at the waiting area, she stopped and looked back toward the dining room where Edwards was enjoying his meal, her boot tapping against the floor.

He's right, she thought. If she hadn't been so close to the case she would have thought to look at all the possible ways the ketamine could have gotten into Kelly and Anchorman. Hadn't he even told her he didn't remember drinking the bourbon, or even when the bottle was opened? That alone should have sent off alarm bells that Anchorman had already been drugged.

She sighed and absently tucked a thick strand of hair behind one ear, then reached into an inner pocket of her parka and drew out a credit card. Approaching the hostess station, she held it out to the woman standing behind it. "Do you see that man sitting alone over there? The obnoxious one in the sports coat?"

Without so much as batting an eye, the woman turned and looked over her shoulder. "Oh, yes. Agent Edwards. He had dinner with us last night as well."

"Great. I'd like to pay for his dinner tonight."

Chapter 28

"So Edwards is saying that it wasn't the bourbon that was spiked with the drug? It was the water for the coffee we had at dinner?" They were back at their own hotel, walking toward the lobby doors, when Anchorman asked the question for the third time.

"That's what he thinks," Ricki confirmed again. "And more importantly, he doesn't think you shot Kelly."

"I didn't hear him say that," Anchorman replied.

Clay pulled open the lobby door and held it for both Ricki and Anchorman. "Yeah, he did, in a cop-speak, superior kind of way. And I'm thinking he'll be talking to the federal prosecutor in the morning and telling him that you aren't their guy."

Ricki nodded. "Which means we have to find whoever is their guy so we can get Kelly his justice and we can all go home. I'm hoping Dan comes through." When they walked into the lobby, Trey was sitting on the sofa nearest the fireplace, a pair of crutches leaning against the back of the cushions. He looked up from his phone as they walked through the doors, immediately grabbing his crutches and struggling to his feet.

"It took you long enough to make that trip to the shooting range. Did you run into trouble?"

"No. We made a detour afterward." Ricki frowned, giving his injured leg a pointed look. "Aren't you supposed to be in the hospital?"

"The bullet went straight through. Nothing major was damaged. It just needs some time to heal up."

"Yeah. In a hospital bed," Anchorman asserted. "If you don't give that wound time to heal properly, you might end up with a limp for the rest of your life."

"I'll take my chances." Trey hopped on one leg as he read-justed the crutches under his armpits. "What did you find out at the shooting range?"

Ricki handed him the picture she was carrying. Trey studied it before raising his gaze to meet hers.

"Who is this?"

"One of our shooters. The other one was getting into the driver's seat of that very black truck with the tinted windows." Ricki nodded when Trey's eyes widened just before they dropped back to stare at the picture again. "They followed Kelly and Landers to the shooting range, then were stupid enough to go inside where all kinds of cameras picked them up." She pointed at the picture in Trey's hand. "They both managed to avoid any face shots, except for this one as they were leaving. It seems our boys didn't notice the lone camera attached to the light pole near the far end of the parking lot."

"Too bad for them." Trey handed the picture back to Ricki. "Anything else?"

"Uh-huh." Ricki eyed the crutches propped under Trey's arms. She quickly brought him up to date, including recounting the conversation with Edwards at the Margari-taville Restaurant. "Now that you know what we know, maybe you'll explain to me how you got out of the hospital?"

The NCIS agent's expression was all innocence as he stared back at her. "The doctor signed my release, and I walked out." He grinned at the skeptical look on her face. "Fine. The doctor signed my release as soon as I signed an AMA form."

Anchorman laughed. "Against Medical Advice. Yeah. I've signed a few of those myself."

"Which is not something to be proud of," Ricki snapped. "And how did you get yourself back to the hotel? Don't tell me you drove here."

Trey tried not to grin but failed miserably as his mouth twitched upward. "No. As far as I know, my car is still in that parking lot up near the Huskey Trailhead. I hired a rideshare."

She threw her hands up into the air. "Wonderful. But your car is here. We drove it back after everyone hiked out."

Clay looked over at the remains of a sandwich left on the coffee table in front of the sofa. "It looks like you've had dinner. Is there anything else we can do for you?"

"Yeah," Trey said. "Bring me up to speed and give me something to do."

"Here's something you can do." Ricki pointed to the cell phone lying next to the abandoned sandwich. "Agent Edwards has been trying to get hold of you, so you can give him a call."

Ignoring that, Trey cocked his head to the side. "What about the symbol? Did your research guru find anything out about that?"

"Parking sticker," Anchorman said, then lifted an eyebrow when Ricki glared at him.

"Now that's a break. It shouldn't take too long to find a company using that image for its logo." Trey grimaced as he shifted his weight. "What are you going to do once you have that company's name? It could be located anywhere."

"I'm betting it's not too far away, so we'll be paying them a visit," Ricki said, earning her a sharp look from Clay.

"I want to go along." Trey frowned when he was faced with three people shaking their heads at him. "Just hear me out. I can help. You said these guys are probably military, or former military. Once you have their names, I can get their service records faster than even your research guru. And I can help with any logistical problems or making calls."

Ricki lightly gnawed her lower lip. He had a point about the military records, and they could also use some help in one critical area. "Can you get hold of a semiautomatic tonight?"

Anchorman quickly nodded. "That would be good." He turned an intense gaze on Trey. "Can you do that?"

Trey rolled his eyes. "Is that a rhetorical question?" He focused on Ricki. "But only if I get to tag along."

She crossed her arms over her chest, and her boot started tapping. "You'd trade our safety for a personal demand?"

Trey didn't flinch at the frost in her voice. "Is that a yes?"

Annoyed that her attempt to guilt him into simply getting hold of the semiautomatic for them without any strings attached had failed, she made a mental note to never again deal with military helicopter pilots before reluctantly nodding her agreement. "But you stay in the car," she added. "That is not negotiable."

"I don't have a problem with that," Trey said. He shifted one of his crutches from under his arm, then bent over and scooped up his phone. "I'd better make some calls." He readjusted his crutch and had taken two hobbling steps when Ricki's phone rang.

Everyone looked at her, holding their collective breaths when she nodded. "It's Dan." Lifting the phone to her ear, she told him to "go ahead," and then listened. She hung up with a simple "got it," followed by her gaze slowly scanning the expectant faces around her. "Tactical Solutions, in Concord, North Carolina. Dan couldn't get us an appointment with their CEO, but Hamilton did. We're expected tomorrow morning." She looked at her watch and did some quick calculations. "According to Dan, it's a four-hour drive from here, so we'll be leaving at 0600 sharp, which will give us some wiggle room for any last-minute problems."

"Concord," Trey repeated. "Got it. Then I'll see you here in the lobby at 0600."

While he continued his awkward walk toward the elevators, Anchorman gave a quick thumbs-up and followed him, leaving Clay and Ricki standing alone.

Once the elevator doors had closed, Clay gave her a considering look. "What's up?"

"About?"

He smiled. "You know what about. How did you know that Tactical Solutions would be close and not in Texas or Hawaii, or even someplace overseas?"

"Because I don't think Kelly was the target, or at least not the final one. I think Anchorman was, and probably still is." She looked down at her phone, zeroing in on the email she'd received from Dan late the previous night, along with its attachment. "We can talk about it up in our room. And then I need your help."

Chapter 29

THE NEXT MORNING dawned cool and clear as the last of the night was chased away by the steady rise of the sun. Three people loitered in the hotel lobby, holding disposable cups filled to the brim with the coffee Duane had brewed early for them at Ricki's request.

When Trey showed up empty-handed, she scowled, holding his cup of coffee out of reach. "Where's the semiautomatic you promised to secure for us?"

"I did arrange it," he protested. "We'll need to pick it up along the way. I set up a meet point about a mile from the Tactical Solutions headquarters. It will be there."

She stared at him, weighing the pros and cons of taking him at his word, finally handing him the coffee. "Okay. But if it isn't, we're leaving you by the side of the road."

They piled into the SUV, holding their cups steady as Clay made the turn onto the highway that would take them across Tennessee and into the neighboring state of North Carolina. The conversation over the four-hour trip was sporadic and mostly involved various sports teams. Tuning it out, Ricki read over the report Dan had sent on Tactical Solutions. She frowned over the careful wording. It sounded like Dan was trying to tell her something without actually stating it.

Since she was sitting in the back, having given up her usual shotgun seat to Trey and his two crutches, she leaned forward and tapped him on the shoulder to get his attention. "Do you know anything about Tactical Solutions? This report of Dan's says that they provide security for military contractors working overseas."

Trey shook his head. "No, but then I spent both of my six-month tours on a ship." He pointed to Anchorman. "Ask him. He was on land."

When Ricki turned toward Anchorman, he also shook his head. "I don't remember any outfit that went by that name." He lifted his broad shoulders into a shrug. "But then it's been awhile since I was overseas, and I never hung around the guys with the security companies anyway. They were mostly there for the money and the adrenaline rush of being in a war zone."

Giving up, Ricki put her phone away and leaned back against her seat. She closed her eyes and a minute later, was sound asleep. She didn't stir again until Anchorman gently shook her awake.

"We're coming up on Trey's meet point for the gun."

She managed a nod and then yawned, covering her mouth with one hand as she stared with bleary eyes out the front windshield. They were passing mostly through the country-side, with isolated enclaves of houses surrounded by empty fields waiting to be developed.

"We've already passed by the Concord city limits sign, and we're near the north side," Clay told her before glancing down at his phone. "We're about five minutes away from Tactical Solutions."

"Pull into that convenience store," Trey directed, pointing at the lone store along the highway. "And drive around to the back."

Clay did as he was told, pulling the SUV around to the rear of the small store. In the dirt lot in back, concealed from the road by the building, was a black sedan. Ricki sighed. Why did all the federal law enforcement agencies, with the exception of the ISB, drive dark-colored, four-door cars?

"Stop here." When the SUV came to a halt, Trey opened the door and hopped out. Grabbing his crutches, he made his way over to the sedan while Ricki watched from the back seat of the SUV. One male exited the passenger side of the car. He waited for Trey, and then the two of them moved to the rear. The trunk opened, and they both disappeared behind it. Ten seconds later, Trey reappeared, signaling for Clay to pull the SUV forward.

Once Clay had complied, Trey opened the rear passenger door and handed a sleek black rifle, with a scope on top, to Anchorman. As Trey hobbled around the front of the SUV, Ricki was startled when her door opened and a box was dropped onto her lap. She stared down at it, then at the rifle Anchorman was carefully looking over.

"Here's the magazines," she said, dropping the box onto the empty space between them on the seat as Trey climbed back into the SUV.

While Clay backed away from the sedan, heading out to the main road, Trey twisted around in the seat. "I asked for an M4 carbine. I figured you'd be familiar with it."

"I am," Anchorman said. "So is every grunt in the military." He looked up and quirked an eyebrow at the NCIS agent, who glared back at him.

"Which includes the navy," Trey growled.

It only took another five minutes to reach the concrete-and-glass, three-story building that had a small, discreet sign at the entrance identifying it as Tactical Solutions. Ricki said "stay in the car" to Trey just before Clay tossed the agent the car keys.

"If you see us running across the lot, start the engine," he told the disgruntled Trey with a grin.

The front door of the building was made of smoked glass, reminding Ricki of the truck the two shooters drove. It appeared to be a common theme of the company's. The lobby area was spacious, with gleaming tile floors and blown-up photographs of cities from all over the world. A long counter stood directly opposite the entry doors, with a large replica of the picture Kelly had drawn suspended from the wall behind it. A big man with a steely-eyed stare watched them cross the lobby.

His gaze roved over each of them, settling on Clay. "Special Agent James?"

Clay simply pointed at Ricki, who smiled at the annoyed look that crossed the man's face.

"I'm Special Agent Ricki James, with the ISB. I believe we're expected by your CEO, Dannon Campbell?"

"You're on the list," the man confirmed. "His assistant will be down shortly to escort you to his office." He slapped a blue-colored label bearing Ricki's name and title onto the counter, then stared at Clay. "Your name?" Once he'd produced Clay's name tag, he repeated the process with Anchorman, finishing just as the elevator door to the right of the desk opened. Another man, who could have been the brother of the one at the lobby desk, stepped out and walked right up to Ricki.

"Agent James? If you and your party will follow me?"

She trailed after him, and the four rode to the third floor in silence. They walked to the end of a long hallway that ran the length of the building and ended in a small reception area with a desk guarding a set of double doors behind it. Their escort skirted the desk and knocked once on the doors before opening them and silently stepping aside.

Feeling as if she were entering the Kingdom of Oz, Ricki walked into a large corner office with banks of windows on two sides. The decor of muted browns and blues didn't overwhelm the senses, but it did emit the feeling of both calm and success.

A tall man, with dark hair in a short buzz cut and the military bearing to go with it, stood behind an enormous desk. He wore a perfectly tailored dark gray suit, with a paisley tie in several colors of lavender. He had the tips of his fingers braced against the desktop as his gaze immediately focused on Ricki.

"Special Agent James? I'm Dannon Campbell." He didn't come around his desk to greet them, but stayed where he was, waiting with an odd stillness that she'd only seen once before. And that was in Anchorman. Which told her a lot about the CEO's personal background in the military.

She drew a silent breath, then gave him a polite smile. "I'm Agent James," she acknowledged. "And these are my colleagues—Chief of Police Clay Thomas, and retired Marine sniper, Anchorman." She deliberately paused for half a beat. "But I'm sure you're already aware of that."

Campbell's smile reached his eyes, and he appeared genuinely amused. "It's my business to know who everyone is before they walk into my office." He turned his head slightly to look out the window. "Including those who don't walk in. The meeting was scheduled with four names. Where is Special Agent Treynor Robard?"

"Waiting in the car. He recently sustained an injury that makes it difficult for him to walk."

"I see." Campbell stepped away from his desk and strode toward a small conference table with five chairs clustered around it. "Please. Make yourselves comfortable. Can I offer you some coffee, or something else to drink?"

Ricki shook her head. "We're fine. Thank you."

Once Campbell had taken his seat, he turned toward Ricki. "Did Captain Robard's injury occur during his investigation of Sergeant Dorman's murder?"

Not really surprised at how much Campbell knew about them, Ricki nodded. "Yes, it did."

The CEO leaned back in his chair and studied Ricki's face. "You're building quite a reputation for solving murders, Agent James. Didn't your last case involve tracking down the Traveler?"

She shrugged. "That's what the press called him. Monster fits just as well."

Campbell smiled. "Yes, it would. It's too bad I don't have a need for an investigative agent." He shot a glance over at Clay. "Or a homicide cop. If I did, you two would be at the top of my recruitment list." His gaze swiveled to Anchorman. "I've read your résumé and know it would be useless to include you on that list. You don't have any interest in our work."

"No, I don't." Anchorman's voice was flat and his tone devoid of emotion.

"But Agent Robard?" the CEO continued, returning his attention to Ricki. "He has quite a few unique experiences in his record. I would be interested in talking to him."

Ricki considered that for a long moment. "I'll pass the message along, and in return, would like some information from you."

Campbell cocked his head to one side. "Such as?"

Ricki set the folder she was carrying on the table and laid her hand on top of it. "Exactly what kind of services does your company provide, Mr. Campbell?"

The CEO's smile was back. "Exactly what our website says, Agent James. Security. Mostly for civilian military contractors working abroad. Many of them are in high-risk zones."

"Military contractors," she repeated. "Those would be companies?"

"Large corporations, for the most part," Campbell confirmed.

"And you hire military veterans to do this work?"

Beginning to look puzzled, the CEO slowly nodded. "Military experience is certainly a plus and something we definitely look for."

"Do you do any work stateside?"

Now Campbell hesitated, his gaze narrowing. "Some. Why do you ask?"

"Is all your work with companies? Do you ever take on other clients?"

"What kind of clients are you referring to?" Campbell's voice took on a hard edge, and the fingers of his hand resting on the table flexed inward.

Ricki tilted her head to the side, her gaze never wavering from his. "Individual clients. The kind who might need private security."

Campbell's hand uncurled, and his jawline relaxed as he shook his head. "You mean bodyguard work? No. We don't do that. We protect job sites, not single individuals."

Clay leaned forward until he got Campbell's attention. "Do any of your employees moonlight?"

"It's allowed if it doesn't interfere or conflict with their jobs here. And if they get permission first."

Ricki took that as the perfect opening. She reached into the folder and slowly drew out the printed image of the black truck and its passenger. Laying it flat on the table, she slid it across to Dannon Campbell. "How about this guy? Did he get your permission?"

When the CEO's gaze dropped to the photo, Ricki saw it. The small tightening of the jaw and twitch of his cheek. Little telltale signs that he recognized the face in the picture. But his gaze was cool when he lifted it back to hers. "What makes you think I would know who this is?"

"Well. That's your truck with your parking decal on it, and he's getting into it, so I'd say he's either a friend of yours or an employee."

"I do not recognize him," Campbell said without blinking

an eye. "But I have hundreds of employees, and a small fleet of those trucks, so it's possible that he's on staff. I'll look into it."

When he reached for the picture, Ricki slapped a hand on top of it. "We're under a time crunch here, Mr. Campbell." When he nodded, she lifted her hand and let him take the picture.

The CEO got to his feet and walked over to the desk, his stiff back giving away the anger he was hiding behind the frozen mask on his face. He didn't take a seat in the tall-backed leather chair, but simply reached down and pressed a button on his phone. "Come in here. I have an urgent task for you." When their building escort appeared, Campbell held out the picture. "Make a copy of this for us, and then take it down to Human Resources and have them identify this individual and bring me his file."

Once his assistant had exited the office, closing the door behind him, Campbell stayed where he was as he looked at Ricki. "This might take an hour. Two at the most. In the meantime, I suggest you get something to eat. There's an acceptable café three miles south, right next to the road you came in on. I'll call you if I find any pertinent information. If I don't get in touch within that time frame, you can assume I found nothing to tell you."

Taking that as the ending of their meeting, Ricki, Clay, and Anchorman all stood up. After the two men had passed through the double doors, Ricki turned and faced Campbell.

"We'll be waiting for your call."

The CEO barely nodded before he sat down and picked up the phone's handset from its cradle. "Thank you for stopping by, Agent James. If I find anything relevant to our conversation today, I'll be in touch."

Chapter 30

RICKI STARED out the window from her seat in the café, idly wondering if it was going to rain. The café had proven to be both cozy and quaint, decorated with a lot of gingham and lace at the windows and faded pictures of the surrounding area on the walls.

It was coming up on the two-hour mark since they'd left Dannon Campbell's office at Tactical Solutions. The food had come, been consumed, and plates cleared away as they waited for a call. After her third cup of coffee, Ricki had switched to water, and was now nursing her second glass, watching the clock on the wall tick off another five minutes.

"Do you think the jerk lied to us?" Anchorman posed the same question that she'd been asking herself for thirty minutes.

"Possible," Clay said. "But our options for tracking this guy down are pretty limited."

Trey shifted in his chair, trying to find a more comfortable position for his injured leg. "If the guy works at Tactical Solutions, he probably lives close by. I can get a canvass of the area started in the morning. Maybe we'll get lucky."

Anchorman's lips curled into a sneer. "I think the high and

mighty CEO is lying through his teeth, and we should pay him another visit."

"He said two hours. Let's give it to him," Ricki said quietly.

"Why?" Anchorman demanded. "He runs a company that is just short of employing mercenaries." He snorted in disgust. "And that's giving him the benefit of the doubt."

"Because our mystery guy was made." She looked around the table as her boot started tapping against the floor. "Campbell knew the man in the photograph, and he was fuming about something the minute he saw him."

Clay nodded his agreement. "Yeah. I'm betting Mr. Black Truck and his buddy were working a side gig without getting permission from the big dog. So I vote with Ricki. Let's give him the time he asked for."

It was exactly two hours since they'd driven out of the parking lot at Tactical Solutions when Ricki's phone rang. The caller ID listed the number as unknown, so she had no idea if it was Dannon Campbell or someone wanting to sell her something. She inhaled a quick breath and connected the call.

"This is Special Agent Ricki James."

"Agent James, I'm calling as promised."

Ricki snapped her fingers together and nodded, bringing a charged silence descending around the table. "I'm listening, Mr. Campbell."

"The name you're looking for is Austin Hall, twenty-nine-years-old. He separated from the army two years ago with an excellent record and came to work for us eighteen months ago. He has a house here in town." The CEO rattled off an address which Ricki repeated out loud along with the name. "Mr. Hall shares that house with another employee of ours by the name of Kevin Baker. Also former army, and twenty-nine-years-old. The two seem to have a great deal in common. Both like to hunt, both are certified on several types of aircraft, and they both like pancakes and sausage for breakfast." There was a pause while Ricki barely breathed, straining to hear the low-voiced conversation on the other end of the phone. "And it seems there is something else the two men have in common—an apparent dislike for following protocol."

She could read between those lines easily enough. Clay had been right. Hall and his partner, Baker, had colored outside the lines without permission, and at Tactical Solutions, that wasn't allowed.

"Unfortunately," Campbell continued in a smooth voice, "that is grounds for termination. Which was done at their place of residence thirty minutes ago." There was another pause before he added, "Unfortunately, since they are no longer in our employ, we have no other information to give you. This terminates our conversations, Agent James. Good luck with your hunt."

When the phone went dead, Ricki held it away from her ear and stared at it. "Crap." Possibilities raced through her mind as she carefully tucked her phone away. "Our two guys are Austin Hall and Kevin Baker, both former army and both twenty-nine." She stared out the window as Trey immediately began furiously tapping a message on his phone.

"I'm requesting their military records now," the NCIS agent said.

"What else did Campbell tell you?" Clay asked. "There was something else that bothered you. What was it?"

She frowned, going over the conversation in her mind, hearing what Campbell had said, and what he hadn't. At least not out loud. "He stated that the two hadn't followed protocol, and their employment was ended by someone going to their house thirty minutes ago and informing them about that little fact of life."

Trey's face grew red, with an expression contorted into anger. "He told them they had breached protocol and then fired them?" He beat a fist against the table, drawing a startled look from the cashier and waitress gossiping at the other end of the café. "So now they know we've tracked them down?"

"We have to assume that's a yes," Ricki said. She tapped a finger against the arm of her chair, her brow furrowed in thought.

"And they've got a thirty-minute head start on us? Well isn't that just great," Trey continued to fume.

Clay reached out and clapped a firm hand on Trey's shoulder, but his gaze was centered on Ricki. "Hang on there, Trey." Clay waited until the man subsided. "What are you thinking, Ricki?"

"I think Campbell was trying to warn his employees and serve them up to us on a platter at the same time."

Anchorman stirred in his chair. "It could be. Giving his employees a warning would keep his reputation as supporting the brotherhood, but at the same time, he wouldn't shed any tears if they ended up in prison, otherwise he wouldn't have called you at all."

Ricki nodded. That made sense. "Campbell said that Hall and Baker had a lot in common. They liked to hunt, eat pancakes." Her chin suddenly jerked up. Her eyes widened as she met Clay's calm gaze. "And they were both certified on different kinds of aircraft." She grabbed Trey's phone right out of his hands. "A map. We need a map of the area."

Trey snatched his phone back. "Here. Let me do it. What am I looking for?"

"An airport. There has to be a small airport around here somewhere. And their house. We need to know how far it is from their house."

"We passed a small airport about seven miles from here," Clay said. "When you were still sleeping."

Trey jumped in his seat, hard enough to knock his crutches over. "I have it. Yeah. About seven miles away." He looked up, his eyes glittering. "And better yet, we're closer to it than their house is." He looked around the table. "If I were certified on small craft, which I am, and needed to get away fast, that's exactly what I would do. Head to the nearest airport. And if I couldn't get a plane quick, I'd steal one."

They all got up at the same time and sprinted to the parking lot. Clay threw several twenty-dollar bills at the astonished cashier as he passed her register. Trey was the last one into the SUV, literally diving into the back seat and stretching his arm to its full length to get the door shut. The car rocked violently as they careened out of the parking lot, heading northeast toward the small private airfield.

The first thing Ricki saw was a black truck with heavily tinted windows parked near the small hangar. Clay skidded to a halt next to it and jumped out of the SUV, running for the rear hatch. Ricki met him there, and they both hauled out the rifles. Clay tossed one to Anchorman, who already had the M4 carbine secured by its strap to his back.

"There might be innocent people around. Don't use that thing unless you absolutely have to," Ricki warned him.

"I won't," Anchorman said, handing her the rifle he'd just expertly loaded, exchanging it for the one she was holding out to him.

It was less than another minute before they were racing toward the hangar, leaving Trey to fend for himself. The wide tarmac was dotted with small craft, their wings anchored to the ground by heavy ropes or light chains. Ricki squatted down next to the hangar's opening, looking for any human activity in the wide cement space inside. She saw nothing. The runway at her back was empty. Her stomach sank at the thought that they might be too late, but the place had to be carefully checked out.

The trio split up, with Ricki going left, Clay going right, and Anchorman climbing the rickety set of stairs to the office area above. Ricki had reached the door to a maintenance closet, set into the wall she was following, when she stopped dead in her tracks. On the other side of the wall was the noise of an engine starting up. A second later she heard the sound of heavy boots pounding against a metal floor overhead. Anchorman was running. She instantly took off as well, heading for the wide-open door of the hangar. She reached it just after Clay, with Anchorman not far behind. They raced around the corner of the building and were immediately met with a bullet ricocheting over their heads. Ricki flattened herself on the ground, her rifle firmly set against her shoulder as she scanned the area in front of her through her scope.

It didn't take long to spot the small helicopter a football field's distance away. Its rotors were turning, and she could make out the pilot sitting just behind the glass bubble. Next to her, Anchorman opened fire. She swept the barrel of her rifle to the left and spotted the figure, crouched next to a small plane parked halfway between them and the waiting helicopter.

More bullets hit the tarmac in front of her as she and Clay returned fire. There was a furious volley from the shooter that had Ricki ducking her head to avoid flying chips of concrete. When the firing stopped, she saw the gunman racing across the tarmac, heading straight for the helicopter.

She was on her feet in a second, her long legs eating up the distance right beside Clay and Anchorman. They were still fifty yards away when the craft lifted a few feet into the air. Two rifles spat out fire with the staccato snap of the M4 joining in a few seconds later.

Suddenly Trey's voice sounded in her head. *Rear rotors.* She blinked. *You can take a helicopter down by damaging the rear rotors.*

Anchorman was kneeling ten feet to her right. She sprang up, startling him enough that he looked over at her.

"Rear rotors," she yelled. "Aim for the rear rotors."

The barrel of the M4 instantly adjusted to the right, opening a barrage of fire as Ricki turned her head and screamed the same thing to Clay. Their rifles joined the constant bang of the M4. Through her scope, she saw the helicopter suddenly lurch and start to spin in the opposite direction of the main rotor blades. It dropped ten feet, its blades tilting downward, making one smash into the ground was enough force to flip the helicopter over and slam it down again with the screeching sound of metal violently scraping across concrete, creating a tail of sparks behind it. When it came to rest, the underside of its long skids faced the sky, and the cabin had collapsed in on itself.

Ricki stood, her jaw dropping to her chest. She'd never witnessed anything like that before, and it took her a minute to realize both Anchorman and Clay were running across the tarmac toward the mangled aircraft. She took off after them, upping her speed until the muscles in her legs screamed in protest and her lungs started to burn.

She reached the smoking ruins just as Clay hauled a limp body from the twisted metal. Anchorman reached out to take the injured man to the ground, then hooked his hands under his armpits and dragged him back to safety. When Clay jumped down and grabbed Ricki's arm, forcing her away from the smoking crash site, she looked over her shoulder and pulled against his hold.

"What about the other guy? We have to get him out," she shouted at Clay.

"It wouldn't make any difference," he yelled back.

Understanding, Ricki quit trying to pull away and ran with him, chasing after Anchorman. He stopped one hundred feet from the crash and dropped to his knees next to the injured man. Ricki sucked in several breaths, then took out her phone and punched in 9-1-1.

Chapter 31

"MY GUESS he died on impact, but we won't know for sure until we get him out of there. And that's going to take some time." The fire chief peered closer at Ricki. "The paramedics will be happy to give you a look over, Agent James."

"Thanks. I'm good." Ricki added a nod of appreciation, then absently sipped a steaming cup of coffee while she watched him walk off.

She was sitting cross-legged on the ground since there wasn't anything else available on the tarmac. Clay sat on one side of her, with one leg bent at the knee and the other straight out in front of him, while Anchorman sat on the other. Trey stood behind them, leaning on his crutches, taking in the chaotic scene spread out all around them.

The small airport had been invaded by an army of first responders. Besides the firemen and paramedics, there were police from Concord and nearby Charlotte, as well as state troopers. Everywhere you looked, vehicles, their lights flashing, were parked at odd angles to each other and around the planes anchored to the ground.

At the center of the frenzied activity was the mangled helicopter with Kevin Baker's body still trapped inside. The survivor, who had been identified by Trey as Austin Hall, was on his way to a hospital under heavy guard. Ricki had already told Trey that NCIS could have the chore of interrogating him, provided he ever woke up. She had already pieced together what she needed to know and was sure she could hang the murder of Stu Landers around his neck, as well as Kelly Dorman's.

Trey gently nudged one of her knees with a crutch. "Are you sure you don't want the paramedics to check you out?" His gaze swept to Clay and then Anchorman. "Any of you?"

As the two men refused the offer, Ricki tilted her head back and stared up at Trey. "How are the arrangements coming?"

"My guys will be in place in an hour. Which is about the same amount of time the drive will take."

She looked away and closed her eyes. Tired. What she really wanted to do was go back to the hotel and sleep for the rest of the day instead of taking an hour-long drive north. But it couldn't be helped. This whole mess needed to be finished, and then they could all go home.

With that thought as motivation, she unfolded her legs. Planting her boots firmly on the ground, she pushed herself to a standing position, swaying slightly until she locked her knees to catch her balance.

"We need to go," she told the two men staring up at her. They both winced but got to their feet and picked up their weapons.

Anchorman handed the M4 over to Trey. "Thanks. It was a big help."

"Anytime." The NCIS agent slipped an arm through the strap and smoothly anchored the rifle across his back.

"There isn't going to be another time," Ricki stated. She was going to make sure of that. "The SUV should still be in front of the hangar. You take shotgun, Trey. I'll sit in back. Let's go."

Ten minutes later, Clay turned onto Interstate 85, heading north. Ricki leaned forward from her rear passenger seat and tapped him on the shoulder. "Do you have the address?"

"It's in my GPS," he said.

She settled back again, going over the plan she'd put into motion as Anchorman reached a long arm over and lightly slapped the back of Clay's seat.

"Hey, genius. You're going the wrong way. Pigeon Forge is south of here and you're headed north."

"He's going the right way," Ricki said quietly. With a mental sigh, she turned her body in the seat and looked a confused Anchorman in the eye. It was time to tell him the truth, no matter how painful.

"The case isn't closed yet. We have another arrest to make." At least she hoped it was only one. It would be much easier on the retired Marine if it was only one arrest instead of two.

"What are you talking about?" Anchorman crossed his arms over his chest and stared at the back of Clay's head before his gaze jumped over to her. "Is there something everyone else in this car knows except me?"

Better to get it done as quickly as possible, she thought. "Kelly wasn't the target. At least not the only one."

The big man sitting next to her frowned. "The only other dead guy is Stu Landers. Are you telling me Kelly was killed by mistake?"

She shook her head. "No. I'm saying that both you and Kelly were targets, but you had a bigger mark on your back."

"I wasn't the one drugged and then killed and dragged a mile down the trail." He gave her a level look, the fury banked in his gaze. "They could have done that easily enough. But they left me and went after Kelly, then shot him in the back like cowards."

"Because of the money," she responded calmly. "It was always the money."

"What money?" He snorted his disbelief. "It all goes to his mom and brother. The house, the savings account, the life insurance, all of it. They never would have gotten hold of one dime. I would have made sure of that."

"I know." Ricki's voice gentled. "There's not one drop of doubt that you would have made sure of it. But you and Kelly had an arrangement. You told me so yourself. Your money all went to Kelly, who would be sure that your Aunt Sally got the bulk of it, with the rest going to your sister. Isn't that true?"

Anchorman shrugged. "Yeah. So? Like I said, I wasn't the one they killed."

"And with Kelly dead, his money goes to you, and you would see to it that his mother and brother go every penny. Isn't that right?"

"Yeah. I already told you that."

Ricki nodded. "So, if Kelly is dead, once his estate is settled, then his money would go to you first."

"What?" Anchorman jerked in his seat and his eyes shot wide open. "What are you saying?"

"It's simple, really. The minute Kelly's estate went to you, your combined life insurance money would have been three-quarters of a million dollars. Before you have a chance to transfer it to Kelly's payout to his family, you have an unfortunate accident. Or maybe kill yourself because you're depressed about losing your best friend, and suddenly all that money goes to your heirs. Not Kelly's." The took in a breath and held his gaze. "That's the only reason you weren't killed at the same time as Kelly. You had to be alive long enough that you would be recognized as Kelly's heir. Even a couple more days would have done the trick in a court of law."

He shook his head in denial. "But then most of it would have gone to Aunt Sally. You can't believe she would have . . ."

Ricki bit her lower lip when he trailed off, seeing the truth slowly creep into his gaze. "Your Aunt lives alone. I'm sure she would have had a tragic accident of her own."

"Which leaves Dina." He turned anguished eyes to her. "She's my sister."

"I don't know if Dina is part of it. Your sister said she doesn't know that much about her husband's company. And I don't think she was lying about that. She might be aware that it's failing though."

"What are you talking about? They have that big house and take all those trips and buy every damn thing under the sun. They're doing fine."

"No, they aren't," Clay said from the driver's seat. "I saw the report on Fitz's company that Ricki asked Dan to research. Your sister and brother-in-law are in debt up to their eyeballs."

"What report?" Anchorman waved an agitated hand in the air. "The report she ordered was on Stu Lander's company. I was there when she asked Dan to look into it."

Ricki blew out a soft breath. "No. I never said the name of the company out loud, you just assumed it was Stu's framing business. But I sent Dan the name of Fitz's furniture company. It was something Trip said about the price of wood getting so high that Stu's company was in trouble. And so was Fitz's custom-made furniture business. That's why he was trying to get you to invest in it. He'd gone so far into the red that he needed a big infusion of cash. Dan thinks he won't last more than six months, but that would be long enough to settle Kelly's estate, kill you before you had a chance to distribute the funds, and then use your combined life insurance as collateral to keep his predators at bay until he could get his hands on the money." She tucked a stray lock of hair behind one ear.

"You're saying my brother-in-law hired Baker and Hall to first kill Kelly and then me?" Anchorman's big hands dropped onto his lap. He stared down at them, carefully flexing his fingers. "How would he have known when and where we were camping? We weren't going around announcing the information."

"No," Ricki said. "But you did tell your Aunt Sally, and Dina talks to her once a month. And Kelly would have received an email confirming the campsite reservation. Dan says email isn't that hard to hack into if you know what you're doing." She watched his jaw slowly harden, his inner turmoil written in the deep lines in his cheeks, and mentally damned Fitz and his weak spine to hell. "If he found Baker and Hall, he could find a hacker. And now we're going to find that hacker too."

There was a drawn-out moment of silence that had Ricki holding her breath.

"I get to talk to them," Anchorman finally said. "I'll know if Dina was part of this." He didn't utter another word but turned his head and stared out the window.

Ricki leaned back in her seat and let the silence settle around her. She figured Anchorman had a right to confront his family. But it wasn't up to her. It was Trey's case and his call.

Thirty minutes later the GPS chirped out directions, sending them to Willow Creek on the western side of the High Point area. As they neared the house, Clay was instructed to stop behind a plain white van parked on the street. In less than ten seconds, the back doors opened and a man in jeans and a dark vest with FBI emblazoned on it stepped onto the street and made his way to the passenger side of the car.

Trey opened his window and had a short conversation, which confirmed that Dina and her husband were in their house. Once the FBI agent had returned to the van, Clay pulled out into the street and continued driving the half block, turning into a wide driveway, and parking next to a cream-colored Mercedes-Benz.

Anchorman was out of the car first and heading for the

door before Trey could use his crutches to maneuver his body to the ground. Ricki jumped out as well and chased after the big man, with Clay close behind her. They caught up to the Marine just as he stabbed a finger into the doorbell. Behind it, there was the click of high heels walking across a stone floor, followed by one side of the huge oak doors swinging backward. Dina stood in the opening, blinking at Anchorman, who stared back at her.

"Can we come in?" Not waiting for an answer, Anchorman simply walked forward, forcing Dina to step aside or get run over.

She stared after him, her mouth open, finally finding her voice when she spotted Ricki. "What are you all doing here? Is my brother under arrest?"

"We generally don't arrest people and then take them to a family home," Ricki said as she walked past Dina, following Anchorman into a spacious room that featured a floor-to-ceiling marble fireplace and a bank of glass doors overlooking the pool and the large expanse of lawn surrounding it. Clay was right behind her, nodding at an astonished Dina as he walked across the tiled foyer and through the arched entry into the main living area.

Dina rushed after them, coming to a stop in front of the fireplace. She put her hands on her hips and glared at her brother. "What is going on? You and your friends can't just barge in here without an explanation."

Anchorman slowly looked around before his gaze returned to Dina. "Where's Fitz?"

"Why?" she demanded. "I can assure you that my husband would not appreciate your behavior, either."

Anchorman's gaze narrowed on her face. "I wanted to let him know I met two of his business associates. A Mr. Austin Hall and a Kevin Baker. Now, where is Fitz?"

"I'm here." Fitz stepped around a wall separating the kitchen from the living room. He held a pistol in one hand, pointed right at Ricki. "I don't imagine it would bother you a bit to get shot if it allowed you to get your hands on me, dear brother-in-law, or Dina either, for that matter. But I wonder how you'd feel about her getting shot? Could you live with that?"

Ricki and Clay automatically started to move apart, but Fitz immediately waved his pistol back and forth. "Stay where you are. Nobody moves or Agent James will be the first one I'll shoot."

Dina wrung her hands, her voice sliding into a wail. "Fitz? What are you doing?"

His upper lip curled into a sneer. "Come on, Dina. You don't seriously think I'm going to go along with you playing the innocent do you?" He looked at Anchorman. "This was your dear sister's plan as much as it was mine. She enjoys her higher lifestyle. There was no way she was going to give it up."

Anchorman's expression remained carved in stone as his gaze shifted from Fitz to his sister. "Why, Dina?"

His quiet question had his sister's eyes narrowing and her mouth stretching out into a sneer. "Why? Our parents doted on you. The only son and heir apparent to their little diner. Nothing for me, because after all, I would have a husband to look to for support. Did you think I was going to lift a finger to make sure you got your precious inheritance?" She put her hands on her hips and let out a nasty laugh. "I was glad to hand it over to the lawyers. And whenever you came home? Do you think the decorated, conquering hero could offer me anything? Let me shine in a bit of his light?" She sniffed then lifted her chin in a show of defiance as she waved a hand in the air. "Even our aunt wouldn't stop talking about you. God, I was sick of it. You left me to deal with everything at home. That diner, our parents getting sick — everything. You owed me and offered nothing. So why shouldn't I take it?"

"Vicious, isn't she?" Fritz said with an undertone of amusement, drawing Dina's glare to him. He shrugged it off and turned his gaze back to Ricki. "How did you figure it out? Did those two idiots I hired make a deal?"

"We haven't talked to them," Ricki said. "One is on his way to the hospital, the other one to the morgue." She shifted her weight to one hip and cocked an eyebrow at him. "It was killing Sergeant Dorman and not Anchorman. If it had been a random thing, that made no sense. Which led us to the money, Fitz. You and Dina shouldn't have been so greedy and settled for Anchorman's share. Trying to steal Kelly's too was a big mistake."

She paused to smile at the leap of anger in his eyes. "And you shouldn't have shown up in Pigeon Forge. Anchorman never talks about you, and he told me he never sees you, even though he came this way every time Kelly was back in the country. He would go see his Aunt Sally and was here hunting for your cousin Ryan's killer a few years back. But he never went to see you and Dina. Then suddenly, you both show up in Pigeon Forge." She shook her head, deliberately letting her smile grow another inch. "A bad habit of guilty people. They tend to do things out of their normal behavior." She paused, then shrugged. "But you have another problem."

"Oh, don't worry, Agent James. I have an escape plan." Fitz switched his glare over to his wife, whose eyes were shooting daggers at him. "Unfortunately, honey, it's only for one."

"What?" Dina shrieked.

He ignored her. "And I think I had better get moving. If both you and the chief would be so kind as to slowly take your guns out and put them on the ground? One at a time, please." He glanced at Clay. "You first."

Ricki didn't move, raising her voice to be heard over Dina's rant at her husband. "You still have that problem that I mentioned, Fitz. Apparently, you can't count."

He scowled. "Count? What are you talking about?"

"I'm sure you've noticed that there are three of us

standing here. But back in Pigeon Forge, there were four of us."

Dina's yelling turned into nasty laughter. "You jerk. Where's the other agent, huh? Where do you think he is? Outside with the rest of his NCIS friends?"

"Actually," Trey's voice came from the large opening into the kitchen just before he appeared behind Fitz, holding a gun pointed at the middle of the man's back. "I'm right here. Put your gun down, Mr. Pollack. The house is surrounded. You aren't going anywhere."

"You always were dumber than dirt," Dina jeered.

Fitz didn't say anything, he simply smiled before swiveling the barrel of his gun around, aiming it at his wife, and pulling the trigger. Dina's tirade was cut short, and without another word, she crumpled to the ground as Clay leaped forward and tackled Fitz.

Ricki spun on her heel and ran to where Dina was sprawled on the expensive wood floor, but Anchorman got there first. He knelt beside his sister, pressing his hands against the wound in her abdomen. In the background, Trey was calling for an ambulance while the rush of footsteps came at them from all directions.

Ricki dropped to her knees and put two fingers against the pulse in Dina's neck. She looked at Anchorman and nodded.

"Keep the pressure on. If we can slow the bleeding, she might make it to the hospital."

Trey limped over, his gun back in its shoulder harness. "Ambulance is five minutes out. How's she doing?"

"She needs help." Ricki looked over at Fitz, who was lying facedown on the floor, his hands cuffed behind his back. "He admitted to hiring Hall and Baker. If you can get Hall to admit to killing Stu Landers, I'd appreciate it."

"I'll let you know as soon as he does." Trey looked around as two FBI agents hauled Fitz to his feet. "He's a piece of work." He glanced at Anchorman, who was bent over Dina. "Family. Sometimes it's hard to figure."

Clay walked over and held out a hand, helping Ricki to her feet. "The ambulance just pulled up." The words were barely out of his mouth when the paramedics rushed through the wide-open front door. One of them took over from Anchorman, who rubbed his bloody hands down the sides of his jeans before walking over and joining Ricki and Clay.

"My sister," he said quietly.

Ricki laid a hand on his arm. "Family has always been your blind spot. I guess it always will be."

Anchorman turned a shattered gaze on her. "I don't even know what I'm going to tell my Aunt Sally. She's all the family I have left."

"That's not true. The rest of your family lives in the Bay. And they're waiting for you there." As Clay nodded and pulled Ricki into his side, she gave a mute Anchorman's arm a gentle squeeze.

"Let's go home."

Epilogue

THE DOOR to the Sunny Side Up was wide open, kept in that position by the strategic use of a large rock. The hand-printed sign in the window said Private Party, which meant anyone who lived in the Bay was welcome. Light, music, and noise poured out of the opening and spilled onto the sidewalk, drawing even more people inside to join the party until the dining room was bursting with bodies.

Ricki stood behind the back counter, one arm entwined with Clay's, an indulgent smile on her face as she watched her son have a one-sided, mile-a-minute conversation with Anchorman. Eddie and his two school friends had edged out Pete and his crew, as well as the mayor, to claim Anchorman's attention. And judging by the awestruck expressions on the faces of both his friends, her son was undoubtedly going down a list of the former sniper's exploits.

When Eddie gestured toward her and then waved his arms around while Anchorman crossed his arms over his chest, Clay gently nudged Ricki in the side. "Uh-oh. I think the guest of honor tonight might want to have a word with you."

When the big Marine caught her attention, he lifted one eyebrow and shook his head. Ricki sent him back a cheeky grin. Whatever story her son was regaling his friends with, it was undoubtedly embellished to the point of making Anchorman give her that we-need-to-talk look, but that was fine with her. Every boy needed a hero. Looking around, she felt a warm glow flow across her cheeks. Judging by the large turnout tonight to welcome Anchorman back home, it seemed that not just the boys needed a hero.

The smile stayed on her lips as Anchorman made his way through the crowd, his arm around Cheron's shoulders to keep her firmly anchored to his side as he made his way toward the back of the diner. When they finally reached Ricki and Clay, Cheron was breathing heavily. She lifted a hand and brushed her wispy bangs aside before drawing in a long breath of air.

"It's like wading through molasses in here," she declared, but her gaze beamed out from behind the lenses of her glasses. "It's a wonderful party. And wasn't that check from the VFW so generous?"

Ricki laughed. Anchorman had first been touched when Bill, as the VFW commander, had presented him with the check, and then stunned when he'd seen the amount. When he got his voice back, the former Marine quickly took Bill aside and tried to give the check back, but the older man had refused, and told him to spend it on whatever he wanted. And when he'd tried to give it to Clay to pay him back for the attorney fees and bail money, the chief had also refused to take it and repeated exactly what Bill had said.

"And Kelly would be so grateful for the way Norman is going to use the money," Cheron went on. When she patted the front pocket of her pale green, satin blouse, Ricki guessed that the doctor had taken charge of the check.

Curious, Ricki shifted her smile to Anchorman. "So? What do you intend to do with it?"

"Buy an Airbnb and give it to Sondra to run. So she can

have her own business. Unless she'd rather have a bar. I'm going to call her tomorrow and talk to her about it." When Ricki's mouth dropped open in surprise, he ducked his head, and lifted his free arm to rub the back of his neck. "Kelly loved her, and would have made some arrangements for her if he'd had more time. He would want her taken care of. Her and her boy."

"That's a really sweet thought, Anchorman." Ricki's simple statement had the big man's cheeks bursting into flames.

"Sweet," he muttered under his breath before letting out an exasperated sigh. He lifted his gaze and frowned at her. "Not so sweet if you listen to your son. He's over there telling his friends that I singlehandedly took down a helicopter while bullets ricocheted off just about every damn thing around me."

When Ricki laughed, his eyes narrowed on her face. "He's going way overboard."

She grinned back at him. "He's a teenager. That's what they do."

"Did the police catch those license plate forgers?" Cheron asked loudly, smoothly cutting off Anchorman's tirade before he could even get started. "Norman said that one of those awful men you caught had traded the name of the man who made those license plates in exchange for some kind of deal to keep him off death row?"

Ricki nodded. "Yeah. The federal prosecutor agreed to it at the request of the North Carolina attorney general. It turned out there was only one guy working out of his garage, and he is now spending time as a guest of the state.

"What about Fitz?"

Anchorman's quiet question took Ricki by surprise. He hadn't said a word about his sister or her husband during the hours they'd spent on the airplane coming home, or anytime since then.

"Dina called from the county jail where she's being held," Cheron supplied. "She's the one who asked about Fitz."

Anchorman shrugged then looked away. "Cheron, honey, she doesn't have anyone else to ask."

"She was more concerned about money than her husband," the doctor sniffed. "That woman spent a good twenty minutes whining about being almost penniless, and not being able to afford a decent attorney. She even said that it was now Norman's job to look after her since he got her husband arrested." Cheron curled one lip up in distaste. "Can you imagine that? After the horrible things she said to her only brother?" She glanced up at a silent Anchorman and frowned. "And I do not want to see that guilty look on your face. You didn't know she didn't get anything in your parents will. And you know very good and well that you would have given her half once you found out."

Ricki glanced over at Anchorman. Knowing how protective he was of family, even the ones who didn't deserve it, she wouldn't put it past him to cave in and send his sister whatever she demanded, despite everything. "Since she was directly responsible for Kelly being murdered," she said, deliberately reminding him of that fact. "I hope you told her to get a public defender?"

Cheron beamed at Ricki. "Oh. I wish I had thought of that. But no, I told her that Norman wouldn't pay for her attorney, and that she should sell her house if she needs more money."

Covering her mouth as she choked back a laugh, Ricki had to wait a moment before she could say anything. "How did that go over?"

"Not well. It seems the thing is mortgaged to the hilt," Cheron said, her tone turning brisk. "But I won't have her taking advantage of Norman. He needs someone to protect him from people like that."

Anchorman's whole expression changed as his eyes lit up

along with his grin. "Hear that, Thomas? I need protection." His gaze shifted pointedly to Ricki. "Maybe you ought to figure out how to get some of your own."

Not waiting for any answer, he swung Cheron around and headed back into the crowd. Clay stared after him for a long moment and then shrugged. Tilting his head down, he smiled at Ricki. "I need some air. Do you think we can sneak away and duck out back for a few moments?"

With the noise and heat level rising to even greater heights with each passing moment, Ricki was more than happy to make an escape. When Clay took her hand in his, she followed him through the kitchen doors and right out the rear exit into the back alley.

Her lime-green jeep, parked in its usual spot at the alley's entrance, practically glowed in the dark as they walked toward it, side by side, enjoying the cool air and the quiet. When he reached the jeep, Clay turned around and leaned against the hood, drawing Ricki into his arms. He bent his head and gave her a long, warm kiss. She closed her eyes, losing herself in the magic of his touch and the night surrounding them.

When he lifted his head, he smiled, holding her gaze with his. "I wanted to let you know that I'm done thinking, and I've had a talk with Eddie. He's fine with us getting married, so I'm asking you." When she only stared back at him, he inclined his head to one side. "I'll get down on one knee if you want me to."

She shook her head. "No. I had that the last time I was asked, and it didn't work out so well. Except for Eddie of course."

"For me either." Clay lifted a hand and ran one finger over her cheek. "So what do you say, Richelle McCormick James? Will you marry me?"

She rose on her tiptoes and placed a soft kiss on his mouth. "Of course I will." When his expression turned to smug satisfaction, she laughed. "But we can't make it official until you get a ring."

"I thought we'd go into Seattle tomorrow and find one you like."

Ricki was shaking her head before he even finished. "Oh no, Clayton Thomas. You go into Seattle and pick one out. I'd like to see what kind of ring appeals to a homicide cop."

"I'm not the one who will be wearing it," he protested.

She kept smiling as she shrugged. "Too bad. You aren't getting out of this."

"Great," he muttered. "No pressure there."

She kissed him again before laying her head on his shoulder. "I'll tell you what. You don't have to rush into Seattle tomorrow. Take your time and think about it."

Author Notes

Thank you for reading The Blind Spot! If you'd like to keep up with Ricki James and her team, No Place To Hide is now available for presale on Amazon. Ricki, Clay, and Anchorman will be working together again to trap a murder-for-hire killer. Lex Thomas, Clay's deadly brother, is on the move, and according to the FBI, heading to the Northwest. Pre-Order your copy today by clicking Here. Order No Place To Hide

You can follow C.R. Chandler, by subscribing to the author's free newsletter. In addition to receiving notifications to any upcoming books, you will also be able to download a free e-book, Backcountry Murder. It not only has a case for Ricki to solve, but also tells the story of how Ricki and Anchorman met, long before he showed up in her hometown. Backcountry Murder is a prequel to the Special Agent Ricki James series, and is only available to anyone who signs up to receive the free Author's newsletter. To sign up today, click here:

Subscribe to Free Author Newsletter here!

I'm always interested in hearing opinions and suggestions from readers. If you like a particular character, or book, plot, setting (or if there is one you really didn't like!), I'd love to hear your thoughts. Or—if there's a national park you'd like to see in a book, or more of a favorite character or storyline—let me know. Interacting with readers on a one-on-one basis is one of the better parts of my day. (I will admit, I am not very good on the larger social media sites since I'm a little on the introverted side on those kind of stages. . . but I'm working on it). Drop me a line: <u>Send an Email to CR Chandler</u>

I do have a Facebook page if you'd like to drop by there as well—and maybe remind me I should be posting to it on a regular basis: https://www.facebook.com/crchandlerauthor/

And for those of you on BookBub, here is the link to follow me (and much appreciated!): https://www.bookbub.com/authors/c-r-chandler

To visit my website, click here: https://www.crchandlerbooks.com/

Made in the USA
Middletown, DE
19 February 2024

50064163R00181